A Light in the Window

An Irish Love Story

A Light in the Window

An Irish Love Story

JULIE LESSMAN

The characters and events portrayed in this book are fictitious. Any similarity to real persons, living or dead, is coincidental and not intended by the author.

Text copyright © 2013 by julie Lessman

All rights reserved.

Printed in the united States of America.

No part of this book may be reproduced, or stored in a retrieval system, or transmitted in any form or by any means, electronic, mechanical, photocopying, recording, or otherwise, without express written permission of the publisher.

ISBN-13: 978-0-9887691-5-1

Interior format by The Killion Group
http://thekilliongroupinc.com

I am the light of the world:

he that followeth Me shall not walk in darkness,

but shall have the light of life.

John 8:12

A Light in the Window

Chapter One

Boston, Massachusetts, Summer 1895

I will not throw up … I will not throw up … Eighteen-year-old Marceline Murphy set her overnight case on the O'Rourke's wraparound porch and pressed a quivering finger to the brass doorbell, a battalion of butterflies barnstorming her stomach. The last time she'd been this nervous was at the age of eleven when she'd frozen on the top limb of a massive pine tree in the backyard of her best friend Julie O'Rourke. The memory of Julie's older brother Sam climbing up to rescue her made her hands sweat even now, his body close behind as he helped her down, limb by limb. At the bottom he'd tugged on her pigtail with that dimpled grin that had always fluttered her pulse. "Best keep your feet on the ground and your nose in a book, Marceline," he'd whispered in her ear. "You'll want to stay far away from danger."

Danger, yes. Marcy swallowed hard.

Heights and Sam O'Rourke—two things that made her dizzy.

She heard the thump-thump of hurried footsteps on the other side of the door and nervously smoothed her hair. Carefully puffed and pulled back on the sides in the new Gibson Girl style with a tortoise-shell comb, the rest of her long blond curls trailed the back of her powder-blue shirtwaist. Adjusting her wide black belt, she slid a damp palm down her cream gabardine skirt that loosely hugged her hips before it spilled into a bell shape at her ankles. Children's laughter floated on the summer breeze while a pink sky reflected in shiny parlour windows, casting a rosy glow on a white wicker swing. Marcy breathed in the fragrance of the scarlet pillar roses that coiled and tangled on a trellis at the end of the porch, their scent recalling summers playing jacks with Julie or discussing favorite book heroes while lazing in the swing.

It had been five years since she'd seen her best friend, five long years since Papa had whisked them away to New York for his new job as a vice president for Reading Railroad. But he hadn't counted on an agricultural crisis that would result in a worldwide economic depression in 1893, costing him and thousands of others their jobs. Some of Marcy's excitement over returning to Boston ebbed as her thoughts strayed to the financial crisis in which a quarter of the nation's railroads—including the company Papa worked for—went bankrupt. In New York alone, unemployment among industrial workers exceeded twenty percent, which meant Papa had been forced to return to Boston to look for work. Squaring her shoulders, Marcy shook off the malaise that always settled when she thought of Papa out of a job, but she had no doubt that her faith—and that of her parents— would see them through. Even so, tonight she was back home with her best friend, and she refused to let anything dampen her excitement of seeing Julie again. *Especially Julie's brother.*

With her dog-eared copy of *Jane Eyre* clutched tightly in one hand, she pinched her cheeks with the other and waited, hoping she appeared more grown up and confident than the pale-faced girl she'd glimpsed earlier in her bedroom mirror.

The door flashed open, and she grinned at the high-pitched squeal of the best friend she'd ever had. "You're here—you're really and truly here! I could just kiss your parents for letting you stay over the very first weekend you moved back!" Julie launched into her arms with a husky bubble of giggles that brought a sheen to Marcy's eyes.

Oh, Jewels, I missed you so …

Breathless, Julie pulled away, fingers clamped tight to Marcy's arms as if she wouldn't risk her ever leaving again. Creamy white cheeks dolloped with a soft blush were framed by wisps of shiny black curls as laughing ebony eyes studied Marcy head to toe. "I knew it!" she announced with a smug smile. "You've grown into a beauty, Marce, just in time to turn heads our senior year." She squeezed her again, her whisper, brimming with tease. "Especially Sam's."

Marcy gulped, her hour-glass corset suddenly feeling two sizes too small. Heat burnished her cheeks while her gaze darted into the O'Rourke's cozy foyer and back. "Jewels, hush," she whispered, "I came to see my dearest friend in the whole wide world, *not* her brother." She paused to nibble her lip. "He's not home, is he?"

Her friend's laughter filled the air with beautiful music while the scent of lemon oil and apple pie filled the foyer with beautiful memories. "No, you goose, it's Friday night, for pity's sake—Sam wouldn't be caught dead at home on a weekend."

The pinch of Marcy's corset eased considerably. "Oh, thank heavens," she blurted with a sigh of relief.

Julie's low chuckle echoed in the foyer as she

pulled Marcy in and closed the door. "I doubt the 'heavens' have anything to do with it, Marce, or anything else Sam or Patrick are involved in."

And don't I know it. Marcy's cheeks burned at the tales Jewels had written in her letters about Sam and his best friend Patrick O'Connor. At eighteen, Marcy was older than Julie, held back by sickness in the first grade, and although she had experience with rogues in New York, Sam's wayward ways never failed to shock and sadden her. Growing up, Sam had been her hero—the mischievous O'Rourke who had made her smile and laugh and feel as protected and secure as he had his little sisters. The only boy she'd ever trusted—bold but honest, teasing but true, and as rock solid as the knuckles he'd often raised in defense of Julie and her.

Marcy sighed. Unfortunately, his best friend changed all that. Like Marcy, Sam started school later due to a bout of flu that slowed the pace of his education, pairing him up with Patrick O'Connor, who was a year younger. But at twenty-one years of age, there was certainly nothing "slow" about Sam O'Rourke today. According to Julie, he had a reputation on the streets of the Southie neighborhood second only to Patrick, stealing hearts as easily as they'd stolen kisses in the coat room of church after mass.

Patrick O'Connor. Mere mention of Sam's best friend always brought a pinch to Marcy's mouth, reminding her of the man she blamed for Sam's moral demise. Patrick had always been the boy every little girl swooned over for as long as Marcy could remember, instilling a cockiness she couldn't abide. And, based on Julie's letters, apparently he *still* wielded the same annoying charm, not only over Julie, but over every female he met.

Except me, thank God. From what Marcy

remembered, Patrick had been a nice boy who'd turned mean at the age of ten when rumors flew about his family, a scandal Marcy's parents had spoken of in hushed tones. It seemed from that point on, Patrick had picked on little girls unmercifully, especially Julie and her, sometimes playing cruel tricks on them when Sam insisted they be allowed to play. Now as a man, he stirred up strife with big girls as well, without the slightest remorse, at least according to the rumors Julie had shared. The man apparently had no compunction whatsoever about flirting with some while dallying with others, even cozying up to one girl while seeing others behind her back. Marcy shivered. She'd met more than her fair share of scoundrels like that in New York, all out for one thing. No, where Sam had always been kind to her, Patrick had not, and Marcy had never forgotten that.

Lips tight, she huffed out a sigh, grateful Patrick O'Connor left her cold and wishing he did the same to Sam, who joined him on nightly jaunts to Brannigan's Pub for decadence Marcy didn't even want to think about. A lump dipped in her throat. Or so she'd heard from Julie, who had this cock-eyed notion of her brother falling for her best friend—"a good girl who could help him fly straight."

Fly straight? Not likely with her own stomach whirling in circles at the very thought. As much as she'd dreamed of Sam O'Rourke over the last five years, Marcy knew he wasn't the boy for her—too wild, too handsome, too cocky, and way too far from the faith she held dear. Definitely not the man she needed. But wanted? Her stomach melted like heated butter, sliding a warm shiver down her spine. Oh, heaven help her, yes. Which is exactly why she would resist Julie's matchmaking hopes with every breath in her. Because the truth was she didn't trust a dangerous boy like Sam O'Rourke. With a hitch of her pulse, his pirate smile invaded her mind, and her legs wobbled a bit. But even more disturbing was the awful suspicion that gnawed deep inside.

Can I even trust myself?

"My family's gone to a wedding," Julie said, looping her arm through Marcy's to usher her to the back of the house, "but Mama made an apple pie when she heard you were coming." She paused on the threshold of the unusually large kitchen to give Marcy a firm hug. "Oh, Marce, I'm *so* glad you're home!"

"I know," Marcy breathed, the smell of pie, boiled coffee, and bleach making her feel like she'd never left. Thirsty for memories, her eyes drank in the warm and welcoming room where the O'Rourkes virtually lived, with its brick hearth and sunny yellow walls. Rich oak cabinets with glass fronts displayed an endless array of blue Wedgewood china and cobalt blue glassware while fluttering blue and white gingham curtains ushered in the scent of honeysuckle from the garden outside. Her gaze caressed the scarred and scuffed country table, its oak surface and edges worn smooth from so many happy hours spent baking cookies, doing homework, or eating dinner with the O'Rourkes. Her home away from home, she thought with a homesick sigh, and the type of family she'd longed to be a part of from the very first day. Julie tugged her to one of the spindle-back chairs, and the familiar squeak in the worn plank floor was music to her ears.

But instead of sitting down, she gripped Julie's arms and stepped back. "Wait—let me look at *you*," she said, admiring the glossy black knot of curls at the back of Julie's head and the pink cambric blouse with a white cascade frill. "Goodness, Jewels, talk about a beauty!"

She tilted her head with a wry smile. "I'm sure Patrick O'Connor has taken notice, although I doubt that's a good thing."

Julie scrunched her nose and pulled out a chair, tapping it to indicate Marcy should sit. "Well, if he has, he sure hasn't let me know it," she said with a playful pout in her tone, retrieving saucers from the cabinet before pulling a knife from the drawer. "Although you are right—it probably wouldn't be a good thing if he did. With his and Sam's dangerous reputations, I can't help but wonder if Sam has forbidden Patrick to even look my way. I swear the man avoids me as if I were Sister Francine's shadow, which is hard to do when he practically lives here half the time." Her smile tipped. "You know, code of ethics among rogues?"

"Now there's an oxymoron if ever there was," Marcy said with a giggle. She propped an elbow to the table and sighed, chin on her fist. "Wouldn't it be nice if boys like Sam and Patrick treated all girls with the same gallantry and respect they show to their sisters?"

Mischief sparkled in Julie's eyes as she cut two pieces of pie. "Sorry, Marce, but I'm not sure I'd want Patrick O'Connor treating me like a sister, because the truth is the man races my pulse every time he walks through that door." Fishing two forks from the drawer, she delivered the pie to the table with a melancholy smile. "It's just a crying shame he's the Southie's number one heartbreaker."

"Yes, and your brother is number two," Marcy said with a warning lift of her brow, "which is why I think we *both* need to steer clear." She stabbed at her pie, venting her frustration over handsome men with little or no faith who thought they were God's gift to women. She'd had more than her fill of that in New York and no inclination to start again here. *Especially if his name is*

Sam O'Rourke. Marcy took a bite of her pie, rolling the tart apples across her tongue with an appreciative moan before giving her friend a smirk. "And 'crying shame' is certainly an appropriate term based on what you said in your letters. If you ask me, 'crying' and 'shame' are the only things a girl can expect from the likes of them."

"I know ..." Julie rose to pour them both a glass of milk, giving Marcy a sheepish smile over her shoulder. "It's just so hard to keep that in mind, you know? Especially when I'm drowning in clear gray eyes as deep as the purest spring."

Yes, I know ... An image flashed of hooded black eyes the same color as Julie's. Marcy gulped her milk and set it back down, pushing it aside along with thoughts of Sam. "All I remember about Patrick O'Connor was he was too handsome for his own good five years ago, so I can't imagine how cocky he must be by now. Trust me, Jewels, you're better off without him."

And me, too, without your brother ...

"I suppose ..." Julie picked at her pie with a mournful sigh before pushing it away. She suddenly sat up with a bright smile. "Well, pooh—I'm not going to let a scalawag like Patrick O'Connor ruin my joy over your homecoming. So, tell me," she said, shimmying close to fold her arms on the table, "did you talk to Sister Francine about the Christmas-play fundraiser for the parish soup kitchen?"

All thoughts of Sam O'Rourke, Patrick O'Connor, and the poor economy slipped from Marcy's mind as she leaned in like Julie, arms on the table and eyes agleam with the thrill of spearheading the parish fundraiser. "I did, as a matter of fact, just this afternoon after I registered for school and guess what? I got the job!"

Julie hopped up with a squeal and embraced her. "Oh, Marce, that's wonderful! I know the pay isn't much for all the hours, but at least it's something, and with you having been head of the drama club at your old school, you're a perfect fit."

"I think so too," Marcy said with a shy smile. She tilted her head. "Of course, I told her I couldn't do it without help, and naturally I'll need someone musical who can play the piano and assist ..." Her teeth tugged at the edge of her smile. "Know anybody like that?"

Julie shrieked and hugged her again. "Oh, I was soooo hoping you'd ask, and we are going to have soooo much fun!"

"I know!" Marcy squeezed her hand, her own body buzzing with anticipation. "And all while raising money for a worthy cause *and* helping the parish."

"Absolutely. So ... when do we start?" Julie asked, as giddy as Marcy.

"Well, we have a planning meeting with Sister Francine, Father Fitzgibbons, and the director of the soup kitchen Tuesday evening at seven. Can you make it?"

Julie's lips bent in a wry smile. "Wait, let me check my calendar first—I may have a prior commitment." She rolled her eyes. "Of course I can make it. It's summer, what else do I have to do?"

Marcy grinned and waggled her copy of *Jane Eyre*. "Oh, I don't know—reread and discuss our favorite books *and* spend lots of time with me?"

"Sounds like heaven," Julie said, carrying their dirty plates and utensils to the sink. She shot her an imp of a smile. "Now throw in an outing or two with Patrick O'Connor, and I do believe I see the pearly gates twinkling up ahead."

A chuckle rolled from Marcy's lips as she deposited the dirty glasses on the counter with an affectionate smile. "You always were blind as a bat, as I recall," she said, giving her friend a squeeze. "Because I hate to tell you, Julie O'Rourke, but that 'gate' isn't 'up,' it's down, and those pearls you see twinkling in the distance?" Marcy tickled her waist and gave her a wink. "It's fire."

Chapter Two

"I knew there was a reason you're my best friend ..." Sitting on the floor of the confessional, Sam O'Rourke took a swig of a bottle before handing the unconsecrated sacristy wine back to Patrick O'Connor with a flash of white teeth. "Other than being as good-looking as me." He swiped his mouth with his rolled sleeve and slanted a boot to the wall, his vested shirt open at the collar. "Knowing where Father Fitz keeps the key is a definite plus."

Patrick upended the bottle with a wry smile. "Well, it's not a cold beer at Brannigan's by a long shot, but it'll do in a pinch till we get paid." He hiked a foot to the wall like Sam, his six-foot-two frame cramped on the padded bench where Father Fitzgibbons absolved the faithful. The maple and vanilla scent of Black Cavendish pipe tobacco and Wrigley's spearmint gum merged with the smell of stolen port, and suddenly guilt soured Patrick's stomach as much as the wine. Closing his eyes, he took another swig, but it was no use—his friendship with Father Fitz was spoiling the taste. Heaving a penitent sigh, he handed the half-empty bottle back to Sam. "Here, one more drink, then let's get out of here and go to Brannigan's. Maybe Lucas'll run us a tab."

"And waste perfectly good wine?" Sam squinted at Patrick like he'd lost his senses rather than his desire to drink. "When I shadow the threshold of Brannigan's tonight, I want to be primed and ready to go, my friend." He took another long swallow, bottle straight up, assessing Patrick through curious eyes beneath the brim of his flat cap. "Unless you'd rather pay a visit to the McPhee sisters." His sly grin appeared distorted, as much from the light streaming through the overhead grid as his wayward intentions. "Hear tell Alice is smitten."

Patrick paused to study his best friend, reflecting on the McPhee sisters and their apparent fascination with Sam and him. A fascination shared by most of the female population of the Southie neighborhood, it would seem, and the thought lured a smile to Patrick's lips. No question they were a worrisome pair to many a mother. At six foot two, Patrick was taller than his best friend's six foot one, but both sported muscular builds hard-sculpted from hauling steel bins of chemicals, cumbersome rolls of newsprint, or heavy machinery on the dock of *The Boston Herald*. Because of their height and dark hair, some mistook them for brothers. Patrick's thick curls were a brown-black while Sam's were a gleaming ebony that matched his eyes, his slight hook nose and heavy stubble lending a blackguard's air. On their own, they certainly dallied with a female's peace of mind, but as a team? They appeared to be diabolical. Patrick's lips quirked. A perfect contrast for an angel from heaven. His mind flitted back to the blonde beauty he'd seen at St. Mary's, and the McPhee sisters quickly lost all allure. He squinted at Sam and shook his head, a pucker at the bridge of his nose. "Nope, not interested."

Sam angled a brow. "Not interested in free wine *or*

pretty Alice McPhee?" He shook his head and took another draw. "You sick, O'Connor?" An unruly grin slid across Sam's face. "Or just contemplating a brief respite of fidelity in the name of love before you break Emily Fischer's heart a third time?"

Patrick winced, Sam's barb niggling his conscience more than he liked. Emily was the girl he cared for more than anyone else, but it was a caring that fell far short of honor when tempted by the numerous Southie lasses always vying for his attention. Pushing the sliver of guilt aside, he chuckled, eyeing Sam through lidded eyes as he rested his head against the wall. "If I am sick, I've died and gone to heaven, then, 'cause I saw my first angel today."

"Did you, now?" Sam leaned back, a gleam in his eye as he hooked an arm behind his head. "Who and where?"

Patrick exhaled slowly, pulse picking up. "No idea who she is, but I saw her walking into the convent with Sister Francine today when I was playing basketball with Father Fitz and the guys …" He shot Sam a silly grin, but didn't care. "And all I can say is—I'm in love."

Sam's laughter ricocheted in the tiny quarters, and Patrick jostled him with his toe. "Hey, keep it down, O'Rourke, will ya?" His whisper was harsh. "You want Father Fitz to know we're here?"

"Sorry, Patrick, but I have a hard time seeing you take after a girl who spends time in a convent." He shook his head and took another drink. "Holy blazes, you barely know how to pray."

"Trust me, Sam, for this one? I'm willing to learn."

Setting the bottle down, Sam angled to the wall, cushioning both hands behind his neck. "So, what's she look like, this celestial creature?"

A slow smile eased across Patrick's face at the memory of a woman he had every intention of getting to know—*well*. He had never believed in love at first sight before, but he had a gut feeling this girl could shackle him to sobriety and spoken vows faster than he could say, "I do." A tenuous exhale drifted from his lips. "I swear, Sam, this girl had hair the lightest shade of blonde you have ever seen on a woman's head, and it spilled and shimmered down her back in soft, loose curls like spun gold."

"Spilled and shimmered? Spun gold?" A grin split Sam's swarthy face. "Blue blazes, O'Connor, you must be in love." He glugged more wine. "Or sicker than I've ever seen."

Patrick folded his arms with a contented sigh, enjoying the vision that burned in his brain. "I'm sick all right—of any other girls after seeing this one. I don't know, Sam, she just seemed different somehow—almost ethereal—kind of a sweetness and calm that went bone-deep, you know? And the eyes?" He gave a low whistle. "So blue, they could have been snatched from the sky after a hard rain."

"Okay, now I know you're sick. The last time I heard verse like that was in Sister Francine's literature class, which come to think of it," Sam said with a scratch of his jaw, "you carried me through with your confounded A's."

Patrick ignored him, seeing only heaven in his mind while his body grew warmer by the moment. "And so help me, the fullest, pinkest lips you have ever seen—" He glanced over with an unprincipled grin. "Or kissed—in the Southie neighborhood and probably all of Boston. She's a little bit of a thing, maybe five foot two or three, but trust me—every single inch is sheer perfection."

Creases buckled Sam's brow. "So, you didn't try to find out who she was? Where she's from?"

Patrick's lips went flat. "Are you crazy? Of course I did, but Sister Francine wouldn't give me the time of day, and Father Fitz just said he thought she was a new senior, moved here from out of town."

"Tarnation, O'Connor, sure hope you see her again." He winked. "Or I do."

Patrick scowled. "This one is mine, Sam, so keep your distance."

Sam grinned. "If you can find her ..."

"Oh, I'll find her all right, you can bet on that." Patrick stood with a groan and a stretch, then reknotted the tie he'd loosened after work. He tucked his white shirt into his gray trousers and snapped his suspenders in place, then lifted his flat cap before wiping the sweat from his forehead with the back of his arm. "Blast it, O'Rourke, it's hotter than the devil's kitchen in here," he groused, whether from the wine, the cramped space, or pure guilt over drinking stolen sacristy wine in Father Fitz's domain. His scowl softened as he tugged his cap back on. *Or maybe haunting blue eyes?* He stepped over Sam, rolling his sleeves to reveal biceps still sore from a hard day at work. "Let's go to Brannigan's and get some decent brew." Unlatching the door as quietly as possible, he winced when it eased open with a truly annoying squeal.

"Ah, Mr. O'Connor and Mr. O'Rourke ..." Father Fitz stood not two feet away, chin high and hands clasped behind his back. He jutted a silver brow in a smiling face reminiscent of a cat stalking a canary. "Eager to be confessing your sins, are you?"

The heat in Patrick's body converged in his face before the blood iced in his veins. "F-Father Fitz," he stammered, feeling like that little boy who'd been caught smoking in the choirboy closet at the age of ten. "We needed a quiet place to talk ..."

With an imposing height that nearly equaled Patrick's six-two, the fifty-year-old priest appeared to lift on the balls of his feet, his stocky frame leaning forward with a casual sniff. "Talk, yes," he said with a careful nod. "About the virtues of sacristy wine, no doubt."

Heat suffused Patrick's cheeks as Sam slithered out of the booth empty-handed.

Brows wrinkled, the priest flicked impatient fingers at the confessional. "You might at least clean up after yourself, Mr. O'Rourke," Father Fitz said. "After all, you're a proud graduate of St. Mary's, young man, not a street hooligan littering an alley with empty bottles."

"Yes, sir." Sam ducked back in the booth to retrieve the near-empty port, then took his place beside Patrick, bottle limp at his side.

Father Fitz held out his palm with a snap of fingers, and Sam relinquished the wine. The priest righted the bottle with a quick flick of his wrist to squint at the label, giving an appreciative nod. "Ah, yes, port—one of my favorites." He peered up at Sam, then veered to Patrick with a lidded gaze. "Yours as well, evidently."

"Father Fitz—"

The priest cut Patrick off with a stiff hand in the air. "Save your breath, Mr. O'Connor, please. There's not a single word you can say in your defense unless it's behind the screen of that confessional."

"Yes, sir." Patrick dropped his gaze to the marble floor.

Father Fitz snapped his fingers again, and Patrick's head shot up. "I believe you have something of mine, Mr. O'Connor?" he said with an extension of his palm.

Fire scalded Patrick's neck as much as the key

scalded the hand in his pocket. Clearing his throat, he placed it in the priest's palm. "Sorry, Father."

"So am I, Patrick. I thought we'd gotten beyond this."

"We have, sir," Patrick said, his voice no more than a rasp. Regret seared in his chest, hotter than that blasted key. Senior year, he and Father Fitz had forged an unlikely friendship when the priest discovered Patrick's dreams to go to college and write for *The Boston Herald*. Despite Patrick's propensity for breaking rules and endless detentions reported to Patrick's father by Father Fitz himself, the priest had reached out in ways his father never would. A man who was not even blood, singling him out for games of basketball, football, and discussions of literature. Taking him under his wing like the son Patrick could never seem to be for a father who harped and hounded. A reedy sigh of remorse shuddered from his lips as he looked up, his gaze connecting with the priest who was more of a father than his own. "And you have my word, Father, this will never happen again."

The priest's measured gaze seemed to burn straight into his. "Your word, Mr. O'Connor," he repeated quietly, lips compressed in a bare hint of a smile. "Tell me, if we traded places right now—would that be enough?"

Shame scorched Patrick's face as he hung his head, hands slipping into his pockets like dead weights. "No, sir," he whispered.

A hearty chuckle rose in the darkened church, expanding into laughter that echoed clear up to the vaulted chamber past the gothic arches overhead.

Patrick sucked in a harsh breath and looked up, the lingering scent of incense and lemon oil filtering into his nostrils as shock filtered across his face. *Sweet chorus of angels—he's laughing?*

"Well, you see, Mr. O'Connor, that's where you're different from me, and when I'm done with you, young man, it's my hope you'll be different as well." His burly black cassock shifted with a slack of a meaty hip. "Of course I'm in the business of forgiveness, which makes me different as well, so this is your lucky day, gentlemen—I'm ready to absolve you of this regrettable stunt."

The breath Patrick had been holding seeped from his lungs in an audible sigh. A shaky smile made its way across his face. "Sweet soul-saving mercy, Father—you won't regret this."

"No, I don't believe I will, Mr. O'Connor, although I'm not so sure about you and Mr. O'Rourke. You see, we're not explicitly talking 'mercy' from the throne of God here," he said with an ominous chuckle. "You know, 'As far as the east is from the west, so far hath he removed our transgressions from us'? No, rather more of an absolution of a wrong committed where retribution is due."

Sam cleared his throat, his stance as awkward as Patrick's. "If you don't mind my asking, sir, what exactly does that mean?"

Father Fitz glanced at Sam, a ghost of a smile on his lips. "Ah, Mr. O'Rourke has found his tongue, I see, which is excellent because you're going to need it, young man."

Staring straight ahead, Patrick actually heard Sam gulp. "Sir?"

A grin twitched at the corners of the priest's mouth. "For the play, Mr. O'Rourke, for which you and Mr. O'Connor are not only going to build sets or whatever else Sister Francine may need you to do, but perform as well." A smile bloomed on his face. "Oh, and I'm quite

A Light in the Window

sure your time spent in the soup kitchen will be most rewarding, although the Southie lasses are sure to miss you, no doubt."

Sam began to hack, and Patrick commenced to absently pounding him on the back, eyes fused to the priest who'd proven himself a most capable mentor. But this? An infraction that extracted more penance than Patrick was willing to pay? He gouged the back of his neck, the priest's semblance of a smirk giving rise to Patrick's temper. "Look, Father, we appreciate your leniency, but can't you just give us some Hail Mary's and Our Father's and be done with it? Both Sam and I work 40-hour shifts every week, sir, and we have no extra time for things like play practice or a soup kitchen."

Father Fitz arched a definitive brow, his gaze flicking to the confessional and back. "Yes, Mr. O'Connor, I can see that your spare time is put to excellent use."

Patrick had the grace to blush.

With a cumbersome sigh, Father Fitz tucked the bottle under his arm. "No, gentlemen, I'm afraid Hail Mary's and Our Fathers have run their course here." He shook his head with a grimace. "Trust me, I've stockpiled them for you both since you crossed the threshold of St. Mary's, so now it's time to put your money where your mouth is." His chin inched up with a steeled sobriety Patrick had seen many a time. "And since time is money, you will pay through the nose with as much community service as I can possibly bleed from the both of you."

"And if we won't do it?" Sam said, a spark of challenge to his tone.

Father Fitz studied Sam with a firm tilt of his head, the faint shifting of a jaw that Patrick recognized all too well from countless hours of detention with a man few students defied. "You know, it's a curious thing, Samuel—your mother has been after me to come to dinner for months now, so perhaps I should come next week, imparting some information that just may batten your hatches a wee bit."

Patrick's eyes weighted closed. *Great. Another knock-down, drag-out with Pop.*

"I think I may just chance it, Father," Sam said, the dark stubble on his jaw as menacing as the stubborn gleam in his eye. "I can live without my mother's approval."

"Ah, yes, Mr. O'Rourke, but the question remains—can you live without money?"

Sam blinked. "Pardon me?"

Humor played at the edge of the priest's mouth, which was compressed like his jaw in a battle of wills. "Money, Mr. O'Rourke. You know, remuneration for a job well-done that allows you to buy a round a drinks at the corner pub, dazzle a pretty girl with an ice-cream soda, or purchase the proper clothes befitting the neighborhood rakes?"

The blood drained from Patrick's face as quickly as it did from Sam's.

"Yes, well, you see, gentlemen," Father Fitz continued in a tone as matter-of-fact as his smile, "a priest has friends in high places in addition to the Almighty, you know. Such as, shall we say, the *Herald*?"

Patrick's eyes lumbered closed, the lump in his throat as tight as the noose Father Fitz was cinching around their necks. Both he and Sam needed their jobs at the *Herald* if Patrick was going to go to college and Sam was going to rise to management.

"I don't know if I've ever told you boys, but Arthur

Hennessey and I go way back." Father Fitz nodded with a faint smile, eyes trailing into what apparently was a fond trip down Memory Lane. "Actually coached him on the parish league, if you can imagine that." He snapped out of his reverie, his smile brightening considerably. "Of course that was way before he took over as CEO of the *Herald*, you understand. Although I have to admit, nobody tossed a meaner knuckleball."

Patrick stifled a groan. *Except you, Father Fitz ...*

"So ... " Patrick jolted when the priest clapped his hands, his grin almost as loud. "I look forward to seeing you gentlemen at the fundraiser meeting next week, where you'll learn all about just why absconding with the sacristy wine is not a good idea."

"This is blackmail, Father," Sam said with a scowl.

Father Fitz blinked, a wedge popping at the bridge of his nose. "Yes, I suppose it is, Samuel ..." He quickly dismissed his concern with a wave of a hand. "Well, no never mind," he said with a shrug of his shoulders, his smile veering into dazzling, "I'm on good terms with the Man upstairs—I'll just absolve myself."

With a near-jaunty turn, he made his way to the door, pivoting when he placed his hand on the knob. "You know, I really should be thanking you gentlemen for helping me out. I'm afraid Sister Francine has been on my tail for weeks now, badgering me for able-bodied men to assist her new fundraiser chair." His lips parted in a gleam of white. "And after a senior year of English Lit with the woman, I'm sure you boys can appreciate the kind of duress I've been under." He hoisted the bottle of wine in the air. "You know, I believe I may owe a debt of thanks to this tasty port ... and to you as well."

He turned to leave, but not before needling them with a knowing smile tempered by a stern gaze. "But a word of caution, gentlemen. When it comes to the drink, make no mistake—there are always debts to be paid. So if I were you, I'd weigh the cost carefully before you imbibe anytime soon." He tipped the bottle in a salute and opened the door. "Tuesday, seven sharp at the rectory—don't be late." He winked. "The top of the evening to you, gentlemen, and I bid you good night."

Patrick stared open-mouthed as the arched wooden door squealed closed with a thud, the air in his lungs as slack as the line of his jaw. "A good night?" he repeated, staring at Sam with a dazed shake of his head. "Well, it certainly was, but not anymore."

Chapter Three

"Something smells awfully good in here." Mr. O'Rourke ushered his wife and three daughters through the kitchen door with a sleeping boy in his arms, a warm smile on his face that reminded Marcy so much of Sam, her stomach skipped. Handsome in a charcoal sack suit complete with black-striped bow tie, his black eyes twinkled like Julie's as he tossed his homburg hat on the counter and snitched a warm oatmeal cookie. He gave Marcy a wink. "It's awfully good to have you back, Marcy," he said with a swipe of two more, his sweet tooth obviously explaining a bulkier frame than she remembered. "Especially if it means I'll have fresh-baked cookies on a more regular basis."

Julie shot her father a mock scowl, feigning insult as she spooned cookie dough onto a sheet. "Papa, I've baked for you a lot without Marcy here, I'll have you know."

Shifting Julie's five-year-old brother Max to his other shoulder, Mr. O'Rourke sidled over to dispense a hug before depositing a kiss on Julie's head. "Ah, yes, but not as well or as often, eh?"

"Papa!" Julie laughed, pretending to elbow him away.

"Oh, go on with you," Mrs. O'Rourke said with a

playful butt of her hip, bumping her husband out of the way so she could hug Marcy good and proper. The familiar scent of Pears soap and her trademark hint of lavender tickled Marcy's nose along with the feather from a hat that crowned blue-black hair wisped with silver. "Goodness, Marcy, I almost don't recognize you, you've grown so much in five years." Her gaze was affectionate as she buffed Marcy's arms. "How are your parents?"

"They're well, Mrs. O'Rourke, although Papa's still looking for work."

Julie's father slipped a thick arm around his wife's shoulder. "It's pretty dismal out there right now," he said, his look suddenly sober. "But I know for a fact Gunther Machinery is hiring, so tell your father I'll be happy to put in a good word."

"Thank you so much, Mr. O'Rourke," Marcy said with genuine relief. "I'll be sure to let him know."

"Do you remember me?" A miniature version of Julie stepped forward from a trio of female O'Rourkes, two of which were Julie's twelve-year-old twin sisters who appeared either tired or shy. The fireball looked up at Marcy with dark eyes beneath a pert straw hat that complemented a white sailor dress. "Because I don't remember you."

Marcy laughed and bent to give Julie's seven-year-old sister a hug. "Of course I remember you, Erin, but you were only a toddler when I left, so I don't expect you to remember me."

"Julie says you're the best friend she's ever had." Erin tilted a head of black curls, and the navy ribbon on her hat followed suit.

Marcy sent Julie a fond look. "Mine too."

"She says you're gonna sleep here tonight," she said with an innocent blink. "Maybe you can sleep in Sam's bed because he doesn't use it a whole lot anymore."

Marcy's jaw went slack, the heat in her face giving the oven a run for its money.

"Erin, hush," Julie said with a blush that most likely matched Marcy's. "Marcy will sleep with me because Sam needs his bed when he finally comes home."

"'When' being the key word," Mrs. O'Rourke said with a weak smile in Marcy's direction. "I wish Sam wouldn't keep such late hours—it's a poor example for the others." A rueful sigh floated from her lips as she shot her husband a look of resignation. "But I'm afraid his father refuses to lay down the law."

"Sam's a grown man now," Mr. O'Rourke said with a wry twist of his lips as he filched his fourth cookie and homburg from the counter. He gave Marcy a wink that suggested he might have given his parents the same problem. "After boys graduate and begin working fulltime, they tend to burn the midnight oil and then some."

"But he won't need his bed if he stays at Patrick's," Erin reasoned.

"Sam mentioned staying here tonight, darling, although it's safe to say they'll be late." Mrs. O'Rourke kissed Julie good night and hugged Marcy before prodding Erin toward the door, her husband close on her heels. "Come on, little one, it's almost eleven, and we need to get you and Max to bed." Her gaze lighted on Marcy with affection. "Marcy, I can't tell you how good it is to have you home again, not just for Julie, but for us too. We've missed you."

Tears misted Marcy's eyes. Being an only child had never been easy for her, but Julie and the O'Rourkes had eased the loneliness considerably. "Me too, Mrs. O'Rourke—more than I can say."

"Sleep in as late as you want, girls, and we'll catch

up in the morning, either over breakfast or lunch, all right?" Julie's mother blew them a kiss and traipsed down the hall with her husband and daughters in tow, the creaks and groans of the polished staircase rousing even more wonderful memories in Marcy's mind.

Melancholy laced Marcy's tone as she transferred the last few cookies from a cookie sheet to a platter already stacked high. "Goodness, Julie, I just love your family," she whispered with a sigh of longing.

"Mmm ... even Sam?" Julie teased, licking icing from her finger.

Marcy slipped her a patient smile. "I like your brother, Jewels, you know that." Her lips crooked to the side. "I just like him a whole lot better when he's not around."

"I doubt that," Julie said with a wink. "Hey, I have tons of icing left, so how 'bout one more batch, but iced sugar this time?"

Marcy's gaze darted to the clock and back. "I don't know, what if Sam comes home?" Her tongue swiped her teeth in nervous habit. "I really don't want to be down here if he does."

"Come on, you little chicken, you have to see him eventually, and you may as well get it over with, right?" She fetched a clean bowl. "Besides, I already told you, Sam is always out late on the weekend."

Marcy puffed out a sigh. "Okay, but if he comes waltzing through that door while we're baking cookies ..." She threatened her with a spatula. "You are in big trouble, Miss O'Rourke."

"I'll say," Julie said, mischief twinkling in her eyes. "Because you know who will be with him."

Marcy shook her head and laughed. "You are incorrigible, you know that?"

"Nope, that would be my older brother, so I suggest

we get a move on before you find out firsthand."

Marcy chuckled. Whether it was the lively chatter of her best friend, the O'Rourke's homey kitchen, or the steamy warmth of a summer night laden with smells of cinnamon and vanilla, she wasn't sure. All she knew was she hadn't felt this relaxed and happy since before Papa had taken them away to New York. Overnight she'd been thrust into a stiff and snooty society in which Marcy had no desire to fit in. Debutante balls and society teas were not her idea of home, and she found herself craving the simple and unpretentious life she'd left behind in Boston. A life where family and faith meant more than money and prestige, and where she could be who she was meant to be—Marceline Rose Murphy, a woman who loved family, friends, and faith with a passion.

And Sam O'Rourke?

No! Marcy jumped up to slide the last of the sugar cookies into the oven with shaky hands, then carried dirty bowls and utensils to the sink, eye on the clock. "Okay, Jewels, all done. Let me help with those dishes so we can get to bed."

Julie handed her the milk bottle she'd just rinsed. "Here, set this out on the porch, then you can help dry the last of these dishes, okay?"

"Yes, ma'am," Marcy said with a smile over her shoulder as she opened the door, "and then I'm ready for sweet dreams—"

"Oh, me too ..." a husky voice said.

Marcy bounced back into the kitchen with a tiny squeak after colliding with an immovable object so tall, her face was flush with his chest.

"Do I know you?" Sam asked, and Marcy was sure she'd melt into the floor. And oh, sweet saints, how she wished that she could! Her limbs and lungs had ceased upon impact, rendering her helpless to do anything but stare unblinking into a pin-stripe shirt open enough at the collar to expose a hint of dark hair. She tried to respond, but all words adhered to her tongue, the air rasping from her throat in thick, heavy breaths that refused all utterance. Her muscles were so paralyzed, she was totally incapable of even lifting her head. But she didn't have to—she knew who it was. If the low, gravelly tone didn't give him away, the lemon scent of William's Shaving Soap certainly did, intoxicating her as if she'd had one too many of her grandmother Mima's whiskey eggnogs. The shock of his presence caused her to sway on her feet, and her breath caught in her throat when his hands burned through her cotton sleeves like the cookie tins through the potholders. "Whoa ... are you all right?"

No! Somehow she managed to lunge back, milk bottle clutched to her chest as if it were a prized possession.

Julie's laughter floated somewhere behind, foggy and faraway—like Marcy wished she could be. "She's changed a wee bit, hasn't she, Sam?" Julie said.

"Mar-cy?" His tongue sounded slow and thick like hers, the intonation of his question heavy with shock.

Her eyelids lifted in a sluggish sweep of lashes as if each were made of lead, her gaze lighting on the face that had haunted her dreams since she'd been a little girl. "Hello, Sam," she whispered.

Black eyes that had always held a hint of a dare traveled her body so deliberately, her legs nearly buckled as heat pulsed in her cheeks. The burn of his hand returned when he steadied her once again, and his thumb was a torch setting fire as it kneaded her arm. "Well, I'll be ... Marceline Murphy," he said softly, the very sound of her name on his tongue quivering her stomach. As if it had a mind of its own, his gaze slowly swept down and up once again while a perilous grin teased on his lips. "Blue blistering blazes," he muttered, "who would have thought *this* was hiding beneath that little bookworm afraid of her own shadow?"

"She's gorgeous, isn't she, Sam?" Julie's voice fairly shimmered with pride.

"Oh, yes, ma'am, she most certainly is ..." he breathed, grazing her chin with his thumb as if he couldn't believe it was her. Marcy jolted, and he chuckled. "But still the same shy and tongue-tied little girl, I see." He turned and draped a loose arm over the friend who stood behind him, then nodded her way. "And you said it wasn't a good night, O'Connor. You remember Julie's best friend Marceline Murphy, don't you?"

Patrick O'Connor remained as mute as she, the lines of his chiseled face sagging in shock as he stared, dark-bristled jaw slack while light gray eyes all but swallowed her whole. He was every bit as handsome as she'd expected, if not more so, and her trust factor for beautiful men like him sank to an all-time low. She'd seen his type in New York and witnessed first-hand the damage they could do, and she would never allow herself to fall in love with a man like that. A man like Nora's fiancé, who made eyes at Marcy while he made love to her cousin.

The clearest gray eyes she'd ever seen continued to stare, and cold fingers of warning slithered Marcy's spine. Dark curls framed his Adonis face, easily securing Patrick O'Connor's reputation as the Southie's leading Lothario. And, Marcy suspected, a cocky demeanor as well. His hard-chiseled features matched a hard-chiseled body with shoulders as broad as his ego, no doubt, and she couldn't help but bristle, her guard immediately edging up. She'd encountered his type in New York society more than she liked, and their swagger and conceit grated, convincing her once and for all that he was as dangerous for Julie as Sam was for her.

———

Patrick could do nothing but gape, tongue pasted to the roof of his mouth as surely as his lids were pasted to the sockets of his eyes, denying even a blink. "Marceline Murphy," he finally rasped, almost to himself, voice tinged with awe. The breath he'd been holding slowly expelled with a duck of his Adam's apple while he stood rooted to the floor, the angel of his dreams barely two feet away. "It was you ..."

Sam squinted at him. "It was *her*?" he said, awareness dawning in a pinch of brows. "*She's* the one?"

"The one what?" Julie wanted to know, hooking the angel's arm to steer her to the counter. Handing Marcy a towel, she commenced to washing dishes, eyes wide in question as she peered over her shoulder.

Patrick swallowed hard, his gaze flicking to Sam in silent threat before shooting Julie an easy smile that belied the sweat slicking his palms. "The 'one' I saw Sister Francine drag into the convent today," he said casually, striving for nonchalance as he ambled over to help himself to a cookie. He butted against the counter with legs crossed, giving Marcy a wink. "Hope she wasn't plying vocations, Marceline, because that would surely make grown men cry."

"Me included," Sam said with a grin. He swiped a cookie and straddled a chair, eyes twinkling as he chewed. "The cookies are great, ladies, but we'd enjoy them a whole lot more with a glass of milk and pretty company—"

"No!" Marcy dropped a spoon, cheeks bruised with color. "I m-mean we're t-tired, especially your sister since I've been bending her ear, so we're heading up after the dishes, aren't we, Julie?"

Patrick retrieved the utensil and slipped it back in the dishwater, grateful Marceline Murphy was apparently as nervous as he. He grinned. "You could always warm the milk, you know, maybe take the edge off to ensure a good night's sleep?"

Sam reached for another cookie. "You've had Marcy to yourself all evening, Jewels. Can't you give us a few minutes to catch up?"

Julie's nervous gaze flicked to Patrick, and he met it with a crooked grin. "Come on, Jewels," he said softly, coaxing with his trademark smile, "one glass of milk and you two'll be tucked in bed before you know it."

With a chew of her lip, Julie peeked at Marcy, her manner hesitant. "One glass of milk won't hurt, will it?" she said under her breath, as if she didn't want him to hear.

Patrick's pulse stalled at the reluctance in Marcy's eyes, those full pink lips compressing almost imperceptibly. Her chest rose and fell with an audible sigh. "One glass," she emphasized carefully, blue eyes locked on Julie's face with clear warning.

The breath that had lodged in his throat slowly seeped through his lips. He turned to retrieve four glasses from the cabinet before offering Marcy a boyish smile. "I'll be happy to warm yours if you like."

"Thank you, but no," she said in a distant tone he wasn't used to hearing from a woman, abruptly turning away to finish drying a bowl.

Patrick blinked, then strolled to the icebox with a crimp in his pride. *The cold shoulder? From a girl?* He bent to grip the milk bottle, his resolve as firm as the glass in his hand. *And just as breakable?* Maybe, but then Marceline Murphy obviously didn't know with whom she was dealing. He had never struck out with a girl in his life, and he wasn't about to start now. He poured four glasses of milk, only half listening to the conversation while a thin line of determination steeled his smile. Because other than Sam O'Rourke, *nobody* knew how to warm up a cold shoulder better than Patrick Brendan O'Connor.

"How did you like New York?" Sam asked after the girls had finished the dishes.

Knuckles gripped on her empty glass of milk, which she'd obviously bolted to hurry things along, Marceline expounded on the last five years of her life, her voice shy and soft with the barest hint of a brogue. Patrick was more than content to let Sam steal and steer the conversation, taking the opportunity to study the new Marceline Murphy with an admiring eye. He remembered her well, of course, because she and Julie were always thick as thieves, just like Sam and him, although he'd barely ever spared her or Julie a glance. Probably because he and Sam had been "early bloomers" as Mrs. O'Rourke liked to say, two boys who'd matured sooner than most. Tall at fifteen and fourteen with a hint of stubble just beginning to shadow their jaws, Sam and Patrick quickly developed an eye for the older, shapelier girls who welcomed their attention, stoking their desire for more of the same. He slowly twirled his glass on the table. Skills with women he'd easily acquired with little or no effort, or at least until now. He took a drink, resolve trickling through his body like milk trickled down his throat. Marceline Murphy—his very first roadblock.

And my last.

A Light in the Window

He rested his head on the back of his chair with a loose fold of arms, watching her through lidded eyes while his pulse thudded slow and sure. He was mesmerized by the pale gold that tumbled her shoulders, transfixed by the soft shape of her mouth, the silk of her skin. A summer-scented breeze fluttered tendrils of her hair against an alabaster neck, teasing both Patrick and the delicate lobe of her ear. He imagined suckling that very ear and his throat parched dry, compelling him to take another swig of his milk. He forced himself to focus on the person rather than the woman, and a calm settled like nothing he had ever experienced before. There was a reserved innocence that intrigued him and a gentle depth that called, both to his body and his soul. And although he didn't know much about the grownup Marceline Murphy, he did know one thing for dead sure. This was a woman he wanted to know better—and in every possible way.

"So, Marcy," Sam said, crossing his arms on the table. "Tell me you weren't seeking a vocation today, or I'm afraid some hearts and hopes will be sorely dashed."

Patrick prickled at Sam's attempt to dazzle her with a smile meant to disarm. He didn't know Marcy well, but he did recognize a woman who was uncomfortable with flirtation when he saw it, and he mentally filed her reaction away, noting she was not a girl won over by easy charm. He observed how the tip of her tongue nervously grazed her teeth before she offered a reluctant smile and surmised she was as modest and unpretentious as she was beautiful.

"No, not a vocation, at least not as a nun." She exchanged looks with Julie before meeting Sam's probing gaze. "But Julie and I will be chairing the Christmas-play fundraiser this year, and we're very excited." Her eyes took on a sparkle for the first time. "Our first meeting is next week."

All air seized in Patrick's lungs. "The Christmas-play fundraiser?" he repeated, his voice a near-croak. He locked gazes with Sam while a slow smile inched across both of their faces.

She glanced from him to Sam, those incredible blue eyes narrowing the slightest bit. "Yes, why?"

Patrick grinned outright. "No particular reason, Marcy, I just think it's commendable of you girls to take on such a huge task for such a wonderful cause. And you can rest assured Sam and I will be at your beck and call if you need any help."

She blinked, his offer obviously catching her by surprise. Those pink lips tipped up in a perfect smile, and his heart turned over. "Why, thank you, Patrick," she said as if she'd just noticed he was even in the room. "That's very kind."

Patrick beamed. "Our pleasure, right, Sam?"

Sam gave her a wink that tinted her cheeks. "Absolutely. In fact, what time is that meeting? We'll be happy to show up and lend our support."

Her mouth dropped a full inch before a flicker of doubt shadowed her eyes. "Oh no, really, that's not necessary ..."

"We insist," Patrick said, tone and chin adamant. "You'll have scenery to build and auditions to run, and we are more than willing to assist with such a worthy cause. We spend a lot of time at church anyway, with basketball and what not, so we may as well put it to good use. What time is the meeting?" His eyes flicked from Marcy to Julie, not daring to breathe as he silently prayed Marcy would agree. The last thing he needed was for this proper lady to discover the infraction that mandated their attendance.

Julie squeezed Marcy's arm. "I think we should let them, Marce," she whispered, "we're going to need all the help we can get."

The blue eyes appraised him for several moments while that delicate jaw shifted ever so slightly, wheels turning, no doubt, in that beautiful head. Her gaze veered from him to Sam and back before she finally heaved a shuddering sigh that seemed to drain all resistance. "Seven o'clock, Tuesday at the rectory, then," she said with a slump of her shoulders that indicated her energy had been sapped. Eyes flitting to the clock over the sink, she rose to her feet. "Ready to go up, Jewels? I'm exhausted."

Julie bounced up, slipping Patrick a shy smile. "Sure. Good night, Patrick, Sam." She hooked an arm to Marcy's waist and ushered her to the door, shooting a crooked grin over her shoulder. "And come morning, there best be more than a few crumbs of cookies left this time, Patrick O'Connor, you hear?"

He pressed a palm to his heart. "You have my word, Julie O'Rourke, there will be cookies aplenty, even if I have to tie up your brother to do it."

"It's good to have you home, Marcy," Sam called after them, and Patrick couldn't agree more.

"Thanks, Sam," she said, her voice fading when she quickly tugged Julie down the hall. "Good night."

The girls disappeared around the corner, and Patrick dropped back in his chair with a grin that stretched ear to ear. He winked at Sam. "It most certainly is."

Chapter Four

I will not throw up ... I will not throw up ... Marcy pressed a palm to her abdomen as if she could somehow quell her nausea, noting that her knees were knocking along with Julie's knuckles as her friend rapped on the rectory door. The neighborhood literally shimmered with summer, but Marcy barely noticed, the shrill sound of locusts vibrating the night like her nerves vibrated her body. The scent of honeysuckle and fresh-mown grass drifted in the air along with the melodic laughter of children playing stickball in a neighbor's yard and hopscotch on the sidewalk. On the church parking lot, a group of men indulged in a new sports rage called basketball where a soccer ball was tossed into half-bushel peach baskets nailed to posts, shouts ringing out when rubber clattered against wood. Young boys hovered to retrieve balls from the closed baskets, little monkeys shimmying up posts much like Marcy's supper threatened to shimmy up her throat.

Hand to mouth, she stifled a burp, prompting Julie to curl an arm to her waist. "You have nothing to worry about, Marce—I've never seen anyone so organized in my life."

Nothing to worry about? Marcy closed her eyes to swallow the panic in her throat, quite sure her supper was destined for the front of her blue, high-collar blouse. Yes, her notes were all neatly typed with Papa's trusty Remington in triplicate several times, and audition flyers and scripts were ready to be mimeographed pending Sister Francine's approval. Julie and she had already begun writing songs for the play, and a tour of the soup kitchen had only stirred their excitement to epic proportions. Her hair was loosely pinned up in the feminine Gibson Girl style for a professional air, and her favorite pale-blue blouse was crisp and comfortable, boosting her confidence because it matched the blue of her eyes. All in all, everything was under control. A reedy breath shuddered from her lips.

Except my feelings for Sam.

After the four of them had talked in the kitchen last Friday night, she and Julie had chatted far into the wee hours of the morning, battling their fascination with two men neither wanted to like. And yet they did, a predicament only exacerbated by Sam and Patrick's willingness to give of their time. Marcy had been caught off-guard, her barriers compromised by their noble offer, and her heart had roiled in turmoil long after Julie had fallen asleep. And now here she was, stomach aquiver and mouth parched as paste.

"Marcy, Julie—come in, come in!" Father Fitzgibbons' welcome smile worked like a bromide, and a tenuous breath wavered from her lips when it helped settle her stomach and banish her fear. Ushering them in, he steered them to the parlour where Sister Francine conversed with Evan Farrell, the new director of the St. Mary's Center of Hope, whom she and Julie had met on the tour. Fresh out of college, Mr. Farrell had won Marcy's respect immediately with his passion for the poor, devoting his skills and schooling to insure financial solvency for such a charitable cause. He glanced up with a friendly nod and a smile before returning his attention to Sister Francine, who appeared to be engrossed in discussion of the ledger in her lap.

"May I interest you in a lemonade, ladies?" Father Fitz indicated frosty tumblers floating with lemons, and Marcy's mouth instantly watered.

"Oh, thank you, Father, that would be lovely," she said, setting Papa's leather attaché next to the striped love seat where she and Julie sat down. Sipping her lemonade while Julie chatted with Father Fitz, Marcy's stomach tumbled again, but this time with excitement. Never had she been part of something so important before, so vital to the community, so sanctioned by God, and her anticipation suddenly billowed like the parlour sheers in the warm summer breeze.

"Good evening, Miss Murphy and Miss O'Rourke—I'm excited to hear your plans for our fundraiser." Sister Francine laid her ledger aside, her moon-shaped face beaming like the sun.

"As am I," Evan Farrell said, his kind smile making his bookworm face as handsome as Patrick O'Connor's to Marcy's way of thinking. He was not as tall or as brawny as the Southie Casanova, but he had a pleasant face with honest blue eyes enhanced by wire-rim glasses and a spray of freckles that gave him a simple air. But thirty minutes spent with Evan at the center, and Marcy knew his intellect was anything but. Valedictorian of his college class, Evan Farrell had bypassed a number of lucrative jobs to serve the poor instead, according to Sister Francine, who spoke as if the man walked on water.

Marcy all but glowed at the prospect of what lay in store for her and the others in this room. The Christmas play was the highlight of St. Mary's calendar events, a way to reach out to the poor in the community, both financially and spiritually, and a way for her to reconnect with home. To give back to her beloved Southie neighborhood where she hoped to settle down some day and raise a family of her own. Marcy's throat tightened. Because if the city of New York and the financial Panic of 1893 had taught her anything, it was that when all was said and done, nothing mattered more in life than God and family.

"Shall we begin?" Sister Francine said, the starched flaps of her white cornette headdress dipping when she checked the watch pinned beneath the white bib of her black habit. Marcy's gaze flicked to the grandfather clock across the room that read 6:59, her heart beating double time. *Please, Lord—maybe they won't show.* Calmed by the thought, she hefted Papa's portfolio into her lap to withdraw her papers. Snapping it closed again, she placed it back on the floor just as the clock chimed seven, relief coursing through her veins. *Thank you, God!*

Boom, boom, boom. Marcy's eyelids fluttered closed at the sound of the front-door knocker, her body jolting along with Julie's. She felt her friend's gentle squeeze on her arm and opened her eyes to give her a shaky smile. Father Fitz's thunderous voice filled the foyer, and within three heartbeats, Marcy's pulse registered double time as Sam O'Rourke strolled into the room.

If one measured by natural beauty, Sam was not a man most would call handsome—nose too long, eyes too dark. And yet … he was. Even as a boy he possessed a dangerous mystery about him, a lazy grin that could capture Marcy in a slow blink of black eyes. He carried a strawboater, as did Patrick, who followed behind in a pin-striped shirt with suspenders and tie.

Sam's white high-collar shirt with a stylish bowtie accentuated the dark shadow of his beard while pushed-up sleeves revealed muscular forearms, one of which was draped with a navy jacket.

"Ah, reinforcements," Father Fitz said with a cuff of Patrick's shoulder, directing them to matching gold wing chairs across the way. He offered them drinks, which they gladly accepted before he introduced them to Evan. Personable and polite, they responded to Evan's questions with grace and Sister Francine's queries with humor, updating their prior teacher as to their activities since graduation two years ago. Their laughter seemed to fill the room, and although the exchange was brief, it allowed Marcy to study them unaware.

The same charm Julie claimed they exercised with the young women of the Southie neighborhood they now lavished on Sister Francine, the twinkle in her eyes proof that when it came to females, age posed no barrier to their allure. From Patrick's classic good looks and chiseled features to the rugged recklessness of Sam's olive skin and aquiline nose, they made an irresistible pair. They were truly a dangerous duo, possessing a presence and aura that went well beyond handsome faces or charismatic personalities, emanating a confidence few men their age could claim. Although both were bright and articulate according to Julie—Patrick excelling in literary studies while Sam was proficient in math—their academic strengths were often offset by a streak of rebellion that wore a path to Father Fitzgibbons' door.

"Marcy, I trust you've gotten reacquainted with these two young men?" Father Fitz said, seating himself on a spare chair absconded from the dining room.

Swallowing hard, Marcy offered a penitent smile.

A Light in the Window

"Yes, Father, and I hope you don't mind that I invited them tonight, but Sam and Patrick were kind enough to offer their help."

"Were they, now?" Father Fitz said with an arch of a brow, his pointed look burnishing Patrick's neck while Sam merely grinned. "Noble and selfless service is a rare commodity indeed, gentlemen, so you are to be commended." He gave Marcy a nod. "You have the floor, Miss Murphy, and our most ardent attention as well, so by all means—proceed."

"Thank you, Father, and everyone," she said with a shy sweep of the room, stuttering when Sam delivered a wink. "I c-can't t-tell you how excited and honored Julie and I are to be working on this very important project with you, and without further ado, we'll get right to it."

Julie rose to hand out copies of the agenda and Marcy nodded her thanks, her hands sweaty as she shuffled her own papers into a neat, little pile, tongue glazing her teeth. With a clear of her throat, she delivered a stiff smile. "Item one on our agenda tonight is to establish a monetary goal for our fundraiser. To do that, Mr. Farrell—"

"Call me Evan, please," Evan interrupted, his encouraging smile as calming as Father Fitz's had been upon arrival.

Drawing in a quiet breath, Marcy offered a grateful smile. "Certainly, Evan. As I was saying, Evan has been kind enough to provide me with final figures for last year's fundraiser as well as a projection of his needs for the upcoming year, which has helped us to establish this year's goal of ..." Marcy paused, surveying the room with sober eyes. "Eight hundred dollars. Now I know that may seem like a high figure, but Julie and I feel we can accomplish this in a number of new and creative ways over and above the cost of a ticket.

"One ..." She ticked the point off with a finger. "By selling punch and cookies donated by the parish before and after the production and during intermission. Two, by circulating flyers at each parish in Boston rather than just in the Southie neighborhood. Three, by utilizing as many parish children as possible, which Julie and I hope to accomplish with a number of choir scenes. Four, by increasing the number of shows from the usual three over one weekend to nightly for a solid week. Five, by selling raffle tickets for prizes donated by our local merchants during the months up to the event, which will not only help advertise it, but build anticipation. And finally ..." Marcy said with a conspiratorial lift of her brows, a smile twitching on her lips, "six—printing programs that not only list the names of those who performed in or helped with the play, but any local merchants who donate raffle prizes." Her smile broke free. "Donors will be listed as 'Friends of St. Mary's,' of course, with a special note of thanks to those who made a fixed-minimum contribution or more to the center."

Sister Francine unleashed a hearty chuckle. "Bravo, Miss Murphy," she said with a rousing clap of her hands. "Excellent ideas, just excellent!"

Marcy blushed. "Thank you, Sister. Julie and I have been working on this since you and I spoke last week."

"Well, it certainly shows, young lady. By all means, continue."

Adrenaline surging, Marcy dove in to the rest of the plan, so excited she almost forgot Sam and Patrick were still in the room. She explained Julie's role as musical director to write, teach, and play the music as well as her own duties as overall administrator, drama director,

A Light in the Window

and designing and sewing costumes for the main cast. In record time, she covered audition and rehearsal schedules for cast, choirs, and volunteers who'd handle everything from stage assistance, tearing tickets and ushering, to concessions, set design, and scenery production. At mention of set and scenery, she sent a shy smile in Sam and Patrick's direction for their willingness to help in those areas in particular.

Edging towards her conclusion, she paused to inhale deeply, her tone almost breathy as she divulged her final point with a skip of her pulse. "But," she said with a twinkle in her eye, "in the end, a Christmas-play fundraiser is only as good as the play itself, which is why I am so excited about the theatrical presentation I am proposing this year, pending committee approval, of course."

Setting her notes aside, Marcy perched on the edge of her seat, hands clasped in her lap and face surely aglow. "It's called *A Light in the Window*, and befitting a neighborhood revered as the heart and soul of Irish America, it's based on the Irish custom of placing a candle in the window on Christmas Eve through Epiphany to welcome the Holy Family. It's the story of a poor family of eight whose parents sacrifice to give their children a wonderful Christmas, only to share their meager gifts and food with three unlikely strangers at various times, each responding to the candle of welcome in the window. Grumpy at first over the depletion of their Christmas food and gifts, the children are puzzled to find themselves a wee bit more joyful with each gift given away. When a fourth visitor arrives on Epiphany, they are saddened because they have nothing left to give, but lo and behold, it is an angel from the Lord, sent not to take, but to give, bestowing on them the true gift of Christmas ...." Marcy swallowed hard, the power of the story, as always, eliciting a sting of tears in her eyes. Her smile all but trembled as she peeked around the room. "Christ giving His peace and joy to those who give their hearts to Him and to others, shining bright in a dark world like a light ablaze in the window." Embarrassed by her reaction, she offered a feeble grin. "Of course, just as the candle is meant to draw strangers as if welcoming the Holy Family, I hope to replicate that same welcome to those who attend our play with fir boughs and candles in each of the auditorium windows."

Suddenly overcome with emotion, Marcy blinked wide to deflect the threat of more tears. "You see, this is a story in which we, too, can shine our own light of Christ's love through the windows of our eyes … our hearts … our actions …" Her voice tapered off to a reverent hush as her gaze slowly scanned each face in the room. "At a time and place in history when our own community not only desperately needs it, but the very God we serve ordains it."

The room was silent, and for a split second, she froze, gaze darting from Father Fitz to Sister Francine. And then all at once, Father Fitz rose to his feet in a resounding ovation in which the others quickly followed suit, swelling her heart with joy despite the discomfort of praise. She glanced at Sam, and he winked again, that pirate grin sending her stomach awhirl. And then her gaze flitted to Patrick, and her breath hitched in her lungs. No smile, no praise, no applause. Just staring with mouth agape and a sober look of respect in eyes she could have sworn held a sheen of moisture. Her heart tipped.

"Oh, you were wonderful," Julie whispered, stealing her attention with a tight hug.

"Congratulations, young lady, that was a stellar

presentation if ever there was." Evan extended his palm in a hearty shake.

Marcy rose to place her hand in his, offering a wobbly grin. "Thank you, Evan. We certainly couldn't have done it without you or your passion for the center *or* the information you provided."

"Young lady ..." Sister Francine approached, towering over Marcy with an imposing breadth and height that surely intimidated students large and small. "I don't mind telling you that the weight of the world has slipped off my shoulders tonight." She surprised Marcy with a near-crushing embrace before rattling her with a sound pat on the back. "You are an answer to this old woman's prayers, and the saints be praised that your father brought you home from New York."

"Thank you, Sister," Marcy said, tugging Julie close to share in the accolades. "But I couldn't have done it without Julie."

"Obviously a match made in heaven, ladies." Father Fitz advanced with a broad smile while Sister Francine dispensed an equally devastating hug to Julie. "I think it would behoove us to meet biweekly here at the rectory for status reports and marching orders from these two dynamos, eh?" Hands clasped to his back, he slanted back on his heels. "Does seven on Tuesdays work for you ladies?"

"Oh, yes, Father, absolutely," Marcy said while Julie echoed her approval.

"Sister Francine, is that suitable for you and Evan as well?"

Both agreed and Father Fitz nodded, his gaze straying to Sam and Patrick who stood patiently in the background, hands in their pockets. "Gentlemen? I trust that meets with your busy schedules?"

"Yes, sir." Patrick's response was immediate, his

gaze meeting Marcy's with an intensity that triggered an odd warmth in her chest.

"Thank you, Patrick." Father Fitz zeroed in on Sam, one silver brow jagged high. "And you, Mr. O'Rourke?"

Sam hesitated, eyes flicking to Marcy and back. "Some Tuesdays, Father, of course, but I can't guarantee all as there will be evenings Patrick or I work late at the *Herald*."

"Ah, dedication, yes—a commendable trait in an employee, Mr. O'Rourke, as is commitment to a cause as noble as ours. And I have no doubt Arthur Hennessey will feel the same way." He cocked his head, brows lifted in question. "Would you like me to ask him for you? We're long overdue for lunch and I've been thinking of calling, you see, so I'd be happy to assist."

A nerve flickered in Sam's swarthy jaw. "That won't be necessary, Father. I'll just decline overtime hours offered on Tuesdays."

"An excellent idea, Samuel, and one I'm sure Miss Murphy will be most grateful for, along with your sister."

"I hope so," Sam said with a faint smile, those black eyes searing Marcy to the spot until she thought she couldn't breathe.

Her body jumped at the clap of Father's hands. "Excellent! That settles it, then. Two weeks, same time, same place. Evan, if you have a moment, and Sister Francine, I'd like a word with you both, but you ladies are free to go. Good night."

Bidding the others goodbye, Julie and Marcy made their way to the door, Marcy's stomach as skittery as Julie's, no doubt, over the prospect of Sam and Patrick possibly walking them home. *Please, Lord, no* ... Her heart caught in her throat when someone's arm brushed hers in a race to open the door, and she glanced up.

"Thank you, Sa—"

She stopped, taken aback at the nearness of Patrick, unsettled by the serene smile on his lips and the startling clarity of gray eyes so close and so calm. Something in the way he looked at her gave her pause, a quiet confidence as if he expected her to succumb to his charm like every other woman. She caught a distinct woodsy scent similar to pine or sandalwood, and it triggered the faintest of flutters that immediately put her on guard. "Thank you," she whispered softly, *but no thank you.* She quickly turned from both her unwelcome reaction and a man to whom she had no desire to become a notch on a post. *And God willing, neither will Julie.* Looping her arm through that of her best friend's, she hurried Julie down the steps, hoping to steer them both far away from the two men behind.

"Marcy, wait up." Sam touched her shoulder on the bottom step, and her pulse took off in a sprint the same time her body jerked to a stop. "Patrick and I will walk you girls home," he said with a casual air.

"No, Sam, that's not necessary, truly—we've already taken enough of your time." Marcy's breaths were uneven, as if she had just jogged a mile or two. And, oh, sweet saints, how she wished she had—miles and miles away from Sam O'Rourke!

"No, we insist," Patrick spoke up, shoring up Julie's other side.

Marcy inwardly groaned. Why couldn't these two just go pester women who really cared? She gulped. Or at least women who cared enough to want them around? "Honestly, I'm sure you and Patrick have other things to do on a lovely summer night like this—"

"Mr. O'Rourke? Mr. O'Connor?" Father Fitz

bellowed at the door, and Patrick's low groan brought a half-smile to Marcy's lips as he and Sam slowly did an about-face. "Might I have a word with you gentlemen before you head out for the night?"

Marcy heard Sam's heavy release of air along with Patrick's own noisy sigh, and she couldn't resist a tug of her lip as her eyes smiled at Julie.

"Yes, sir," Patrick said, lumbering back up the steps.

Sam hesitated, a hand to Marcy's shoulder and eyes intense. "Will you wait?"

A cleansing breath filled her lungs before she unleashed it in a grateful sigh. "I'm sorry, Sam, but Julie and I invited several girls to my house tonight to solicit their help for the play." Her eyes scanned skyward, taking in the pink glimmers of dusk slowly fading into the deep hues of night. "We shouldn't keep them waiting."

A gruff clear of a throat drew their attention. "Mr. O'Rourke?" Father Fitz held the door, and Marcy bit back a grin at the challenge in the old priest's eyes. "I meant tonight, of course."

Sam's broad chest expanded and released. "Yes, sir."

"Good night, ladies," Father Fitz said, a secret smile lighting on his weathered lips. He slipped them a knowing wink while the boys shuffled back inside, their broad shoulders sagging in a slump. "And bless you."

Marcy grinned and spun on her heel, tucking her arm through Julie's once again, while a hint of laughter twinkled in each of their eyes. "Oh no, Father Fitz," she said with a playful squeeze of her best friend's waist. "Bless you!"

Chapter Five

"I want her, Sam." Patrick stared aimlessly at the endless rows of bottles beneath the smoky mirror of Brannigan's Pub, his elbows limp on the cherrywood bar while he twiddled the mug in his hand. "*Now*, in my life, as soon as possible."

All around him, the buzz and hum of people conversing and laughing filled the smoky air along with off-key singing to the lively piano tunes of Tommy Thomkins while couples danced and flirted. But Patrick didn't hear a thing. His mind was so foggy he didn't know if it was the alcohol or if he was in love, but either way, his body buzzed at the mere thought of Marceline Murphy. He tossed back another swallow of beer, then pushed the half-empty glass away, his taste for alcohol suddenly as flat as his desire for other women. He peered up at Sam out of the corner of his eye. "I never believed in love at first sight, O'Rourke, but I gotta tell you—something about that woman took me down the minute I laid eyes on her." He shook his head, a grin sprouting at the mere idea of Marcy wanting him too. "What can I say? She's ruined me forever."

Sam's eyes narrowed as he nudged Patrick's beer back his way. "I'll say—I've never seen you turn your nose up at a beer before." He took a swig of his own, troubled eyes appraising Patrick over the rim of his glass. Setting it back down, he shifted on the stool to face him, tone droll as his thumb absently glazed the side of his mug. "The lass doesn't appear to be taken with either of us, Patrick, which is part of the attraction I suppose—a woman who plays hard to get." His lips took a slant. "And that's the dilemma, my friend—she's not playing, she *is*."

"Doesn't matter," Patrick said with a firm press of his jaw. "I want her in my life, Sam, and I mean to have her."

Sam's mouth curved in challenge. "As do I."

Patrick tilted his head, studying his best friend through eyes as thin as his patience. "What are you talking about, O'Rourke? I saw her first."

Upending his glass, Sam guzzled the rest, then clinked it down to signal Lucas for another. His grin edged toward predatory with just a touch of tease. "Not technically." He canted against the bar, long legs stretched out. "She's been sleeping in my house since she was six years old, remember?"

"So have I," Patrick said with a scowl, "but that's irrelevant since neither of us paid her any mind until now."

Sam slid him a hooded gaze. "No, what's irrelevant, my friend, is how you or I feel. It's not up to us, it's up to Marcy to decide who she'll allow to darken her door."

Patrick straightened on the stool, back square and Irish up. "We've been friends a long time, Sam." A nerve flickered in his jaw. "I'm asking you to stay away."

Sam regarded him carefully with the barest of smiles. "Why? Afraid to lose?"

A Light in the Window

Patrick laughed outright. Snatching his half-empty beer, he downed it in one furious gulp, then slammed the mug on the counter. He nodded his thanks when Lucas delivered two more and held his aloft with a broad grin, foam slithering the sides of his glass. "I've never lost yet."

A low chuckle rumbled in Sam's chest as he raised his in salute. "Ah, but then we've never gone head to head before, now have we?" He took a long swallow of brew, gaze fixed on Patrick as the beer glugged down his throat. Swiping the side of his mouth with his sleeve, he angled his head, the glint of a dare glittering in dark eyes. "So she's to be a contest, is she now?"

The smile faded from Patrick's lips, the thought of Marcy as the prize in an unsavory competition not settling well. "No," he whispered, shoving the beer away a second time. "That's not what I want. I'll not have her hounded by the likes of us, torn in two different directions in some unholy tug-of-war."

"What, then?" Sam said. "Because make no mistake, Patrick—I mean to have her as well."

A nerve pulsed in Patrick's temple as he stared, fist clenched on the bar. He and Sam had been best friends most of their lives, but never had he wanted to bloody that Roman beak of a nose more. His voice carried a warning. "So, you're going to allow a woman to come between us?"

The bristled plain of Sam's jaw hardened while both a question and a challenge burned hot in his eyes. "No ... are you?"

Patrick slammed a fist to the counter. "Blast you, O'Rourke, no, but I'll not cheapen her in a wager either, like so much loose coin. One of us has to back down."

Sam eyed him for several seconds, gaze pensive.

Releasing a heavy exhale, he finally reached in his pocket and tossed a coin on the bar, lips crooking when it spun to a stop. "All right, Patrick, not a duel to the death, then, or even a tussle that will tear Marcy apart." He quirked a brow. "But perhaps a toss to decide who shall woo her first? If you win, I'll bow out and leave her completely vulnerable to your devastating, pretty-faced charm." He lifted his glass in a toast. "And if I win, you'll do the same, agreed?"

Sweat licked the inside of Patrick's collar as he stared, weighing the risk in his mind. He finally shook his head. "No, I'll not chance it."

"You don't have a choice," Sam said evenly, his black eyes nearly piercing him through. "It's either a toss or our friendship—you can't have both."

Patrick met his gaze, realizing for the first time that Marcy's pull on Sam was obviously as strong as her pull over him and he swallowed hard, suddenly aware he might well lose. He bludgeoned the counter again with a knotted fist and swore under his breath. Eyes itching hot, he seared the man with a look that might have to come to blows if not for their fifteen-year friendship. "I have a mind to spit in your eye and do what I bloomin' well please."

Sam grinned. "But you won't, because our bond is like blood." He hoisted another toast, giving his friend a wink. "And we both know blood is thicker than lust."

Sam's comment barbed, and that's when Patrick knew Marcy meant more than a fling or a conquest, more than just the favors and affection of a pretty girl. His pulse seized for a split second when comprehension assailed his mind, as sweet and intoxicating as the scent of lilac water when she'd passed him at the rectory door. For some reason he couldn't ascertain, she mattered more to him than just the race of his pulse over eyes as blue as the sky, more than the heady warmth when he lingered on those lush pink lips. More—*far more*—than mere physical attraction, and the very thought stunned because for the life of him, he didn't know why. He scowled. All he did know was that the sound of the word "lust" in regard to Marcy made him want to blacken Sam's eye. His voice came off as a hiss. "It's more than lust this time, Sam."

"You're right, Patrick—it is—and I feel it too. Marcy is ..." He paused, eyes shuttering closed as if attempting to decipher the mystery of Marceline Murphy. "Unique, special, somehow different than most girls with whom we associate, almost as if she's wiser, more caring." His eyes opened to reveal a rare glimpse into a more vulnerable Sam. "A woman capable of eliciting great things from a man without ever letting him know." His gaze trailed into a reflective stare. "And perhaps a woman who would love a man so much, he could almost love himself." He glanced up with a melancholy smile, the effect somehow soft and so out of character for Sam O'Rourke, that Patrick could only blink. "We barely know this slip of a girl and yet here we are, the both of us, besotted over an ethereal beauty who is sure to steal our hearts as effectively as she has stolen our thoughts. A woman definitely worth fighting over." He glanced up, the rake returning once again with a twinkle in his eye. "But we won't. We will toss for the privilege of pursuit and cheer the winner on, eh?" He brandished his beer as if it were a call to battle.

Patrick gouged the back of his neck, then expelled a weighty sigh, his eyes locked with Sam's. "If I win the toss, you'll step aside and leave her be?"

He acquiesced with a dip of his head. "I will." His eyes glittered. "And you'll do the same. Unless the winner fails, that is. Then all bets are off, and it's each man for himself."

"Fail." It was more of a statement than a question as Patrick stared. Jaw grinding, he clenched his lips in a tight line. "I don't fail, Sam."

Sam responded with a flash of white teeth. "Nor do I, Patrick, but something tells me Marceline Murphy is more than capable of making fools of us both. So ... shall we have Lucas toss the coin to put at least one of us out of our misery?"

Stomach in knots, Patrick glanced over his shoulder. "Lucas—can you help us out over here?"

"You boys needin' another brew?" Lucas Brannigan ambled forward, wiping the sweat from his brow with a muscled arm.

"Soon," Sam said with a grin, "but for now, we need an impartial party in the toss of a coin."

"Do you, now? And to what are we tossin', might I ask—the cost of six beers?"

"Nothing so crass, Mr. Brannigan, I assure you." Sam gave Patrick a wink. "And something far more satisfying, although I suspect the headaches may be far worse."

He tossed the coin and Lucas caught it with a chuckle. "Now you boys have me intrigued."

Sam hooked an arm around Patrick's shoulder with a laugh. "A woman, Lucas, of the very highest caliber who, most likely, would only entertain the notion of one rogue at a time."

Patrick grunted, giving Sam a sideways smile. "If any at all."

"Oh, she'll entertain all right—it's just up to Lucas as to whom." Sam deferred to the barkeep with a bow of his head. "If you will, Mr. Brannigan, our fate is in your hands."

Lucas polished the silver coin against his white apron in a show of ceremony before placing it on the side of his fist. He peered up beneath bushy red brows. "Who makes the call?"

Sam slapped Patrick on the shoulder. "Let my friend call it."

"All right, then, Patrick calls it in the air. Ready, gentlemen?"

Palms damp, Patrick nodded, his breath stifled as if the blasted coin lodged in his very throat.

In a blur of motion, Lucas flipped his thumb, and the coin sailed high in the air, spinning like Patrick's stomach. "Heads," he called, voice hoarse.

The flash of silver twirled several times before plummeting into Lucas's hand a fraction of a second before he sandwiched it with a meaty palm. Nobody breathed as he lifted a finger to take a peek, a broad grin spanning the whole of his ruddy face. "Well, the devil take it," he said with a wink. "Now here's a lass in trouble if ever there was ..."

Chapter Six

Clipboard to the chest of her high-buttoned shirtwaist, Marcy stared wide-eyed at the church auditorium teeming with people, tongue gliding her teeth at the rate of four times a minute. She gulped, fingers digging into Julie's arm as a group of rowdy street urchins almost knocked her down in an impromptu game of shadow tag while a ring of little girls played duck, duck, goose in the corner of the room. Despite windows thrust high along one side of the gym, the summer night was sticky and still, papers rustling as adults fanned themselves and chatted in endless rows of wooden folding chairs set up in front of the stage. From mothers patting babies over their shoulders to the tattered and curious homeless who wandered in from Evan's soup kitchen next door, it seemed they had a full house. Expelling a shaky sigh, Marcy couldn't help wonder if she'd bitten off more than she could chew. "I had no idea we would have such a turnout," she whispered into Julie's ear as her friend played a scale on a battered upright piano.

Julie chuckled, fingers carefully plunking to test each ivory while she glanced across the crowded, high-ceilinged room that shimmered like a sea of noisy humanity. Music and mayhem bounced off white-

A Light in the Window

washed, wood-planked walls and a scuffed hardwood floor that creaked and moaned when children darted or adults shifted in chairs. She peeked up at Marcy with a bit of the devil in her eyes. "Just punishment, I'd say, for a woman who near wore off my feet handing out flyers to every house in the Southie neighborhood."

Marcy nipped at her lip. "Do you think we went a wee bit too far?"

Julie rose to tweak the back of Marcy's neck. "Not 'we,' my friend, you!" She gave her a quick hug. "But then nothing is too far when it comes to people or a cause you hold dear, which is one of the reasons I love you so much. Besides, between Sister Francine soliciting students to help and our very successful volunteer meeting at your house last week, we are more than amply endowed with the help we need." She patted Marcy's arm. "So rest easy, my friend." Her smile turned devious. "About the auditions, that is, not about my brother. He hasn't taken his eyes off you since he walked through that door."

Marcy's gaze flicked to where Sister Francine spoke with Sam and Patrick at the back of the stage, frantically motioning at the proscenium arch with a pointer as if angels alighted there. A lump bobbed in her throat when Sam's eyes met hers, his look as penetrating as if he were only two feet away. She fumbled the clipboard, causing it to drop to the floor with a clatter. Quickly ducking to pick it up, she wished she could hide behind the piano forever or at least until the fire died in her cheeks. Head high, she rose with as much grace as she could muster to glance at the clock, venting a grateful sigh when Sister Francine marched to the front of the stage and blew a loud whistle.

As if a billowing sheet had snapped into the air, silence fluttered and settled like a thick shroud, riveting all eyes on the rotund taskmaster whose legendary rap of the knuckles could make the most fearless of men tremble. She cleared her throat, the sound as threatening as it was practical, a squint of blue eyes almost disappearing into the heavy folds of soft, creamy skin dotted with two circles of pink. "I'd like to welcome you to the St. Mary's auditions for this year's Christmas fundraiser. Before we begin, if you did not receive a sheet to fill out at the door, please raise your hand and our volunteers will provide one. This sheet must be completely filled out with all pertinent information as well as the various positions for which you would like to audition, be it cast member, stagehand, scenery production, or various volunteer options."

Chairs squeaked and clothing rustled as whispers rose and hummed into chatter.

Crack! Sister Francine's pointer lashed the podium with cool intent, stilling the room into submission as she lanced a group of particularly noisy boys with a deadly glare. "Might I remind you there are a limited number of positions available in all areas, so it would behoove those who truly wish to participate to be on their best behavior." She pivoted to the side, waving Marcy forward with an impatient twitch of fingers.

With a quick glide of her teeth, Marcy hurried to the front of the stage to join Sister Francine, the leg o' mutton sleeves of her lavender blouse swooshing against her bodice while her heeled shoes clicked across the planked wooden floor. She was quite certain her corset had shrunk several sizes for she could barely draw a breath as she stood with a stiff smile, clipboard clutched to her chest like a shield.

Sister continued, tone taut. "Miss Murphy is our chairman this year, and I expect you to give her your fullest cooperation." For apparent emphasis, she slapped the podium with her stick once again, causing Marcy to jump and the audience to titter. "Anyone who gives this young woman any problems whatsoever will answer directly to me, is that clear?" Sister nodded at Marcy and stepped away, hands clasped while her pointer rested on her formidable stomach.

Marcy cleared her throat. "I'd like to thank each and every one of you for taking the time to be here tonight. If you filled out a form, you should have a number that will be called when it's your turn to audition. Those applying for volunteer positions will be asked to meet with Father Fitzgibbons in the rectory for a brief interview, and those wishing to audition for a part in the play or choir will remain in the auditorium. As you can see from the overview sheet you received at the door, we have roles for seven adults and eight children in the actual play itself, but we'll need at least twenty people for the adult choir and twenty for the children's choir, so please specify your preferences on the sheet."

Marcy pointed to the right of the stage. "When your number is called, you will bring your completed sheet to Sister Francine and myself in the first row, then enter the stage from the steps on the left. Please advise Miss O'Rourke at the piano if you wish to audition for the choir, the play, or both, and she will provide you with the music and/or a script. You will have approximately twenty seconds to sing or read, and when the whistle sounds, we ask that you exit the stage on the right and quietly return to your seat." She smiled at the crowd with a lift of brows. "Any questions?" A hand waved in the air from the second row, and Marcy nodded. "Yes?"

"When will we find out if we made it?" a young girl asked.

Marcy's smile was warm. "Callbacks will be announced at the end of this evening, and those selected will return for a second audition next week. Final cast, choir, and crew will be chosen then and given a rehearsal packet with everything they need to know. Anything else?" She glanced to and fro throughout the auditorium, ignoring Sam and Patrick who grinned at her from where they stood in the back, slanted to the wall with arms folded. "Then, let's begin."

Two hours later, Marcy had a headache from off-key singing, slaughtered diction, and Sister's Francine's whistle, giving her pause as to her sanity in agreeing to the job as fundraiser chair. Kneading her temple, she glanced up to see a young boy who had auditioned for the cast pushing a small girl in a wheelchair to the front of the stage.

With a scrub of shaggy brown hair, he approached with a solemn smile and a nod of respect. "Sister, Miss Murphy, my name is Nate Phillips, and this here is my sister Holly." He took another step forward, cap in hand and voice fading to a whisper. "She's only seven, but Ma asked me to bring her 'cause, well you see, Holly doesn't get to do too much on account of she's crippled, you know, so Ma thought …" His Adam's apple wobbled several times. "Well, she hoped you'd consider letting Holly audition because of her name and all, seeing it has to do with Christmas and that's her birthday too." He leaned in, a glimmer of moisture in his eyes as he twisted his hat with his fingers, voice lowering all the more. "You don't have to pick her, understand, just let her read and sing 'cause she's real good at both, you know, and Ma just thought that alone would be enough to make her happy."

Marcy blinked, the boy's face watering into a blur. She swallowed hard to fight a heave, but it was no use, it broke from her lips in a shuddering rasp.

Sister Francine patted her arm and spoke to the boy

with a firm lift of her chin. "If your sister took the time to come and audition tonight, young man, then audition she will." She glanced up at Julie. "Miss O'Rourke, will you please hand this young man both a script and music for his sister, please."

The young boy, all of twelve, looked as if he might break down and cry himself, jaw aquiver while tears welled in his eyes. "Thank you, Sister," he whispered, then grabbed Marcy's hand, shaking it as if he were pumping water for a man dying of thirst. *Or maybe a sister ...* "Bless you, Miss Murphy, and you too, Sister Francine—Holly ain't never had nothing like this happen to her before, so bless you!" He whirled around and rushed to give Holly a hug, then took the papers that Julie gave him and handed them to her as well. With a squeeze of her shoulders, he stepped aside.

Marcy took a quick swipe at her eyes and leaned forward, awarding Holly the brightest smile she could muster. She noted the faded calico dress the little girl wore that appeared three sizes too big and a pale face that made her appear like a china doll with liquid-brown eyes. "Holly, are you ready to read from the script?"

The little girl nodded, chestnut hair trailing fragile shoulders as she gave Marcy a sweet smile. "Yes, ma'am," she whispered, her voice so soft and wispy, Marcy worried that no one would be able to hear.

"Start at the beginning, then, sweetheart, reading the script just like you're that little girl in the play who's excited about Christmas, all right?"

Holly nodded again and paused ... right before she belted out the lines as if they were coming from an entirely different little girl.

"Excellent!" Marcy said with a grin when Holly had finished. "Are you ready to sing, and do you know the

Christmas carol, *Oh, Holy Night?*"

"Yes, ma'am."

"Perfect!" Marcy glanced up at the piano. "Julie, let's try C major, all right?"

Whether it was the fact that it was late and everyone was tired or whether it was the sight of a frail little girl in a wheelchair who longed to be a part of the play, the room stilled to a hush. Marcy's breath suspended as she waited, the pounding of her own pulse in her ears drowning out Julie's musical intro. And then, in the sweet and soulful song of a little girl, a steamy and noisy auditorium became the gate of heaven itself as a sound so poignant rose in the room, Marcy had no power over the tears that slipped from her eyes.

For several thudding heartbeats after the last note was sung, the silence was almost painful, an ache in Marcy's chest over the loss of a voice that had ushered them into the very presence of God. And then, in a blast of applause that swelled to the ceiling, the audience shot to their feet along with Marcy and Sister Francine, dewy-eyed over a delicate little girl who may not be able to walk, but whose voice could soar to the sky.

After a whisper in Sister Francine's ear and Sister's subsequent nod, Marcy hurried to give Holly a hug, kneeling to clasp the little girl's hands in her own. "Holly, that was simply the most beautiful thing we have ever heard," she said with a sheen in her eyes, "and we want you to know right now, young lady, that not only are we giving you a part in this play, but we want you to sing that very song as well. Would you like that?"

Brown eyes as glossy as Marcy's blinked back when Holly nodded, her rosebud mouth quivering along with her jaw. "Oh, yes, ma'am," she whispered, flinging herself into Marcy's arms with a chuckle that broke into a sob.

Marcy squeezed the little sprite of a thing, eyes closed and heart rejoicing that even now, before this play came to pass, it was changing lives as Marcy had hoped and prayed. That it wouldn't just be a mere fundraiser, but a spirit raiser as well, touching people with the grace of God. Jumping to her feet, she hurried to pull two rehearsal packets from Papa's portfolio and handed them to Holly's brother, who now stood by her side. "Nate, please give these to your mother so she knows the exact dates Holly and you will need to be here. There's a full script inside each packet, so you need to practice both of your parts together. You will play the part of Daniel, and Holly will play the part of Sara—" She paused, her eyes softening as they lighted on his sister once again. "No, wait—Holly will play herself." She glanced up and gave Nate a wink. "Since it is a Christmas play and all."

He stared, mouth agape before it curved into a silly grin. "Yes, ma'am, and thank you, ma'am!" he gushed, cranking her hand so hard once again, she was sure she'd be sore come morning.

"Why don't you take Holly home now so you can tell your mother the good news, and no need to come back until the first rehearsal date, all right?"

"Yes, ma'am!" he shouted, and took Marcy by surprise when he bowled her over with a hug that had her grinning ear to ear. She watched Nate wheel his sister away and sighed, returning to her seat next to Sister Francine.

"I'll tell you what, young lady," Sister Francine said with a smile that displayed a rare show of tenderness, "it's moments like this that weaken my resolve to be an old crab."

Marcy grinned. "It can be our secret if you like,

Sister, although it may serve good purpose in keeping your students a wee bit off balance."

The old nun laughed, a deep, throaty chuckle that Marcy—or Sister's students, she supposed—seldom heard. "I knew I liked you," she said with a firm pat of Marcy's arm, "a woman after my own heart." Her lips tipped off-center. "Which may well be an insult."

"Not likely, Sister." Marcy nodded to a group of boys against the wall who were apparently getting antsy and loud. "I'm going to need all the attributes you can spare, I'm afraid, and then some." She glanced at her gold pendant watch pinned to her blouse and then the handful of audition numbers yet to call. "We best get a move on, I suppose, if we're going to finish by nine."

Rising to her feet, she turned to call the next number, a smile tugging when she noticed Sam stretched out in a chair in the back, arms folded and eyes closed. She began to turn, and her gaze collided with Patrick's, a connection so strong it was as if he willed it, the gray eyes holding her captive for several powerful thuds of her heart. The faintest of tremors quivered her stomach, and she spun around and dropped in her seat so fast she was dizzy, shock stealing the strength from her limbs. *No!* She would *not* respond to a man like Patrick O'Connor. Too attractive to be trusted, too used to getting his own way, *especially* with women. Thoughts of her cousin flashed in her mind, and Marcy's eyes fluttered closed for the briefest of moments, anger resurging over the injustice of it all. How men like Patrick O'Connor pushed and prodded and promised the moon to a woman like Nora, putting a ring on her finger that became a noose around her neck. Marcy's heart listed, breaking all over again. A cousin so dear, ruined forever. And all because of a handsome face.

"Thank you, Mrs. Miller," Sister Francine said and Marcy jolted up, ashamed she'd missed the woman's audition.

Slipping a peek at the nun beside her, Marcy offered a hesitant smile. "So, what did you think?"

"A definite callback." Sister scratched a quick notation on her sheet, then rifled through a basket to select the next number. "Mercy me, this has been a long night, but we're almost done," she said with a teasing roll of her eyes, "and then we can send the bad ones packing and be done with the lot of them." She gave Marcy a wink. "Won't that be nice?"

The bad ones. Marcy blinked, Sam and Patrick coming to mind. Oh, to send them packing and be done with them both! Exhaling a weary breath, Marcy managed a half smile that veered just shy of droll. "Oh, goodness, me, Sister—you have no idea."

Chapter Seven

"So ... what's your name?"

Hammer in hand, Patrick paused, one nail lodged in his teeth and another positioned against a kitchen cabinet façade while he, Sam, and a few other men built scenery. The smell of sawdust and popcorn filled the noisy auditorium along with thick, humid air from the sweltering summer night. One of the little girls from the play blinked up at him, obviously more interested in pestering him on her break than playing duck, duck, goose with the rest of the kids in the cast. He studied her out of the corner of his eye, her impossibly thick eyeglasses magnifying her hazel eyes at least double in size. His lips quirked, angling the ten-penny nail straight down. "Atrick," he mumbled, dropping the "P" in the absence of being able to press his lips together.

The little squirt squinted, nose wrinkling almost clear up to her eyes. "What kind of name is that—Aa-a-a-a-aaa-trick?" she said, grinding it out. "Sounds stupid to me." She slapped a molasses-colored braid over her shoulder like a challenge.

Patrick pounded one nail into the wood, then spit the second into his free hand, righting it in the air. "*P*-atrick," he enunciated, popping extra "puh" into the "P." He placed and buried the nail with a single

A Light in the Window 67

deafening whack, eyeing her with a slant of a smile. "And you are?"

"Matilda," she said with a sharp thrust of her pointed little chin. "But my friends call me Tillie."

He wiped sweat from his forehead with the side of his upper sleeve. "They do, do they? So, what should I call you?"

She cocked her head, assessing him through slivers of golden brown eyes. "You can call me Tillie, I guess, but only 'cause you're cute."

His lips parted in a grin. "Funny, I was thinking the same thing about you."

The little dickens actually blushed. "No you weren't neither," she said with a scowl. "Nobody thinks I'm cute."

He jagged a brow, tucking a nail in his teeth while he fixed another to the wood. "I do."

"No you don't."

Thwack! He drove the nail home and angled to face her, removing the other one from his mouth. "You calling me a liar, Miss—?"

"Dewey. Matilda Dewey." She jutted her chin even higher. "And you bet I am, mister, 'cause ain't nobody ever called me 'cute' afore, so you gotta be lyin'."

Huffing out a sigh, Patrick scratched the back of his neck with the hammer, then peered up beneath slatted lids, his heart going out to the little dickens who couldn't be a day over six. "Well, I'm not lying, Miss Dewey, and for your information, I happen to know a thing or two about pretty women."

She folded her arms. "Ha! That proves it. I ain't no woman yet neither, and I ain't pretty, leastways not accordin' to Omer."

He slacked a hip, hammer loose at his side while he scanned her head to toe, taking in the frayed grayish pinafore he supposed had been white at one time. Underneath, it masked an even more rag-tag calico dress that hung like a scarecrow, hem resting on top of scuffed shoes. Her sleeves were so long, only the tips of dirty fingernails peeked out. She could have been only six, given her small bone structure and slight frame, but her attitude suggested way older, as did cynical eyes that hinted at too much experience with ridicule. He sighed. "A girl is just a woman not fully blossomed yet, Miss Dewey, and it's easy to see you're gonna be a pretty one when you're finally in full bloom." Hammer in hand, he motioned toward her head. "For instance, take your hair. Sure, it's in pigtails now, but it's the color of summer wheat at the edge of dusk, with just a glow of pink about it. And those eyes?" He shook his head as if he had no earthly idea why she couldn't see what he saw. "Like polished amber, guaranteed to turn more than one male head down the road."

Her nose rumpled in a scrunch. "What's amber?"

"Ever see the eyes of a tiger, darlin'?" he asked, face in a squint.

"Nope."

"Well, they're the prettiest honey gold you ever did see, downright hypnotize a man if he isn't careful."

Her face squished again. "What's hip-no-tize?"

He shifted his weight to the other leg with an exhale as thick as her glasses. "You always ask this many questions?"

"More," she said, eyes wise beyond her years and all too sober. "Which is why Omer hauls off and whacks me sometimes."

The hammer suddenly felt like a 2-ton sledge. "Hits you?" he bit out, jaw clenched. "Who the blazes is this moron, anyway?"

She shrugged her shoulders as if getting whacked

were an everyday occurrence, and Patrick's gut felt like he'd swallowed a handful of those blasted ten-penny nails. "Ma's friend. He don't like it when I talk too much, so he whacks me." She pulled up the sleeve of her arm, displaying a rash of ugly bruises from wrist to elbow and beyond, no doubt. "He done this and lots more I cain't show ya on account of it ain't proper, but see this?" Finger sliding her neck, she rubbed a whole patch of gray he'd just assumed was dirt, lips pursed as if it were a badge of honor. "Tried to whack my mama, but I spit on his boots, so he throttled me instead," she said with no little pride. "Hurt like perdition, but at least Mama got away."

The hammer clunked to the floor when Patrick squatted to his knees, jaw hard but grip soft as he clutched her skinny arms in threadbare sleeves, the feel akin to twigs wrapped in tissue paper. "Why the blazes does your mama let him come around, Tillie? Why doesn't she just kick the bum out?"

Her tiny rib cage expanded and contracted, deflating like the pride in her eyes. "For crying out loud in a bucket, mister, don't ya think she tried? But he keeps coming around, drunk as a skunk and ain't nobody can make him go away."

A knot jerked in Patrick's throat as he rose, eyes as steely and pointed as the nails in his pocket. "Can you give this Omer a message for me, darlin'?"

She tucked those dirty fingernails into the tattered pockets of her pinafore. "Sure, I guess."

He pointed the hammer like a threat. "You tell that worthless sack of dung that if he lays another finger on you or your mama, that me and my hammer are gonna pay him a visit, you hear?"

A grin split her face, complete with a missing tooth. "Jumpin' toadstools, mister, shore would pay good money to see that! Iffen I had any." She tilted her head as she studied him through those larger-than-life amber slits. "Say, how old are you, anyway?"

"Old enough to arrange a few of Omer's teeth," Patrick said with a wink.

She chuckled, a surprisingly low rumble for such a little girl. "Gosh, mister, that's for dead sure with them there muscles of yours. Omer's pert near twice your size, at least in his belly, and he shore don't look half as pretty or strong as you."

He chucked her chin. "Is that a fact, Miss Dewey? And how old are you?"

"Mama says a lady ain't s'posed to tell her age, but seein' I ain't no lady yet, I guess it's okay." She rocked back on her heels. "I'll be seven week after next, but Mama says I'm ma-chure for my age."

Patrick grinned and propped another nail to the façade. "True enough."

"What's ma-chure mean? Mama told me, but I forgot."

He pounded the nail in place. "It means you're a whole lot smarter than most people, including that sludge Omer."

A shrill whistle blew and Tillie scowled as Sister Francine herded everyone back up to the stage. "I swear on a crate of nickels that penguin woman's gonna swallow that thing one of these days, and people are gonna be paradin' like the Fourth of July." She thrust out her hand. "Nice to meet ya, Patrick. You're not so bad for a boy."

He shook her hand, her little fingers frail as bird legs. "Thank you, Miss Dewey, you're not so bad for a girl, either," he said with a tap of her nose. "And a pretty one at that."

With a smile and a wave, she hurried to join the

others, and Patrick's gaze followed her all the way up the side steps where Marcy stood with a clipboard. Hammer in hand, he rubbed his forehead with the back of his wrist, eyes now riveted on the only woman alive who didn't give him the time of day. Or the benefit of a glance, a smile, or a kind word. He expelled a noisy sigh. No, that wasn't fair. She said thank you whenever he opened a door for her, nodded hello and goodbye whenever he came and went, and responded in a polite tone whenever he asked her a question. The edge of his lip crooked. Not exactly a heated affair. And certainly not what he was used to, which pricked his male pride more than he liked. The only positive was she avoided his gaze, which meant he could brazenly stare. And right now he wished she didn't look so blasted pretty in that fitted pinstripe blue shirtwaist that matched her eyes and accentuated every single curve. For weeks she'd avoided almost all eye contact, all conversation, all indication she even noticed he was alive, and his only consolation was that she treated Sam the exact same way. With one major difference. A satisfied grin tipped his lips.

I won the toss.

"It would appear the famous O'Connor charm has made yet another conquest." Sam strolled up, mopping his brow with a rolled sleeve of an old shirt liberally spotted with both paint and sweat. He nodded toward Tillie, who waved at Patrick with a cheeky grin. "But not exactly the eye you were hoping to catch."

Patrick waved back, giving Tillie a wink. His pulse stuttered when Marcy finally looked his way, apparently to see who the precocious Miss Dewey was waving to. He vented a weary sigh when Marcy did a quick about-face. "That's okay, I'm just biding my time. The woman doesn't like me, that much is clear, and for the life of me I don't know why, so I'm sure in the blazes not going to rush her."

Sam chuckled. "I don't think there's any danger of that, Patrick, but it has been three weeks now, and I'm a wee bit concerned you're losing your touch." He latched an arm to Patrick's shoulder. "You may have won the toss, man, but I'll be dashed if I'll wait forever."

Patrick flicked Sam's arm away, tone bristling. "I plan to make my move tonight, O'Rourke, so you can put your tongue back in your mouth." Patrick watched as Marcy bent to give Tillie a kiss, and his heart warmed. "Since you and Julie have to leave early for your aunt's birthday party, I plan to walk the lady home."

"And if she prefers to walk alone?" Sam's eyes glittered with tease.

"She won't," Patrick said with far more confidence than he felt. He forced a cocky grin. "You may not know this, O'Rourke, but I can be very persuasive."

"That's good, Patrick, because you'll need all the persuasive skills you have to turn Marcy's head in the next two weeks."

Patrick shot a sideways glance at his best friend. "Why two weeks?" he asked, the bridge of his nose pinched in annoyance.

Sam slapped him on the back. "Because that's all the time I'm giving you, O'Connor—four weeks to win the woman's heart before I move in." He turned to go.

"That wasn't the deal." Patrick halted him with a grab of his sleeve.

Sam paused, gaze flicking from the hand on his arm to Patrick's face. "You won the toss, Patrick, what more do you want?"

"For you to stay away altogether," he said, voice

harsher than intended.

Sam regarded him for several moments before quietly removing Patrick's hand. "Well, then, let me ask you a question, my friend, and I want an honest answer." Sam's eyes bore into his with a candor he'd come to expect from the best—and most unconventional—friend he'd ever had. "If you were in my shoes—would you?"

Patrick stared, reminded once again that the man before him was as drawn to Marcy as he and if not for the toss of a coin, would be pursuing her even now. He blasted out a heavy sigh. "No." He gouged the back of his neck and glanced to the stage where Marcy worked with the children. He muttered a rare curse under his breath. "It's as if the blasted woman has put a hex on us both, and God help us."

The sober intensity in Sam's eyes glinted into humor. "I'm not sure God's inclined to helping the likes of us," he said with a low chuckle, giving a nod toward Marcy, "but we sure in the blazes better hope He isn't helping her. Or you and I, my friend, may well never see the light of day with the woman of our dreams."

A grin creased Patrick's lips, the truth of Sam's statement lightening his mood for some strange reason. He chuckled in spite of himself. "Saints almighty, O'Rourke, it's enough to make a grown man cry, isn't it?" He cuffed Sam's shoulder with a firm grip, his words low and laced with a thin thread of hope. "Or pray ..."

Chapter Eight

"Marceline, you are a wonder! The progress we've made tonight is remarkable." Sister Francine paused to place a hand on Marcy's arm, the geese flaps of her starched white cornette appearing as limp as Marcy felt at the end of the third rehearsal. Marcy stifled a yawn, and the wings of Sister's headdress drooped even more when she leaned in, a crimp in the fleshy ridge of her brow. "Dear girl, this won't be too much with your studies and then school starting soon, will it?"

Marcy tucked her master script into Papa's portfolio and smiled, the blissful silence of an empty auditorium making her sleepy. Her gaze flitted to the clock on the wall, noting that at almost ten o'clock, this was their latest rehearsal yet. "No, Sister, I'll be fine, really. Julie and I will attend to most of the fundraiser details on the weekends so we can focus on schoolwork throughout the week." She followed suit when Sister Francine lumbered up, yet another yawn sneaking past her lips as she stood and stretched. "But I am particularly tired tonight, I suppose because it went so long."

"Well, you best be heading home, young lady." She paused, one thick gray brow angled dangerously high as she and Marcy made their way to the double doors at the front of the auditorium. "You're not walking home alone, I hope?"

"Just tonight, I assure you. Julie and I usually walk together, but she had to leave early." Marcy waggled Papa's leather portfolio with a tired smile. "But it's not too far, and I can always smack an assailant with this if need be."

With several loud clicks, Sister Francine flipped a row of tap switches, slowly dousing the gas lighting throughout the auditorium until the room went dark. Fishing a ring of keys from her pocket, she proceeded to lock the doors, tugging to make sure they were secure. "Well, I shall pray there is no need for use of your portfolio for anything other than carrying papers. Good night, my dear."

Sister turned and halted, eyes wide. "Good heavens, Miss Dewey, whatever are you doing out here by yourself?"

Marcy whirled to see Tillie perched atop a brick column at the bottom of the steps, skinny legs dangling and a gleam of white from her gap-toothed grin. "Waiting for you, Miss Murphy. We're going to walk you home."

"We?" Marcy said, brows in a scrunch.

"Yes, ma'am." Tillie's eyeglasses gleamed as bright as her smile in the light of the streetlamp overhead. She nodded to the next brick column partially obscured by a thick lilac bush. "Me and my friend."

"Your friend?" Marcy peered past the bush at a shadowed span of long legs crossed at the ankles, too long and too large to belong to Tillie's young neighbor who always walked her home. The shadow straightened and ambled forward, and Marcy's stomach lurched at the face she saw illuminated in the glow of the lamp. *Oh, Lord, no ...*

"'Evening, Sister, Miss Murphy." Patrick gave a

slight bow, eyes fixed on Marcy with a calm smile that produced an effect in her stomach that was anything but. "If you'll permit—Miss Dewey and I are at your disposal."

Marcy was shaking her head before the words could even stutter past her lips. "T-thank you, t-truly, but that's not necessary."

"It most certainly is," Sister Francine piped up, tone indignant. "Mr. O'Connor and Miss Dewey, thank you. I had misgivings about Miss Murphy walking home alone, so I am indebted to you for your thoughtfulness."

"Our pleasure, Sister," Patrick said, transferring Tillie from the column to the ground in one easy sweep. He took the little girl's hand in his while his gaze reconnected with Marcy's, that maddening smile still in place. "Since I'm walking Tillie home anyway, we figured we'd wait for Miss Murphy as well."

"No, truly—"

"Nonsense, Marceline," Sister said with a decisive wave of her hand. "I'll feel much better knowing a strapping young man is escorting you home, right up to your front door, making sure that you're safe." She swished her fingers as if to shoo them away. "Now, scoot, the lot of you. Good night."

Safe. Marcy gulped. Not a word any woman associated with a rake like Patrick O'Connor.

Keys jangling, Sister scurried off in the direction of the convent, leaving Marcy at the mercy of the Southie's most infamous Romeo. She expelled a weighty sigh. *At least Tillie will be along.* She switched hands on Papa's portfolio while she descended the steps, avoiding his eyes.

"It was Patrick's idea to wait," Tillie said, her scrawny, little chest puffed out like a proud mama. "He said you'd need somebody to walk you home too."

Marcy slid Patrick a sideways glance and a stiff smile. "Thank you," she whispered, taking the hand that Tillie offered. "But why isn't your neighbor walking you home, young lady?"

"Aw, he was in an all-fire hurry tonight, and I wanted to stay and talk to Patrick." She peered up at Marcy, bright hazel eyes filling the whole of her glasses. "He's my new friend, Miss Murphy, and I like him a lot." Her little matted head tipped to the side. "Don't you?"

Patrick chuckled. "I doubt Miss Murphy shares your opinion, Tillie." He extended his free hand, gray eyes sparkling. "Here, Marcy, let me carry that for you."

"No, really, that's—" He reached across Tillie and wrested the portfolio from her hand, her face burning while he gently pried her fingers loose. "Thank you," she said softly, quite sure the heat in her cheeks had nothing to do with the warmth of the night.

"My pleasure." The husky timber of his tone unsettled her all the more, and she quickly turned her attention to Tillie.

"You're a quick study, Tillie." Marcy smiled as the little girl tried to swing between them, dragging on their arms while she bunched up her legs. "Nobody has memorized their lines as well as you."

"Mama helps me," Tillie said with another sway between Patrick and her. Skinny legs skidded back to the sidewalk as she blinked up. "And guess what, Miss Murphy?"

"What's that, Tillie?" Marcy breathed in the scent of summer, fresh-mown grass, and honeysuckle, making her wish the warm weather could last all year.

"Patrick thinks I'm cute and that I'll turn heads when I'm in full bloom."

Marcy blinked, her gaze flicking up to Patrick's. He

gave her a wink, and she quickly looked away. "Well, he's absolutely right," she said with a reflective nod, "and that was a very nice thing for him to say."

His rumble of laughter merged with the trill of tree frogs and crickets. "Contrary to opinion, Miss Murphy," he said softly, "I have been known to be nice at times."

She chanced a peek, slipping him a faint smile. "I have no doubt, Mr. O'Connor."

"Sure you do," he said quietly, the tease in his tone fading to serious.

"And guess what else?" Tillie tugged on Marcy's hand, attempting to swing once again. "Patrick says he's gonna hammer Omer if he ever whacks me again, ain't that swell?"

Marcy's heels skidded to a stop, along with her heart. "W-who's Omer, and what do you mean he 'whacks' you?"

"Aw, he's just Mama's friend who hits me sometimes," she said in a nonchalant tone, feet flying through the air.

A shiver skittered Marcy's body as her eyelids fluttered closed for the briefest of moments, memory of bruises on Tillie's neck invading her mind. *Oh, Lord ...*

Tillie's throaty giggle floated in the warm breeze along with her little body as she sailed back and forth, legs tucked. "But holy mackerel, almost wish ol' Omer would pop me again just so Patrick can hammer him good."

Marcy opened her eyes. Her gaze converged with Patrick's, the sobriety in his look matching her own. She swallowed hard, heart breaking over Tillie's lot in life. "You're lucky to have Patrick for a friend," she said quietly, unable to look away while tears stung. "Thank you," she mouthed.

"I know," Tillie said with the utmost assurance. She chattered on as they continued several blocks out of the way to the little girl's flat in a questionable part of town, making Marcy most grateful for Patrick's presence. "Well, here we are!" Tillie bounced back to the ground in front of a three-story brick tenement. Her tiny palms slipped from Marcy's as she turned to give Patrick a hug. "Thanks, Patrick—you're swell."

He squatted to give her a hug back, then gripped her arms with a serious look, nodding down the street. "Tillie, I live about six streets down and four blocks over, #17 Hastings Street, brick house, green shutters. If Omer or anyone lays a hand on you ever again, you come get me, understood?"

"Okay."

He gently pushed her glasses up and tugged on her braid. "Okay." With a final kiss to her nose, he stood to his feet. "You go on, darlin'—we'll wait till you get inside."

"G'night, Miss Murphy." Tillie rattled Marcy's arm with a hard shake of her hand before turning to go. "Bye, Patrick," she called, darting to her building with a palm flapping in the air.

"Tillie, wait!" Marcy's cry stopped the girl midway. She ran over and stooped before her, throat convulsing as she wrapped Tillie in a fierce hug. "I'm so glad you're in the play," she whispered, eyes squeezed tight to contain the moisture welling beneath her lids. "I have a feeling you'll be one of the stars of the show, sweetheart." She pressed a lingering kiss to the little girl's cheek.

"Gosh, Miss Murphy, thanks!" Tillie gave her an eager hug back before tearing down the sidewalk and up a series of cracked steps into her flat, waving all the way. A heavy wooden door slammed behind her with a loud thud.

Marcy stared after her, her chest in a vice. She sensed Patrick close behind her. "That breaks my heart," she whispered.

"Me too," he said, his voice as melancholy as her own. He offered his arm to help her up. "She's a cute kid."

Accepting his help, she rose to her feet and quickly withdrew her hand, the warmth of his palm staying with her. "That was really nice of you to tell her she was pretty," she said, suddenly seeing Patrick O'Connor in a whole different light. More tears sparked. "I don't think she has a lot of friends because the other children tend to avoid her."

He gave an awkward shrug of his shoulders that seemed out of character. "I don't understand why— she's a friendly little thing." His Adam's apple shifted as he buried his hands in the pockets of his workpants, as if to deflect the emotion he felt. "Waltzed right up to me tonight bold as you please," he said with a sheepish smile, looking so much like a shy, little boy that Marcy smiled back. He grinned in return. "Told me I was cute."

She shook her head and started walking again, face forward and humor tipping her lips. "Oh, and I suppose you've never heard *that* before."

He laughed and snatched something from a tree overhead. She peeked out of the corner of her eye to see him bobbling an acorn before he sailed it nearly a block away. "Well, there's no accounting for taste, I suppose." He paused, as if weighing his words. "I've never seen anyone as good with children as you, Marcy—you make each and every one feel special."

She smiled, staring straight ahead as she kept a brisk pace. "Well, blame it on the fact I'm an only child who wishes she were from a big family where love flows like water." She breathed in the loamy scent of a garden they passed, expelling it in a contented sigh at the mere mention of family. "Goodness, I love children."

Pause. "And would that 'love' extend to men who act like children, I hope?"

A soft chuckle escaped her lips as she shook her head again. "It does not, Mr. O'Connor, but I'm quite sure there are enough lovely lasses in the Southie neighborhood to more than accommodate."

He slowed her with a gentle hand, coaxing her to a stop. His voice held a tease, but his eyes were as deadly serious as they'd been at the revelation of Tillie's home life. "And what of the man bewitched by a lass who can't abide him?"

She hesitated to speak her mind, his handsome face in and of itself a warning of the smooth speech of a man like him. The same kind of man who betrayed her cousin with empty promises and an even emptier engagement. Her defenses immediately notched up. And the same kind of man as Elsie's father, her best friend in New York. A devastatingly attractive man who'd swept Elsie's mother off her feet with lots of tingles and tremors, only to trap her in an empty marriage in which he shamelessly pursued other women.

Marcy heaved a weary sigh, unwilling to succumb to such a fate. "Especially a man like that," she said quietly, hoping her smile would soften her response. After all, it wasn't Patrick O'Connor's fault he'd been born so handsome. But it *was* his fault how he'd misused that gift from God.

Head bowed, she picked up her pace, uncomfortable with the fact she'd obviously hurt his feelings, given his silence on the remainder of the blocks home. But it couldn't be helped. Beautiful men like Patrick O'Connor who made women swoon were not to be trusted as Marcy soon discovered with the various good-looking Don Juans who'd sought her out in New York. Unlike her cousin and Elsie's mother, she had no desire to allow passion to steer her into such a marriage. No, she longed for friendship first, not flutters in her stomach, a man who could make her feel safe and steady without all those dangerous palpitations that could muddy a girl's thinking. Sexual attraction was a measure for love to most girls, she supposed, but not for her. Give her a godly and studious man like Evan Farrell any day of the week over a handsome face with shuttered eyes and a dangerous smile. A shiver skittered through her, and she clutched her arms close to her waist while she hurried toward her home on the next block. At the turn, she stopped and nodded down her street, offering Patrick a hesitant smile while she reached for her portfolio. "I live just a few houses down, so I'll take this, and you can double back to Hastings." She tugged, but he didn't let go.

"Excuse me, Miss Murphy," he said with a jag of a thick, dark brow. "But Sister Francine would have my hide if I didn't deliver you safely to your door, and you've been absent five years, so you've no idea the terror she strikes in the heart of men."

Marcy sighed, lips quirking into a wry smile. "A terror well deserved, no doubt. And 'safely' is one of those points that's a matter of opinion, Mr. O'Connor." She chanced a sideways glance with just a sliver of a smile. "At least given your reputation in the South end of Boston."

A slow grin traveled his lips, and Marcy all but scrambled to her front gate, alarmed at the feathery feeling in her stomach. She fumbled with the latch while his words drifted behind, warm and low and husky with tease. "So I'm subject to penance with you as well as Father Fitz, am I, Marceline?"

Racing down her flagstone walk, she quickly mounted the steps to her front porch, finally facing him at the door with what she hoped was a serene air. "Thank you for walking me home." She extended a hand. "If you'll give me my portfolio, I'll bid you good night."

He hesitated, fingering the attaché as he studied her through cautious eyes. "Even Father Fitz forgives me of my sins, Marceline," he said quietly, "and those are the ones I know about. With you … I've no earthly idea what I've done to make you dislike me so."

Marcy folded her arms, a hint of shame warming her collar. *But not enough to let my guard down.* She softened her tone, praying he would not take offense at her response. But she knew full well that she needed to be blunt to dissuade a man of his confidence and reputation. "I'm sorry, Patrick, and I don't dislike you, truly, but I suspect you may be flirting with me, and if so, it's best to let you know up front that I have no interest in flirting back."

Attaché in hand, his thumb slowly traced the side of it with sober eyes. "Do you mind if I ask why?"

She released a weighty sigh, not wanting to be indelicate, but well aware she needed to tell him the truth. Cautious of his feelings, she chose her words carefully, cushioning her tone with a gentle smile. "Well, it's certainly no secret you're a very handsome man, and unfortunately …" She tugged the side of her lip with her teeth, peeking up with a tentative gaze. "I've had some awful experiences with handsome men, so I'm afraid the truth is I simply don't trust them." Her heart sank at the hurt in his eyes, and she quickly laid a hand to his arm, desperate to ease the sting with a laugh that felt forced. "Well goodness, as the infamous Southie Lothario, I'm sure you can understand why I'd rather not risk flirting with danger?"

He nodded. "Fair enough," he said quietly, "but all flirting aside, Marceline, I wish you'd give me a chance to get to know you better."

She drew in a fortifying breath, determined to nip this in the bud once and for all. "Most certainly, and we shall, Patrick—as friends during the play. But in a romantic sense?" She gave a faint shrug of her shoulders, sympathy edging her smile. "I'm sorry, but I'd rather not add my name to your long lists of conquests."

He shifted, his jaw stiffening enough for her to notice. "I beg your pardon, Marcy, but you don't even know me."

"I know your reputation," she said softly, "and frankly, that's more than enough to give me pause." She held out a hand for her portfolio, her eyes gentle. "Thank you again for the escort, truly."

A nerve pulsed in his cheek as he stared her down, making no move to return her father's attaché. "One outing," he whispered, "and if I don't behave, you can throw me out on my ear." The intensity in his eyes matched the plea in his tone.

She studied him in the moonlight, the dark ringlets tumbling his forehead making him look like a little boy. Penetrating gray eyes that usually teased and flirted were now stone somber with an air of humility she didn't expect. She felt the tug, the pull of his petition, wondering if it were actually possible that a Casanova of Patrick O'Connor's ilk could ever be trusted, ever be faithful, ever embrace the same intimate faith in God as she. Nora's tear-stained face and swollen belly came to mind, and a shiver wisped across Marcy's shoulders like the summer breeze that stirred the hair against her neck. Wooing her, winning her with its silky warmth ... only to usher in the cold sting of winter. She shuddered and took a step back, arms to her waist. "Please forgive me, Patrick, but you and I—we're nothing alike."

"It would be dull if we were, Marcy," he said softly. "Surely you've heard the expression that opposites attract."

Her smile was kind. "Maybe so, but not spiritually."

His handsome face screwed in a frown. "I don't understand—we share the same faith."

She sighed and buffed her arms, not from the cold, but from the awkwardness of his statement. "Yes, we both belong to the same church ..." she said carefully, "but we both don't live by the same rules."

He frowned. "I'm confused—I go to church, to confession, and I'm good friends with Father Fitz ..." He slacked a hip, her father's portfolio limp at his side. "What more do you need?"

She drew in a deep breath, not wanting to wound him, but intent on speaking the truth. "More, I'm afraid. You see, to me it's a matter of faith that is real and deep and alive."

He flinched. "I have faith," he said, a bristle of hurt in his voice.

"Yes, of course you do," she said quickly, gaze gentle as she tapped a finger to her head. "Up here." She slowly slid a hand to her heart, taking great pains to soften her words. "But based on what I know of a man of your ilk, I worry that it doesn't live here." She studied the confusion in his face and tried again. "I believe that in your mind, your faith is deep—doctrine, precepts, catechism—but when it comes to living it?"

Her smile was sad as she curled her hand over her chest. "I suspect it may be heart shallow."

"And how would you know that, Marceline?" A spark of fire glinted in his eyes for the very first time. "As I said before, you don't even know me."

Releasing a tired sigh, she regarded him with a look of sadness that clearly bled into her voice. "No, but as *I* said before, Patrick, I know your reputation with women, your flirtatious ways, your disregard of rules ..." A lump dipped in her throat as she paused, determined to make him understand once and for all. "Your lust for things of a more ... carnal nature."

—

Blood gorged his cheeks at the way she said it—like he was one of the degenerate sots that littered the alleys of Ann Street like garbage—and it stung his pride with the heat of humiliation. He blinked, suddenly feeling like a little boy instead of a man, and the very notion angered him. Never had a woman turned him away before, and frustration prickled the back of his neck like a thousand needles of guilt, telling him he would never measure up, never make the grade. "You're a waste of a man, Patrick O'Connor," his father would say, "selling your soul to the devil instead of living for God." But then it was "God" Who belittled him through the very judgment in his father's eyes, rejected him through the condemnation in his father's barbs. While the devil had only given him free reign to be accepted and approved, if only in the eyes and hearts of Southie lasses. Defiance steeled his jaw. *All but one.* His gaze flicked up to blue eyes soft with pity and an angel's face gentled with empathy that was nothing more than condescension in disguise. Oh, how he craved to turn his back on the very faith she espoused.

But he was nothing if not determined and no one if not a man used to getting his way with the gentler sex, and so he controlled the anger that smoldered inside, taming his tone. "Marceline," he said quietly, "I'm asking you to give me a chance, that's all. I've been drawn to you from the moment I saw you, and I would like to know you better."

Seconds passed like eons before she finally shook her head. "I'm sorry, really I am. I like you as a person, Patrick, truly, but in the romantic sense, I have no desire to be involved with a man like you, a rogue who so casually equates lust with love."

A man like you.

A failure, a sinner, someone not worthy of love. To his parents, and now, apparently, to Marceline Murphy. Her pious judgment detonated his temper. Fists clenched, he leaned in, looming over her with fury itching in his eyes. "So you're judge and jury, then, condemning me without knowing me?"

Her jaw notched up, his tone apparently sparking her own anger. "I may not know *you*, Mr. O'Connor, but I *do* know this neighborhood is littered with broken hearts and tarnished reputations at your hand, so if you'll kindly return my portfolio, I won't detain you any further."

She might as well have spit in his face. He stood paralyzed except for the white-hot fury that scorched through him, stunned at her blatant rejection. Once again, Christian piety at its very best—judging him, condemning him, telling him he would never measure up. Deemed imperfect by imperfect people. The leather portfolio burned in his palm like the angst burned in his gut, and he could hardly fathom that the one woman he longed to know condemned him just like his father. The very notion caused the blood to pound in his brain, and his response was swift, defiant and rash, determined to throw in her face all she obviously thought him to be. "Yes, I'll return your portfolio," he said with a strained whisper. "But first ... you revile me as a rogue, Marceline? I'll give you a rogue ..."

Flinging the attaché to the floor, he jerked her close with a sharp catch of her breath, temple throbbing as he silenced her protest with his mouth, stilling the lash of her arms with a steel hold. Fury pulsed through his veins as he took his fill of a woman who had cut him to the core, wounded his pride and spurned him as cruelly as his own blood. The stolen kiss of a rogue—just punishment for a woman who had stolen his heart, crushing it beneath the heel of faith in a so-called loving God.

His trigger reaction had been prompted by revenge, but she tasted of peppermint and lilacs and a summer so warm, his anger flamed into desire, filling him with a fierce possession. "Marceline," he rasped, voice hoarse as he cupped her face in his hands. "This is not how I meant it to be ..."

She lurched away, the stinging jolt of her slap vibrating his jaw till his teeth nearly rattled in their sockets. "How dare you!"

He blinked, the strike of her anger diffusing his own and breaking the spell the kiss had cast. "How dare I?" he whispered. "How dare I do anything else, Marceline, but be all you've proclaimed me to be?" Throat constricting, he bent to retrieve the portfolio, the same sick feeling of shame shuddering through him as when he fought with his father. He held it out, and her hand quivered when she took it back with tears in her eyes, making him feel like the despicable lowlife she and his father believed him to be.

He met her eyes with a look of grief that exposed

him for the lost soul that he was. "My most humble apology, Marceline, for losing my temper and causing you pain." Head bowed, he lowered his voice to a bare whisper. "And although the word of a man of my 'ilk' may mean nothing, you have it nonetheless, along with my abject sorrow." He looked up then at the one woman he wanted more than any other, painfully aware his temper and pride had just cost him any chance he might have had. "You have my promise—I won't bother you again."

Without another word, he turned and walked to the street, hands in his pockets and shame in his throat. He was giving up without a fight, he knew, something he'd never done a day in his life, but he'd seen the truth in her eyes—she despised him—and with just cause. One foolish slip of his Irish temper had sealed his fate, confirming once and for all to Marceline Murphy what his father so blatantly proclaimed—he was not a man to be trusted.

Head down and heart heavy, he plodded toward home, giving up any hope of ever turning her head. But then maybe he was more like his parents than he knew, giving up on the things that mattered most—one's children, one's marriage, one's self-respect. Somewhere an owl hooted, and the mournful sound echoed the despair and loneliness that had plagued him since he'd found his father in the arms of another woman at the age of ten, betraying both his wife and his two sons. A pillar of the Church who chose lust over family, self over flesh of his own flesh and bone of his bone. A hypocrite who chastised his son for public sins he practiced in private.

And served a God just as false.

Patrick's jaw tightened. No, he would never be the type of man Marceline Murphy wanted because he'd just proven he possessed a vile temper and a "lust for things of a more ... carnal nature." But by sweat and by blood, he would earn her respect with the worth of his word. A vow he would keep, unlike his father. He stopped in the street in front of his house where lights glimmered and glowed without any warmth, determined to show her he was worthy of love even though she would never give it. And he would do it in the only way he knew how.

He'd leave her alone.

And leave her to Sam.

A rogue like himself, yes, but a rogue who possessed one less flaw. Marcy was a woman who craved family and fidelity, hearth and home. Who longed for the wholeness of loving parents and siblings who cared. Something Sam could easily provide. Patrick opened the door to his house of despair.

And something he definitely could not.

Chapter Nine

Heart thundering, Marcy plastered herself against the inside of her front door, eyes squeezed shut and the back of her head pressed to the wood while saltwater swam in her eyes. The memory of Patrick's kiss inflamed both her cheeks and her blood, spiking her anger. *How dare he!* A warning shiver pulsed through her and she was reminded just how deadly a man like him could be—kisses that coaxed and begged for more, disarming a girl's will to say no. It had been a man just like him that had disarmed her cousin, but it would never—*ever*—happen to her, no matter how much his kiss had tingled her skin and surged her pulse. Hand trembling, she swiped at her eyes, the taste of his mouth still burning her lips and quivering her stomach.

"Marceline—are you all right?"

Her eyes popped open with a harsh catch of her breath. "Mother!"

Worry flickered across Bridget Murphy's face as she hurried down the steps, her blue dressing gown fluttering wildly. At thirty-eight, her mother was a beautiful woman with a fair amount of sass in sky-blue eyes that matched Marcy's to a T. Waist-length pale-blonde hair—the exact shade of her daughter's—was loosely tied with a sash at the back of her neck, spilling over shoulders now squared with worry. "Something's wrong—what is it?"

Marcy forced a smile, hoping to calm her mother's frantic look. She laid her father's attaché on the foyer table and quickly embraced her, breathing in the comforting scent of Pears soap and rose water. "Nothing's wrong, I promise."

Her mother held her at bay, gaze narrow as she studied her daughter. Her tone was no-nonsense and to the point, so like Bridget Murphy herself. "No, your eyes are red and your face, flushed—something's wrong."

"Nothing, truly," Marcy soothed, "just a wee bit upset over something that happened tonight, but it's nothing serious, I assure you, so you can go back to bed."

Bridget buffed her daughter's arms before prodding her toward the kitchen at the back of the house. "Your father's snoring up a storm and I need chamomile, so we'll talk." She pressed Marcy into a spindle chair at a polished oak table graced with cottage roses that infused the kitchen with the scent of summer. Filling her trusty copper teapot with water from the tap and a hefty dose of tea, her mother set it to boil on the cast-iron stove before retrieving two floral cups from the cabinet. Eyelet curtains billowed with a gentle wind scented with mulch while her mother shimmied into a chair, hands folded on the table and brows arched. "So ... what happened?"

Marcy's heavy sigh could have fluttered the curtains along with the breeze. She kneaded the bridge of her nose, avoiding her mother's eyes. "Nothing terrible, I suppose," she said carefully, "it's just that Patrick O'Connor walked me home tonight, and he ..." A muscle dipped in her throat as she paused to swallow.

"Well, he ... made advances."

"What?" Bridget Murphy sat straight up, nose pinched in a frown. "That hooligan friend of Julie's brother? What kind of advances?"

Marcy picked at her nails, gaze fixed on her hands. "He kissed me," she whispered, feeling the heat of his lips all over again, along with an annoying flutter in her belly.

"Good heavens, you didn't like it, did you?" Her mother's tone bordered on alarm.

"Of course not," Marcy fibbed, desperate to convince herself as well as her mother that the sparks she'd felt were from anger and shock rather than attraction. A shiver whispered through her mind. Passion had no place in her life except passion for God, and she intended to keep it that way. From everything she'd seen and felt in New York, romantic passion only led to trouble for a woman, blinding her eyes and clouding her judgment. No, Marcy wanted none of that. Yes, she wanted to be attracted to the man that she would eventually marry, but an attraction based on friendship and a keen mind, not sweet talk and swoons. She'd learned through the heartaches of her cousin and best friend's parents that palpitations and promises were no basis for a happy marriage. And if there was one thing Marcy intended to have, it was a happy marriage. Her lips quirked. A near impossibility with a handsome rake like Patrick O'Connor. "He reminds me too much of Nora's ex-fiancé," she said with absolute certainty. "You know, too handsome to be trusted, too experienced with women."

"Good." Her mother's jaw shifted in a familiar grinding motion as her eyes narrowed to slits. "I certainly hope you slapped him silly."

Marcy nodded, chewing the edge of her lip as

mischief tugged at her smile. "I think I may have rattled the poor man's brain."

"Humph ... nothing 'poor' about a scoundrel like that except his manners, and you have to have a brain before you can rattle it." Bridget leaned in, a glint of warning in her eyes. "You stay far away from the likes of him, Marceline, do you hear? And the same goes for Julie's brother. Cocky lots the both of them, preying on young girl's affections."

Julie's brother. A shaky exhale parted from Marcy's lips. *Affections, yes.*

The teapot whistled and her mother jumped up, straining the steaming brew into each cup before she delivered them to the table. The sweet smell of apple swirled in the air along with the steam as she bustled back for spoons, milk and sugar, then returned to her seat, eyeing Marcy while she stirred the cream in her cup. "Where was Julie and why was that scalawag walking you home in the first place?"

Marcy blew on her tea and sweetened it to taste. "Julie and Sam had a family function to attend, so Sister Francine insisted Patrick walk me home."

"Sweet mother of mercy, does the woman not realize the type of reputation that boy has? Goodness, Loretta McPhee asked for prayer at our sewing circle just last week concerning those Lotharios, the two of them forever sniffing around her daughters."

Hot liquid pooled in Marcy's mouth, burning far less than the mention of Sam with another girl. She wrinkled her nose and added more sugar. "I think Sister Francine was so relieved I didn't have to walk home alone, she overlooked that it was Patrick who offered."

"Well, just see to it that it doesn't happen again."

Marcy bent to sip her cup, her thoughts lost in its golden depths.

"Marceline?"

She glanced up, idly warming her fingers on the sides of her cup. "Yes?"

Her mother squinted to study her face. "You don't have feelings for this O'Connor boy, do you?"

She absently shook her head, her gaze fading back into her tea where the kiss played out once again, warming her skin like the steam from her cup. Tremors rolled through her stomach as she abruptly pushed the cup away, golden liquid sloshing in her saucer. *Not if I can help it.* "Of course not," she whispered.

"Good, because the boy comes from bad blood, make no mistake, so it's best to stay far away from a man like that." She wrinkled her nose while she tasted her tea. "After all, the apple doesn't fall far from the tree."

Marcy glanced up. "What do you mean?"

Bridget paused, assessing her daughter over the rim of her cup. She huffed out a weary sigh and slowly placed her cup back in its saucer. "I suppose you're old enough to know of such things now, especially in light of the O'Connor boy's advances, but it's not a pretty story."

"What happened?" Marcy whispered, her breathing suspended.

"Well, it seems Patrick's father—a church board member, mind you—had an affair with the sixteen-year-old daughter of the next-door neighbor."

Marcy sucked in a harsh breath.

Bridget clucked her tongue. "Yes, I can assure you it was shock to everyone. The poor family up and moved so quickly that everyone just knew the girl was pregnant."

"No ..." Marcy clutched a hand to her throat.

Bridget nodded. "The man has since repented and

mended his ways, of course, but he's never been the same, I can tell you that." She gave a short grunt. "And spawning a rake for a son certainly didn't help." She took a drink of her tea, lips pursed in a scowl. "The sins of the father, you know."

Yes, Marcy knew. *And he did that which was evil in the sight of the Lord, as his fathers had done ...*

"Mark my words—it's in the boy's blood. A young woman would do well to study the father if she wants a glimpse of the son ..."

Thoughts of Sam popped in her mind, and her heart sped up. Although not overly devout, Mr. O'Rourke was a God-fearing man who attended church with his family. Without question, he loved his wife and children, ensuring a close-knit bond among parents and siblings to provide the kind of family Marcy desperately craved.

She shook off her reverie to give her mother a sad smile. "I knew something terrible had happened to the O'Connors, but I never really knew what." Marcy tucked her arms to her waist, warding off a shiver. "It certainly explains a lot."

"Yes, regrettably it does, so it's best to keep that scoundrel at arm's length." Bridget paused, teacup hovering at her lips. "And the scoundrel's friends as well, Marceline."

Eyes averted, Marcy quickly sipped her tea while heat scalded her cheeks.

The chair squeaked against the wood floor when her mother shifted to lean in, eyes shrewd. "Did you hear what I said, daughter? That includes Julie's brother."

Marcy's eyelids weighted closed as the tea clotted in her throat. She gulped it down hard, the sharp bob of her throat prompting a catch in her mother's breath.

"Oh, Marceline, no—not Sam O'Rourke!"

Upending her tea, her mother clunked her cup back in her saucer. "The saints preserve us."

Marcy peeked up, her voice frail. "I've always had a fondness for Sam, Mother, you know that."

Bridget slammed a palm to the table, her jaw grating as she peered at her daughter. "But that was five years ago! I hoped that time and distance would diminish that schoolgirl crush."

Marcy's hands quivered as she sipped, her mother's disappointment no more than her own. "Trust me, Mother, I have no intention of acting on it."

Her mother grunted in unladylike fashion. "It's not you I worry about trusting. Sam may not be as tempting as Patrick O'Connor, but those two are cut from the same cloth, make no mistake." She rose to pour herself more tea. "So much for sleeping tonight after that bit of news—it'll take the whole bloomin' pot." She plopped back into her chair and drowned her tea with more milk. "I've a mind to forbid you to stay the night at Julie's anymore."

Marcy's cup clattered against her china saucer. "No, please! I love Julie and I love her family, and that would be so unfair."

"No, young lady, 'unfair' would be if I lost my daughter to the likes of Sam O'Rourke."

"You have nothing to worry about, truly." Marcy reached to stroke her mother's arm, ducking her head to capture her gaze. "I intend to fall in love with a man who shares my faith as deeply as I do, so trust me, please? Besides," she said with a hint of a smile, "Sam is somewhat of a flirt, yes, but he's not as worrisome as Patrick, for heaven's sake. He's not near as handsome nor cocky and he comes from a stable home."

"Humph. He may not be as devilishly handsome as the O'Connor boy, but the two share the same shadow, you mark my words. And I love Julie and her family, you know that, but I would be lying through my teeth if I didn't tell you that you having feelings for Sam O'Rourke puts the fear of God in me."

Marcy chuckled. "And me as well, I assure you. But, who knows," she said with a wiggle of brows, suddenly giddy at the thought. "Maybe I could put the fear of God in him as well."

"Now *that* I would like to see," Bridget said with a wry smile. "Only with someone else's daughter rather than mine, thank you very much. Half the mothers in the Southie neighborhood would owe a debt over that, you can be sure, including Mrs. O'Rourke."

Draining her tea, Marcy rose to bestow a kiss to her mother's head, suddenly exhausted as she carried her cup to the sink. "Me too," she said with a yawn. She washed her cup and dried it, sending a tired smile over her shoulder. "Sam could use a touch of God in his life. Mrs. O'Rourke and her children are very devout, but Sam seems to be a bit of a black sheep, taking after his father at the same age, I think."

Bridget chuckled. "Wolf in sheep's clothing, you mean, black or otherwise." She joined Marcy at the sink, rinsing her cup as well.

Marcy laughed. "Honestly, Mother, Sam's not all that bad. Did you know he and Patrick volunteered on their own to help at the center *and* with the play?"

"Now why does that worry me?" Bridget's lips took a wry twist.

"Because you're a mother?" Marcy asked, hooking her mother's waist to press a kiss to her cheek.

"A mother with a nose for trouble when it comes to her beautiful daughter," she emphasized with a lift of her brows. She dried her cup and put it away, slipping Marcy a narrow gaze out of the corner of her eye. "And from where I'm sitting, neither of those boys smell all that good and a wee bit like a skunk." Pulling the kettle from the boil, she turned to follow her daughter to the door. "And that's a stink you'll be wanting to avoid, Marceline."

A weak laugh bubbled from Marcy's lips, as tired and slap-happy as she. "Well, seeing I'm neither too fond of either skunks or rogues, I think it's safe to say I plan to steer clear of both."

Bridget doused the light and gave her daughter a warning squeeze. "Well, just see that you do, darlin' girl," she said with a crook of her mouth, "just see that you do."

Chapter Ten

"Come again?" Sam stared at Patrick with eyes as wide as the gape of his mouth.

Patrick exhaled a weary sigh. It wasn't even midnight, and Brannigan's was in rare form, crawling with thirsty men—and in the realm of love—even thirstier women, flirting to their heart's content. Particularly muggy for late summer, sweat gleamed on smiling faces as men coaxed and ladies teased, dancing, chatting or crooning to the tunes of Tommy Thomkins while he caressed the keys of his battered piano. Patrick wrinkled his nose, the scent of stale whiskey and cheap perfume more potent than normal and surprisingly void of its usual thrill.

"Patrick!" Sam shook Patrick's arm, bringing him back to the crowded bar where a haze of smoke hung as thick as the fog in his mind. He looped an arm over his best friend's shoulders and bent to peer in his face, tone urgent. "Are you crazy? Colleen's uncle is gone for the weekend, and Jenny is spending the night. And *you're* going home?"

Crazy? *Apparently.* Patrick expelled another noisy breath, in total agreement with Sam that he had, indeed, lost his mind. *Or my heart.* He glanced at the privy door at the back of the bar where Colleen and Jenny had gone to "freshen up" before heading to Colleen's uncle's flat, then exhaled again. He was reluctant to admit to his best friend that for some strange reason, intimacies shared with Jenny no longer held any appeal.

Some strange reason? Patrick grunted and tossed the rest of his beer to the back of his throat. Some strange girl, more likely, a holier-than-thou angel who had ruined his taste for other women. Pushing his mug away, he scrubbed his face with his hands, wanting nothing more at the moment than to just go home to bed—*alone*. He tossed payment for his tab on the bar and lumbered to his feet, slapping Sam on the back with an apology in his eyes. "Sorry, buddy, but I'm spent and so is my money."

Sam cinched his arm, gaze flicking to where Colleen and Jenny were inching through the sea of patrons, heading their way. He turned back, dark eyes pleading. "Look, Patrick, we don't get this opportunity all that often, and the girls are more than willing, so what's your problem? I thought you liked Jenny?"

"I do," Patrick said. He glanced her way, noting the blatant stares of other men as Jenny passed by. She sent a smile in Patrick's direction and he returned it, scanning from her shapely shirtwaist to the soft curve of her hips as they swayed beneath a skirt that skimmed her body like every man longed to do. Except for him. His smile went flat. At least lately. He shook his head. "But not tonight, Sam—just not in the mood."

"Not-in-the-mood?" Sam enunciated slowly, thick brows bunched in disbelief. He placed a palm to Patrick's forehead, his shock evident in the rasp of his voice. "The chance of a lifetime and you're *not* in the mood? That settles it, O'Connor—you're sick, and I'm taking over even if I have to drag you all the way."

Patrick laughed. "You would have to, Sam, because

I'm exhausted. I worked three double shifts this week, remember?"

"Yeah, I remember," Sam said with grunt, "but that's never stopped you before."

"Ready?" Colleen appeared at Sam's side and ruffled his dark curls, her brown eyes sparkling with tease. She tossed a loose strand of auburn hair over her shoulder with a pretty arch of brows, gaze flitting from Sam to Patrick.

Sam hooked Colleen close, making her giggle when he nibbled her ear. "I certainly am, but I'm afraid Patrick here is 'not in the mood.'"

Patrick groaned. "Come on, Sam, I told you I'm just exhausted."

"Not in the mood?" Jenny said with an innocent blink of blue eyes that was purely for show. She sidled up to Patrick and slipped her arms to his waist, lifting on tiptoe to graze his stubbled jaw with her lips. "Why, I take that as a personal challenge, Mr. O'Connor," she whispered, the warm mold of her body racing his pulse. Hooking a hand to his neck, she pulled him down to weld her mouth with his, and Patrick groaned and finished the job with a kiss so deep, heat seared him head to toe. Blood pumping, he devoured her neck, sweeping away honey-hued curls to suckle her ear.

And then in one jagged breath, pale gold tendrils on an alabaster neck came to mind, and Patrick's heart thudded to a cold stop. His lips stilled on Jenny's ear, all desire suddenly as lukewarm as the dregs of beer at the bottom of his glass. Eyelids sinking closed, he stifled a groan before pressing a lingering kiss to her cheek. He pulled away, regret softening his gaze as he tenderly buffed her arms. "Jenny, as tempting as that kiss was, I have another double shift tomorrow and really need to head home." He lifted her chin with his thumb. "Give me a rain check?"

"Come on, Patrick," Sam said, "don't leave the woman high and dry. One or two hours, and then you can head home for that sleep you so desperately need."

"Sorry, Sam, but I guarantee after that last kiss, not only wouldn't I be leaving in one or two hours, but I wouldn't get any sleep." He gave Jenny a wink, then cuffed Sam's neck. "Good night, all," he called over his shoulder. "Don't do anything I wouldn't do." Fielding flirtations from various ladies on his way to the door, Patrick stepped outside and inhaled a deep draw of crisp air, glad to be free of the noise and smoke and temptation for which he suddenly had no stomach. Hands in his pockets, he vented his frustration with a noisy blast of air, head bowed as he absently made his way down the street.

"O'Connor!"

Patrick turned, a silent groan lodged in his throat when he saw Sam loping toward him, shadowed jaw as ominous as the dark glare of black eyes. He exhaled loudly, waiting for Sam to catch up while Brannigan's music filtered down the near-empty street.

"What the devil is your problem tonight?" Sam snapped, chest huffing as he came to a stop, hands on his knees to catch his breath. "You not only ruined Jenny's evening, you ruined mine."

Slacking a hip, Patrick pinched the bridge of his nose. "Come on, Sam, you're a big boy. You don't need me along to have a good time."

"No, but we're a team—it's not the same without you."

One side of Patrick's smile crooked up. "Since when do you need me along to woo a woman, O'Rourke?" He slipped his hands in his pockets and started walking again, pinging a rock into a lamppost with his toe.

Sam fell in to step beside him with a scowl. "Since Colleen doesn't cotton to Jenny being alone in the next room, listening to everything going on." He kicked a stone of his own, sailing it half a block down the street until it ricocheted off a fire hydrant. "Thanks a lot for ruining a sure thing."

"Just as well," Patrick said with a squint at the sky, his thoughts melancholy as he studied the full moon. "Colleen and Jenny aren't exactly the type of women we hope to marry someday."

"Marry?" Sam's voice almost cracked as it rose several octaves. "Bloomin' saints, O'Connor, who's talking about marriage? I'm talking about the needs of a red-blooded American male here, not 'till death do us part." He stared at Patrick's profile. "What the devil's gotten into you, anyway?"

Patrick delivered a sideways glance at his best friend, his gaze pensive. "You ever worry we won't be able to find a decent girl to marry? You know, given our tainted reputations?"

Sam halted on the sidewalk. "*Tainted* reputations?" he said, tone incredulous. "Blue blistering blazes, we're two of the most sought-after males in all of South Boston, hard workers both, slated to do well. You as a writer and then maybe editor at the *Herald* someday, and me as prosperous businessman." He grunted and scooped up another pebble, lashing it down the cobblestone street. "Trust me, my friend, when the time comes, we'll have our pick of decent girls and our 'tainted' reputations, as you call them, will have naught to say about it."

A low chuckle parted from Patrick's lips. "Trust *you?*" He slid his friend a crooked smile. "If all the Southie lasses and their mothers don't, why should I?"

"Ah, but you're the pretty-boy Lothario they really don't trust. Me? I'm just your average side-partner along for the ride." Sam's teeth flashed in the glow of a flickering streetlamp. "But what a ride it's been, old boy, at least until tonight." He hooked an arm over Patrick's shoulder. "Which leads me to my original question—what the blazes has gotten into you? If I didn't know better, I'd say you've been paying too much heed to Father Fitz."

No, not Father Fitz ... Patrick sighed, his smile fading along with his good mood. Waiting for a horse-drawn carriage to pass, he sprinted across the street along with Sam, sidestepping a pile of manure before resuming his slow pace on the other side. "I don't know, sometimes I wonder if we're being selfish, you know? Caring more about our own pleasure than the reputation of the women we meet."

"What?" Sam stopped again, jaw dangling.

Patrick shot him a wry smile. "Don't look so shocked, O'Rourke, you're the one who threatens me within an inch of my life if I so much as glance your sister's way. You go to great lengths to protect Julie from bums like us and yet neither of us bat an eye over taking advantage of other girls."

Sam shook his head, hands loose on his hips. "It's different with girls like Julie, and you know it. She's a good girl who wouldn't darken the door of a pub on a bet, but there are plenty of girls who do, and trust me—they're there for the same reasons we are. Good grief, we're men with needs and desires—it's natural to crave the affections of women. Besides," he said with an off-center grin. "Judging from our success, I'd say they like it as much as we do."

"Not all of 'em," Patrick muttered. He jumped to swipe a hickory nut from an overhead limb and hurled the nut with so much force, it sounded like a gunshot against the wood gutter of a storefront.

"Well, that's true—we've certainly dabbled with our share of prudes ..." He paused, coming to a complete standstill as he gripped Patrick's arm. "Wait a minute ..." he said with a faint smile that slowly inched its way into a grin. "This is about Marcy, isn't it?"

Patrick shook Sam off and kept walking, forcing his friend to follow with a low chuckle. "Well, what do you know?" There was a touch of awe in Sam's voice. "The angel reforms the devil. I thought you said nothing happened when you walked her home."

"I lied," Patrick said, lips flat. "Something happened all right. She dislocated my jaw."

Sam laughed outright. "No kidding?" He slapped Patrick on the back. "That could be the best news I've heard all night, old buddy. So, what happened?"

Patrick huffed out a sigh, hands back in his pockets. "I tried to charm her, but it didn't work—she turned me down flat. Claims she wants a man with a deeper faith."

Sam chuckled. "That would be three quarters of the sots at the soup kitchen."

"Yeah, well, you're not exactly a choir boy, O'Rourke," Patrick said with a tight edge to his tone. He sucked in a heavy dose of air, his spirits dampened considerably by the memory of Marcy's rejection and his subsequent anger. "I lost my temper," he said quietly, "and was stupid enough to force myself on her and she ..." A muscle jerked in his throat. "Well, she hates me now." He glanced over, giving Sam a listless smile. "Which means I struck out, O'Rourke, and you're up to bat. There's just one thing I ask."

"And what's that?" Sam studied Patrick with a cautious eye.

Patrick paused, pinning his best friend with a

warning stare. "Treat her decently, Sam. She's one of a kind, and I'll not have you taking advantage of her." The edge of his mouth crooked up. "Not that she'll let you."

Sam nodded, gaze dropping to the sidewalk. He hesitated for several moments before peering up, face somber. "I'm sorry, Patrick."

Patrick glanced up, smile faint. "No, you're not, but you will be if you don't treat her right."

A rare sobriety stole across Sam's features as he walked quietly beside Patrick, hands in his pocket and head down, as if considering whether Marceline Murphy would be worth all he would need to give up.

"Sam?" Patrick paused, suspicion creeping into his tone.

Sam looked up, his lips in a thin line.

"Your intentions *are* honorable, right?" Patrick searched his friend's face.

Sam's solemn expression lightened with a sparkle in his eyes. "Since when, Patrick, are my intentions ever honorable?"

Patrick stayed him with an abrupt hand, turning to face him head-on without the slightest bit of humor. "This isn't a joking matter. Marcy's something special, and I'll not have you ruining her, do you hear? If all you're out for is more of the same, then I'll ask you to leave her be."

Sam shook his head. "You've really fallen hard, haven't you?" He dragged a hand through unruly curls at the back of his head, his chuckle strained. "Well, I can see now that we have a dilemma on our hands, because you may be ready to sell your soul to a woman, but I'm certainly not." He unleashed a heavy sigh, head cocked as he assessed his friend with a reflective air. "All right, Patrick. I'm intrigued by our Marceline

Murphy, so I'll treat her honorably, I assure you." Sam latched an arm to Patrick's shoulder, giving him a wink. "Heaven knows there are more than enough lasses with whom I can be dishonorable, eh?"

Patrick's smile was sour. "Unless you commit to her, and then if I see you squiring other women, I'll break your arm."

"Fair enough." Sam grinned. "Tell me, does Marcy have any idea she's stumbled upon an unlikely guardian angel who hails from decidedly south of the Pearly Gates?"

"Not yet," he said with a dry smile, "but I aim to rectify that soon enough by winning her friendship, hopefully to shift this blasted attraction into something far less annoying."

Sam's laughter echoed down the shadowed street. "Please tell me this celestial duty will not keep us from enjoying the benefits of warmer climes with ladies who leave their halos at home?"

Steeling his heart against the influence of Marceline Murphy, Patrick cuffed an arm to Sam's shoulder, merging his laughter with that of his friend. "Perish the thought," he said with a tinge of his Irish temper, delivering a defiant grin. "I may be besotted, O'Rourke, but I'm not crazy."

Chapter Eleven

"Pinch me—I can hardly believe my brother volunteered to build furniture for the soup kitchen." Peeling potatoes at the kitchen table, Julie stared out the window of St. Mary's Center of Hope, where Sam worked in a sunny courtyard with Evan and Patrick, building tables and benches for the newly expanded soup kitchen. The smell of sawdust and sweat seeped through a bank of open windows at the back of a black-and-white linoleum room crowded with commercial cast-iron stoves, scarred wooden prep tables, and several large iceboxes. A wistful sigh floated from Julie's lips as she gazed with longing at Patrick O'Connor, whose muscled forearms gleamed with sweat while he sanded a table, the sleeves of his sweat-stained work shirt tightly rolled. The thin, damp material strained hard against intimidating biceps with every thrust of the sander while limp dark curls bobbed over his forehead with each grinding motion. She plopped another peeled and quartered potato into a bowl for the vegetable beef soup that would be served for dinner and sighed again. "Because heaven knows where Sam goes, heaven follows."

Marcy's gaze trailed Julie's, narrowing considerably at the sight of a man too handsome for his own good—

and Julie's. Her thoughts wandered to the night he'd kissed her and heat broiled her cheeks that had little to do with the boiling cauldron of soup. "Heaven, indeed," Marcy said with a grunt, forcing her gaze from Patrick's muscled body to Evan's tall, lanky frame, which although not as sculpted as Patrick's or even Sam's, was not altogether unappealing. Marcy's lips pressed thin. "Hmmm ... more likely the netherworld, I'd say." She tossed more penny carrots into her bowl and nudged Julie's shoulder with her own. "And I'll be pinching you for sure, Julie O'Rourke, if you don't take your eyes off that scalawag right now." She scrunched her nose. "It's beyond me what women see in the likes of him when there are decent men like Evan Farrell around."

Julie grinned with a tweak of Marcy's neck. "Yes, Evan's attractive in his own way, I suppose, but honestly, Marcy, if you can't see in Patrick what every other woman sees, then I suspect you're sorely in need of glasses."

"I'm sorry, Julie, but there's more to a man than good looks." Marcy whacked at a particularly thick carrot, whittling it down to size like she wished she could do with Patrick O'Connor after that stunt he pulled on her front porch. "Give me a man far less handsome who is trustworthy and kind and thinks of others instead of himself, and I'll consider being smitten." She hurled the carrots into the bowl with a plunk, lips compressed as a warm shiver prickled her skin. "But not with someone like him."

"Goodness, I've never seen you so severe with anyone before." Julie tossed the last of her potatoes into the bowl while she studied Marcy with a curious air. "What on earth has Patrick ever done to you, anyway?"

You have no idea, Julie, nor will you. I wouldn't

hurt you that way. Marcy set her paring knife down, eyeing the clock to assess when Miss Clara might return from the store. "I just don't trust a man as good-looking as him, that's all. My cousin cured me of that—along with the father of my good friend in New York and all the insufferable womanizers who came to call."

Julie's throaty chuckle echoed off stark white walls newly hung with freshly painted, white-wood cabinets and a shiny selection of steel pots and pans. "Yes, but you have to admit that what Patrick doesn't inspire in trust, he certainly makes up for in beautiful scenery." She brushed black curls from her forehead with the back of her hand, then followed Marcy to the stove to dump their potatoes and carrots into a simmering pot. "And although I'll never have the chance to find out, I don't mind telling you, Marcy, I do enjoy looking."

Marcy laughed and shook her head, snatching a dishrag to wipe down the counter. "Julie O'Rourke, you are utterly incorrigible!"

"Uh ... that doesn't have to be a bad thing, you know." Patrick grinned at the door, one muscled arm flush with the door frame as twinkling gray eyes peeked through the screen. He flapped the front of his damp shirt, several buttons open to reveal a tan chest with a whisper of dark hair. "Sorry to disturb, ladies, but we're wondering if you might show mercy to several very hot and thirsty, albeit 'incorrigible' men." His playful gaze flitted from Julie to Marcy, and something warm swirled in her belly when he gave her a wink. "Or at least two ..."

"Oh, absolutely!" Julie said with a start, cheeks fusing scarlet as she bustled over to the icebox to retrieve the pitcher of cool tea. "Come in—please."

Patrick continued fanning his shirt, sweat glazing his skin. "Better not. Miss Clara will have my head if I track sawdust all over her clean floor. Besides, 'incorrigible' is one thing," he said with a crooked grin. "'Ripe' is something else altogether."

"That's an understatement if ever there was." Sam joined him at the door, and Marcy's pulse skipped a beat, noting that although he was leaner than Patrick, Sam's body appeared as toned as his friend's. *Beautiful scenery, indeed,* Marcy thought, Julie's earlier statement braising her cheeks.

"Good gracious me, glad to see you taking care of my boys," a gravelly voice said behind the two men, and both turned to greet Miss Clara Rumsfeld, Commander in Chief of the St. Mary's Center of Hope kitchen. Affectionately referred to as Sarge by both Patrick and Sam, the crusty sixty-year-old ran a tight ship with all volunteers, although Marcy couldn't help but be annoyed by her obvious favoritism for the Southie Lotharios. Large, butterscotch teeth flashed in a round ebony face that gleamed with sweat and good humor, while wisps of black and silver hair fluttered about a disheveled chignon.

"Here, give me that bag, Miss Clara," Patrick said with a boyish smile, "you're too delicate of a woman to be lugging heavy groceries around."

Marcy fought the urge to roll her eyes as she followed Julie to the door with the third glass of tea, noting how quickly both Patrick and Sam alleviated the ample-sized woman of two sacks of groceries. She shook her head while Julie held the door for everyone to enter. Copious charm with women of all ages, apparently, Marcy thought with a silent grunt, exceeded only by an endless supply of blarney. She wrinkled her nose, more from the easy banter between Miss Clara and her "boys" than from the rank smell of sawdust and sweat. Her smile brightened when Evan appeared with several more bags retrieved from a small wooden wagon parked in the alley beyond.

"Fiddle-dee-dee, but it's an oven out there," Miss Clara announced, fanning herself with a copy of *The Boston Herald* that she fished from one of the bags. A button nose too small for her face scrunched in distaste when she sniffed the air, scouring all three men from head to toe. "You best march those sweaty bodies right back outside, gentlemen, afore you sour my soup."

"Aw, come on, Sarge," Patrick said with a playful scoop of Miss Clara's generous waist, "we're just working ourselves to the bone for a woman we love."

Miss Clara shooed him away with a good-natured swat, black eyes glittering as much as the moisture on her brow. "Oh, go on with you, you silver-tongued rascals, the lot of you. And we'll be needin' those new tables and benches lickety-split before you'll be takin' your leave. Last night the food line shuffled clear out the door, and I aim to pack 'em in tighter tonight, understood?"

"Aye, aye, Captain," Sam said with a salty salute, luring a smile to the old woman's lips.

Miss Clara promptly pinched both Sam's and Patrick's cheeks with a toothy grin. "I don't care how bad you two smell, you are about the prettiest volunteers this old girl has ever seen." She prodded them to the door. "Now, git, and don't you two rascals teach my boy Evan any bad habits, ya hear?"

Patrick paused at the screen door, a crimp of hurt between dark brows. "I'm wounded, Miss Clara, that you would think we would be anything but a good influence."

"Ha!" Marcy's cheeks burned when she realized she'd spoken out loud.

Evan chuckled, wiping his forehead with his sleeve

while he grinned at Marcy. "You'll be glad to know I'm holding my own, Miss Murphy, but who knows?" He delivered a wink so out of character that Marcy wondered if Patrick and Sam weren't making greater inroads than Evan suspected. "Perhaps I'll be a good influence on them."

Miss Clara's chuckle was throaty and rich and brimming with fun as she bustled over to wash her hands at the sink. "Not likely, Mr. Farrell, but we can always hope."

Marcy and Julie exchanged glances before both of them broke into giggles. Slipping an apron over her head, Marcy tied it behind her white shirtwaist and navy skirt, sending Miss Clara a look of supreme doubt. "Yes, we can, Miss Clara," she said with a sassy grin aimed in the men's direction. "But if it's all the same to you, we won't be holding our breath."

Hazy shafts of sunlight and smells of the city spilled through the open windows of the St. Mary's Center of Hope, where fresh asphalt and manure from the busy street outside mingled with body odor, musty clothes, and vegetable beef soup. Crammed window to wall with a sea of humanity that was more than a little pungent and considerably hungrier, the dining room buzzed with sounds that made Patrick feel more alive than all the piano music and shots of whiskey Brannigan's had to offer. From the tinkle of utensils and china to children's giggles and shrieks laced with adult conversations, few things shocked Patrick more than the fact he actually enjoyed working here, serving others instead of his own lust for pleasure. Whether building furniture all day in the blistering heat or returning after a fresh shower and shave to help Miss

Clara with the dinner shift, being here made Patrick feel worthy and whole for the first time in his life.

He heard the soft cadence of a female giggle rise above the hum of the room and his lips quirked. Of course, the frequent presence of Marceline Murphy certainly didn't hurt. Patrick paused at a table where an elderly man he'd chatted with before hunched over his near-empty bowl, spooning the remains with great care. Shifting a tray stacked high with dirty dishes, Patrick cuffed the man's shoulder. "Another lemonade, Luther?"

The man looked up, gray hair straggling over his threadbare collar while tan, leathery skin wrinkled with a grin that contained very few teeth. "Yes, sir," he said with a bobble-head nod, the foul odor of his ragged chambray shirt smelling worse than Patrick had after a day building benches and tables in the sun. A shabby cowboy hat lay on the table beside him that appeared more battered than he.

"The name's Patrick, not 'sir,' Luther, so don't you be giving me airs," he said with an easy grin. He glanced down at the bowl of soup that was almost empty, then back up at the hollow cheeks of a man who probably owned nothing in life but the clothes on his back. "Another bowl of soup?" he asked, heart tugging at the man's skeletal frame.

The sun peeked through vacant eyes clouded by poverty. "Yes, sir, Patrick, that would be mighty nice."

Patrick grinned and nodded toward a long opening that separated the kitchen from the dining hall where Marcy and Julie served soup and bread to a rag-tag parade of poor souls. "How about if I have that pretty blonde over there dish it up for you?" he said with a wink.

Sunlight sparkled in the old man's eyes, and for a

brief moment, Patrick could almost see him as he might have been as a young man. Luther's grin reached epic proportions that exposed black teeth at the back of his mouth. "I do believe that would make it a might tastier, if you know what I mean."

Patrick chuckled, gaze flitting to Marcy and back. "Yes, sir, I most certainly do."

Luther paused, shaggy head cocked. "She your gal, Patrick?"

My gal. His heart twisted at the futility of such a longing as his gaze tracked to where Marcy glowed while she smiled and served a young mother with two small children. He shook his head, his good humor flagging somewhat. "Naw, Luther, that lady is way too good for the likes of me."

One silver brow jutted up. "Look here, mister, I may be half blind, deaf as a post, and pockets as empty as those dishes on that there tray, but there's one thing an old coot like me learns on the streets might quick and that's how to judge the character of a man." Rheumy blue eyes flitted to Marcy and back before they squinted up at Patrick with a mock scowl. "Yes, sir, one glance, one word, one nod of the noggin—that's all it takes, and from where I'm sittin', son, you're the type of man I'd be right proud to have as a friend."

Son. Friend. Patrick swallowed hard to fight the sudden sting of tears, shocked at the emotion that swelled in his throat. Oh, to hear those very words from the lips of a father he could never please. But, no, they'd been uttered by a stranger instead, one some people might even discount as a human being. Wiping a palm against clean trousers, Patrick extended his free hand, his smile tight lest it quiver and convey how needy he was for the acceptance of a father. "Patrick Brendan O'Connor, sir, and it's my extreme pleasure to call you a friend as well, Luther—"

"Tuttle, Luther P. Tuttle, young man," he said with a surprisingly firm grip for a man so frail and thin. "I've been coming to this here soup kitchen for a while now, and I don't mind tellin' you, son, you're a rare sight, indeed."

Blood broiled Patrick's face. "I'll just get that soup for you," he said quickly, the old man's words shaming him to the core. *A rare sight, indeed.* And he wouldn't be here at all except for what his father called the hooligan behavior of a smart-mouthed punk. He winked at several little girls who gaped as he passed, then unloaded his tray of dirty dishes onto the soapstone counter by the kitchen sink. Snatching a clean bowl from the end of the serving counter where the ladies worked, Patrick placed it on his empty tray and patiently waited for Marcy to finish conversing with a dirty-faced little boy. "Ahem," he said when she was done, nudging her with the tray.

Sky-blue eyes widened as she glanced over her shoulder, and he couldn't help but smile when those perfect pink lips parted in surprise. Handing her the bowl, he nodded to where Luther was flashing his toothless grin. "Mr. Luther P. Tuttle humbly requests a second bowl of vegetable beef soup served specifically by you, Miss Murphy." He leaned close to her ear, voice husky as the scent of lilacs stuttered his pulse. "Don't look now, Marceline, but I think the gentleman's smitten."

Shoulders as stiff as her smile, she plucked the bowl from Patrick's tray and ladled while she sent Luther a shy nod. "Now, why do I suspect this is your bad influence at play, Mr. O'Connor?" she said under her breath, all the while smiling at Luther.

"Because Luther and I obviously share good taste?"

he said, lowering his voice for her ears alone.

Those very ears tinged pink as she handed the soup back. "Here," she said, clunking a particularly thick end slice of crusty sourdough onto his tray. "You might tell him not to bite off more than he can chew," she said with a definite smirk that bordered on tease. "And you, Mr. Connor ..." One beautiful blonde brow jagged high. "Would do well to follow suit." She abruptly turned and continued to serve, and he grinned outright when Luther gave him a thumbs up.

Spoon in hand, Luther's eyes followed Patrick all the way over to his table. "Not real partial to ye, is she, son?" he cackled when Patrick set the steaming bowl of soup before him.

"What do you mean?" Patrick shot a glance Marcy's way, somewhat encouraged by her obvious tease.

"I mean the woman all but wrinkled her nose, boy, when you butted her with that tray." He peered up beneath wiry brows, his expression thoughtful. "Appears you have a ways to go to make that little filly your gal."

"My gal?" Patrick's smile sloped off-center as he stacked more dirty dishes. "I've got news for you, Luther—I've got a ways to go before I make that 'little filly' my *friend*."

Luther swooped into the soup with gusto, eyeing Patrick while he slurped the broth from his spoon. He struggled to bite off a piece of the bread, gumming it a few times before pert near swallowing it whole. "I'd say from the roll of those blue eyes and stiff set of those pretty shoulders, there's no question that little gal's got a hankerin' to give ye a piece of her mind." A grin split his weathered face, wrinkling it more than his rumpled shirt. He actually winked. "And nothing else, if you know what I mean." The few teeth he had tore at the bread like a dog tussling a bone. "So, what put the burr in her saddle, son?"

Patrick's gaze flicked past Luther to the others at his table, satisfied that the noisy kids sitting beside him were too busy squabbling and tossing pieces of crust at each other to pay him much mind. A heavy sigh gusted out as he parked hands low on his hips. "She claims I'm a rogue with one thing on my mind," he said with a hint of frustration, wondering why on earth he was opening up to some down-and-out cowboy in a Southie soup kitchen. But then, who else was there to talk to? He wasn't comfortable talking to Sam anymore with his designs on Marcy, nor any of his other friends because his pride was at stake. His brother Paul would only chide him, mocking him unmercifully because he resented Patrick's easy success with women, and Father Fitz was simply out of the question.

Luther squinted, chomping more bread. "Well, are you?"

"Used to be, I guess," Patrick said, sending an idle glance Marcy's way, realizing his thinking had shifted on the subject the moment he'd laid eyes on her. He turned back to Luther, venting with a noisy sigh. "Yeah, I suppose I was, Luther, at least before I saw her. But since?" He shook his head, reaching to wipe the section of table across from Luther with a wet dishrag. "Suddenly I have this crazy desire to be a better person."

A raspy chuckle rolled from Luther's lips as he sopped up the remaining soup with what was left of his bread. "Well, then, I'd say you're in a heap o' trouble, Patrick Brendan O'Connor, 'cause that's what the right gal'll do for a man—first she lassoes his heart, cleans it up a might, then grows it real big till afore you know it, you're a-givin' rather than a-takin'." He nodded toward

Marcy, sourdough rolling around in his cheeks like chaw. "You best not let that one get away, son."

Patrick's laugh was harsh. "Yeah, well, it's a little late for that. The woman despises me and I lost a bet with my best friend who intends to court her now, so the only hope I have is friendship." He loaded more dirty dishes on his tray from the gaggle of kids who just left and wiped down the table in time for several middle-aged men who sat down. Nodding at the men, Patrick hefted the tray of dishes, giving Luther a thin smile. "Which I'm hoping will help cool these other feelings I have for the lady." He gave Luther a salute. "But for now? I've got dishes to wash."

Luther's laugh crackled. "I wouldn't count on friendship coolin' you off any. It can warm a body a whole 'nuther way than just a-courtin', if you get my drift."

Patrick chuckled. "You could be right, Luther, because feelings hot or cold, friendship or dishes—any way I look at it," he said with a wink, "I'm still in hot water."

"Jewels, quick—over here!" Hiking her navy muslin skirt high above her ankles, Marcy darted away from Sam with a squeal, all but leaping into the air to seize the beanbag Julie shot her way before Patrick could stop her. Wild cheers rose from Mrs. O'Rourke and each of her daughters along with groans from the men and giggles from the girls in a game of keep away in the O'Rourke's spacious backyard. Sam's sister Erin and little brother Max whooped and danced in circles while Marcy sprinted across a lawn freshly manicured and mowed by the man who now pursued her. Laughter bubbled up as she glanced behind her, heart slamming against her ribs when Sam lunged for the bag. "Noooo!" She skidded to a sharp stop and ducked away before he could snatch it. "Mrs. O'Rourke!" she screamed and fired the bag to Sam's mother, not ten feet away.

Mrs. O'Rourke yelped when her husband ambushed her from behind with thick arms to her waist, spinning her around while trying to wrestle the bag from her hand. Fist in a death grip, she squirmed and squealed to get loose, but to no avail. Her younger daughters instantly rushed in to batter their father with giggles and shrieks while he derailed their mother with a kiss. Watching them, Marcy reveled in the joy of family, her wispy exhale drifting in the air along with the scent of fresh-cut grass, sap from the massive pine overhead, and the barbecued chicken Mr. O'Rourke grilled for dinner.

"Papa, no fair!" Julie yelled, making a mad dash to pry the bag from her mother's hand before her father could steal it away. "Kisses are off limits!"

"Mmm ... too bad," Sam whispered behind Marcy, and she jolted, pulse jumping along with her body when she glanced over her shoulder to see his mischievous grin. He winked and flashed past to join the noisy fray of O'Rourke's attempting to steal the bag, and Marcy splayed a hand to her chest to slow the sputter of her heart. She grinned when Sam scooped Max up on his shoulders before hooking Julie at the waist just as she stole the bag. "Hold on, Max!" he shouted, whirling his sister in the air to make her dizzy, no doubt, while he bellowed for his father to grab the prize. Fending his wife off, Mr. O'Rourke swooped in to reclaim the win, but his efforts only unleashed a squall of female O'Rourkes, tackling in a breathless blur of laughter and limbs.

Marcy sighed, fighting the melancholy that always descended whenever she witnessed the love and laughter of a large family like the O'Rourkes. She adored her parents with every breath in her, but she would be lying if she denied that Julie's family was everything she'd ever longed for—a house full of children, siblings to spar and play with, and parents who were clearly in love and made no bones about it. Her parents had a deep love as well, of that she was certain, but a quieter, more private one, with a reserved and gentle father who was clearly not one for public displays of affection.

Marcy chewed the edge of her lip when Mr. O'Rourke tugged Julie's mother from the fracas to distract her with another sound kiss, leaving Sam, Max, and Patrick to battle Sam's sisters in pursuit of the bag. "Oh, what I wouldn't give for a family like that," she whispered, ignoring the twinge of guilt that always accompanied this deep-seated desire. Too ashamed to voice her next thought out loud, she allowed her mind to stray to the dream she'd harbored since she'd been a little girl stuck in the pine at the edge of their yard. *And, oh, to be part of the O'Rourkes rather than just an outsider looking in ...*

"Marcy!" Somehow, Julie managed to abscond with the bag while Patrick chased her down, capturing Marcy's attention when she hurled it her way. Not missing a beat, Marcy launched a full foot in the air, nabbing the bag in a long stretch that landed her on the ground with a grunt and a jolt. Laughing too hard to catch her breath, she gasped when two powerful arms hooked her from behind, twirling her off the ground like Mr. O'Rourke had done with this wife.

"Don't fight it, Marcy," Sam whispered in her ear, grappling to remove the bag from her hand as he spun her around. "I aim to steal it away …"

She gulped. *Too late.* He'd stolen her breath the moment he'd touched her, the scent of lemons making her dizzier than her body while it whirled through the air. With high-pitched squeals, she attempted to dislodge his hold, chest heaving with laughter when he locked a massive hand over hers, capturing both the bag and her attention with a winded warning. "Let it go, Marceline," he whispered, "or I'll be forced to employ my father's tactics."

"Not … on … your … life … O'Rourke," she ground out with a breathless giggle, fighting him with everything she had until his words finally registered. *His father's tactics?* She felt something nuzzle her neck, and in a ragged beat of her heart, she was paralyzed in his arms, unprepared for the heat that blasted through her at the warm touch of his lips. As if singed by a coal from his father's grill, she dropped the bag so fast, her legs wobbled when Sam pirated it away, leaving her breathless and weak with a wayward wink.

"The men reign supreme!" he boasted, tossing the bag to Patrick as he looped an arm to Julie's waist. He deposited a kiss to her cheek, then spun her around once more. "It was a valiant effort, ladies, but that'll teach you to challenge the men, eh, Miss O'Rourke?"

"Samuel O'Rourke, you put me down this instant!" Julie shouted through her laughter, but Sam only whirled her faster, finally leaving her dizzy and staggering while he pounced to do the same with each of her sisters.

"You're as bad as your father, young man, you know that?" his mother said in a good-natured scold, her face aglow when her husband curved an arm to her waist.

"And that's a bad thing?" Mr. O'Rourke said,

halting her with a lingering kiss.

Yes, Marcy thought, still feeling the burn of Sam's lips on her neck.

Sam's mother playfully pushed her husband away, dodging his hands when he attempted to pull her back. "Only when one cheats in keep away by manhandling the opposition." She hurried to the kitchen door, tossing a grin over her shoulder. "Next time there will be a no-touch rule—no kisses, no twirls, no distractions—just pure, unadulterated skill, understood?"

"You still won't win," Sam said, pitching the beanbag to Max in an impromptu game of catch. "Girls aren't any good at keep away when they play with men, right Max?" He grinned, catching Marcy off-guard when he lobbed the bag her way.

His jaw fell when she deftly caught it one-handed with a jag of her brow. "Wanna bet?" She tossed it high in the air again, neatly catching it with a sassy smirk. "You obviously haven't been challenged by the right girls, Mr. O'Rourke, *or* played fair and square. Because when it comes to playing keep away from rogues such as yourself and Mr. O'Connor?" Marcy shot a smug smile while she linked arms with Julie on their way to the kitchen. "Some of us are better than others."

Chapter Twelve

"Merciful heavens, what a day!" Stifling a yawn, Marcy rolled a kink from her neck as she pitted the last of the cherries for tomorrow's cobbler just as Miss Clara pulled a piping hot confection from the cast-iron oven. The moment the warm rush of air infused the kitchen with brown sugar and cinnamon, Patrick and Julie ceased their horseplay while washing dishes at the sink. All eyes—and noses—were held captive by the cobbler in Miss Clara's hand, even Evan's, who managed to tear himself away from his beloved bottom lines. Closing her eyes, Marcy took an appreciative sniff. "Goodness, Miss Clara, that cobbler makes me wish I was working the soup kitchen tomorrow instead of helping with Mother's sewing circle." On cue, Marcy's stomach emitted a noisy rumble that warmed her face as much as the oven warmed the room.

Miss Clara flopped a potholder on the scarred oak table where Marcy and Evan worked before clunking a bubbling pan of cobbler on top with a grunt. "Well, seems to me that anybody who worked as hard as you young people did today has earned a fine piece of this here cobbler, wouldn't you say, Mr. Evan?"

Leaning back in his chair with a groan, Evan scratched the back of his neck with the blunt side of a well-worn pencil. "And then some." Despite facial muscles that appeared to sag from fatigue, he offered Marcy a tired smile. "At this rate, that fundraiser can't come soon enough. Today was our biggest day since I've been here—over 650 meals served." He huffed out a weary sigh, fingers pinching the bridge of his nose. "I'm just grateful Father Fitz expanded the dining room on last year's budget because we're barely eking by at this point for groceries alone."

"Now, you just hush up 'bout money tonight, Mr. Evan," Miss Clara said with a wave of her hand. She deposited a stack of plates and utensils on the table and started dishing cobbler, her brusque tone a poor mask for the concern in her eyes. "We may not be fancy here, but my mama done taught me how to stretch a dollar when it comes to putting food in a belly, so we'll be fine till this here angel of mercy fills up them coffers."

"Mmm ... angel of mercy," Patrick said with a grin, pulling out a chair to seat Julie before claiming his own next to Evan. He leaned in, eyeing Marcy with a glint of tease, pinstripe sleeves rolled to display hard-sculpted arms casually folded on the table. "Dare I hope that extends to more than fundraising?"

"You in need of mercy, Mr. Patrick, is that what I'm hearin'?" Miss Clara plopped a hefty piece of cobbler onto a plate and slid it his way, her affection for the rogue evident in the twinkle of umber eyes.

Marcy fought the inclination to roll hers and gave him a patient smile. "I'm not sure 'angels,' are prone to extend mercy to one with a bit of the devil, Mr. O'Connor, but you're in luck—the Lord requires it of human beings."

"Good to know," he said with a slow smile, before digging into his cobbler.

"Well, bit of the devil or no," Evan said with a

friendly tap of Patrick's back, "this man has certainly outdone himself in his volunteer work on heaven's behalf. I honestly don't know what I would have done without you or Sam this summer, Patrick, so please accept my profound gratitude for your time and the sweat of your brow."

"Hear, hear!" Miss Clara bellowed, pounding a meaty palm on the table.

"I agree." Julie hiked her chin, the gleam of pride in her eyes unmistakable. "Even Mama and Papa are all but glowing that you and Sam have given so much of your time to a charitable cause."

With an awkward bent to his smile, Patrick quickly shoveled more cobbler. His face—as red as the cherries on his spoon—caused Marcy to pause mid-chew, surprised at his humility.

"Although ..." Julie said with a smirk and a taunt, "the 'devil' is plainly afoot when the man helps with the dishes, as the dampness of my shirtwaist will quickly attest."

Patrick grinned and flapped the front of his equally damp pinstripe shirt. "Might I remind you, Miss O'Rourke, that yours was the first splash."

A giggle tripped from Julie's lips, soft blotches pinking her cheeks. "Now there's a bit of the devil talking, I'd say. Ladies do not instigate water play, Mr. O'Connor."

"No, but minxes do, Miss O'Rourke," he said with a challenging gaze, and Marcy's lips firmed at the flirtation between the two. Gulping the rest of his cobbler, Patrick pushed the empty plate away, mischief lacing his tone. "And be it devil or angel, there's a heavenly host to affirm that you threw the first splash."

"I did not—"

"Ahem ..." Evan placed his fork on the empty plate

and peered up at Julie. Patrick's devilment was obviously catching, judging from the trace of tease in brown eyes usually prone to be serious and shy. "Actually, Miss O'Rourke," he said in his usual gentle tone, "I believe I saw the first wave of soap bubbles coming from your direction, if I'm not mistaken." Marcy blinked, mouth all but gaping like Julie's at the hint of the devil in the man's smile, a smile that promptly toasted Julie's face with a pretty blush. His gaze flicked to Marcy and back. "Of course, in lieu of Father Fitzgibbons, I'm sure our angel of mercy can always absolve this innocent infraction on your part. That is," he said with an uncharacteristic wink, "if you promise to behave in the future."

"Thank you, Evan, my man," Patrick said with a sound slap on his back. "Heaven knows I can use all the support I can get with these two ladies." He had the audacity to follow Evan's lead and give Marcy a wink. "Especially our angel of mercy."

Miss Clara lumbered to her feet, stacking the cut tray of cobbler beneath a tower of others, all slated for tomorrow's dinner. "You people can splash all the livelong day iffen those dishes are clean and the floor wiped up after," she said with a low chuckle, cutting a piece of wax paper to cover the top tray. "Now, people, it's nigh on ten o'clock, and this here woman is tired and heading home, so I suggest you do the same."

Marcy and Julie rose to clear the dishes, but Miss Clara shooed them away. "You girls, scoot. Mr. Evan and I draw a salary here, not you, so we'll finish up." She poked a stubby finger in Patrick's direction. "And you, Mr. Devil-In-His-Eye, will see these young girls home, safe and proper, you hear?" A pixie grin split her full face. "Although I'm thinkin' neither 'safe' nor 'proper' likely pertains to a handsome devil like you."

Patrick placed a peck to Miss Clara's glossy cheek, giving the rotund woman a side hug. "Now, I'm not sure if that's a compliment or not, Miss Clara."

"It's not," Marcy muttered under her breath, and Julie hushed her with an elbow to her side.

"Thanks for filling in today, everyone." Evan shuffled his papers and stood to push his chair in. "With several of our regular volunteers out sick, you girls were lifesavers." He extended a hand to Patrick. "And I know you passed on an overtime shift with Sam tonight to pitch in, so I can't thank you enough."

"My pleasure." Patrick shook Evan's hand, his humor softening into a sober smile. "It feels good to help out, and I find I like myself more when I do. I admire what you do here, Evan, and I'm proud to be even a small part."

Marcy blinked. *Sincerity? From a rogue?*

"Well, go on now, you young'uns, git." Miss Clara prodded them out the back door. "G'night, all."

Patrick donned his sack coat and cap, then helped Julie on with her bolero jacket before ushering the girls out. The lock clicked behind them, and Marcy instantly clutched her arms to her thin shirtwaist. Feeling a nip in the air, she was sorry she hadn't brought a jacket of her own given the unseasonably cool evenings of late.

"Cold?" Patrick shuffled his jacket off broad shoulders while they traveled the alley between the center and auditorium on their way to the street in front of the church.

"No, really—" she began, but he draped his coat over her shoulders anyway, cloaking her in the warmth from his body. "Thank you," she whispered, wishing he would just stop attempting to be so nice. She remained silent while he and Julie chatted and laughed about the colorful characters that frequented the soup kitchen, including Luther who'd taken a shine to Patrick. The woodsy smell of pine from his shaving cream mingled with the spiciness of Bay Rum to envelop her in his scent, annoying her when it caused her stomach to loop.

"You're awfully quiet tonight, angel of mercy," he said casually, the huskiness of his voice merging with his scent to warm her more than the infernal coat.

"I wish you'd stop calling me that," she said with a stiff smile she hoped came off as a tease rather than the truth. "I am neither an angel nor inclined to mercy where you're concerned, Patrick O'Connor."

"Marcy!" Julie's tone held a playful scold.

A scold that found its mark—Marcy felt awful for the grudge she obviously still harbored toward Patrick despite her boatload of prayers. *Lord, forgive me* ... She tempered her tone with humility, pushing aside her distrust of the man. "My apologies, Patrick, truly—that was uncalled for." The words no more left her tongue when his stolen kiss suddenly popped in her mind for the umpteenth time. Her jaw instantly tensed. "Even for a rogue."

"Goodness, Marcy," Julie said with smile agape, "poor Patrick will think you don't like him!"

Poor Patrick, indeed! Poor reputation, poor morals, poor manners on a girl's front porch ...

Patrick's low chuckle only raised Marcy's temperature. "That's okay, Julie. Our Marceline is rather like a wild Irish rose—skin as soft and dewy as its silky petals, but enough sharp thorns to keep predators away." He scooped up a spiky sweet gum ball and bobbled it back and forth before he lobbed it a quarter block away. "But everyone knows the sweetest-smelling roses have the worst thorns, so I consider it a small price to pay for true joy and beauty." He slid Marcy a secret smile. "As long as one keeps his hands to himself, that is, far from the prickles."

"I thought you worked the same shifts as Sam," Marcy said quickly, desperate to derail a conversation that might hint at the advances Patrick had made. She picked up her pace in an effort to hurry the last few blocks to Julie's house, grateful she was spending the night and Patrick needn't walk her home alone.

"I usually do, especially the overtime shifts like tonight." He buried his hands in gray trousers, his gait as relaxed as Julie's while the two lagged behind. "But I've already clocked three double shifts this week, so I figured I needed the rest."

"Not much rest building tables and benches in the hot sun," Julie said with a note of respect, "nor on your feet all night serving food, clearing tables, and doing dishes."

"Or staving off water nymphs?" He gave Julie a wink that lured a giggle from her lips.

Marcy kept up her staunch march, blowing a stray hair from her face with no little exasperation. *For the love of decency, Julie, open your eyes. The man is an insatiable flirt.*

"Seriously, I admire your work ethic," Julie continued, her obvious admiration irking more than Marcy wanted to admit. "Sam says you almost have enough saved for college."

College? Marcy chanced a peek at his chiseled profile, almost wishing he had an unsightly wart. She fought the tickle of a grin. *What, now they have higher learning for rogues?*

"I do, as a matter of fact," Patrick said, and it was hard to miss the note of pride in his tone. "I've worked odd hours at the *Herald* through high school and full time since graduation, so I've been able to save some."

Marcy's prior humility died in a silent grunt.

Whatever you don't spend at Brannigan's, I guess.

A man on a bicycle whizzed by, and Patrick instinctively pulled Marcy close, out of its path, sending a jolt through her body. He released her just as quickly, as if no more than an afterthought, then faced Julie once again as he continued on. "I hope to begin next semester at Boston College, taking it one year at a time, of course. But I think I can do it working part-time at the *Herald*." As if privy to Marcy's negative thoughts, he turned to deliver a lazy grin. "So, you see, Miss Murphy, Brannigan's doesn't get all of my money."

"Oh, we're here," she breathed, hurrying up Julie's sidewalk so Patrick wouldn't see the hot blush of shame she felt in her cheeks. Nerves twitching, she waited for Julie on the front porch while she and Patrick took their time strolling the walk.

"Thank you for walking us home," Julie said with a smile that glowed as bright as the harvest moon overhead. She tilted her head with a shy tease, an impish grin on her lips. "I don't care what Sam says about you, you're a very nice person."

The husky rumble of his laughter warmed Marcy's skin, reminding her she still wore his coat. "Well, you should know better than anybody you can't believe everything your brother says."

"Yes, thank you very much, Patrick, for both the escort and the coat." Marcy slipped it off her shoulders, immediately missing its warmth. She handed it back, and caught her breath when a spark ignited at the touch of their fingers.

His lips curved despite the intensity of a serious gaze. "Sorry. It's wool," he whispered, as if that could explain the erratic pounding of her heart. "Static electricity, you know."

She stepped back and nodded, anxious to be inside

and as far away from Patrick O'Connor—and the sparks he ignited—as humanly possible. "Yes, well, thank you again," she said in a strained voice.

He offered a short bow of his head. His eyes flitted from Marcy to Julie and back, gaze lingering enough to make her uncomfortable. "Good night, ladies."

"Good night," Julie called as he strolled toward the street. She angled a brow at Marcy while turning the knob of the front door. "Whatever has gotten into you?" she whispered, shooting a quick glance over her shoulder as if to make sure Patrick was gone. "If I didn't know better, I'd say you seemed a bit rude to the poor man."

Julie held the door open while Marcy barged through, jaw stiff at Julie's obvious blindness to a rake like Patrick O'Connor. *Oh, Julie, if you only knew!* She whirled around mid-foyer, her anger resurfacing over her unwanted attraction to a man she didn't trust. She crossed her arms in challenge. "I just don't know what you see in him. The man's little more than a cad cloaked in nice manners."

Julie paused, hand on the lock. "For mercy's sake, Marcy—what has Patrick ever done to you?"

Marcy's lips gummed tight. *Trust me, you don't want to know.*

Hanging her jacket on the coat rack, Julie turned to counter her best friend, hands plunked to her hips. "I happen to think he's a very nice boy, one of the few who actually has ambition to go places."

Marcy jutted her chin. "Maybe so, but when it comes to women, I doubt the places he wants to go are very commendable. Merciful Providence, Julie, he's not exactly a man of faith, except in himself."

"Come on, that's not fair." Julie made her way to the kitchen. "Patrick really seems to be trying."

"That may be, but you and I both know he's the very reason Sam has gotten so far off track in the first place, changing your brother into a womanizer just like him. Why, Sam is from a decent family, for pity's sake, raised to know better, always looking out for girls instead of taking advantage of them, but hobnobbing with Patrick has certainly changed all that."

"Really, Marcy, you can't blame everything on Patrick—"

Marcy arched a brow. "Do you deny he's been a bad influence on your brother?"

"No ...." Julie tugged at her lip. "But I truly think he's changing—"

"Oh, Jewels, you just have your head in the clouds when it comes to that man." Marcy followed her down the hall, grateful the rest of the family had obviously gone to bed. She flopped in a chair and snatched a cookie from a plate on the table, lips in a scowl.

Julie's soft giggle helped to soothe Marcy's sour mood. "I don't think so," her best friend said in a sing-song tone, tossing a sly grin over her shoulder on her way to the ice box. "At least ... not anymore."

Marcy sat straight up, a molasses cookie lodged in her teeth. She quickly chewed and gulped. "And what's *that* supposed to mean?"

Julie sashayed from the icebox to the counter, milk bottle in hand. She took her time pouring two glasses.

"Julie Mariah O'Rourke! If you don't tell me right now what that means—"

More giggles floated in the air as Julie scurried to the table, delivering two tumblers of milk. Plopping in a chair, she reached for a cookie and leaned in, nibbling while her eyes danced with mischief. "Well ... it means that I think I may have found someone who can race my pulse as much as Patrick O'Connor."

Marcy's jaw dropped, cookie limp in her hand. Her mind scoured the possibilities. The male lead in the play, Peter Martin? Peter's friends who came to volunteer and flirt with the girls? The new boy from France that all the girls were swooning over who would be in their class? Marcy's brow crimped in thought, considering the possibilities.

Julie laughed outright, shimmying to the edge of her chair. "Come on, Marce—who do we spend time with three days a week at the soup kitchen?"

Marcy blinked before her eyes went wide. "Saints almighty, you don't mean Evan Farrell, do you?"

A becoming shade of pink dusted Julie's cheeks as she giggled. "I do." She propped her chin in her hand while a dreamy sparkle lit her eyes. "Did you notice him tease me tonight?" A sigh feathered her lips. "I've caught him watching me more than once, and one day at the center last week when you had your father's birthday dinner?" She nervously chewed on her thumbnail. "He helped me wash dishes, then walked me home."

"You didn't tell me that!" Marcy stared, jaw distended.

"Because I thought I might be imagining it at first, but he flirted with me tonight—you saw it. Didn't he?" She slanted in, awaiting Marcy's answer with a nibble of her lip.

Eyes squinted in thought, Marcy thought about it before finally glancing up, a chuckle bubbling to her lips. "You know, I believe he did. I guess my mind was busy somewhere else."

"I'll say—busy picking at Patrick, I'll wager."

Marcy's smile crooked. "Most likely." She jumped up to give Julie a hug. "Oh, Jewels, I love Evan. I just never thought of him in a romantic light before because he's a bit older than us, although he certainly is a wonderful man—kind, giving, dedicated."

"I know." Julie beamed. She paused, her smile dimming. "Wait—you didn't have designs on him, did you?"

Marcy shook her head. "Absolutely not. I think he's a sweet man who's perfect for you." She huffed out a sigh of relief. "And good heavens—anyone's better than Patrick O'Connor."

Julie dipped her head, studying Marcy through eyes that were no longer playful. "Patrick's a good person," she said quietly, "and I honestly think he's trying to be better. I even heard Sam grousing at him in the kitchen late one night, complaining that Patrick is spending more time at the center than he is at Brannigan's."

Marcy steeled her mind. The last thing she needed was to disarm her distrust of a pretty-boy Don Juan who wreaked havoc with her pulse. "That may be so, but it will take more than a few nights a week at the center for me to trust him." Marcy vented her frustration with a weary sigh. "Look, I'm sure he's a very nice person in some ways, but as a man a woman can trust?" She grunted and grabbed another cookie. "I doubt I will ever change my mind about him." She took a bite and chewed slowly, reflecting on the type of man she hoped to marry someday. A man who could stir her faith more than her pulse and who trusted in God as much as she. As far as she was concerned, that was the only guarantee for a happy marriage and family, and she sure wasn't about to risk falling prey to the deadly charm of a sweet-talking Casanova. She washed the cookie down with a drink of milk, then gave Julie a patient smile. "I know you like Patrick, and he's nice enough as a friend I suppose, but the truth is he's not a man of faith like Evan, so I'd just as soon avoid him altogether."

Drawing in a deep breath, Julie eased back in her chair, slowly twirling her glass on the table while she assessed Marcy with a sad smile. "You know, he might become a man of faith if he saw an example in us."

Marcy stopped chewing while the cookie turned to sludge in her mouth. She gulped hard, and it sank to the pit of her stomach as she put a hand to her eyes, conviction watering her gaze.

Julie gently touched her arm. "I'm sorry, Marce," she said softly, "but this isn't like you. You're usually the one whose heart is so soft and tender, the girl who never speaks ill of anyone. And yet with Patrick, you seem to be so hard, so unforgiving. I don't know what he ever did to you, but I think you need to see him for the person he is, as well as the man he can be. Aren't you the one always saying that faith is the great equalizer? Helping us to love others no matter who they are or what they've done? So they, in turn, can love themselves and ultimately others, just like Christ did for us?"

Marcy nodded and closed her eyes. "I'm sorry," she whispered. "I guess I see Patrick in the same light as my cousin's ex-fiancé." Her voice hardened at the thought of the man who used Nora for his own pleasure and then left her in shame to bear a baby alone. "Men too handsome to be trusted, able to make women swoon with a glance or a kiss, only bent on satisfying their own lusts."

"They're not all like that," Julie whispered, rubbing Marcy's back with tender strokes, "and even if some are, we're called to forgive and pray for them, aren't we, Marce?" She released a fragile sigh. "Sam flirts with the lasses, but I know in my heart that faith and family are important to him and Patrick, too, I'm sure, at least deep down. I honestly believe both of them would do the right thing if need be, heaven forbid."

"Heaven forbid, indeed," Marcy said quietly, memories piercing her heart. "Heaven forbids them to steal a girl's innocence, and yet it's done, Julie, more than either of us know." Her eyelids weighted closed, haunted by the image of her friend Elsie's handsome father cornering her in their kitchen pantry, attempting to kiss her, grope her, stealing her very innocence by the mere look of lust in his eyes.

Julie's soft sigh blew warm in her ear as her friend gave her a squeeze. "All the more reason to win the hearts of such men with our faith, matching our strength against their charm, wooing them with kindness." Julie brushed loose strands from Marcy's face, an imp of a smile twitching her lips. "I'll tell you what—my mother and I would certainly like to see what you could do for Sam."

Lips pursed, Marcy shook her head, fighting a smile. "You are relentless, you know that? You are not going to rest till I give Sam a chance, are you?"

"Nope." She returned to her seat and snitched another cookie, eyeing Marcy while she chewed. Her grin faded into a soft smile. "You'd be good for my brother, Marce, I just know it, and I honestly believe he needs you in his life."

Sam? Needs me? A warm chill scurried down Marcy's arms, melting her from the inside out. *Oh, Lord, if only ...*

Julie finished her cookie and dusted the crumbs from her hands, lumbering up with a groan. She carried the glasses to the sink and washed them, leaving them to dry in a dish basket on the counter. "Well, I don't know about you, but I may just have to crawl up those steps because I don't believe I've ever been this tired before."

A Light in the Window

"Worn out from batting those eyelashes all day?" Marcy tweaked the back of Julie's neck.

Dousing the kitchen light, Julie laughed and looped an arm to Marcy's waist to usher her up the creaking stairs. "Well, I had no idea romance was this exhausting," she whispered, keeping her voice low to keep from waking the others. Tiptoeing down the hall, she gave Marcy a soft giggle. "Goodness, who knew that being smitten could make you so weak in the knees?"

Weak in the knees? Marcy held her breath as they passed Sam's empty room on their way down the hall, the lemon scent of William's Shaving Soap all but melting her bones to fresh-churned butter. The image of Sam lying on his bed in the dark with tousled curls and chest bare suddenly quivered her stomach, a quick reminder that passion was dangerous when one was smitten. *Who knew?* Her tongue swiped her teeth once and then twice before she swallowed the gulp that wedged in her throat. *Sweet heavenly host, Jewels ... that would be me.*

Chapter Thirteen

"Julie, are you asleep?"

Silence.

"Julie!" Though Marcy's whisper carried a soft urgency, it was only met by the wispy cadence of her best friend's shallow breathing, the covers on Julie's side of the bed rising and falling as steadily as Marcy's relentless thoughts. Up, down, up, down ... just like her mood since her head had hit the pillow over three hours ago. Should she open her heart to Sam? *Yes, no, yes, no.* True, she'd always cared for him, but could her faith keep her strong until it changed him into the man she needed him to be? *Maybe, maybe not, maybe, maybe not.* Lord, please—should I even risk it? *Yes, no, yes, no ... yes ... yes ... yes.*

Chewing her lip, Marcy lay in the dark, wishing more than anything that Sam was asleep behind the closed door of his room so she could steal down to warm some milk. But, alas, all she'd heard for the last three hours was Julie's gentle breathing, the occasional squeak of the bed, and the deep bong of Mrs. O'Rourke's antique grandfather clock proclaiming the hour. No click of the front door, no creak of the stairs, no water running while he got ready for bed. She needed to be alert to help with Mother's company tomorrow, and she could ill afford to be tired, but sleep evaded her as neatly as all sensible thought while she pondered Julie's words. *"My mother and I would certainly like to see what you could do for Sam."* Marcy gulped as the clock chimed two. True enough, but what, pray tell, would *he* do for her other than provide dangerous temptation?

No! She rolled over on her side, drawing in a calming breath. *This is Sam*, she reminded herself, *not Patrick O'Connor*. This was the boy she'd idolized from little on, the hero who'd always made her feel safe and protected. For goodness sake, this was her best friend's brother and a member of a family she loved and longed to be a part of since she'd been a little girl. Patrick O'Connor had been a bad influence, certainly, and Sam now shared Patrick's infamous reputation, but unlike Patrick, Sam had always treated Marcy with affection, kindness, and respect, so surely that wouldn't change?

Would it?

Venting with a groan, she swung her legs from the bed, almost wishing the movement would wake Julie up. She didn't want to risk going downstairs alone if Sam wasn't home yet, but what choice did she have? Snatching Julie's quilted robe from the closet, Marcy quickly buttoned it and moved to the door, jerking the sash tight. She held her breath as she peeked out a crack, then slowly opened it wide, well aware that Sam's door was the only one still open. With all the stealth and care of a thief on the prowl, she stole down the steps, stopping after each to chance a fractured breath, hoping against hope to still any creaks that may whine. Easing down the main hall, she was relieved to find the kitchen dark as night, lit only by the moonlight that streamed through the windows. The faint whiff of apple pie from Mrs. O'Rourke's dinner taunted her stomach, but a cookie would be much easier—and faster—to snatch on her way back up to Julie's room. Barely daring to breathe, Marcy carefully retrieved the milk from the icebox, then rifled around in the dark for something in which to heat it. She winced when the pots clattered after she pulled a saucepan out, but forged on, determined she *would* sleep tonight. The flames of the gas stove sizzled and licked against the steel pot until the steam from the milk rose to her nostrils. Her heart hammered as she fished a mug from the cabinet. *Almost there ...*

A shadow at the back door nearly wrenched a cry from her throat, until she heard the key in the door. And then her body flashed with heat as hot as the milk boiling in the pan. *No!*

The door slowly opened and a tall silhouette froze, infusing the kitchen with that deadly lemon scent that thundered her pulse. It paused, moonlight revealing a shirt haphazardly open at the collar and a grizzled jaw. "Marcy?"

She quickly doused the flame and poured the milk in a cup, hands shaking so much, liquid spilled onto the counter. "Oh, fiddle," she hissed, stomach lurching when she heard the deadly click of the lock. Plucking the dishrag from the sink, she mopped up the mess, hands quivering as much as her stomach, then chanced a timid peek over her shoulder. "Hi, Sam," she whispered. "I couldn't sleep."

"Apparently." He hung his jacket on the coat rack by the door and strolled in, brushing her arm as he reached for a glass from the cabinet above her. His touch singed, and she jerked back, prompting a low chuckle from his lips. "Not sure that warm milk will do it—you appear pretty jumpy. But I'll wager a touch of honey and whiskey would do the trick, if you want."

"N-no!" She cinched the robe to her neck, cheeks burning when she realized the top button was unfastened. With shallow breaths, she fumbled with the catch to no avail, palms sweating and fingers as clumsy as sausages ... and just as slick.

"Let me," he whispered, paralyzing her when he slowly looped the catch around the quilted button, fingers lingering several seconds too long.

"T-thank you ..." she stuttered, stumbling back a step. "Good night—"

He stayed her with a hand to her wrist. "I'm hungry," he whispered, thumb circling her skin while fireflies circled her stomach. "Mom said she'd save me some pie—want some?"

She shook her head vehemently, the long curls that trailed the front of her robe shivering with the motion. "I'm not hungry," she lied, terrified he could feel the throb of her pulse.

"Then keep me company?" He ducked his head, searing her with a pleading gaze. "Please? I hate to eat alone, and if you can't sleep, maybe a chat will calm you down."

With you? A lump shifted in her throat. *Not likely.*

He reached behind him for a half-eaten apple pie that waited on the counter. Palming it with one hand, he waved it before her nose, his grin gleaming white in the dark. "Come on, Marceline," he whispered, "you know you want some, and I've had a horrendous night at work. But I have the utmost faith that you are my redemption."

Faith. Something Sam needed desperately. She swallowed hard. And she as well, evidently ... at least at the moment. *And redemption?* Hope warmed in her chest like the steaming cup in her hands. *Oh, Lord, let it be!* Drawing in a fortifying breath, she slowly released it again, uttering a silent prayer for strength. "All right," she said with a waver in her voice, "but we best turn on the light."

He reached for the brass lamp over the sink and switched the tap to turn the gas on before carrying the pie to the table, a soft glow filling the room to give it a cozy feel.

Too cozy, Marcy thought as she fished a knife and forks from the drawer and followed with her mug of milk and two plates. She placed the items on the table and attempted to pull out a chair when Sam unnerved her by seating her instead. He pushed the chair in and then claimed his across the table, his laughter warm and low as he cut two pieces of pie. "Not hungry, eh?" he said with a sparkle of black eyes, sliding her pie across the table.

She forced a shaky smile and almost wished they were still in the dark so he couldn't see how nervous she was. Or *she* couldn't see hard-corded arms beneath rolled sleeves and dark hair peeking from an open collar where a tie straggled free. A thick shadow of stubble bristled his jaw while one unruly black curl defied all restraint from the Brilliantine he usually wore, dangling over his forehead. Hard-sculpted features and a distinctive Roman nose captured the essence of the pirate he always reminded her of, a presence so dominating, it never occurred he wasn't particularly handsome. Certainly not in the manner of a Greek god like Patrick, but a dark charisma all his own that never failed to trip Marcy's pulse. *Like now.* She averted her eyes to her pie, hoping to just gobble and run because if ever a man *looked* dangerous, it was Sam O'Rourke. And if ever a man was? She had no idea, but the very thought clogged the first bite in her throat.

"So ... talk to me, Marceline. Why can't you sleep?"

The next taste stalled in her throat and she started to cough, lunging for her hot milk to wash it free. It burned going down—but not as much as her cheeks.

"You okay?" he asked, a crimp of concern in dark brows.

She nodded, eyes on her pie and breathing sporadic.

"Marcy."

Her head shot up. "Yes?"

He leaned in, a ghost of a smile on full lips while ridges furrowed above his nose. "Have you always been this nervous around me?"

She blinked, realizing that, yes, it had always been this way around Sam from little on. Skittish nerves, flutters in her stomach, appetite as weak as her knees. Her throat dipped and she looked up, warming at the affection in his eyes. Nibbling on the edge of her lip, she felt the tug of a smile. "I think so."

He grinned. "Then take a deep breath and blow it back out again, Marceline. Because I assure you, the only thing I'm going to gobble up tonight is this pie, agreed?"

Her chest expanded and contracted in compliance, sucking in a wellspring of air that eased her anxiety before she expelled it again.

"Better?" he asked, opting for a second piece of pie.

Her grin broke free. "Actually, yes—thank you."

"My pleasure." He nodded to her barely eaten dessert. "I'd offer another piece, but you seem to be having trouble with that one." He attacked his second helping. "So, you didn't tell me—why can't you sleep?"

Thoughts of helping Mother tomorrow came to mind and Marcy pounced on it. She explained how she'd worked at the center all day because several volunteers were sick, leaving little time for preparation of desserts she'd promised to make for her mother's sewing circle. Consequently, she needed to rise early to bake as well as help clean. "So I've been tossing and turning for hours now, knowing I need a good night's sleep," she said, "but that only makes it worse."

"I have just the thing." Sam jumped up and headed to the pantry, pulling a bottle of whiskey from the top shelf, along with a crock of honey and cinnamon sticks.

"Oh, no, not whiskey—"

He crooked a brow. "Not much, just enough to take the edge off and help you sleep. It's Pop's own personal hot toddy, I promise."

She watched him while he reheated her milk, biting the edge of her lip when he added too much whiskey to suit, but she finally blew out a sigh, desperate enough to try anything. Sam entertained her with stories about Patrick and him on the docks and within minutes, he handed her a steaming cup of milk with a cinnamon stick. "Drink up, Marceline," he said, reclaiming his seat with a grin. "Your sheep await."

Shaking her head, she closed her eyes to sip the brew, soaking in its warmth and wonderful smell. "Thank you," she whispered, suddenly shy.

"You're welcome." He leaned back in his chair with arms folded, eyes a twinkle while he regaled her with stories that made her giggle and relax. He talked about the play, the center, and work at the *Herald*. She felt literally aglow, laughing over his tales of the antics of his sisters and brother in the warmth of his kitchen, as if she were an O'Rourke herself. And, oh, how she'd wished over the years that she were, her heart swelling when he mentioned church with his family and how much it seemed to mean to him the older he got. By the time she reached the end of her cup, her body felt warm and languid, as if sweet dreams were only moments away.

Disappointment set in when he stood to his feet, carting the pie and plates to the sink. She followed suit and commenced to washing dishes while Sam dried, stowing them away once again before he doused the light. "Goodness, I believe I could sleep for days after that toddy," she said, her eyelids suddenly as heavy as her body. She moved toward the door, hazily aware that he followed. "I don't know how to thank you, Sam."

His low chuckle warmed her belly as much as the toddy when his fingers slid over hers. She turned, a gasp catching in her throat as he slowly tugged her back. "Well, I do," he whispered, gently nudging her to the wall. "Accompany me on a picnic, Marceline," he said, intensity fairly shimmering in his gaze.

Her eyes went wide as the possessive hold of his hands fairly seared her arms, the back-and-forth stroke of his thumbs liquefying the tendons at the back of her knees. He towered over her with a smoky look, gaze lighting on her lips until she could barely breathe. Caressing the side of her face, his hand glided into her hair as if it were silk, brushing it aside while his fingers fondled the lobe of her ear. Her eyelids quivered closed, every traitorous nerve in her body surrendering to his touch. "Sam ..." she rasped, "I—" Her words faded into his mouth when his lips took hers in a slow, languid kiss.

He pulled away and her body seemed to follow, almost a physical pain at the parting of his lips. When she opened her eyes, she saw the same fire that pulsed through her reflected in his. "Marcy," he said quietly, "say you'll come out with me."

No, Sam, I can't ... "Yes," she whispered, too weak

to resist, too bewitched to say no.

His chuckle glazed her lips like heated honey, sweet and warm. "Good. This Sunday, then, a picnic after church ..."

"I h-have a brunch with my parent's friends," she stuttered, the words a quiver of tremulous air. "And my father's birthday is the Sunday after ..."

He dazed her with another tender graze of his mouth, his breath warm and scented with apples. "The following Sunday then ..."

"I ... have a s-status report due to Father F-fitz on that next T-tuesday," she whispered, eyes closed while the blood thrummed in her veins.

"We'll do it together ..." His lips swayed softly against hers, and she could do nothing but nod. "Three weeks, Marceline," he said, and taking her by the hand, he led her up the stairs, far more silently than the drumming of her heart, past his own room to Julie's. Without a word, he bent to deposit a gentle kiss to her nose and steered her inside, carefully closing the door behind.

Body limp, she sagged against the paneled wood, pulse pounding in her ears as she heard him get ready for bed. The heat that had throbbed from his kisses slowly began to recede, and with it any strength in her limbs, nearly buckling her knees. Tears stung as she disrobed and silently slipped in beside Julie, her gaze a blank stare at a ceiling she didn't see, feeling a deep-rooted passion she didn't want to feel. The enormity of what happened slowly sank in, chasing all hope of slumber away. She hadn't wanted this and yet deep down inside, she knew that she did, and that was what scared her more than anything. For all of her hero worship and hidden feelings, Sam was still a rogue she had hoped to avoid. A rogue who had stirred a passion within her she could not afford to indulge. And yet here she stood, on the threshold of just such a relationship, and the very thought wrung a slow trail of tears from her eyes. "Oh, Lord, what have I done?" she whispered, wishing she had never ventured from Julie's room. Her eyes lumbered closed while she uttered a silent prayer. "And God help me, what will I do?"

Sam hesitated before he silently shut his bedroom door, sorely tempted to fix a hot toddy himself. He had a feeling Marcy's insomnia was catching tonight, especially with her lying in his sister's bed a mere room away. Stripping off his shirt, he hung it back in the closet then dropped his trousers and did the same, opting to sleep in nothing but his knee-length underdrawers. There was a definite chill in the air, but you couldn't prove it by him, not after that kiss. Or *kisses*, he reminded himself, unable to help feeling a wee bit smug that he'd succeeded with Marcy where Patrick had not. Life-long friends, Patrick and he were closer than brothers, and yet there was a silent rivalry that neither ever acknowledged, although Patrick usually bested him with the ladies. His lips tipped in a faint smile as he slipped into the narrow bed he shared with his five-year-old brother.

Until Marcy.

He cocked his arms behind his neck and grinned at the ceiling, both over the husky, little snorts Max emitted as he snuggled close and the notion that there was finally a woman who'd chosen Sam over Patrick, a rare occurrence, indeed. A veritable blue moon, he thought with a gloat before a niggle of guilt set in, dimming his smile. Patrick was smitten beyond anything Sam had ever seen, and it pained him to be the one to stand in his way and yet, it had been Marcy who had chosen, had it not? Spurning Patrick for the affront of a stolen kiss while all but melting into Sam's arms? The grin returned, accompanied by a chuckle of wonder and awe.

When Patrick had asked if his intentions with Marcy were honorable, he'd balked, wondering why it even mattered—Marcy was no different than the scores of other women with whom they'd dallied, at least to Sam's way of thinking. But to Patrick's? The woman had obviously bewitched him. And yet in the space of several kisses, Sam suddenly knew why. There was a little-girl innocence about her uncommon to the women they squired. A purity and decency that called to the very core of who his mother had raised him to be, a place where faith, family and integrity resided, buried deep by parents who cared. Unlike Patrick, whose home life was not only barren of love and kind words, but of that tenuous thread of faith that still anchored Sam to his roots. Somehow touching Marcy tonight, kissing her, had stirred those very roots, awakening a need for something other than the things he'd sought thus far.

A need for commitment?

Marriage?

He fought the inclination to shiver. The cool of the night settled on his bare chest, chilling him into sobriety. Someday, perhaps, but certainly not for a long, long time. Which definitely posed a problem. Marcy was a woman who deserved more than he'd ever given before—a white picket fence with babies on her lap—and Sam wasn't willing to go that far just yet. He closed his eyes and exhaled a weary sigh. Which meant he should just leave her be as Patrick had warned. And yet ... he could not.

He saw her in his mind's eye in the shadows of the

kitchen, the face of an angel caught by surprise, fragile and quivering in his arms, and the seed of a thought took root. Julie and his mother were always hounding him to seek out "good girls," the kind of cool, passionless and pious women that always left Sam cold. But a few chaste kisses with Marcy had convinced him that she was anything but, a veritable wellspring of passion just waiting to be tapped. A slow grin made its way across his face. Not only the ideal wife someday, but the ideal way to keep his mother and sister happy until he could say I do. Till then, he'd follow his father's sage advice to sow wild oats before settling down with one woman.

Exhaling a slow breath, Sam suddenly realized he wanted Marceline Murphy to *be* that one woman—the one he protected and cared for. His grin faded to soft as he recalled the glow of innocence in her face when he'd kissed her in the kitchen, and for the first time in his life, the need to protect a woman was greater than the need to have her. Somehow, the very idea of staying chaste with Marcy made him feel more like a man than all the sated lust he'd experienced before. While talking with her in the kitchen, certainly his references to family and faith had been calculated based on what Patrick had told him, an effort on his part to soften any resistance to his renegade past. She'd turned Patrick away because of his lack of faith and wild reputation; Sam had no inclination to suffer the same fate. But he'd not expected to *want* to protect her from his own advances, and yet he did, proving that Marceline Murphy wielded a pull over him unlike any girl he'd ever known.

"Something special," Patrick had called her, and for the first time Sam understood. He suspected she was a woman who could elevate the lowest of men to the rank of a king, enabling him to scale mountains to become all he could be, something that tempted Sam fiercely. To scale the heights of fidelity like his father finally had with his mother, rising to the peak of happiness with one woman, one wife. Shifting in the narrow bed, he tucked Max to his side with a kiss to his head, enjoying the feeling of holding his little brother close while his lips took a dry slant.

Now ... if he just didn't have an aversion to heights ...

Chapter Fourteen

After a final skim of the razor, Patrick wiped the residue of shaving cream from his jaw, not sure he liked the image in the mirror, clean-shaven or no. Working three double shifts this week and several nights at the center were taking their toll, leaving him with shadows of fatigue beneath gray eyes that appeared way too glassy and lifeless. His mouth shifted to the side. At least for a man who was about to spend an evening at Brannigan's with his best friend and a pretty girl or two.

Unleashing a sigh, he rinsed his razor and put it away before slapping Bay Rum on his face. There was a time when he liked what he saw in the mirror—the chiseled nose, the rock jaw, pale gray eyes that appeared to drive some women wild. He applied Mum deodorant paste under his arms while he assessed his bare chest, arms sculpted with thick muscles still sore from hours of heavy lifting on the dock of the *Herald*. To most women, his face and form were pleasing, but suddenly those veiled looks from the ladies and obvious flirtations no longer brought him satisfaction. Not when the one woman he wanted saw his good looks as nothing but a curse.

He reached for his clean underwear from the back

of the commode and slipped them on. The soft flannel material of the long-legged and long-sleeved union suit soaked up the dampness from his bath while he pondered why Marceline Murphy would take a shine to Sam instead of to him. Certainly his "lust for things of a more carnal nature," as she had so painfully pointed out, was no different than Sam's, nor the faith aspect either. As far as Marcy's distrust of handsome men, although Sam wasn't what most would call classically good-looking, he had a bold and rugged air that appealed to many, and yet Marcy had said yes to Sam and no to him. Patrick scowled as he buttoned his shirt and put on his trousers. No—morals, faith, and good looks aside—the woman just flat-out didn't like him, and he'd be dashed if he knew why.

Bam! Bam! "You about done in there?"

Patrick sighed. *And she's not the only one.* The edge in his brother's voice and the fist to the door told him Paul was in one of his moods. He had hoped to be gone by the time his brother got home from his job at the steel mill, but obviously luck wasn't running his way.

"Give me twenty seconds," he called, no energy to butt heads with either his brother or father tonight. The scent of coconut oil teased his nostrils as he applied Macassar oil to his damp hair before combing it back in a part on the side, annoyed that the dark curls seemed to have a mind of their own, springing back in a wayward fashion. Rushing lest Paul bludgeon the door again, he quickly fastened his suspenders, then adjusted his tie before slinging his dark wool sack coat over his shoulder.

He opened the door and forced a tight smile. "It's all yours," he said casually, attempting to sidle past his younger brother with whom he'd been at odds most of his life. Clearly his father's favorite, Paul could do no wrong and took every opportunity to make sure Patrick knew it. Of course Patrick was often prone to do the same with Paul's obvious lack of success with girls, something he knew bothered his brother greatly. Where Patrick had inherited his father's height and dark curly hair, Paul had inherited their mother's straight brown hair and slight frame. His face, which usually bore a scowl, might have been handsome if not marred by acne, but between it and his frequent dark moods, he had few friends.

"Smells like a bloomin' whorehouse in here," he muttered, shoving Patrick out of the way as he pushed into the bathroom.

"As if you would know," Patrick mumbled when the door slammed behind him, well aware that Paul was both painfully shy with women and jealous of Patrick's success with the fairer sex. Taking great care on the stairs, he quietly made his way to the front door, hoping to slip by his parents in the parlour without notice.

"Patrick!"

A silent groan trapped in his throat at the needling sound of his father's voice. "Have you paid your mother rent for this month?"

Patrick paused, door ajar and head bowed as he sucked in a deep swallow of air. "Not yet, but I will," he called, knuckles pinched white on the knob. "Tomorrow."

"No—*now*! Before you drink it all away."

Heat stung the back of his neck while he ground his jaw, biting back the sharp retort that sprang to his tongue. His father and he shared a mutual lack of trust that ran as deep as their mutual lack of respect. Slamming the door closed, he strode into the worn parlour where Joseph O'Connor sat like a king in his battered leather wingback chair. Feet propped up on a matching ottoman, he peered over the top of the *Boston Herald* splayed in his lap, his trademark scowl typically reserved for his eldest son.

Patrick's eyes flitted to where his mother sat, posture bent as she knit yet another afghan in a house that needed all the warmth it could get. Eyes downcast, she dare not lift her gaze to speak in her son's defense lest she anger the man who ruled with an iron fist.

Avoiding his father's critical glare, Patrick fished his wallet from his pocket and hurled several bills onto the coffee table before rounding on his heel to bolt for the door, desperate for escape. The last thing he wanted was another row with his father, something that was becoming increasingly easy to do. He couldn't afford to live on his own just yet, not with college to save for, and his father knew it, baiting him, barbing him, every chance he got. But, not tonight.

"Don't you dare turn your back on me, you ungrateful punk!"

Patrick halted, eyes weighting closed with a heavy exhale before he slowly turned at the parlour door, hands shoved in his pocket.

His father hurled the paper aside with that lethal glint in his eye that told Patrick he was looking for a fight. He lumbered to his feet, face pinched above a perfectly tied Windsor knot and buttoned vest. "Don't think I don't know what you're doing all night," he said in a caustic tone that set Patrick on edge. "Drinking, carousing with the worst kind of women, and God knows what else. If you can spend that kind of money on whores every night of the week, maybe I need to be charging more rent."

Patrick's jaw hardened along with the clench of his fists in his pockets, a nerve flickering in his cheek as he struggled to control his temper. His father had been itching to raise his rent for a while now, and Patrick knew it, but he'd be dashed if he'd give him the chance. "I'm saving for college, Pop, you know that. And I'm not spending money every night of the week *or* on 'whores.'" He ground the word out, his anger seeping through. "I volunteer at the center several nights and work overtime most of the rest."

His father grunted. "You think you're fooling anybody working at that soup kitchen, boy?" He strolled forward to thump several taut fingers on Patrick's chest, raising Patrick's blood pressure. "You got your eye on a girl there, is that it? Because I can tell you right now that no decent girl would look twice at a scoundrel like you." His lips twisted into a sneer, a look Patrick had long become familiar with, at least since high school when he'd finally given up trying to win his father's approval and respect.

No amount of good grades or obedience seemed to satisfy Joseph O'Connor, not since that fateful day when Patrick had been sent home sick from school midday at the age of ten. He'd stumbled in on the upstanding Joseph O'Connor in bed with the next-door neighbor's flirtatious daughter while Mom was visiting Aunt Rose in New York. Rumors of the daughter's pregnancy had flown through the parish as quickly as the neighbors had flown from the neighborhood, scarring Patrick's reputation for years to come. From that moment on, it seemed his father had taken his anger and guilt out on his eldest son until Patrick finally rebelled in high school, battling his father at every turn, their relationship little more than a bomb ticking away. Pop had long since cleaned his life and reputation up, but Patrick's reckless ways apparently rubbed salt in the man's wounds, which suited Patrick just fine. Until lately. Now all Patrick wanted was to save money for college, get his degree, then kiss the devil goodbye.

"Don't bother coming home if you knock some hussy up, you hear?" Pop shoved him with the ball of his hand, and his mother's gasp echoed in the room, a frail indication of shock that never seemed to make its way into protest or support on Patrick's behalf.

Patrick staggered back, tendons tight with restraint as his arm wrenched up in a knee-jerk reaction, grinding to a stop before he could ram a fist in his father's gut. *No, I won't give you the satisfaction, old man.* Air sucked through his clenched teeth as he knotted his hands at his sides, satisfied that the dangerous flush on Pop's face had whooshed into a deathly pale.

"You gonna hit me, boy?" he whispered, a cold glaze of triumph in gray eyes that matched the color of sallow skin. "Go ahead, you worthless punk, because there's nothing I'd like better than to toss your sorry carcass out into the street. Let's see how many skirts you can lift when you're taking all your meals in a soup kitchen."

Sweat beaded Patrick's brow from the exertion it took not to bludgeon that unholy smirk off his father's face, his body literally quivering from the effort.

"Shaking in your boots, are you?" Joseph O'Connor laughed, a sickening grate that complemented the crazed gleam in his eyes. "That's good, because the fires of hell are licking at your boots if you keep on the way you're going. And no amount of soup dished out by dirty hands is gonna save you." His eyes narrowed to slits. "Or are you counting on some pretty, little angel to save your worthless hide? Trying to cloak your sins by cozying up to a decent woman, maybe that pretty Murphy girl Father Fitzgibbons introduced as the center's fundraiser chair?"

The blood drained from Patrick's face at the mention of Marcy's name, and his father laughed, the sound so sinister, Patrick may as well be wrestling with the devil.

"That's it, isn't it?" Pop stepped close enough for Patrick to smell the garlic from the shepherd's pie Mom fixed for dinner. "You got a hankering for a decent woman, do you now, Patrick? Just aching to get your filthy hands on her, eh? Well, I got news for you, boy, decent women like the Murphy girl would rather die than be caught with a fornicator like you."

"I'm sorry, Patrick ... but I've no desire to be involved with a man like you ..."

Muscles twitching, Patrick spun on his heel to escape before he did something he'd regret, but his father yanked his collar from behind, thrusting him hard against the wooden frame of the parlour door. Needles of pain splintered his skull.

"Joseph!" His mother found her voice for the first time Patrick could remember, the fear in her tone as thick as the bile coating his tongue.

Rage like Patrick had never known exploded in his brain, and he whirled around to shove his father away with such force, the man's arms flailed in the air before he hit the ground hard, head crashing against the ornate leg of their brass parlour stove. "A fornicator like me?" he said, eyes bulging with fury, "well, that's like one step better than an adulterer, isn't it, Pop?"

His mother screamed and flew to his father's side as Patrick watched, chest heaving while his temper slowly waned into shock when his father didn't rise to his feet. "Pop?" Voice strained, he dropped to his knees. "Pop, I'm sorry—please forgive me ..."

"G-get out," his father whispered, chest pumping raspy air while he lay dazed on the floor, blood oozing from a cut to his head. "You'll p-pay for this with d-double rent, you no-good punk, and you'll change your vile w-ways or I'll kick you out for good, do you hear?"

Patrick stared, sleet slithering through his veins. Sweat beaded his father's brow and his skin took on an ashen hue that would have alarmed Patrick if he hadn't been so outraged by the old man's punishment. A nerve jerked in his cheek while he slowly rose to his feet, too angry to respond as he picked his jacket up off the floor. Teeth clenched, he slammed the front door behind him, a nerve throbbing in his temple. Striding down the walk, he hurled the front gate open. It battered against the white picket fence, which declared a normalcy that was nothing more than façade. A meticulously clean cottage with green painted shutters and manicured bushes, where parlour lights streamed from windows dressed in lacy sheers. The outside all trussed up for the neighbors while the inside was barren of love and caring and the so-called faith his father proclaimed.

He trudged down the street, head down and hands shoved in his pockets while his jacket hung limp over his arm, counting the days until he could finally move out and be on his own. But that took more money than he could make working the docks at the *Herald*, especially now that he had double rent to pay. It would take moving up in the ranks to copywriter, then reporter, copy editor, news editor and someday, Editor-in Chief of one of the most influential newspapers on the Eastern seaboard. To do that, he needed college under his belt, and he was almost there. Just a few more months of saving and he could enroll in the spring, and from there it was just a matter of time. He could put up with almost anything until then—even a hypocrite who chastised his own flesh and blood for sins he'd committed himself.

Staring at the bright lights of Brannigan's down on the next block, he heard its music drifting on the cool night air, inviting him to forget his troubles for yet another evening.

"Don't bother coming home if you knock some hussy up, you hear?"

Patrick's facial muscles calcified. "Don't worry, Pop, I'm not my old man," he hissed, "I've got dreams to go somewhere and be somebody, and I guarantee you, it won't be with a 'hussy.'"

Thoughts of Marceline Murphy sifted through his mind like a shaker of salt on the fresh wound his father just inflicted, burning his temper as much as his soul. Since the night he'd made advances, she'd been civil but cool, and although he didn't blame her, her obvious disapproval continued to fester like an open sore. Squaring his shoulders, he reached for the tarnished brass knob of Brannigan's front door, the peeling green paint reminding him he needed to strip himself of aspirations for Miss Murphy as well, which he fully intended to do. And once purged, he would find himself a woman just like her in every way—gentle and pure, beautiful and bright, and completely and utterly besotted.

With him.

His smile thinned as he entered the noisy bar, knowing full well he would never find her in the smoky confines of Brannigan's Pub.

If she even existed at all.

Chapter Fifteen

"Bravo!" Standing before the children's choir, Marcy clapped wildly, face aglow at how wonderfully they'd performed. Twenty children, ages seven to twelve, stood proudly on risers hand-crafted by Evan, Patrick, and Sam, each and every face radiating the same exhilaration Marcy felt in her own. Only a month and a half into practice, and already everything was falling into place. A sigh floated from her lips. *Thank you, Lord!*

"You were all wonderful," she said, "and as a reward, please quietly line up by the door. Sister Francine and Father Fitz will take you to the center for refreshme—"

Her announcement brought cheers and giggles that drowned out the rest of her sentence, and Marcy grinned, unable to keep a smile from her face. The shriek of Sister Francine's whistle instantly restored calm as she prodded the troops next door to the center with a stern look, her steely gaze in stark contrast to the warm twinkle in Father Fitz's eyes as he greeted each child at the door. She shook her head and turned to address Julie. "Goodness, Jewels, you've done wonders with them in mere weeks."

Julie beamed, the smile on her face as bright as the

shafts of sunlight that bathed the gymnasium with the cozy warmth of a sunny Saturday afternoon. She stood up from her wooden piano bench with a groan, stretching her arms high overhead. "They're a talented lot, they are, our St. Mary's youngsters, so I surely can't take all the credit." Flexing her fingers, she offered Marcy a teasing grin. "And then, of course, there's no denying the power of Sister Francine's whistle."

Marcy laughed and reached for the script she'd laid on the back of the piano. "Worth its weight in gold, it is, along with Sister Francine herself." She perused her script, then glanced at the watch pinned to her blue, mutton-sleeved blouse. "We have just enough time to run through the second act with the cast." Her gaze traveled the noisy auditorium where the play principals sat laughing and chatting, awaiting their turn. Marcy squinted. "Mmm … everybody seems to be here but Tillie and Holly," she said, brows in a bunch. "I wonder where they could be?"

Julie stood and straightened her music, a lopsided smile on her face. "My guess would be outside with Patrick and Sam. Tillie's practically Patrick's shadow these days and now that she's befriended Holly, so is she." She walked to the edge of the stage to peek out the windows overlooking the side yard where Patrick and Sam were painting scenery while Tillie and Holly "helped." Her smile dimmed considerably as she turned back to Marcy. "But to be honest, I think Patrick needs Tillie right now as much as she needs him. I can't imagine losing one's father so suddenly like that from a heart attack, and from what Sam told me, just hours after he and Patrick had a horrific fight." Julie released a fragile sigh. "It's so hard to believe—here one week, gone the next. Sam said Patrick was devastated even though he and his father were not very close."

A shiver rattled Marcy's shoulders, the thought of losing her own father shaking her to the core. "My heart goes out to him for sure," she said quietly, "especially since Sam mentioned Patrick refuses to talk about it, which is not good. It's only been two weeks and yet the man acts as if nothing happened. But, God bless him, I suppose everyone grieves in their own way." She huffed out a heavy breath and gave Julie's shoulder a quick squeeze. "Well, I best drag Tillie and Holly back in," she said with wink. "I'm questioning how wise it is to let two innocent little girls spend time with boys who can hardly be considered a good influence."

Mischief glimmered in Julie's dark eyes as she bumped Marcy's hip with her own, giving her a tiny pinch. "Probably not, but then neither is it wise for innocent big girls to spend time with boys who can hardly be considered a good influence either, now is it, Marce?"

Heat crept up the back of Marcy's neck. "W-whatever are you t-talking about?" she whispered, gaze darting to the side door and back.

Julie folded her arms and arched a brow, a smile squirming as she tapped her toe on the wooden stage. "Just exactly when were you planning to tell me—at the wedding?"

Wildfire flamed in Marcy's cheeks.

Julie's throaty giggle caressed Marcy's neck as her friend squeezed her in a tight embrace. "Oh, Marce, I couldn't be happier that you agreed to go out with Sam—it's an absolute answer to my prayers."

"He told you?" Marcy whispered, eyes wide as she held Julie at arm's length.

"Of course he did!" Julie assessed her with a mock scowl. "What I want to know is why my best friend didn't?"

Marcy sat down on the bench and pulled Julie along, her voice lowering to a whisper. "I'm sorry, Jewels, but to be honest, I wasn't sure if I was going to keep the date or not."

"Why not?" Julie asked, tone laced with worry. "I have to tell you, I've not seen Sam this excited in a long time. He never tells me anything about his dealings with women, but he hunted me down the moment you left after spending the night, just to ply me with questions."

"Questions?" Marcy blinked. "What kind of questions?"

"What your favorite food is, dessert, flower, color," she emphasized each point with a back and forth bob of her head, "not to mention your favorite things to do, your favorite books, poets, you name it."

"He did?" Marcy swallowed the shock in her throat. "But why?"

"Because he's smitten, you goose, and I just knew he would be." Julie gave her another fierce hug. "He told me he's taking you on a picnic and wants everything to be perfect. Oh, Marce, promise you'll give him a chance, please?"

Marcy's eyelids fluttered closed over Julie's shoulder. What was she going to do now? She hadn't told Julie on purpose because she wasn't sure she would go and, in fact, after praying about, had decided to cancel. But now? How could she?

"Julie, I don't know …" she whispered, unwilling to face the joy in her best friend's eyes. "Sam asked me when I spent the night, yes, but he also …" A lump bobbed in her throat. "Well, he … he kissed me—"

A tiny squeal erupted from Julie's throat as she shook Marcy's arms. "You didn't tell me that—why didn't you tell me that?"

"Because I was embarrassed and more than a little scared." She locked eyes with her best friend. "Kissing Sam completely disarmed me, made me forget how I feel about men like him, womanizers who can't be trusted." She gulped. "And to be honest, Jewels, his kisses made me feel like I couldn't be trusted either."

Julie tipped her head, offering Marcy a smile that was soft with affection. "But this is my brother, Marce, he knows what kind of girl you are and I think he'll respect that and keep his distance." A gleam lit her ebony gaze. "And if he doesn't, he'll answer to me because I'll scratch his eyes out."

A faint smile shadowed Marcy's lips. "You will, will you? And what about me? What if I don't keep *my* distance?"

"Oh, you will, I have no doubt. I know you too well, Marceline, and my brother has met his match in you, make no mistake. And maybe—just maybe—that match will last a lifetime, and my best friend will become my sister!"

Hope fluttered in Marcy's heart like a feather, slowly drifting until it lighted as soft as a kiss. Was it possible? *Could Sam be the man for me?*

"Miss Murphy?"

Marcy's head jerked up, heat staining her cheeks as if the young girl before her was privy to her thoughts. "Yes, Adelaide?"

The female lead offered an apologetic smile. "I'm sorry, but my mother asked me to be home to babysit by four o'clock, so I was wondering if we'd be done by then?"

Taking a quick peek at the watch pinned to her blouse, Marcy flashed a reassuring smile. "Most definitely, Adelaide, and we'll start right now. If you wouldn't mind herding the others up to the stage, I'd be most grateful."

"Yes, ma'am," Adelaide said, hurrying over to rally the group of principals for the practice.

"So ... will you keep the date, then?" Julie asked, a plea in her eyes that said she worried Marcy would say no.

Marcy sighed, exhaling her resignation. "Yes, I will keep the date, but only if you promise to keep me covered in prayer. Your brother has always had a disastrous effect on me, and well you know it."

Julie giggled. "Yes, but now you have the same effect on him, so between me, prayer, and your will of iron, this should be a walk in the park." She winked. "Or maybe I should say 'picnic.'"

"I don't care what you say, as long as your prayers go along with it." Marcy glanced at the group of principals chatting on the stage before giving her friend a fond embrace. "Would you mind running scales with the leads while I go hunt down two little girls who seem to have gone astray?"

"Absolutely." Julie nodded and turned to the group while Marcy made her way down the steps of the stage to march outside where the boys painted scenery, head high and heart hammering. She halted at the door, and her hand fluttered to her throat at the sweet scene before her. Patrick was helping Tillie paint sloppy red hearts on the unfinished scenery that would become a backdrop of a snow-dusted barn. Marcy's eyes lighted on Sam's muscled form, and her heart skipped a beat as he worked with Holly. His black curls, damp and wayward, sported a crown of knotted clover stems, obviously fashioned by the girls and a perfect match to a clover necklace strewn around Patrick's neck. Assisting Holly in applying a stroke of paint, Sam bent to press a kiss to the little girl's cheek, and Marcy's legs nearly buckled. Little girls who have gone astray. She swallowed hard and uttered a silent prayer.

Oh, Lord, please don't let one be me ...

"Can we leave our pictures for everyone to see?" Tillie asked, her hazel eyes almost bigger than her tiny body as she blinked up at him behind thick eyeglasses that always brought a tender smile to Patrick's face.

"Sorry, darlin'," he said with a tweak of her pigtail, "but if we let these pictures stay, Miss Murphy would box my ears and maybe yours too." He made her giggle when he pretended to swipe her face, his thumb peeking through his fist as if he had stolen her nose. He leaned close as if to whisper, but his tease was loud and clear. "Our Miss Murphy is one pretty pooch whose bite is definitely worse than her bark."

"Ahem."

Patrick spun around, heat crawling inside his collar at the sight of Marcy in the doorway, arms folded and one beautiful brow spiked.

With an awkward shrug, he gave her a lazy grin, steering Tillie in front while he latched hands to her shoulders. "I did say 'pretty,' did I not, Tillie?"

Tillie giggled and peered up at Patrick with an elfin grin. "Are you in trouble, Atrick?" she whispered loudly, teasing him with her pet name.

"Yes," Marcy said with a twitch of a smile. Her eyes seared Patrick within an inch of his life as she propped the door with her backside, arms and palms flush to the wood. Her gaze dropped to Tillie and softened. "And so are you, Miss Dewey, if two little girls I know don't hightail it to the stage for practice right this minute."

"Uh-oh, Holly, we're in trouble," Tillie said with a giggle. Heaving a grunt, she attempted to push Holly's wheelchair up a slight incline.

"Hold on there, darlin'," Patrick said, whisking Tillie up on his shoulders while he quickly commandeered the wheelchair to steer Holly up the ramp.

Marcy halted him with a hand at the door, gaze flitting to Sam. "Sam, would you mind terribly taking the girls in? I need to speak with Patrick."

Patrick's blood slowed to a crawl as he stared, his Adam's apple dipping several times. "Look here, Marcy, I didn't mean to imply you're a dog …"

Sam laughed and butted Patrick aside. "Too late, O'Connor—I see an ear-boxing in your future, my friend, although I might just take one myself if administered by this beauty." He wheeled Holly through the door, allowing his hand to casually brush against Marcy's as he passed, fingers twining with hers for the briefest of moments. Patrick quickly turned away, Marcy's reaction—a pretty blush, lowered lashes, shy smile—grating his nerves. He preferred to focus on painting scenery rather than Sam's obvious effect on the woman of his dreams. Squatting, he proceeded to stir the paint, anxious to get on with the barn backdrop.

"Patrick?"

"Yes?" He stirred the paint too briskly, causing splotches to fly and splatter his arm. His lips ground tight.

"Would you … would you mind facing me, please?" she whispered, the soft proximity of her voice over his shoulder sending shivers of warmth to the tips of his fingers.

Expelling a noisy sigh, he rose and turned with a

slack of his hip, prepared to fend off her obvious dislike. "Look, Marcy, I didn't mean to call you a—" The words locked in his throat at her nearness, a mere two feet away while those blue eyes peered up with genuine warmth instead of her usual polite civility. He swallowed hard, bewitched by the humility of her gaze, the gentle smile on those full, pink lips, hair the color of white gold, gleaming in the sun. The scent of lilac water and Pear's soap captured him, tangling his tongue—and his stomach—into more knots than the clover necklace Tillie had strung around his neck.

"I know that," she said quietly. The creamy lines of her throat shifted along with his while the corners of that perfect mouth tipped the barest amount. "Although I suspect you'd be more than justified, with all the snapping and growling I've done at you lately."

He was speechless, unable to prevent the sag of his mouth anymore than he could the erratic thud of his heart.

Her smile blossomed like a rose—pink, soft, and slow—and as breathtaking as a garden of exotic blooms. A delicate blush dusted creamy cheeks as dewy as satin, and just as sensual. "I ..." Impossibly long eyelashes the color of dark honey flickered several times as if her words would not come without their gentle prompting. She cleared her throat and exhaled a shaky breath, the action quivering the bodice of a crisp blue blouse the exact shade of her eyes. "The truth is, I owe you an apology, Patrick. I've ... been somewhat distant and cool to you, I know, and I'm sorry."

He blinked. *She's apologizing? No!* How would he remain aloof without the barrier of her silence? Her disdain? All moisture left his mouth, gluing his words to his tongue like a paintbrush left overnight in a bucket.

His silence must have unnerved her because the color in her face heightened and she began to ramble while she picked at her nails, easing his own anxiety in her presence for the very first time. Rather enjoying that he could fluster her as much as she could him, he waited, which given the fact he was dumbstruck, wasn't difficult in the least.

"You've b-been nothing b-but kind to me," she stuttered. When her eyes finally met his, her face fused as scarlet as the paint on the brush in his hand, the memory of his stolen kiss the night on her porch most likely coming to mind. She quickly looked away, gaze drawn to the haphazard hearts he and Tillie had painted. "The only explanation I have is that I have a dear cousin in New York who was engaged to a man who looked a lot like you, you see, and he broke it off after he … he …"

He detected the barest quiver of her chin, and comprehension dawned as clear as the sun-rich summer day. Yes, suddenly he did see … A sheen marred her luminous gaze, and the sight produced a cramp in his chest. "Marcy—"

She raised a palm, as if her own words begged release as much as the tears in her eyes. "No, please—let me finish because I need you to understand the reason for my rude behavior."

He nodded, allowing the breath in his lungs to slowly seep out.

Squaring her shoulders, she raised both eyes and chin, meeting his gaze dead-on with a look of such vulnerability that he fought the urge to gather her in his arms. "You see, she loved this man with all of her heart and he … r-robbed her of her v-virtue, leaving her with a child he conveniently claimed was not his." Her hand shook as she swiped at the single tear trailing her face.

"I cannot even begin to convey the depth of my cousin's humiliation and sorrow ..." She promptly took the handkerchief he offered and dabbed at her eyes. "Or mine."

"Marcy, I'm so sorry—"

She halted him with another hand, brows pinched over closed lids while she struggled to say what she obviously needed to say. "No, Patrick, please—hear me out. This is difficult as it is, but I need you to know just why I've been so mistrustful of you." She sucked in a shaky breath and continued. "Not only did Nora's situation nearly destroy me, but from the moment I came out in society, it seemed I was besieged by handsome rogues who left me with a bad taste in my mouth." Her fingers quivered as they shielded her eyes. "The final blow came when an older man made advances to me ..." She inhaled deeply, chest expanding and contracting while her hand slumped to her side. Her reluctant gaze finally rose to meet his. "He was a very handsome *married* man, you see ..." Muscles shifted in her throat as tears glimmered in her eyes. "And, unfortunately, the father of my best friend."

A ball of regret jerked in his throat. "Marcy, I'm so desperately sorry. Not only about your cousin and your friend's father, but for my despicable behavior that night—"

"Thank you—" she said in a rush, then attempted a smile that came off tremulous at best. "And I believe you truly are. I've seen your kindness with the girls, with Evan and Miss Clara, and even the gentle souls at the center like Luther." The blue eyes sharpened, as if she were really seeing him for the first time. "Julie and Sam and the O'Rourkes love you, and Tillie and Holly adore you ..." One corner of her mouth tilted up. "And you've stolen the hearts of every female south of

Boston proper, including Sister Francine." A genuine smile lit her face—the first she had ever really given him—spilling across her lips like the sweetest of nectars he craved to taste. "I believe I have misjudged you based on the fact that you are ..." The blush was back, staining her cheeks despite the glimmer of tease in her eyes. "An attractive man and notorious rogue."

Notorious rogue. A sharp pain seared his gut. Or in the words of his father—*fornicator*—a word he would never again hear from his father's lips except in the dark recesses of his mind. It was his turn to blush, a completely uncommon occurrence with women. He pushed the painful thoughts of his father aside and attempted to deflect his grief and shame with an off-center smile. "Thank you, Marceline, but rogues need love too, you know."

Her soft chuckle was music to his ears. "Yes, well, one would certainly find it, Mr. O'Connor, if one were inclined to look beyond a pretty face, you know, into the heart and soul."

His smile faded to reveal some of the mourning that clotted thick in his throat. "A lesson learned all too late, I'm afraid," he said quietly. "And only one of many regrets, I assure you."

She blinked, and as if suddenly paralyzed by his words, her stare locked with his while a sheen of moisture marred her gaze, his own grief suddenly mirrored in her face. "I ... never really had the chance at the funeral to tell you how very sorry I am about the sudden passing of your father." She drew in a shaky breath, allowing it to quiver on a fragile sigh while compassion welled in her eyes. "It must be such a painful thing to lose someone you love."

More than you know, Marceline, he thought with an ache only partially caused by the death of his father, his fierce regret and shame greatly compounded by the woman before him.

She broke the spell with a clear of her throat, her manner suddenly as painfully efficient as always. She drew in a deep breath, head cocked as she studied him through questioning eyes. "So ... apology accepted?" she asked with a gentle smile.

He wiped his hand on his stained work pants and extended it, a slow grin wending its way across his lips. "Most assuredly, Miss Murphy. Shall we start anew, then—as friends?"

Her gaze flicked to his proffered hand and back, uncertainty clouding her eyes while her tongue glossed her teeth, a habit he'd noticed whenever she was tentative or nervous about something. She slowly placed her hand in his and he carefully closed his palm around it. Her touch jolted with that same spark of current he'd experienced the last time, tingling his body—and from her sharp intake of breath—hers as well. He felt her start to pull away, and he held on, lingering long enough to give her a firm shake.

Slipping her hand from his, she barricaded her arms to her waist, gaze averted. "Now that we are officially friends, Mr. O'Connor—"

"Patrick," he said quietly, noting she suddenly seemed ill at ease.

She nodded, still avoiding his eyes. "Patrick," she said softly, and the very sound unleashed a shot of warmth that all but stole the breath from his lungs. "I wanted to apologize because I was wrong, certainly, but for another reason as well." Her gaze rose to meet his with a tentative look. "You see, Sam has expressed an interest in—"

"I know," he said quickly, wanting to deflect her awkwardness as well as his own. "He told me."

A Light in the Window

She nodded. "It's no reflection on you, of course, it's just that Sam and I have always had ..." Honeyed brows peaked, as if begging him to understand. "A connection, if you will." A melancholy smile flickered on her lips. "And, of course, Julie has been plotting a relationship between us forever it seems ..."

"It's all right, I understand," he whispered, wishing that understanding alone could dispel the sick feeling in his gut.

Relief eased the strain in her face. "Thank you. You have no idea how much that means to me, Patrick—your sensitivity in this situation." She released a shuddery breath, a sincere smile beaming from her beautiful face once again. "Well, I best be going—a restless mood looms inside, no doubt."

And outside as well ... He forced a smile. "No doubt."

She turned to go, then whirled around at the door with a twinkle in her eye, inclining her head toward the sloppy hearts on the scenery behind him. "I'm hoping you're a wee bit better with barns, Mr. O'Connor, than you are with hearts," she said, a clear jest in her tone.

He watched her disappear through the door and for the first time, he felt the full extent of his grief. "So do I, Miss Murphy," he whispered, "so do I."

Chapter Sixteen

Marcy watched as Sam's three little sisters and brother flew down the grassy hill of O'Reilly Park, shrieking wildly on their way to skip stones in the lake. "Don't go too far," she called after them, stomach in knots. *Please ...*

Palms clammy, she repacked the remnants of their lunch back into the wooden basket Sam's mother had sent along, taking great pains to avoid Sam's gaze. At the time, a picnic in the park had seemed like a good idea as their first official outing, especially since his sisters and brother would be along to chaperone. Marcy gulped as she hooked the basket closed. And she'd had a wonderful time—teasing with his sisters, playing tag on the lawn, laughing with Sam while he taught her how to fish, and even working on Father Fitz's status report together. But now that she was alone with a rake who rippled her stomach as much as the skipping stones rippled the lake, she wasn't so sure, especially lounging on a blanket in a secluded section of the park. Her eyes flicked to the shore where his siblings raced along to the far end of the lake, too distant and too distracted to care what their big brother did, and suddenly Marcy's comfort level was as low as O'Reilly Lake after a rainless summer.

She inched to the edge of the blanket and nervously clasped her hands around tented knees, making sure her ankles were properly covered by her skirt. Hand to her eyes, she scanned the shore of the azure lake as it sparkled in the sun, reveling in the beauty of a perfect late-summer day. The lake shimmered beneath the cloudless sky while boats skimmed its surface and families meandered its shore. Children's laughter and the chatter of birds literally hummed in the air, and a gentle breeze rustled the leaves of the towering oak overhead. Head back, she squinted at the sunlight that flickered through the branches above, imagining the vestige of golden foliage that would come in the month ahead. One half-gilded leaf sailed on a breeze, caressing her cheek, skimming her jaw … just like Sam had that night in the kitchen. Her heart stalled.

Sam.

Swallowing hard, she chanced a peek his way, and her cheeks warmed at his blatant stare, his lean and muscled body sideways in an easy sprawl while he studied her, head propped in his hand. Humor sparkled in his dark eyes. "I'm not going to bite, Marceline," he said in a husky tone, reaching out to graze the arm of her lavender silk blouse with a single finger. "We already had lunch, remember?"

A shaky giggle parted from her lips as she shifted to face him, positioning herself at the far corner of the tattered blanket while she once again encircled her knees like a vise. "I should hope not, Samuel O'Rourke, after the quantity of fried chicken you just consumed." She gave him a playful thrust of her chin, the tease helping to calm her rattled nerves.

He laughed and fiddled with a frayed rose on his mother's old quilt while he peered up beneath dark lashes. "Well, in case you haven't noticed, Marcy, I've grown into a man with a ravenous appetite."

Oh, yes, I've noticed ...

"So," he continued in a casually polite tone, "tell me about Marceline Murphy."

Her head tilted with a squint. "You already know everything about me, Sam—we grew up together, remember?"

"Yes, I do." His fingers gently pulled at a loose thread from the quilt, carefully tugging it free. "I know you're an only child who is a voracious bookworm and my sister's best friend. Julie tells me you were at the top of your class at your old school in New York, the president of the drama club *and* an actual debutante with an official coming out in *high society*." His eyes twinkled on the last two words before he continued. "And I have on good authority that as a little girl, you not only had a propensity for climbing trees that were too high, but getting stuck at the top, too afraid to come down."

She laughed. "Yes, I do suppose I tend to shoot high with goals in life, it seems, only to freeze in terror when I've gone too far."

He cocked his head, assessing her through curious eyes. "And just what are your 'goals,' Marcy?" he said softly, "besides reading books and scaling heights?"

She sighed, the tension in her limbs easing along with it. "Well, originally, my parents had hoped to send me to Vassar College in New York, but when Papa lost his job with the railroad, that all changed. Now they want me to go to Smith College here in Boston next year, provided the vice president job Papa applied for comes through, God willing." She wound her arms around her knees and rested her chin on top. "He thinks it's essential for a well-bred young lady to be well-rounded in every field of study—music, drama, academics. But I have to admit, it's always been his dream, not mine."

Sam abandoned the now unraveled rose for a leftover apple at the edge of the blanket. "So, what is your dream, then?" His gaze fixed on hers as he tossed the fruit in the air, Max's bite marks clearly evident in its side.

Marcy felt a rush of adrenaline, and for the first time all day, it had nothing to do with Sam. She sucked in a deep breath laced with the loamy scent of the mossy bank, the fishy smell of the lake, and the lingering trace of Sam's shaving soap, and quickly released it again. Her voice fairly brimmed with excitement. "I love my parents, I do, but I haven't the heart to tell them that my dreams look nothing like theirs. I'm not happy Papa lost his job, but there's a part of me that is so grateful we were forced to return to Boston, so grateful that …" She absently picked at her nails, guilt working its way into her tone while she peeked up at Sam, hoping he wouldn't think her crazy or worse yet, ungrateful. "Well, that our current financial dilemma may allow me to do what I've always longed to do."

His brow lifted when she paused. "And that is …?"

She chewed the edge of her lip and then grinned outright. "Oh, Sam, I'd give anything to work with the babies at the St. Mary's Infant Asylum and Lying-In Hospital after I graduate instead of college, absolutely anything! Not that I don't want Papa to find a wonderful job, mind you, but nothing thrills my heart more than babies, and if we don't have the finances to send me to Smith next year, well, then I hope to acquire a position at St. Mary's."

Sam's other thick brow rose along with the first. "Blue blazes, Marcy, does that mean you plan to forego marriage and children of your own?"

She gave him a shy smile. "Heavens no—I've longed to fall in love, get married, and have babies since I received my first bisque baby doll the Christmas I was five." A bit of melancholy niggled at the memories of the dozens of dolls she'd collected over the years to assuage her yearning for siblings, vowing she would have a large family like that someday. Her thoughts leap-frogged to her cousin Nora and the precious child she had to give up, and Marcy's euphoria suddenly seeped out with another frail sigh. "But until that happens, I'm content to give my love to those precious little ones who have no mothers of their own," she whispered, thoughts of Nora's broken engagement a stark reminder that marriage wasn't always a guarantee. Shaking off her malaise, Marcy lifted her chin with a warm smile. "There will be plenty of time for marriage if it's meant to be, but until it happens, I hope to serve and love little ones who have no family of their own."

Mouth agape, Sam stared in awe as if she'd just sprouted a halo. "Remarkable," he breathed, the edges of his mouth curling in a slow grin.

"'Remarkable' that I love babies and want to care for them?" Marcy dipped her head in a skeptical smile. "I don't think so. I'm a woman, Sam—that's what women do—they love babies. What's so remarkable about that?"

He chuckled, bunching the blanket beneath his head as a makeshift pillow, elbows cocked and hands braced to the back of his neck. "Nothing if you're a woman with an eye on a gold band to accomplish the feat. But loving babies on your own, with no immediate interest to toss a noose around some man's neck?" He shook his head, his eyes glowing with interest. "That, Marceline Murphy, is truly remarkable." His gaze traveled from her high-collared lavender silk blouse to the black laced shoes beneath her gray gabardine skirt, and his low whistle pierced the air. "Especially for a woman who looks like you," he whispered. "I shouldn't tip my hand, I know, but regrettably, I'm as blunt and honest as I am bold, so I have to say, Marceline, I could find myself falling in love with a woman like you. Trust me—nothing is more appealing to a man like me than a woman who's willing to wait for that white picket fence."

Marcy tipped her head, her stomach swooping along with the seagulls over the water. "A man like you? And what exactly is that?" she teased, hoping to deflect the disappointment his words instilled.

"Oh, you know—a so-called rogue who would like to experience life before settling down." Face to the sun, he closed his eyes while a breeze ruffled the curls on his head. "That is, if one settles down at all."

Marcy's jaw dropped so quickly, she was grateful Sam's eyes were shut. "If you settle down at all?" She covered her shock with a light tone. "Goodness, coming from a wonderful family like yours, I would think marriage would be a given, that having a happy home like your parents would be something you'd want."

He grinned. "Not if you're not the marrying kind, which I considered myself to be until recently when something changed my mind."

"Oh, thank heavens," she said with a hand to her chest, her relief evident in a slow exhale of air. "Goodness, you have the type of family I've always dreamed of, Sam, and to think you might not have the desire to pass that wonderful upbringing on to a family of your own is unthinkable." Feeling worlds better that Sam intended to provide grandchildren for his parents, Marcy relaxed with a flat stretch of her legs, adjusting her skirt before leaning back on her hands, studying him with interest. "So, what changed your mind?"

She waited while another slow grin eased across his handsome face. One eyelid edged up. "You," he said softly. "I never dreamed I'd find a woman like you, Marceline."

"M-me?" Her hand fluttered to her stomach as if she could still the somersaults provoked by the husky sound of her name on his tongue.

"Yes, you ..." He sat up and moved in so close, she swore she felt the warmth of his words on her cheek. He trailed an unhurried finger down the sleeve of her blouse, his touch tingling her skin right through the material. "I'm attracted to you, Marceline," he whispered, "unlike any woman I've ever known, and as God is my witness—I'd run like the devil if you and I weren't of like mind."

"Of ... l-like m-mind?"

He reached to fondle a loose strand of her hair, the flick of his gaze to her mouth stealing her air. "A woman I can love who's willing to wait until I'm ready to say, 'I do.'"

Her heart beat faster than a thousand hummingbirds splashing in the sugar water of her mother's feeder in the garden. *Until he's ready to say I do?*

"Are you, Marcy?" he whispered, thumb tracing her jaw.

"Am I what?" Her voice cracked.

"The kind of woman who's willing to wait?"

Her lips trembled as a lump dipped in her throat. "I don't understand, Sam—what do you mean?"

"I mean you're the kind of girl I hope to marry ..." he said softly, drawing her close with the firm press of his hand at the small of her back. "Someday. But I need to know—if you and I are meant for each other, are you willing to give me time? Will the babies of St. Mary's be enough until I can put a ring on your hand?"

She jerked away, so stunned by his declaration, she could barely breathe. "Are you ... proposing, Sam? Is that what you're saying? Because this is no laughing matter."

"I'm not laughing," he whispered, caressing the side of her face with the palm of his hand, not a trace of humor to be found in his eyes. "*You* are the type of woman I want, Marceline—eventually. Both as my wife ..." His gaze dropped to her lips while his fingers slowly twined in the loose hairs at the back of her neck, "... and in my bed."

Heat braised her cheeks, both at the boldness of his remark and the idea that marriage was even on the mind of a man like Sam O'Rourke. "Are you ... serious?"

"I am," he said softly. "If we're right for each other and you're willing to wait, that is. So, I'm asking you again—are you? Willing to commit to me without a ring or engagement? A courtship of sorts, that may be years in the making?"

A courtship of sorts? Marcy blinked, not exactly sure what that meant. She'd dreamt of a romance with Sam since she was a little girl—the boy she'd longed for and the family she craved—but never had she imagined it might come true. She studied him now, her childhood hero all grown up with a rakish air and mischievous smile, and knew that spending time with him over the summer—at the play, at the center—had only deepened her affection and solidified her trust. So, was she? Willing to wait? For a man who wasn't ready to commit?

Her heart clutched and skidded to a dead stop. *And* for a man who didn't embrace—or live—the same passion for God as she? They belonged to the same parish, of course, and he attended church with his family every week and had always been the one boy she'd respected and trusted more than any other, but Marcy wanted more than a man with a lukewarm interest in God. More than a man who dallied with women, a reputation she knew to be true, both from Julie's stories and Sam's overtures that night in the kitchen. Marcy absently skimmed her teeth. Could such a man change? *Would* such a man change?

For her?

Easing away from his touch, she scooted back, her eyes sad as they connected with his. "I ... don't know," she said quietly, not wanting to hurt him, but not wanting to skirt the truth either. "I need a man who shares my passion for God and although you and I share the same faith ..." She swallowed her hesitation while those ebony eyes bore into hers. "Your reputation seems to indicate that we ... don't apply that faith in the same manner."

"Ah ... my reputation ..." The barest of smiles curved on his lips.

"Yes," she whispered, her words to Patrick returning to shore up her resolve. *Your reputation with women ... your flirtatious ways ... your disregard of rules ...* Marcy inhaled deeply to sustain her nerve, hoping she wouldn't trigger Sam's temper as easily as she had Patrick's. "Like Patrick, you seem to have a lust for things of a more ... carnal nature."

He smiled, and she felt a reprieve from those piercing eyes when he lowered his head for a moment to emit a soft chuckle. He finally glanced up, constricting her air when he braced massive hands to her arms. "Marceline," he said with a conviction that surprised her. "Men change ... and so do their reputations." He grazed the silk of her sleeve with his thumb, triggering her pulse, sparking her hope. His lips curved into that perilous smile that completely disarmed her, defusing all denial. "All it takes is the right woman."

The glide of his hands to her waist derailed her thoughts when he coaxed her body to stand, nearly flush with his. "I have a strong feeling you're that woman, Marcy, and if so, I will share whatever you want me to share—your faith, your dream, your passion ..." Tease laced his tone as he lifted her chin with a finger. "Even your desire for things of a *less* ... carnal nature."

Relief whooshed like a fountain of hope. "Oh, Sam—truly?"

He gave her nose a playful tap as if she were a little girl and he the doting parent. "Truly." His smile faded into soft affection, voice laden with a sobriety seldom heard from his lips. "You stir something in me," he said quietly, stark sincerity in the depths of his eyes. "The desire to be the kind of man who would deserve a woman like you, and I've never felt that before." His gaze seemed to caress her face before finally lingering on her lips, evoking that wayward grin once again. "Of course, you also stir desire of another kind," he whispered, and the warmth of his breath in her ear stuttered her pulse. "I want you, Marcy, and I'm asking you again—are you willing to wait, to allow me to court you until we're both ready to marry?"

She stood paralyzed—afraid to say yes, afraid to say no ...

"Say, yes, Marceline ..." Cupping her face, his eyes sheathed close while he nuzzled her lips.

The soft moan that left her throat was pure surrender. "Yes ..."

The faraway sounds of children's laughter suddenly

filtered through the fog he'd inflicted and she instantly lurched away, chest heaving. "For the love of decency, Sam, we're in broad daylight!" she croaked, taking another step back while her gaze darted toward the lake. Her fingers shook as she tucked a stray hair over her ear, eyes flicking to where his sisters and brother raced up the hill. Each carried cattails they waved wildly until white, fuzzy seeds floated up, up, and away.

Like my heart ...

Sam chuckled and stooped to pick up the blanket. "Forgive my forward behavior, Miss Murphy, but I couldn't risk leaving without the answer I wanted." His grin gentled into a tender smile as he stroked the curve of her jaw. "I think I could be on my way to falling in love with you, Marcy, so if you know what's good for you, I suggest you do the same."

Marcy blinked while Sam shook out the quilt, carefully folding it as he gave her a wink. Tossing the blanket on top of the basket, he turned and laughed when Max plowed into his legs with a loud squeal. Sam swooped his brother high in the air, and Marcy was pretty sure her heart did the same.

If she knew what was good for her?

She gulped. Oh, she knew, all right—in her mind. But in her body? Her tongue glossed her teeth, not once, but twice, because deep down she suspected. When it came to Sam O'Rourke?

Her heart had long since made up its mind.

Chapter Seventeen

"Break it up, you two—*now!*" Father Fitz's voice bellowed across the weedy lot, not boding well for Patrick when the priest stormed to where Dagen Fischer lay sprawled on his back with Patrick on top, pummeling away.

"Mr. O'Connor!" the priest shouted. "Unhand him this instant!"

Giving the smart-mouth quarterback a final clip, Patrick rolled off, breathing hard as he lumbered up. "I suggest you keep your trap shut in the future, Fischer, or I'll lay you out cold."

"What the devil is your problem, O'Connor—you crazy?" Dagen Fischer scrambled to his feet, chest heaving as he brushed mud and rocks from his grass-stained trousers. Swiping his face with the sleeve of his dirty jersey, he shot a scowl at Father Fitz. "That's a clear-cut penalty, Father. You saw it—he tackled me after the ball left my hand."

"Game over," Father Fitz snapped, mopping his own sweaty brow with a handkerchief from the pocket of his rolled-sleeve cassock.

Groans rose in the air from the group of men who convened regularly for after-supper games with Father Fitz's football on the church lot.

"Why don't you just throw *him* out of the game, Father?" Dagen shouted, glaring at Patrick. "He's the troublemaker, not us."

Fischer mouthed a curse his way, and Patrick lunged again, jerking to a stop when Tommy Bandle locked his arms from behind. He tried to break free, Fischer's earlier insults festering like a splinter under his skin, but Tommy's whispered warning stayed his temper. "Leave him be, Patrick."

Eyes narrowed to slits, Father Fitz waggled his fingers at Cecil McClaren who now held the ball. "Turn it over, Cecil—now, and the lot of you—go home!"

"But we just started," Dagen protested.

"I said, game over, Mr. Fischer!" Football safely tucked under his arm, Father Fitz singed the men with a glare until each trudged away, mumbling while shooting scathing looks in Patrick's direction.

Temper seething, Patrick turned to go.

"Not you, Mr. O'Connor," Father Fitz said, tone steely. "In my study—*now!*"

"Curse Fischer's hide," Patrick muttered, slogging behind the priest while he led Patrick into the rectory.

"Sit," Father Fitz ordered. He slammed the door after Patrick plodded into his office, remnants of dusk seeping through imposing shuttered windows to scatter narrow slats of daylight across a fringed Oriental rug. Two walls of oak shelving lined with a vibrant assortment of books bespoke a love for literature that had provided a reluctant bond between Patrick and the priest, a bond that made confrontation like this all the more difficult. And yet tonight, Patrick barely cared for all the angst churning in his gut.

Rounding a desk strewn with papers, a half-empty cup of coffee, and a pipe, the priest settled back in his worn leather chair. Elbows propped on the armrest, he steepled hands against a mouth pressed as tight as Patrick's fingers to the arms of his chair. "So, Mr. O'Connor, in the vernacular of Southie hooligans—what the devil is your problem?"

Jaw clamped, Patrick glared at the front of Father Fitz's polished oak desk, so familiar with the grain of the wood after years of tongue-lashings from the principal of St. Mary's, that he felt personally connected to every golden whorl. He glanced up, Father Fitz's calm expression and the scent of pipe tobacco and spearmint gum quelling his temper somewhat. "Fischer is an idiot," Patrick mumbled.

"That's a given, but then so are you at times, are you not? Like now, for instance?" A squeal of his chair indicated Father Fitz was getting comfortable as he slanted back, hands braced behind thin brown hair shot with silver at the temples. "So, I repeat—what the devil is your problem?"

Patrick blasted out a sigh. "Fischer called me a—"

"I don't *care* what Mr. Fischer called you," Father Fitz interrupted, chin lifted and brows arched. "I care about why a relatively easy-going young man who's demonstrated a true heart for service over the summer is suddenly chewing heads off left and right and spitting them out."

A curse hissed from Patrick's lips. "Blue blazes, Father," he said with venom in his tone, "you just buried my father three weeks ago—doesn't that count for anything?"

"Watch your tongue, you street hooligan." The priest bent forward with a bit of temper of his own. "I'll not have you swearing in my presence, is that clear?"

Patrick dropped his gaze, eyes singeing the front of Father Fitz's desk, certain the priest would find scars there in the morning. "Yes, sir," he ground out, the acid in his tone equally capable of gouging wood.

Father Fitz settled back again, his tone softer. "I'm well aware you lost your father, son, and no one knows better than me how much you must be grieving inside, especially with your guilt over not being able to make amends before he passed."

A nerve twittered in Patrick's jaw as he closed his eyes, his heart cramping over the raw reality that his father was dead and gone and Patrick would never have a chance to mend the relationship. He fought the tears that stung. Oh, what he'd give for a second chance ...

"Is that what this is all about then?" Father Fitz said quietly. "This feud with Mr. Fischer—the fact that your father is gone?"

Yes. No. I don't know ... Patrick steeled his jaw, gaze lost in a hard stare. "Fischer triggered a mood, that's all," he whispered, the sharp bite of his tone and the twitch in his cheek clear evidence the "mood" was alive and well.

"No, Mr. O'Connor," Father Fitz said, slanting in to jolt Patrick with a firm rap on his desk. "This is not just a mood, this is a vendetta of the most blatant degree. Be it that tussle with an indigent at the center last week, almost coming to blows with a parent at the play, or a smart-mouthed teammate you wallop on the field." Father Fitz eased back in his chair, his gaze burning with an intensity that almost made Patrick flinch. "So, I suggest you come clean or I'll be forced to pay a visit to my friend at the *Herald*, which might rob you of much-needed pay."

Another swear word slipped from his lips before he could stop it, and Father Fitz angled a brow. "Sorry," Patrick said, gouging a hand through disheveled curls. He huffed out a sigh and sagged back in his chair, eyes glazed while he kneaded his temple. "It's nothing,

Father, I've just been out of sorts lately, that's all."

Concern beetled the priest's brows. "It's been a grievous month for you, Patrick, no doubt, but somehow I sense a tension over and above your loss, so what is it, son? Has volunteering at the center and play practice cut into your overtime hours at the *Herald*, slowing your college fund? Is that it?"

Patrick almost smiled, his bad mood thawing over the priest's obvious concern—the only one who apparently cared about him other than Sam, and right now Patrick wasn't too sure about him. "No, Father, the fund is on track and I should have enough for the spring semester by Christmas."

"Well, then, are you butting heads with your mother now?" Father Fitz asked, a trace of worry in his tone.

A caustic laugh broke from Patrick's lips. "No, my mother pretends I don't exist as always, which is an improvement over my father, I assure you. But I accepted both Mom and Pop's disdain for me long ago, so I've learned to let it roll off my back." He exhaled again, his eyes veering into a faraway stare. "She's talking about moving to New York to live with my Aunt Rose and taking Paul with her, but not me, which suits me just fine." His laugh was harsh. "As long as I have enough money to fend for myself."

The priest laced fingers on his chest. "I've known you since you and Sam were rolling around in the dirt as youngsters. Despite too-many-to-count detentions in this very office, too many tiffs with your father, and little or no emotional support from your mother or brother, you've always managed to stay above the fray. Suddenly in the last month, I have never seen you angrier, moodier, or more prone to throw a punch." He hunkered down in the chair like a bear in a cave for the winter, lips pursed. "Yes, this could all be related to your father's passing and your mother and brother's disregard, but my gut tells me it's more than that. So I suggest you spill it, Mr. O'Connor, because neither of us are leaving this office until you tell me what's put this thorn in your side."

What? Or who? Patrick scowled, totally frustrated with his best friend over something that wasn't even his fault. Sam and he had always been a team, never been at odds before. *Until now.* Patrick ground his jaw. *Until Marcy ...*

Father Fitz eyed him with a probing gaze, exercising a lengthy pause before his mouth clamped in a flat line. "This wouldn't involve a girl, would it?" he prodded, eyes narrowing considerably.

Patrick grunted and crossed his arms, the side of his fist pressed to his mouth as he debated whether his pride would allow him to divulge Marcy's outright rejection while she swooned at Sam's feet. The last few weeks, the blasted woman had a glow about her whenever Sam was around that made Patrick downright nauseous, the two exchanging tender looks, smiles, and secrets until he thought he might retch. Yes, he'd agreed to step aside and let Sam have a shot, and yes, he'd resigned himself to mere friendship with Marcy, but he hadn't expected *this*—a gnawing jealousy that was eating him raw.

"Patrick," Father Fitz said softly, "I hate to see you do this to yourself—you have too much going for you. You're smart, talented, industrious, and if you continue the path I've seen this summer, you also have a bright future." He squealed back in his chair, hands clasped behind his neck while a hint of humor crept into his tone. "Not to mention the enviable ability to turn the head of any lass in the Southie neighborhood."

Patrick grunted again. "Not all of 'em, Father."

"Ah, so it's a matter of the heart, is it?" Father Fitz chuckled and crossed his arms. "Well, rumor has it you can charm any lass you like, Mr. O'Connor, and judging from that fracas tonight in the dirt, that obviously goes double for Mr. Fischer's sister, whose heart, I'm told, you've recently broken a second time."

Shame scalded Patrick's face at the mention of Dagen's sister, who Patrick had wooed relentlessly, allowing her to believe they were courting while he dallied with others behind her back. He looked away, reluctant to face Father Fitz's incriminating stare. "That wasn't my intent, Father, I swear …" He lowered his gaze, and a muscle dipped in his throat while more heat crawled up the back of his neck. "At least the second time," he said weakly. "I'm fond of Emily, but after I started pursuing her again, well, something happened …"

"Like another pretty face, I suppose." A heavy exhale parted from Father Fitz's lips. "If you've ever heeded a warning before, Patrick, heed this: your history for toying with women's affections will not only backfire, son, but it's an affront to God that may well cost you the woman you love."

Elbows on his knees, Patrick put his head in his hands. "A lesson learned all too late," he whispered, the thought of Marcy with Sam an ache like nothing he'd ever known. "I've already lost her."

"Balderdash," Father Fitz said with a grunt. "You can't lose the woman God has for you unless you flout His will."

Patrick winced.

"Then rectify it!" Father Fitz snapped, angling forward with hands gripped to the arms of his chair. "Repent before God and be judicious and respectful in your dealings with young women from this moment on."

"I have," he whispered, eyes trailing into a cold stare, "but it's too late."

"It's never too late to do God's will. If there's a lass who's caught your eye, then forsake all others and pursue her."

"I'm sorry, Patrick ... but I've no desire to be involved with a man like you ..."

"Patrick!"

His head jolted up, eyes wide while Father Fitz's features sharpened into view. "I'm sorry, Father—what did you say?"

"I said—give it to God."

Patrick blinked, confusion furrowing his brow. "Give what to God?"

"This woman who's won your heart—pursue her, then give it to God."

If only it were that easy. He shook his head. "I can't Father—I lost the bet."

Father Fitz eyed him with a wary pinch of brows. "So now you've added gambling to your infractions, have you?"

A faint smile shadowed Patrick's mouth. "No, sir, but Sam and I tossed a coin and I won the toss, but not the girl."

Father Fitz's eyes lit with understanding. "How so?"

Patrick slumped back in his chair. "She was afraid of my reputation."

The whites of Father's eyes expanded. "But not Sam's?"

"Apparently not."

"I see." He paused, lips pursed in thought. "This girl in question wouldn't by chance be Marceline Murphy, would it?"

Patrick's heart sank at the mere mention of her name. "It would, sir."

Father Fitz nodded, sloping back in his chair. "And you're miserable."

"No, sir," Patrick said with a sick feeling in his chest, "I'm devastated. Because somewhere deep inside … I actually thought …" He swallowed a knot of emotion. "Hoped, really, that she was the one."

"The one …" Father Fitz said carefully, "as in marriage?"

Patrick nodded slowly, not the slightest doubt in his mind.

"Then go after her."

He glanced up, his heart stalling at the meaning of Father Fitz's words. "I can't. She's chosen Sam, not me, and he's my best friend. And to be honest …" His heavy exhale signaled his resignation. "She's something special, Father, and I'm not."

"Ah, but that's where you're wrong, Mr. O'Connor," Father Fitz said, brushing a streak of dirt from his sleeve. "You are what I refer to as a diamond in the rough. A young man lost on his way to respectability." Father Fitz paused, eyes in a squint. "Does Sam feel about Marcy the way you do?"

The question caught Patrick by surprise, giving him pause. *Did he?* "I'm not sure."

"Well, then, let's put it this way. As far as putting Marcy's best interests at heart—are his intentions as honorable as yours?"

"Since when, Patrick, are my intentions ever honorable?" Sam's statement the night they'd left Brannigan's circled in his brain, twisting Patrick's gut, clenching his teeth. "I'm not sure," he whispered.

"Yes, you are, or that tic wouldn't be pulsing in your cheek." The priest folded his hands on his chest, eyeing Patrick with a sharp gaze. "Have you considered forging a friendship with the woman and then praying for more?"

Patrick's jaw dropped as if the man had just suggested entering the seminary. "Pardon me?"

Father Fitz chuckled. "It's not as far-fetched as you think, my boy. Marcy is a very prayerful woman. What better way to win her heart than through friendship and prayer?"

It was Patrick's turn to laugh. "Come on, Father, do you really think God would listen to me any more than Marcy did?"

Father Fitz studied him with a faint smile. "Actually, Patrick, He has a propensity for prayers uttered from the heart, especially when one bows his knee at His throne." He squinted, scratching the edge of his chin. "Tends to be a wee bit partial, He does, to a man after His own heart as I recall. Just look at King David in the Bible—a bit of a rogue such as yourself, lusting after another man's wife, and yet God called him 'a man after His own heart.' Why?" Father Fitz leaned in, his gaze pinning Patrick to the wall. "Because he repented of his sins and moved on to be the man God called him to be—a man who not only lives his life *for* God, mind you ... but *with* Him." He slowly leaned back in his chair, his eyes never leaving Patrick's face. "Something tells me, my boy, that before a man can truly win the heart of a woman like Marceline Murphy, his own heart must be aligned with God's. So ... if this young woman means to you all you say she does ..."

A nerve twittered in Patrick's temple. "She does."

"Well, then, I would think you'd want to hedge your bets with a chat or two with the Almighty, wouldn't you?"

A Light in the Window

Patrick stared, the possibility of prayer working on his behalf with Marcy as foreign as a woman's rejection. And yet ... the very notion fanned the faintest glimmer of hope in his soul. He peered up, his words as thick as his tongue while his heart thudded slow and hard in his chest. "Do you ... think with prayer, Father ... I have even the slightest chance to win her heart?"

A sparkle gleamed in the priest's eyes that matched the peaceful smile on his lips. "Actually, Mr. O'Connor, I'm of the opinion that you don't have the slightest chance *without* it."

Patrick's heart began to pound, the prospect of winning Marcy's heart buoying his spirits for the first time in weeks. He hesitated while his pulse slowed to a crawl. "But what if it doesn't work? What if God says no?"

Father Fitz assessed him through patient eyes, his affection evident in the warmth of his tone. "Then either way, I suspect you'll encounter a peace unlike any you've experienced before because that, my boy, is a by-product of faith ... and prayer."

"Peace?" Patrick shook his head, his smile clearly laced with doubt. "I'm not sure I'd even know what that is."

"It's a mantle of hope, my boy, no matter the circumstances. A cloak of rest that settles the soul. Unshakable calm in the midst of a storm." He slanted in, hazel eyes almost gleaming with a passion Patrick had only seen one other time—in the gaze of one Marceline Murphy. "It's something that can only deepen with a true faith in God, Patrick, and you mark my words—a true faith in God will not only save your soul, but your very life from destruction, unleashing untold blessings in His name. Pursue Him, my boy, and then pursue your young woman, but do it in prayer and obedience to God. Because His blessings don't depend on the whim of a toss or the roll of a dice, but flourish in the fertile soil of faith and obedience."

"Faith and obedience," Patrick whispered, the words a mystery he did not understand. He thought of his father's fraudulent faith and wanted nothing to do with it, and yet ... something honest and real rang true in the words of both Father Fitz and Marcy. Glancing up, he squinted at the priest who was not only a mentor and friend, but one of the few men he actually respected. "I don't even know where to begin," he said quietly, and his unsteady words brought a dazzling smile to Father Fitz's face.

"Ah, but that's where the experience of a doddering, old priest comes in quite handy, Mr. O'Connor, because I happen to be privy to the very first step." Reclining in his leather chair, he girded his hands behind his neck and grinned, giving Patrick a wink. "Brace yourself, my boy, for one of the keys to true happiness—it's called 'prayer.'"

Chapter Eighteen

Wrinkling her nose at the musty smell of the downstairs church storeroom, Marcy peered into the dark closet, holding her carbide gas lantern high enough to scour the third shelf for the Advent wreath Sister Francine asked her to fetch. Spider webs and mouse droppings did not lend a cozy feeling as she slapped at the back of the lace fluted collar of her fitted cream blouse, feeling a tickle she hoped was her imagination. Setting the lantern down on the floor, she buffed her full mutton sleeves and continued to browse until she spied the wreath on the third shelf.

Something warm feathered her neck and she jumped, whirling around with a squeak. Heart in her throat, she whacked a shaky hand to a rock-hard chest, the sight of Sam O'Rourke looming in the shadows doing nothing for her composure. "Sam O'Rourke, you scared me half to—"

His lips effectively silenced her until the thought that someone might catch them suddenly jolted, and Marcy quickly pushed him away. "I-am-going-to-box-your ears," she said in a fractured whisper as breathless as she, failing in her attempt to dislodge his hands from her waist.

His low chuckle tickled her neck as his lips fondled

the soft flesh of her ear. "I'd rather you focus on my mouth than my ears, Marceline," he said in a husky tone, then promptly muzzled her with another kiss.

"Do you need help finding it, Miss Murphy?" Sister Francine's distant shout filtered down the stairs into the dimly lit hall.

"No!" All blood drained from her face as she swatted at Sam's hands on the way to the door. "I'll be right there," she called, grateful when Sister nodded and disappeared. Marcy spun around, two palms flat to Sam's chest. "Sam O'Rourke, so help me—"

He squelched all protest with another kiss, hands sliding the length of her waist to slope the curve of her hip. "I *am* trying to help you, Marcy," he whispered with a chuckle, "but you're not making this easy."

Breathless, she shoved him away, chest heaving as she plunked her hands on her hips. "For the love of decency, what is wrong with you? You've been a perfect gentleman until now, but so help me if you pull another stunt like this, you'll crawl out of this closet with a black eye, is that clear?"

His teeth flashed white in the shadowed light, sparkling as much as the gleam in his eyes. "My apologies, Miss Murphy, but I'm not responsible for my actions when I have you alone in the dark."

She batted him away, snatching the lantern up and holding it out. Using it as a barrier, she pointed to a shelf where a pinecone Advent wreath sat in a shallow box. "Make yourself useful, you scamp, and hand me that box, then tell me—*please*—that no one saw you come downstairs."

"I assure you, no one knows I'm here except for Julie, who told me where you were." He kissed her on the nose and reached for the wreath. "I slipped down the stairs while Sister Francine was ranting at several young ruffians from the choir."

"B-but, what are you doing here? I thought you had to work t-tonight," she stammered, well aware that a dark closet was *no* place to be alone with Sam O'Rourke.

"I do, but I needed the sustenance of your lips, Marceline, to help me get through the long night." He turned around, box in hand, and she immediately bolted from the storage room while he followed, closing the door behind him.

Petrified someone would come down the steps, Marcy hurried down the hall, shooting a strained smile over her shoulder. "Well, those stolen kisses will have to hold you for a good long while, mister, because you are officially on probation for ungentlemanly conduct, is that understood?"

He sauntered behind her with a grin on his face. "Yes, ma'am, but it was definitely worth it."

She wheeled around at the bottom of the staircase, chin in a jut. "I'll take that box now, if you please, and you, *sir*, will stay down here for a good five minutes until I am back up on the stage directing the rehearsal, is that clear?"

"Have I ever told you how cute you are when you're bossy?" he teased, handing the box over with a quick kiss to her nose.

"I am *not* bossy," she said with a mock indignant air, lowering her voice to a whisper, "except with a certain person who has trouble keeping his hands—and his lips—to himself." She skittered up the steps with a giggle before he could deposit yet another kiss. "Good night, Mr. O'Rourke," she called at the top of the stairs.

"Till Saturday night, Miss Murphy," Sam said with a bow. "Seven sharp."

Shaking her head, Marcy smiled as she slipped

through the door, carefully closing it while she made a mental note to avoid being alone with Sam. Face and body flushed, she halted at the back of the bustling auditorium to reposition the box in her hands when a baby's plaintive cry reached her ears, instantly clutching her heart. Maternal instincts swelled, and she swiftly honed in, marching to a row of chairs where sweet Carrie Pagels was frantically patting her baby sister's back. Carrie stared at her with wide eyes and red cheeks, clear evidence of her embarrassment over the ruckus her sister was making. "I'm so sorry, Miss Murphy," she stammered, "but Mama had to see Father Fitz for a few minutes, and Cassandra Rose won't stop hollering."

"Here, let me try, sweetheart." Marcy offered a sympathetic smile, adrenaline coursing her veins at the mere thought of holding a baby. She placed the box on a folding chair and scooped little Cassandra Rose into her arms, body thrumming as if it were Christmas morning. "I'll just bet you're hungry or teething or both, aren't you, little one?" she whispered, pressing a soft kiss to the little girl's sodden cheek before she started to pace, bouncing the baby in her arms. Cassandra Rose continued to howl, and Marcy spied a wet washrag peeking out of Carrie's open satchel nearby. She nodded to it. "Hand me that wet rag, Carrie, do you mind?"

With lightning speed, Carrie handed the rag over, and Marcy quickly cleaned her hand before placing her finger in the baby's mouth to massage her gums, cooing as she soothed with a tender smile. The little tyke immediately hushed, bright blue eyes swimming with tears as she blinked up at Marcy.

"You did it, Miss Murphy," Carrie announced with a shout of pride and Marcy laughed and looked up, her gaze snagged by Patrick's stare from across the gym. He was watching her from the open side door where he was obviously taking a break from building a wooden sleigh. His serious gray eyes seemed to weld her to the spot while a gentle smile shadowed his lips. The intensity of his look caused a strange stir in her belly, and when it merged with the joy of holding a baby in her arms, heat immediately pulsed in her cheeks. Eyes fused to hers, he cocked a hip to the jamb while he slowly took a drink from a water jug, throat glugging as he continued to stare.

The connection was broken when Carrie's mother hurried up, apologies tumbling from her lips. "Oh, Miss Murphy—Cassandra Rose wasn't crying, was she?"

Marcy held the baby close, heart melting when the infant's glossy blue eyes lumbered closed, her rosebud mouth gently sucking on Marcy's finger. Fighting a sting of disappointment at Mrs. Pagels' return, Marcy handed the sleeping child over to her mother, her arms keenly feeling the loss. "Just a wee bit, Mrs. Pagels," she said, gently stroking the baby's cheek before tweaking Carrie's neck, "but nothing we couldn't handle."

"Marcy?"

She turned to the stage where Julie waved a script in her hand. "We have a slight problem."

"Coming," Marcy called over her shoulder. She bent to give Carrie a hug. "Cassandra Rose is lucky to have a big sister like you, Carrie, you know that?"

"Gee, thanks, Miss Murphy!"

Saying her goodbyes, Marcy grabbed the box and hurried toward the stage, giving Patrick a quick nod before she skittered up the steps to where Julie stood with arms crossed. "Hate to break it to you, Marce, but Peter Martin has the flu."

"Oh, fiddle." Marcy frowned as she set the box aside. "Is Clyde Donaldson here, then, his understudy?"

"Nope. Sister Francine told me Clyde's out of town for his grandfather's funeral."

"Oh, drat," Marcy muttered, scanning the auditorium for a temporary replacement. She sighed, wishing she hadn't cut the adult choir practice short to focus on the second act. Consequently, male attendance was sparse, with only the children's choir present for costume measurements, mothers and toddlers chatting in the back of the auditorium, and the principals sitting on the edge of the stage, waiting to begin. Marcy's eyes honed in on Patrick, still propped in the door while he upended the jug. He swiped his face with the rolled-up sleeve of an open-necked work shirt and set the jug down before turning to go.

Marcy darted to the front of the stage. "Patrick!"

He glanced over his shoulder, and her teeth tugged at her sheepish smile while she shot him a pleading gaze. "I need you ..."

A boyish grin stole across his lips as he sauntered back in, hands in his pockets and mischief in his tone. "I knew it was only a matter of time, Marceline," he teased. Approaching the stage, he latched his thumbs in his trouser pockets while one thick brow angled high, gray eyes twinkling with humor. "At your service, Miss Murphy—how may I assist?"

Flustered, Marcy wrung the script in her hands with a nervous glaze of her teeth. "P-Peter M-martin has the flu and Clyde's grandfather died," she blurted.

Tone somber, the edges of his mouth flickered as if fighting a smile. "My condolences."

Brows inching into a plea, she implored him with a pitiful look. "I need you to stand in, to play the father's role, just for tonight. Could you—*would* you?"

His eyes softened. "For you? Anything."

Relief whooshed from her lungs as she waved him up the stairs and handed him a script. "Oh, bless you!" she said, hooking his arm to drag him to an easy chair. "This is a scene on Christmas Eve where this poor family has almost no gifts and very little food, but their home is full of love." She pointed to his lines in the script. "You play the father, obviously—Jeremiah Brennan—and the scene begins with you reading the paper. A blizzard has the family housebound and the children are getting antsy, so you ask your wife—" She nodded to Adelaide, who sat wide-eyed in a rocker, face as pale as the snow-white knitting bunched in her lap, "to dance while your son plays the fiddle. It's a very tender scene that ends with a gentle kiss just before a stranger knocks on the door." She glanced up and smiled. "See? Not too difficult."

"What if I don't dance?" he asked, the sobriety of his tone giving her pause. He chuckled and gave her a wink. "Now, really, Marceline, would a true rogue not know how to dance?"

A smile twitched on her lips. "Then you must be quite good," she said with a spry tilt of her head.

He leaned close, his whisper brimming with fun. "Aye, and quite adept with a kiss."

Heat swarmed her cheeks as she wheeled around and clapped her hands. "Everyone, Patrick has graciously agreed to fill in for Peter tonight, so let's help him along, all right? Please take your places." She scurried over to position Holly's wheelchair at just the right angle by the painted wooden hearth that Patrick had made. Planting a kiss on the little girl's cheek, she tweaked Tillie's pigtail on her way down the stairs to sit in the first row with Julie.

"Lucky Adelaide," Julie whispered. "Sure wish *she*

were out of town so I could fill in for *her*." Her smile turned impish as she nudged Marcy's arm with an elbow. "Just once I'd like to find out what it would be like to be kissed by Patrick O'Connor..."

"It's a kiss on the cheek, Julie," Marcy reminded patiently, anxious to downplay the flutters in her chest over memories of his stolen kiss.

"I don't care if it's a kiss on my elbow," she said with a low chuckle, "I have a feeling danger lurks in the touch of that man's lips."

You have no idea, Jewels, and thank God! Marcy fanned herself with her script, suddenly warm at the memory of Patrick's kiss on her front porch. *Danger, indeed*, she thought with a sigh. But then, no more so than with his best friend, Marcy supposed, given Sam's brazen kisses downstairs. Squaring her shoulders, she blew the whistle around her neck to command the cast's attention, mentally vowing to "command" Sam's attention too, at least on the subject of moral restraint. And *soon*.

She glanced at the watch pinned to her bodice and then smiled at the cast. "I'd like to run through the entire second act at least once since I think it still needs some work. It's important we create a warm family atmosphere for this scene because it underscores the true blessings of God, not only for this family, but for the audience as well, despite the obvious lack of presents and food. So try to imagine this is Christmas Eve in your own home to help conjure the glow of this special holiday, shall we?" Marcy's gaze swept over the cast and halted at the look of dejection on Tillie's face, suddenly reminded of the tragedy of her home life. "Or wait—do you remember the wonderful cast party Father Fitzgibbons and Sister Francine had for all of you in the center last week?" Marcy was relieved when

Tillie's eyes lit with excitement. "Well, try to think of this scene like that, okay?" She turned to thirteen-year-old Bobby Simmons who stood with his fiddle at his side. "Ready, Bobby?"

"Yes, ma'am."

"Adelaide—you'll have to take the lead as much as possible with Patrick, helping him as needed, all right?"

The poor thing gulped so hard, Marcy swore she could hear it, and the girl's face was as red as the cranberries that looped the Christmas tree prop. "Yes, ma'am," she whispered, peeking up at Patrick with so much trepidation that Marcy had to stifle a smile. Almost a year younger than Marcy, sweet Adelaide was painfully shy, and yet on stage she blossomed. Until tonight, apparently, the prospect of dancing *with* and being kissed *by* the Southie's leading Lothario obviously unnerving her. And yet, it was Adelaide's shyness with boys, be it Peter or Patrick, that was the weak spot in act two, and somehow Marcy had a gut feeling Patrick could help. She'd watched his tenderness with both Tillie and Holly and his big-brother camaraderie with the smaller boys, playing catch during breaks, and she sensed he had a gift with people. He winked at Adelaide, and Marcy's lips quirked. Especially women—young *or* old.

"Then, let's get started. Tillie, you have the first line, I believe." Marcy nodded at Adelaide who perched on a love seat borrowed from the convent, commencing to knit while Patrick sat reading a newspaper in an easy chair donated by Father Fitz. Each child took their place—Bobby practicing his fiddle in the corner while Holly's brother Nate played marbles with Michael Sherwood on the floor. Tillie played jacks with Becky Peterson next to Holly, who sat reading a book.

"Mama, I'm bored," Tillie said with a wide yawn,

"can we go outside and play in the snow?"

"Good heavens no, darling," Adelaide said in her most maternal tone. "It's frigid outside, sweetheart, and it's almost time for bed."

"But it's Christmas Eve, Mama," Becky piped in, "can't we start our party for Jesus tonight—just a little? I want to celebrate."

"So do I," Tillie shouted, jumping up to plunk hands on her hips. "And Holly does too, don't you, Holly?" She turned to Holly who looked like an angel in a cream chiffon dress. Holly nodded with a sweet smile while Tillie folded her hands to beg. "Please, Mama, can we, please, please?"

Sneaking a nervous peek at Patrick, Adelaide glanced at the clock over the wooden mantle and released a tired sigh. "I'm sorry, children, but it's really too late for a party tonight—"

"Excuse me, Mrs. Brennan," Patrick said with a grand rise from his chair, script in hand, "but may I remind you that in the Brennan household on Christmas Eve, it's never too late for a party." Children's squeals rose to the rafters as he laid his newspaper aside and promptly offered Adelaide his hand. "May I have this dance?"

Adelaide had no trouble playing the part of a flustered wife as she stared up at Patrick with wide eyes and rosy cheeks. "B-but, Jeremiah, it's nigh p-past ten, and the children really need to be in b-bed ..."

"Nonsense," Patrick bellowed, appearing to enjoy his role as husband and father. He plucked Adelaide up and into his arms, then surprised them all with a quick whirl and a dramatic dip back that burnished Adelaide's cheeks. The children all giggled while he quickly glimpsed at his script and then at Bobby. "Robert—music, if you please."

The lively sound of Bobby's fiddle filled the auditorium while Patrick bowed to his "wife" and attempted to dance with Adelaide, whose smile, unfortunately, was as stiff as her body. Marcy chewed the edge of her lip when Adelaide missed a line, wishing there was some way she could help her relax. She leaned close to Julie, her voice a whisper. "The poor thing needs somebody to show her how it's done, Julie—would you mind?"

Julie turned, brows elevated a full inch. "Oh, no you don't—not me. I'm all talk when it comes to Patrick O'Connor, and you know it. Goodness, I'm likely to be more tongue-tied than poor Addie. Why don't *you* show her how it's done since the man obviously has no effect on you?"

No effect? Marcy worked hard not to gulp, sucking in a deep breath instead. "All right, I will," she said, ignoring an annoying flip in her belly. Rising to her feet with a firm tilt of her jaw, she blew her whistle and marched up the stairs to the stage, hoping her smile softened her "bossy" stance. She ignored Patrick's twinkling gaze and tucked an arm to Adelaide's waist. "Addie, sweetheart, I know you're nervous about this scene, so would you like me to show you how I envision it?"

A lump bobbed in Adelaide's throat. "Yes, ma'am, that might help."

"All right, first I'll show you what you're doing, then I'll show you how I'd like to see you do it instead—would that be okay?"

The young girl nodded and stepped aside while Marcy moved in to stand in front of Patrick. Giving him a crisp smile, she calmly took his hands in hers in a matter-of-fact manner, then lifted them to a dancing position while she glanced at Bobby over her shoulder.

"Music, Bobby, if you please." Stomach skittering, she turned to Patrick with a lift of her brows. "Shall we dance, Mr. Brennan?"

A smile eased across his lips. "My pleasure, *Mrs. Brennan* ..." Taking the lead, he slowly whirled her to the music with effortless grace while Marcy did her best to look stiff as a board, no easy feat with Patrick's obvious mastery of dance.

"See, Addie, you just have to forget that Patrick is the Southie's most notorious rogue," Marcy said with a tease in her tone that elicited several chuckles from the cast. "Or that Peter is the boy in your class that Sister Francine always sends to Father Fitz." She paused to smile at Adelaide, grateful to see a semblance of a smile on the girl's face as well. "Instead, focus on playing the part of an actress who is simply dancing with her husband ... like this." Returning her attention to Patrick, Marcy gave him a perfunctory nod, almost breathless when he took control with a graceful spin as fluid as the flow of Bobby's music. In his arms, she felt lighter than air and with little or no effort, she giggled as they danced, her cheeks flushed with fun while the rest of the cast clapped in time. With an odd bit of reluctance, Marcy stopped and pulled away, then laughed when everyone in the auditorium gave them a rousing ovation. "Why, thank you," she said to the cast, pulse racing from the exertion. She turned to Patrick and gave him a playful curtsy. "And thank you, Mr. O'Connor—you make an excellent husband and dance partner."

Patrick bowed at the waist, the intensity in his eyes at odds with the mischievous smile on his face. "As do you, *Mrs. O'Connor*."

The obvious slip of tongue caught Marcy by surprise, prompting a queer feeling to curl in her stomach. She whirled around. "Did you see the difference, Adelaide?"

The young girl giggled and nodded, shooting Patrick a shy smile.

Marcy gave her a quick squeeze. "All right, then — you can do it, Addie," she whispered in her ear, "I have faith in you, and I'll be praying, okay?"

"Yes, ma'am," Adelaide said with a deep draw of air.

"Okay, everyone, back in position, please, and we'll take it from the top." Marcy hurried off the stage and returned to her seat, eyes fixed on Adelaide while she whispered a prayer.

"So, how was it?" Julie teased. "You seemed to enjoy yourself a little too much up there, if you ask me."

Marcy ignored her—and the heat in her cheeks—to follow Adelaide and Patrick as they danced with far greater ease than before. "I think she may have it," Marcy said, her voice tentative with hope.

Julie chuckled. "No, *he's* the one who has it—that magical charm that just naturally sweeps all women off their feet. Except you, I suppose, which is a good thing." She tweaked Marcy's shoulder. "At least for me and my brother."

"What on earth ...?" Marcy sat straight up when Patrick broke with the script to swoop Tillie up in his arms. He spun her in an impromptu dance that stole all objection from Marcy's tongue before she could even utter a word.

"What's he doing?" Julie asked, the very question stuck in Marcy's throat as the actors on stage ceased being a cast to merge into a joyful family where Adelaide danced with her "sons" and Patrick with his "daughters." So natural was the jubilation and unscripted revelry that Marcy watched in awe as the family on stage embraced her with a longing for just such a family of her own. In the midst of the merriment, Patrick squatted before Holly to whisper in her ear, and in a clutch of Marcy's heart, he gently lifted her from her chair. With playful tenderness, he twirled her in his arms, her cream chiffon dress flying in the breeze while her giggles flew in the air, the little girl's joy as contagious as the tears that glazed Marcy's face.

"Oh, Marce, tell me you're going to keep the scene just as he's done it," Julie said with an equal amount of emotion.

Marcy grinned and swiped at her eyes. "Oh, yes," she whispered with a sniff and a chuckle, "and I just may appoint the rogue director as well."

Julie's sigh blew warm in her ear. "I'll tell you what—the man may be a rogue, but you have to admit—he's a rogue with an awfully big heart."

Marcy swallowed hard, ashamed at just how much she had misjudged him. "That he is, Jewels," she whispered, suddenly no longer seeing him as a rogue at all. "That he is."

Chapter Nineteen

"Gosh, that was the most fun I ever had," Tillie said with a giggle, skipping alongside Patrick while he walked her, Julie, and Marcy down Tremain Street on their way home.

"Me too, squirt." Patrick tugged on her pigtail, inhaling the scent of wood smoke while the trill of tree frogs buzzed in the unseasonably cool air like excitement buzzed in his brain. The invigoration of filling in for Peter tonight as the male lead had taken him by surprise, allowing him to be a part of something that stirred a deep longing inside. Somehow, the glow of that make-believe family instilled a hope that someday he, too, might be a part of a close-knit circle of love that would envelop him with such joy and hope, redeeming him from his own barren upbringing. His quiet sigh drifted out as Tillie grasped his hand, the connection of family—no matter how make-believe—a balm to his lonely soul. He was grateful Sam was working tonight so he could escort the ladies home on his own, somehow prolonging this magical feeling. He squeezed Tillie's hand. "Well, we'll just have to see if Miss Murphy will allow us to do it again," he said with a sideways grin at Marcy.

"Oh, she'll let you, all right," Julie said with a

smirk. "You had her blubbering like a baby."

"Julie Mariah O'Rourke!" Marcy halted with a turn on the sidewalk, mouth agape. "As if you weren't mopping up your own buckets of tears!" Her gaze skimmed past Julie to Patrick, brow arched. "And you, Patrick O'Connor," she said with a noticeable squirm of lips, "railroading the script to steal the show—you should be ashamed." Her eyes twinkled as she delivered a mock glare, wagging a finger at him in obvious tease. "Ashamed you didn't audition for the part of the father, you scamp." She grinned. "You're a natural, you know."

A natural. Her words made him heady ... like he suspected the woman herself would do ... if God answered his prayers.

"But what if it doesn't work ... what if God says no?"

"Either way, Patrick ... you'll encounter a peace unlike any you've experienced before ..."

Patrick tempered his hope with a slow exhale and a melancholy smile. "No, not a 'natural,' Marcy," he said quietly, "just someone who wants a large, happy family as badly as you."

The blue eyes blinked, as if he'd taken her by surprise, and his pulse skipped several beats. *Oh, give me a chance, Marceline, and let me truly take you by surprise ...*

"Patrick, can you give me a piggyback ride the rest of the way?" Tillie peered up, those luminous hazel eyes tugging his heart, as always.

"Your wish is my command, milady," he said with a sweep of her tiny body into the air and onto his back.

She quickly dug her heels in with a giggle. "Giddy-up!"

Julie tickled Tillie's waist. "Goodness, Patrick, my

A Light in the Window

feet are killing me—can I be next?"

Julie's tease unleashed a bit of the devil in him and he slid her a sideways smile with a shuttered look that assessed her head to toe. "Although you're just a sprite of a thing, Julie O'Rourke," he said with a lazy smile, "I'm not sure I'm up to the task." He gave her a wink that promptly colored her cheeks in the flicker of the gas streetlamp overhead. "But I'm always game to try." His gaze eased past to Marcy, stuttering his pulse. "And you too, Marceline, if you promise not to kick too hard." Hope swelled in his chest when she offered a shy grin.

"I wanna go fast," Tillie announced, spurring him on with another flap of her heels, and Patrick jogged the remaining block to her tenement flat. Reaching behind to grab her by the waist, he whisked her into his arms and up in the air, braids and shrieks soaring along with her giggles.

When Julie and Marcy caught up, he deposited a kiss to Tillie's forehead and set her down, squatting to give her a tight hug. "G'night, squirt," he said with a ruffle of her hair.

"G'night, Atrick." She flew at Marcy and then Julie, giving each of them a giant hug around their skirts. "G'night, Miss Murphy, Miss O'Rourke." She peeked up at Marcy, a bit of the imp in her eyes. "Would it be wrong to pray Peter doesn't get well for a while so Patrick can be my dad?"

Patrick's heart stalled in his chest.

Marcy stooped to take Tillie's hands in hers, lips twitching as if she were fighting a smile. "Yes, it would, Miss Dewey, but how about I have Patrick go through the scene one more time, just to show Peter how it should be done? Would that work?"

"I guess," Tillie said with a heavy sigh. "Better than

nothing." She turned to clutch Patrick's legs one more time before trudging toward her flat, her wave listless as she wagged her hand in the air. "G'night, everybody."

"G'night, Tillie," Patrick called, wishing more than anything that Tillie were his sister so he could just take her home. And yet the very thought unearthed a gloom he worked so hard to hide beneath his carefree and easy-going façade. Because other than being spared the occasional beatings at the hand of her mother's no-good beau, there was very little happiness he could offer within the walls of his not-so-happy home.

"She idolizes you, you know," Marcy said softly as they continued their trek, "which I have to admit, shames me a wee bit because you see, in the beginning …" She glanced up with a sheepish tease. "I wasn't sure that was such a good thing—you know, the questionable influence of a notorious scoundrel on a sweet little girl." She sighed, cushioning the blow of a first impression she obviously now believed to be wrong.

Only it wasn't, Patrick realized, inwardly wincing at how selfish he'd been in the past, focusing on his own needs without caring about those of anyone else. He slipped his hands in his pockets and gave an awkward shrug as they continued down the street to Julie's house, marveling at just how much he'd changed over the last few months. His chest constricted. *Since Marcy.* "It wasn't," he said quietly, "a good thing, that is, at least not in the past." He exhaled his regret. "But I'm working on it."

"Well, here we are—home, sweet, home." Julie stifled a yawn before she gave Marcy a hug, hands latched to her arms as she studied her in the moonlight. "You sure you don't want to spend the night? Mother promised French toast."

Marcy shook her head, the wisps of gold fluttering on her neck drawing Patrick's gaze. "No, better not. I promised Mother I'd help sew new curtains, bright and early." Her full lips curved in a beautiful smile. "If you and I spend half the night talking, I'm pretty sure there will be very little 'bright' or 'early.'"

Julie laughed. "All right, but I can't say Sam won't be disappointed."

Patrick averted his eyes to stare at the sidewalk, Julie's remark causing a twinge in his gut. *Yes, Sam, his best friend ... and Marcy's beau.*

Marcy laughed. "Not if it means more French toast for him," she teased. "Good night, Jewels—I'll be over later in the day to study, okay?"

"Sounds good, Marce. G'night, Patrick."

"Good night," Patrick said, waiting until she entered her house before continuing on. They walked in silence, Patrick suddenly nervous. His tongue felt so thick, it was several moments before he managed to eke out a comment. "Sounds like you and Sam have really hit it off." His voice was quiet.

She hugged her arms to her waist, as if the subject made her uncomfortable, but her soft tone told him all he needed to know, causing his heart to sink in his chest. "We get along well," she said carefully, "despite the unlikely match." A nervous chuckle toppled from her lips. "But then, like you, I've been part of the family since I was five, so it's a comfortable fit."

A comfortable fit. Patrick swallowed hard, his response stuck in his throat at the image conjured—Sam kissing Marcy, their bodies so close, the very thought seared the walls of his mind.

His silence must have given her pause because he sensed her tentative glance, and when she spoke, her tone was gentle with a hint of concern. "So, for me, it's the best of both worlds, you see. Not only am I able to grow close with a boy for whom I've had a school-girl crush since I was eight *and* spend time with his family I adore ..." Her hand lighted on his arm with a feather touch, halting both him and the breath in his lungs. "But I have the added blessing of forging a dear friendship with his best friend as well."

A friendship. The words inflicted a blow to his hope as effectively as Marcy's hand had to his cheek the night she'd whacked him for kissing her on her porch. Forcing a casual air, he flashed a bright smile, determined to pursue the friendship Father Fitz suggested. "Then, a winning scenario all around, I'd say."

She grinned, her relief evident in the sparkle of her eyes. "Agreed." She peeked up with a curious smile. "So, Patrick ... how is your college fund coming and just exactly what field of study do you hope to pursue?"

You.

He returned her grin. "Well, by Christmas, I should have the funds needed for the spring semester at Boston College, where I hope to study journalism and English literature."

Her eyebrows rose considerably, as if she were surprised a rogue would entertain any field of study other than women. "Very impressive," she said with a wide span of eyes.

He laughed, the wonder in her tone coaxing another flash of teeth. "Yes, hard as it is to believe, Marceline, rogues can actually read and write too."

She had the grace to blush. "Touché. I seem to be prone to all kinds of misconceptions where you're concerned, so please forgive me."

"Nothing to forgive," he said, burying his hands in

his pockets. "Till now, my reputation for roguery far exceeded my aptitude for the written word, but that's about to change, come January."

"Really?" Her voice held an interest and respect he hadn't heard before, at least not when it came to him. Hands clasped like a little girl, she looked up with such a glow of enthusiasm, it plucked at his heart. "What do you hope to do with your life?"

Marry you, Marceline ... on my way to editorship of The Boston Herald. He cleared his throat, tamping down desires that may never be met. "I hope to write for the *Herald* someday. You may not know this, but I *was* editor of the St. Mary's Gazette two years running, as well as founder and first-year president of the Lantern Club."

She came to a dead stop, the whites of her eyes expanding along with the gape of her mouth. "*You? You're* responsible for the Lantern Club?" she whispered, almost in awe. "But how? Why?"

He chuckled. "Well, contrary to my dismal conduct record at St. Mary's, my grades in literature and English composition were actually pretty good, which is one of the reasons Father Fitz took me under his wing in the first place." He slid her a sideways grin. "I was in his office for detention so much, we discovered a mutual love of books and verse. Turns out we shared the same favorites—Mark Twain and Stephen Crane. So when I read that both Twain and Crane were part of a writers group that formed several years ago in New York, I was fascinated."

"I can certainly see why," she said, her nod of approval a balm to his pride.

He continued, a warm glow from her interest slowly spreading through his chest. "Yes, well it seems this group of esteemed writers actually shared their work during literary banquets held every Saturday evening. One of the members would read a piece they'd written, which the others would then critique. Only negative criticism was allowed, mind you, and the highest regard a reading could be given was complete silence." He shrugged his shoulders, hands in his pockets. "So I suggested to Father Fitz that St. Mary's do the same, and he agreed."

She slowed in front of her house, turning toward him with a hand on the gate. "Goodness," she said with a chuckle, "you couldn't have shocked me more than if you told me you were going to be a priest."

A slow grin curled his lips as he ducked his head to scratch the back of his neck. "Well, I can assure you most wholeheartedly, Miss Murphy, that *that* will *never* happen."

She laughed and opened the gate. "Thank you for walking me home." She paused to study him with a tilt of her head, her smile ebbing considerably. "I misjudged you terribly," she whispered, a hint of sadness in her eyes, "Can you ever forgive me?"

He found himself staring, certain he'd never met a more beautiful woman—inside and out. "I told you before, Marceline, there's nothing to forgive," he said quietly. "You weren't far off in your judgments, I'm ashamed to say, nor with your slap." His smile was sheepish as he rubbed the side of his face, his beard rough against his palm. "In fact, I suspect you may have knocked some sense into me that night on your porch because ever since, I ..." He dropped his gaze to the street, unwilling for her to see the longing in his eyes. "Find myself wanting to be a better man."

When she didn't respond, he glanced up, shocked to see tears glimmering. She gave him a tremulous smile while she quickly swiped at her eyes. "That is possibly the nicest thing anyone has ever said to me." She drew in a deep breath and slowly released it, expelling shaky air. "Thank you."

"No," he whispered, "it's I who needs to thank you."

She shook her head. "But I didn't do anything," she insisted, nibbling the edge of her lip with a guilty smile. "Except slap you silly."

A grin creased his lips. "That you did, but then I deserved it for losing my Irish temper, which," he said with a note of levity, "it appears has met its match."

She chuckled and extended her palm. "How about I forgive you and you forgive me, and then God can forgive us both? Deal?"

He studied her with a squint, ignoring her hand. "You know, I see lots of people who profess God, but not many who live it, at least not like you." He hesitated, trying to understand the quiet depth of faith she seemed to possess. "God is pretty important to you, isn't he?" he said softly, hardly believing he was pursuing a conversation about God with a woman.

Her hand slowly sank to the side of her skirt where her fingers fiddled with the edge of her pocket, gaze drifting to the ground. "Like the air that I breathe," she whispered, so low he almost missed it. When she finally looked up, more tears glistened along with a fierce passion that seemed out of character for the calm and gentle woman he was privileged to know. "No," she said carefully, chin elevated and eyes bright, "He *is* the air that I breathe. The reason I live each day with hope despite trial or tribulation. The strength in my bones when I'm too weak to go on. The very presence in my heart that brings peace and joy to my soul." A soft smile lighted on her lips as her gaze locked with his. "And," she said quietly, the barest trace of sympathy edging her smile, "something I suspect you might relate to as well—the only One Who has ever truly taken my loneliness away."

He blinked, blood heating his cheeks at the notion that she could read his mind, see into his soul the ugly truth he worked so hard to hide. He was alone. No matter the women that jockeyed for his attention or the mother or brother that occupied his home or even the best friend who knew him better than anyone else or a kind parish priest. The simple truth was, he was a lonely human being. A man searching for love through the affections of pretty women ... or peace at the bottom of a bottle or mug. A chill shivered his soul. And somehow the woman before him knew it, as surely as he knew it himself.

He coughed to deflect his embarrassment, stepping back to plunge his hands in his pockets once again. "Well, I guess I better let you go—"

He stilled at the touch of her hand, the terrifying gentleness in her eyes. "He's a force to be reckoned with, Patrick, and you will be too ... with Him by your side." And lifting on tiptoe, she pressed the softest of kisses to his cheek, paralyzing him to the spot. "Good night, dear friend," she whispered.

He followed her to the door with his eyes, unable to move or breath or blink until he heard the click of the lock, and then he sucked in air like sustenance, never surer that she was meant to be his. Bowing his head, he beseeched the Almighty right then and there for the very woman who was leading him home—to God, to the family he'd longed for, and to a life he never dared to imagine.

A force to be reckoned with. He shook his head. *Him?* Exhaling slowly, he made his way down the cobblestone street. "No, Marceline," he whispered, the faintest of smiles tipping the edges of his mouth. "That would be you."

Chapter Twenty

"Goodness, what a day," Marcy said with a groan in the spacious kitchen of St. Mary's Center, sliding into a chair at the scarred wooden table now littered with dirty dessert plates. She offered a tired smile to Julie, Evan, and Patrick, each equally exhausted, no doubt, after one of the busiest Saturdays ever. "How many meals did we serve today, do we know?"

Evan took the last bite of his pie—the sweet reward Miss Clara promised after their full day of service, both chocolate cream and cherry—then pushed his empty dish away. "Haven't tallied it yet, Marcy, but it's a definite record, judging from the lines that wrapped around the building for both lunch and supper." He sank back in his chair, body sagging along with his smile. "Which, I'm not sure is a good thing or a bad thing."

"It's always a good thing to help people in need," Julie soothed, patting his arm.

His smile perked up. "I guess it is, isn't it?" He covered her hand with his own before she could pull away. "I'll tell you what, Miss O'Rourke, after we tackle these dishes, I believe I'll be in 'need' of a soda at Robinson's—you care to 'help' *me* out?"

Julie blinked several times, a blush seeping into her

cheeks as red as the cherry juice seeping onto her plate. "Uh ... sure, Evan." She and Marcy exchanged a look before she returned his gaze with a gulp. "I'd like that."

Glancing at the clock on the wall, Marcy jumped up, her energy suddenly restored now that Evan had *finally* asked Julie out. The two of them had been flirting and fawning over each other for a month now, and Marcy couldn't be happier. "Well, it's six-thirty on a Saturday night, you two, so you'll need to get going to beat the crowd."

"Oh, no, you don't," Julie said, hopping up to collect dirty dishes from around the table. "I'm not leaving until this place is spic-and-span—"

Marcy blocked her at the sink with a stubborn bent of her jaw. "Oh, yes you are." She snatched the pile of dishes from her hands and plopped them on the counter with a clunk. "You and Evan were here before anyone else this morning, so you're officially off the clock—right, Miss Clara?"

"Oh, laws, yes!" The old woman motioned Julie toward the door before she turned to pour a pot of boiling water into the cold rinse in the sink. "Besides," she said, dumping the rest into the dishwater. "I'm tired of looking at you two, now git."

"B-but there's too much to do—the dishes, the floor, the dining room tables to be wiped. You n-need help—" Julie stuttered, ignoring Evan as he stood there with her jacket in hand.

"I beg your pardon," Patrick said, tone indignant. He rose from his chair to gather the rest of the utensils and dishes. "What am I—a piece of the furniture?"

Marcy couldn't help it—her lips crooked in a smile. "Of course not," she said with an innocent tilt of her head, "Miss Clara already has a dumbwaiter ..."

Julie giggled while she slipped an arm into the

jacket that Evan held for her. "Oh, good one, Marce," she said with a wink in Patrick's direction.

"Very funny, Miss Murphy." Patrick strolled to the sink with a dry smile, depositing the dirty dishes on the counter. He added more soap powder to the dishwater and swished with his fingers till bubbles puffed high. "Just for that, you wash."

Miss Clara chuckled and pinched his cheek. "Well, jumpin' Je-hosaphat, he may be dumb, but he sure is cute."

"You ladies are treading on awfully thin ice here." Patrick dried his hands on a towel before tossing it over his shoulder and rolling the sleeves of his shirt.

Marcy scooped up a handful of bubbles and blew them in his face with an imp of a smile. "You mean thin 'bubbles,' don't you?"

"Okay, that's it." Patrick snatched the towel from his shoulder and twisted until it was taut, snapping it at Marcy's skirt. "We are officially at war."

"All right, you two," Miss Clara said, "I'm declaring a truce until those dishes are done, you hear?" She pushed Julie and Evan out the door. "And, you two—skedaddle—before I change my mind."

"You heard the boss, Miss O'Rourke," Evan said with a jaunty salute. Palm to Julie's back, he guided her through the door with a broad smile. "Good night, all."

"Good night," Marcy called, tying Miss Clara's oversized apron around her blue muslin skirt. "Oh, and Julie—tomorrow—are we studying at your house or mine?"

"Yours," Julie shouted before Evan quickly closed the door.

Miss Clara bustled over to the pitiful remains of cherry pie with a low rumble of laughter. "S'pose I best get these leftovers wrapped up and over to the rectory or I'll be saying Hail Marys till the Second Coming." She shot Marcy and Patrick a narrow gaze while she parceled the rest of the pie onto a plate. "That is, if I can trust you two to keep them bubbles in the sink and not flying through the air."

Patrick paused, mid-scrape on a dirty plate. "Why, I'm wounded, Miss Clara," he said, a deep crimp above his nose that was clearly at odds with the twinkle in his eye. "I'll have you know that every water fight in this kitchen has been waged by a woman."

"Mmm-huh." A dubious smile curled on the old woman's lips while doubt emanated from every pore of her pleasingly plump face, dark skin dewy with sweat from working in a hot kitchen all day. Eyes shrewd, she pursed her lips in a smirk as she swaddled the pie plate in wax paper. "I wasn't born in a cave, Mister Patrick, so Miss Murphy best be nigh as dry as week-old corn biscuits when I come back, or there'll be some paying the piper, understand?"

"Me?" Patrick slapped a hand to his chest, muscled forearm tan against his wilted white shirt while a dishtowel dangled from his fingers. "What about her?"

"But I'm the 'angel of mercy,' remember?" Marcy said with a playful flutter of lashes and a quick roll of her sleeves. Grinning, she laid a towel on the side of the sink to absorb the rinse water from freshly washed dishes.

"Angel, my foot." Patrick slapped the towel over his shoulder before resorting to the adorable little-boy grin that used to grate on Marcy's nerves, the flash of dimples now making her smile. "You *saw* her, Miss Clara—the little brat blew bubbles in my face."

"And what a handsome face it is," Miss Clara said, displaying a few dimples of her own. "Now, you two get to work while I deliver this pie, you hear? I need to discuss a few things with Father Fitz, but then I'll be back to make sure you haven't drowned each other, so behave!" Flapping a pudgy hand in the air, Miss Clara bounded out the door.

"'Behave'?" Marcy said with a nudge of Patrick's arm, mischief tilting her lips. She bumped him out of the way and plunged her hands into the suds. "Does she even know you, Patrick 'Rogue' O'Connor?"

A grin eased across his lips as he sidled over to butt a hip to the counter. "I'll have you know I've all but abdicated that title." He took the wet plate she handed him and proceeded to dry.

"Have you, now?" Marcy cocked her head to study him, grateful she and Patrick had become good friends over the last month. Good enough that they were now able to laugh and talk about everything, from religion to politics to her relationship with Sam. *To a point*, she thought with a glimmer of guilt, well aware that Sam's carnal nature was not a subject she cared to broach with his best friend *or* his sister, no matter how much it bothered Marcy of late. Yes, Sam had made her feel safe and protected with his gentlemanly behavior over the last so many months, but over the last few weeks? She sensed a dangerous change coming—in chaste kisses that had suddenly become more passionate. Shaking off the unsettling thought, she offered Patrick a teasing smile. "And what exactly is 'all but' if I may be so bold to ask?"

He gave her a wink, the gray eyes sparkling like polished pewter. "'All but' means I'm only seeing three women at a time instead of six and one visit to Brannigan's a week instead of four."

She shook her head and laughed, tackling a dirty pot. "Well, that's certainly an improvement, I suppose."

"I thought so," he quipped, drying the utensils she'd

placed on the towel. He took extra time to buff a large serving spoon. "And between Father Fitz's influence and yours, my reputation is sure to shine more than this spoon."

"Indeed." Her smile softened as she handed him a wet pot, fondness in her gaze. "I'm proud of you, Patrick—not only for the changes you've made in your own life, but how those changes have affected Sam as well." She nibbled the edge of her lip, never believing she'd have Patrick O'Connor to thank for curbing Sam's wild ways. "Goodness, and his family thinks *I'm* the good influence."

The laughter in his eyes mellowed into gentle affection that spread warmth through Marcy's chest like Miss Clara's oven on baking day. "You are," he said quietly, the intensity of his gaze tripping her pulse before he quickly looked away. He plucked another pot from her hands, focusing on it instead of her face. "You've been a good influence on us both, and I'm grateful for that." He dried the pot and put it away, finally turning to face her with a smile that seemed melancholy. "Sam's a lucky man."

The warmth in her chest crept up to her cheeks. "I'm not so sure he'd agree," she said with a hint of jest. "Being reined in by a woman he's not 'officially' courting."

"No, not officially …" Patrick's tone sounded flat, as if he might not approve of the casual understanding she and Sam shared.

She peeked at him out of the corner of her eye, the tight clamp of his jaw convincing her she had an ally in the reformation of Samuel O'Rourke. "I wonder—do you feel the way Sam does? You know, about postponing marriage till later?"

Marcy blinked in surprise when a ruddy blush

crawled up Patrick's neck to bloody his cheeks. The spatula he was drying slipped from his hands and bounced on the floor, landing on top of Marcy's shoe.

He scooped it up, his face completely aflame. "Of course not," he said, voice hoarse. "Believe me, I've had my fill of dallying with women—I'm hoping to settle down with the right one, and the sooner, the better."

"Really?" Marcy spun to face him, the barest twinge of jealousy that Sam didn't feel the same.

Patrick studied her with a keen eye. "Yeah, really. You and Father Fitz have changed my mind on a lot of things lately, Marceline, including marriage." Two tiny ridges bunched in his brow. "I know Sam has always professed he wasn't the marrying kind, but I just figured after courting a girl like you, that would change."

So did I ... It was her turn to blush, enough heat surging to her hairline to singe her eyebrows. Swiftly wringing out the dishrag, she whirled around to wipe off the table, loathe for Patrick to see the embarrassment in her face. She strove for nonchalance. "Actually, Sam and I are having too much fun getting to know each other to worry about anything more at this juncture." Cupping a palm to the edge of the table, she swiped the remaining crumbs in her hand and turned, her body going cold at the fierce look of concern on Patrick's face.

"I see." The urgency of his next words—barely audible—fairly shimmered in his eyes. "Well, stay the course then, Marcy, please," he whispered, "and stay strong."

Heat scorched her face all over again. "W-what do you mean?" she asked weakly. But she knew exactly what he meant, and the warning in his eyes told her that

A Light in the Window

he knew too. *Sam's carnal nature.* "I'll w-wipe the tables in the d-dining room," she stuttered, bolting to the sink to rinse out the rag before wheeling around, desperate to escape.

He stayed her with a gentle hand, paralyzing her limbs. "You forget I'm a rogue," he said quietly, "and Sam's best friend for nigh on fifteen years. I know how he thinks, how he feels, how relentless he can be when there's something he wants ..."

Her eyelids flickered closed while a knot dipped in her throat.

She felt his grip tighten, as if he wanted to protect her. "The reason Sam and I were both attracted to you in the first place was because you're different, Marcy, special, a woman of strength and moral conviction." His thumb kneaded her arm, its touch suddenly gentle. "Don't change for anyone ... *please.*"

"Of course not," she whispered, his words infusing her with the resolve to curtail all time alone with Sam. She drew in a cleansing breath and patted his hand, avoiding his eyes. "Thank you, Patrick, but I'm fine, truly." Chin high, she hurried into the dining room to complete her tasks, returning just as he was finishing up. "Shall we toss to see who mops the floor?" she asked, forcing a levity she didn't quite feel.

He slipped the now damp dishtowel over a brass hook bolted to the side of the cabinet and turned, a glimmer of tease invading his serious gaze. "Odd, I wouldn't have pegged you for a gambling woman, Miss Murphy." He slanted against the counter, arms folded.

She flipped a stray curl over her shoulders and sashayed into the kitchen, dishrag in hand and a smirk on her face. "Of course I am, Mr. O'Connor—I gambled on friendship with you, didn't I?"

Fishing a coin from his pocket, he shot her a grin.

"That was a matter of intelligence, not risk." He lobbed a nickel at her, and she caught it one-handed, coaxing a throaty chuckle from his lips. "Why do I get the feeling you've done this before?"

"Because I have," she said with a cocky smile, feeling a bit reckless. She strutted over and fisted her hand, thumb tucked and dishrag dangling while she positioned the coin on top. "Julie and I used to toss to see who got to read a book first, you know."

His teeth gleamed white. "How decadent."

Her smile was smug. "No, Mr. Wiseacre, 'decadent' will be me enjoying an oatmeal cookie at the table with feet propped while *you* mop the floor." She arched a brow. "Ready?" With practiced dexterity, she popped her thumb beneath the nickel, and it launched in the air, her breathing suspended while the coin toppled over and over.

Plunk. With a devious smile, Patrick snatched it just inches from her hand and slapped it on top of his. "Call it."

She pursed her lips, eyes squinted as she tried to visualize which side of the coin it might be. "Heads," she said with a confident hike of her chin, praying her intuition was correct.

His groan rose in the air when he lifted his palm. "I hate mopping the floor," he muttered, slipping the nickel back in his pocket.

Giddy over her win, she giggled. "Don't be a baby, Patrick, a little soapy water won't hurt you." Mischief bubbled up along with her laughter as she sloshed the rag in the sudsy dishwater and flicked it at him, intending only to splatter a few drops his way. She gasped when the rag accidentally flew from her hand. Eyes wide, her jaw dropped as it pelted him in the face and fell to the floor, leaving soapy water sluicing down his dark-bristled cheek. "Oh, I am so s-sorry ..." Her voice trailed off into a fit of giggles she could no more stop than the water stains that dribbled down his trousers into a puddle at his feet.

"Oh, you shouldn't have done that, darlin' ..." he said with a glint of retaliation. Whisking the sopping rag up off of the floor, he squeezed it with a lightning thrust of his arm, showering Marcy's torso—and Miss Clara's apron front—with soapy water.

Marcy shrieked and giggled, but not before dousing Patrick's chest with a slash of her hand in the sink, slamming him with a wave of dirty dishwater before she darted away. Flushed with excitement, she felt like a little girl again, having a pillow fight with Julie. Adrenaline coursed while she scrambled to the other side of the table, her breathing hard and hands braced to a chair. "Come on—truce," she begged, tone breathless.

Dipping the dishrag into the dirty water once again, he casually tossed the sodden rag back and forth while he ambled toward the table with a wicked grin. "Sure, Marceline—right after I even the score."

Her stomach skittered as she pleaded, eyes darting to the door and back with a nervous laugh. "Miss Clara will be back any minute, and she said not to start any trouble."

Step by step, his grin never wavered as he rounded the table. "I didn't."

"I'll be good, I promise." Her body pulsed with adrenaline as she skirted the table in the opposite direction, praying Miss Clara would return before she got soaked.

His husky chuckle sent goose bumps up her arms. "I know—*good* and wet."

With a wild shriek she made a break for the door, laughing so hard, she didn't hear him coming until he whirled her around. Her laughter turned to squeals when she tried to get away, but he clamped a steel arm to her waist while he held the rag dangerously close to her neck. "Repeat after me," he whispered, eyes issuing a challenge. "Patrick, I'm a brat, I'm sorry, and I will never do this again."

Pulse sprinting, she giggled, eyes flicking from him to the rag in his hand, weighing her options. "And if I don't?"

One dark brow jutted high as his smile eased into a grin. "You won't have to bathe tonight, darlin'."

His words warmed both her cheeks and her temper. "You wouldn't," she dared.

"Only one way to find out." There was a bit of the devil in his eye, the rag dangling precariously close to her neck

Marcy sucked in a deep breath. "All right, Patrick," she said, skin tingling with mischief and eyes on the rag, "I'm a brat, I'm sorry, and I ... *won't* promise—" Lunging, she whipped the rag from his hands so fast, he never saw it coming, christening him with dirty dishwater like Father Fitz christened babies in the back of the church.

He hooked her waist before she could escape, and her high-pitch giggles merged with his husky laughter as she flailed in his arms, a death grip on the soppy rag thrashing over their heads. Dishwater flew every which way while he tried to reclaim it, but Marcy hid it behind her back with squeals of laughter. Locking her to his chest with one arm, he circled her waist with his other, his breath warm on her cheek as he grappled to claim the win.

"Give ... it ... up ... Patrick," she said, her words punctuated by shrieks and shallow rasps as she tried to wrestle free, "you will ... never win ..."

Her words seemed to paralyze him, and in a single heave of her breath, his body stilled against hers. She could feel the ragged rise and fall of his chest, the hot press of his arm at the small of her back, the wild hammering of her pulse in her ears. All at once, she was painfully aware of his nearness, bare inches away from the dark stubble that peppered his jaw. His hard-muscled chest was so close she could almost feel the dampness of his shirt while the familiar scent of spices and pine whirled her senses. His breathing was ragged like hers, warm and sweet with the faint scent of chocolate from his chocolate cream pie, and when his gaze lowered to her lips, heat coiled through her so strong, it sapped all moisture from her throat.

The silence roared like the blood in her ears as he stared, a battle waging in his eyes that eclipsed to a dark fervor, shocking her when it quivered her belly. "I will never give up, Marceline," he whispered, his lips parted to emit shallow breaths. Fire singed when his glance flickered to her mouth once again.

"T-take it ..." she whispered, alarm curling in her stomach. *Dear Lord, had he meant to kiss me?* Prodding the rag to his chest, she pushed him away while heat throbbed in her cheeks. She took an awkward step back, gaze on the floor as she buffed at her arms with brisk motion. "Goodness, Miss Clara will have our heads," she said with a nervous chuckle, unable to look at him even yet. "You win, Patrick—I surrender." She forced a casual tone and attempted to side-step him on her way to the broom closet.

Her heart seized when he halted her with a gentle hand. "Marcy ..." His voice was somber and steeped with regret. "I'm sorry ..."

"For what?" A deep voice sounded from the door, shattering what was left of Marcy's calm. Sam strolled in the kitchen, screen door slamming behind. His dark eyes flitted from Patrick's hand on Marcy's arm to her face, now sporting a blush that burned as much as Sam's scathing look. "What's going on here?"

Patrick slowly turned, bobbling the rag in his hand with a stiff smile. "Water fight." His light tone belied the tic in his jaw.

"Y-you're early," Marcy stammered, hurrying to give him a soft peck on the cheek.

Sam cocked his head, one thick brow jagging high. "Actually, I'm late." He shot a hard glance at Patrick before returning to Marcy with a cool air. "But it seems you were too preoccupied to notice."

"Knock it off, Sam—it was an innocent water fight and nothing more." Patrick made his way to the broom closet to retrieve a mop, ruddy color bleeding up the back of his neck. "Why don't you two head out, and I'll finish up."

Stomach roiling, Marcy hurried over to grab the mop from his hands. "No, I started the water fight, so I'll wash up the floor."

He gripped the handle, fingers strained white while he issued a grim smile. "I'll have you know I am not a welsher. I lost the toss fair and square—*I'll* mop the floor."

Sam plucked the mop from Patrick's hand. "Go," he said in a tone that brooked no argument. "I'll help Marcy finish up."

Patrick stared at his best friend, his tight-lipped hesitation constricting Marcy's chest. With a heavy exhale, he finally released his hold on the mop and proceeded to unroll and button his sleeves, eyes locked with Sam's. "Have it your way," he said in a clipped tone, and without a glance back, he left with a slam of the screen that rattled Marcy's nerves as much as it rattled the jamb of the door.

"I won't be but twenty minutes—" she said, reaching for the mop.

Sam held it away, eyeing her with concern. "What happened, Marcy?"

She blinked, cheeks burning from his scrutiny. "Nothing, I promise. It was just a water fight like Patrick said, horseplay between two friends, nothing more."

His tone was as tight as the muscles in his face. "No, Marceline, horseplay is innocent—what I saw was not. In fact, I've never seen two people look guiltier." He gripped her arm. "Did he kiss you?"

Her temper flared along with the heat in her cheeks. "For heaven's sake, Sam, *nothing* happened." She attempted to wrest the mop from his hand, but he held on, drawing her close. "I want the truth, Marcy—did he make advances to you?"

"No, of course not!" She pushed away, shocked that he was accusing his best friend, but no more so than over the desire she'd seen in his best friend's eyes. "What is wrong with you? Patrick and I are friends, nothing more. For heaven's sake, he's your best friend—don't you trust him?"

"In most things, yes, but not with you." He cupped her face with firm hands. "He wants you, Marceline, because you're a challenge ... and because you belong to me. So no, I don't trust him where you're concerned."

His words barbed, not only because of the rift she appeared to be creating between two best friends, but because of the implication that Patrick's friendship was merely pretense to lure her away. Her eyes softened at the look of vulnerability in Sam's eyes, something she'd never seen in him before, and somehow it drew her closer. She stroked his face with gentle fingers, his late-day beard rough against her palm. "You have nothing to worry about," she whispered, "I only have eyes for you ..."

He stared for several moments, thumbs grazing the hollows of her cheeks, and then with a low groan, he clutched her close. "I'm falling in love with you, Marceline," he murmured against her lips, gripping her as if he were afraid to let go. "And I don't want to lose you."

She melted against his strong chest, the citrus scent of Sam and soap swirling her senses and sweetening the moment. "You won't lose me." Her words sounded sure and strong to her own ears, relaxing his hold, but they whirled in her mind with the image of gray eyes that both warmed her body and chilled her soul.

"He wants you, Marceline, because you're a challenge ... and because you belong to me."

Hurt prickled that Patrick might actually be the scoundrel she always believed him to be instead of the honest friend she'd come to know and trust, intrigued by a challenge more than a friendship. Closing her eyes, she rested her head on Sam's chest, the thought provoking a profound sadness that ached more than it should. Either way, the look of longing she'd seen in his eyes tonight convinced her that noble or not, friendship with Patrick O'Connor was no longer an option.

At least, not for her.

Chapter Twenty-One

Patrick stormed down the busy street in a fury, three blocks away from the center before he even realized where he was. Halting on the sidewalk where neighbors milled and children played, he gouged the bridge of his nose to ease the headache that was just beginning to throb and almost wished Marceline Murphy had never come back to Boston. With a low growl, he bludgeoned a stone with the tip of his shoe, hurling it at a cast-iron post box, but the bullet-like ping provided little satisfaction for the angst in his gut. Ignoring the wide-eyed stares of little girls playing hopscotch, he continued on, head down and hands in his pocket. His jaw ground more than the electric streetcar that groaned along the tracks of Monroe Street, rumbling past horse-drawn trolleys and buggies.

He sucked in a deep breath to regain some semblance of calm, but frustration crawled in his chest all the more at the stark realization that Marcy belonged to Sam. No matter how natural it had felt to hold her in his arms, how painful the longing to caress her lips with his own, Sam was the one she was falling in love with, not him, and Sam was the one she wanted.

Guilt soured his stomach like bile, rising to parch

his throat with the need for a drink, anything to numb this sick feeling of coveting a woman who belonged to his best friend. The lure of Brannigan's was so strong, Patrick forced himself to turn off on a side street and head for home instead, no desire to seek comfort either with the bottle or in the arms of another girl. A harsh laugh erupted from his throat as he shook his head. The blasted woman had not only stolen his heart, she'd stolen his lifestyle as well—one that had given him a grim sense of satisfaction, no matter how misguided. And now he was stuck in a friendship with her, with no hope of anything more.

"Do you ... think with prayer, Father ... I have even the slightest chance to win her heart?"

"Actually, Mr. O'Connor, I'm of the opinion that you don't have the slightest chance without it."

He grunted and kicked at another rock, sending it disappearing into the dusky night along with his hope. It was pretty clear from the glow in her eyes whenever she looked at Sam that Patrick didn't stand a chance. For the first time in months, the realization that friendship with Marcy was all he might ever have settled in like a deep-throbbing ache. Hand to his eyes, he paused on the sidewalk, not sure whether he could continue to be friends with her or not. Not only did she threaten his heart, but his allegiance to Sam as well, knowing full well that Sam had designs on Marcy that were not in her best interest. Anger surged all over again at the look on her face when he'd warned her not to give in. It had been his fear talking, concerns over Sam's motives with her and nothing more, but she'd validated his unease with a flicker of her eyes and a telling blush. In that moment, he wanted nothing more than to take a swing at his best friend, but that wasn't the answer. No, if he couldn't love Marcy the way he wanted, then God help him, he'd love her the only way that he could—making sure his best friend treated her with respect.

God help him? Bitter irony curved the edges of his mouth into a wry smile. *Yes, God help him, indeed.* He expelled a noisy breath and continued on, hardly able to believe how much Marcy had changed him, introducing him to a God he'd had no desire to know. A God who became clearer and clearer to him with every word out of Marcy's mouth and those of Father Fitz, leading him down a path that had given him a semblance of peace for the first time in his life. All at once, an overpowering urge to play basketball with Father Fitz rose within, far stronger than the need for a drink, but he plodded on toward home nonetheless, reluctant to chance a repeat encounter with Marcy and Sam.

"O'Connor!"

A silent groan stalled in his chest as he halted, unwilling to butt heads with his best friend, not when he had an itchy fist and frayed temper. He kept walking, hoping Sam would just go away.

"What the blazes are you doing?" Sam shouted, jerking Patrick around with a hard clamp of his arm.

Patrick shoved him back, his ire suddenly white hot all over again. "I suggest you run back to Marcy, O'Rourke, because I'm in no mood for you right now."

"No?" Sam leaned in, fists clenched at his sides. "But you were sure in the mood for *her* tonight, weren't you?"

A tic pulsed in Patrick's jaw as he tried to harness his temper. "It-was-an-innocent-water-fight, you moron, which is more than I can say for you when it comes to your intentions with Marcy."

"Innocent for her maybe," Sam spat out, "and you know nothing of my intentions."

"I know you, O'Rourke, and so help me, if you don't do right by her, I'll bloody you good." Patrick curled his fingers into fists, just itching to vent.

A curse hissed from Sam's lips as he turned away, hands low on his hips. He spun back, dark brows slashed low with concern. "Blast it, Patrick, what the blazes are we doing? I don't want Marcy to come between us."

"Then treat her right," Patrick snapped, a nerve throbbing in his temple like jealousy throbbed in his gut.

Sam exhaled and gouged fingers through his hair. "Look, I'll admit that my intentions with Marcy weren't all that honorable in the beginning, but that's all changed now. I plan to marry her."

Patrick's laugh was harsh. "And when will that be? After you ruin her?"

Another swear word defiled the air. "What's that supposed to mean?"

The veins in Patrick's temple pulsed as he slanted in. "It means you're pressuring her, aren't you? I know you, and I could sense it in her manner tonight. You're up to our old tricks again, O'Rourke, pushing for favors under the guise that you'll marry her someday."

"That's a lie," Sam said with a vehemence that took Patrick by surprise. "I have strong feelings for Marcy, and for your information, I'm planning on making the courtship official. And as far as pushing her, you and I both know I take my pleasure at Brannigan's, not with her."

"For now." Patrick cocked a hip with a fold of his arms. "But what about after you make this so-called courtship official?" Patrick studied him through narrow eyes. "I won't stand by and watch you betray her."

Sam stared, a knot the size of Patrick's fists ducking

in his throat. "I won't," he said quietly. "I'm falling in love with her."

The words sliced through Patrick like a blade of jealousy. "Then prove it—court her properly like she deserves or leave her alone."

"Or leave her to you, you mean." He blasted out another sigh, his tone as worn as his manner. "All right. You have my word that I'll do right by Marcy with a courtship true and proper, but I'll not forsake Brannigan's with my best friend."

Patrick peered up beneath hooded eyes, well aware this was a huge concession for Sam. "True and proper, with no other women on the side?"

Sam gave a short nod, jaw firm. "Other than innocent flirtations at Brannigan's with you along to keep me honest."

"Ha!" Patrick said with a hint of a smile. "You don't know the meaning of the word 'innocent,' but I'll keep you honest, you can bet your eyeteeth on that."

Sam held out a hand, his gaze sparkling with humor for the first time all night. "Then all amends are made, aye? Friends again with no woman to come between us?"

Patrick assessed him with a wary eye, well aware this agreement would close the door on any hope he'd ever had for Marcy ... what little there was. His resignation drifted from his lips with a draining sigh. "Aye," he said with a firm clasp of Sam's hand, "no woman between us."

Relief relaxed the muscles in Sam's face as the two shook. Sam gripped Patrick's shoulder in a firm hold. "Marcy's waiting, so I have to get back, but I want you to know—you're the best friend a man could have." Slapping him on the back, he turned to go, a mere shadow in the dim light as he jogged back to the center.

The best friend a man could have. Patrick's lips quirked as he thought of Marcy, his heart comatose in his chest. *Aye, and a woman too.*

Chapter Twenty-Two

"Oh, what a grand time," Julie said with the same glow she'd worn the last three weeks since Evan had first asked her to accompany him for a soda. She sipped the rest of her Coca-Cola through a straw at Robinson's with a dreamy look that matched Evan's as he sat in the booth beside her after the St. Mary's Fall Promenade.

Marcy couldn't agree more, the flush of dancing with Sam throughout the evening still warm in her cheeks despite the ice cream soda she now spooned in her mouth. The dances in New York had never been as magical as this, and Marcy regretted all the years she'd missed with her best friend. *And her brother.* She peeked at Sam out of the corner of her eye, so handsome in his navy suit while he talked with Patrick across the table, who looked equally dapper in a charcoal gray sack suit with dark tie and winged collar. Sympathy squeezed in Marcy's chest. That is, considering the purple bruise around his left eye that was just beginning to fade into a mottled gray and green.

"Good gracious, what happened to Patrick?" Marcy had whispered to Julie last week while they measured Tillie for her costume. When Sam and he had arrived at practice to finish painting scenery, Patrick's left eye had been so swollen and black, Marcy's jaw had dropped along with the pin she'd been holding.

"He hammered Omer," Tillie piped up with no little pride.

"What?" More pins sailed to the floor as Marcy bent to stare in the little girl's beaming face. "What do you mean he 'hammered' Omer?"

Hazel eyes blinked wide beneath thick glasses, the little girl's freckles bunched in a squint. "Well, shoot, not with his hammer like he said, but just as hard with his fist, sure enough. Bloodied Omer's face but good when he whacked me after Patrick walked me home from the last practice. Drew a mite big crowd too, he did, aduckin' and aweavin' when Omer tried to whack him." The little girl's sunken chest actually puffed out with pride beneath the Christmas costume Marcy was sewing as she pushed smudged eye glasses back up her nose. "But Patrick's too fast and smart and strong for that big, ole dumb ox and pert near broke his nose. Told 'im if he ever came around again to bother Ma or me, he was acomin' back to finish the job."

Mouth agape, Marcy's gaze collided with Julie's before she glanced over her shoulder to where Patrick and Sam were talking with Evan at the side door, buckets of paint and brushes in their hands. "Well, I'll be," she muttered, not usually a proponent of fistfights, but her pride in Patrick swelling her chest as well.

Hands to her knees, Julie ducked to peer in Tillie's face, her jaw as distended as Marcy's. "Three days ago? Sweet saints, have you seen Omer since?"

"Shoot no, and don't expect to, neither. Patrick scared him but good, I can tell you that. Said if he came back again, he'd bring his hammer next time and break both his knees to match his nose."

Marcy gulped and glanced at Julie, the both of them biting back a smile.

"I'll tell you what," Tillie said with a worshipful gaze in Patrick's direction, "if I were grown up ladies like you, I'd shore in tarnation be settin' my cap for Patrick 'cause he shore is one prize catch."

One prize catch. Laughter broke into Marcy's reverie, returning her attention to the booth at Robinson's where Patrick was regaling Sam with a funny story. Her gaze drifted to the girl beside him, a dark-haired beauty named Emily Fischer who hung on to his every word—and on to Patrick, for that matter—and something pinched at Marcy's good mood like the corset beneath her aqua chiffon dress.

Emily giggled and whispered into Patrick's ear, and he slipped an arm around her shoulder, tucking her so close that Marcy had to look away. She liked Emily well enough, although she considered her somewhat of a flirt, but the adoring gaze the woman directed at Patrick all evening was starting to grate on Marcy's nerves. As close as Marcy had gotten with Patrick as friends over the last few months, she couldn't understand how Emily could trust him as a beau. Especially not after he'd led Emily to believe he was seeing only her, then dallied with other women behind her back, rumors Marcy knew to be true. She inhaled the rest of her soda with a loud, hollow noise and pushed the glass away, assessing Patrick out of the corner of her eye. *For heaven's sake, what was Emily thinking?* She'd heard he'd broken her heart two times before and was probably on his way to a third. Prior experience with heartbreakers like him stiffened Marcy's jaw. Which meant that Patrick O'Connor may be top-notch as a friend, but in the realm of romance? A cold shiver skittered her spine. She was pretty sure the man was sheer poison.

"Marcy?" A gentle touch from across the table jolted her back and she blinked at the concern on her best friend's face. "Are you all right?" Julie asked. "You were frowning."

"Yes, I'm fine," she said with a bright smile, shaking off a malaise she didn't quite understand. "Just sad about all the years of school I missed with you here in Boston."

"Me too," Julie said with affection, "but you're here now, on the arm of my brother, no less, for the first dance of the year, and that's all that matters, right?"

"Right," Marcy agreed.

"I'll second that." Sam drew her near for a kiss to her cheek. "We best get you ladies home or my parents will have my hide." He leaned close, his breath warm in Marcy's ear. "You *are* spending the night with Julie tonight, yes?"

Her response stalled on her tongue when Patrick glanced her way, one of the few direct looks he'd given her all night, pensive and brooding, as if to underscore the warning he'd given her before the incident with Sam at the center. Since that night, he'd made himself scarce, both at the kitchen and at play practice, working more overtime hours at the *Herald* than ever before, and oddly enough, Marcy was hurt. Their friendship had come to mean more than she'd anticipated and although a part of her welcomed the distance between them since the run-in with Sam, a part of her missed him more than she cared to admit. She quickly averted her gaze to Sam with a penitent smile, deciding then and there she wouldn't spend the night as planned. "I don't think so, Sam," she whispered, "I need to get up early because we have brunch with the Byingtons after mass."

A Light in the Window 249

She knew he was upset by the sudden shift of his jaw. "You're avoiding me," he said quietly, "and I want to know why?"

Her gaze flicked across the table to where both couples were engaged in conversation, then back to Sam with a chew of her lip. "I'm not avoiding you, I just have to get up early."

"You used to spend the night with Julie every other week," he said with a pointed gaze, "but you haven't once in the last month. You're avoiding me."

"No, I'm not, really," she said carefully, stomach cramping at the near lie.

"Then prove it." He angled a brow in challenge. "Come home with Julie tonight because there's something I need to tell you." His thumb caressed the line of her jaw before tracing the curve of her mouth. "Please?"

Her pulse stuttered at the heated look in his eyes. "I d-don't know, Sam ..."

He glanced over at his sister. "Jewels, you said Marcy was coming over tonight, and now she says she's not."

Julie blinked. "But, Marce, we agreed you'd spend the night tonight, and your mother thinks you are too. Besides," she said with an imp of a smile, "we have way too much to discuss for you to go home."

"It's all settled then," Sam said with a squeeze of her hand. "Evan and I will deliver you both safe and sound to the O'Rourke's front door."

Safe and sound. Marcy gulped, wondering just how "safe" it would be to spend even a few moments alone in the O'Rourke's porch swing like Sam would want her to do. After almost four months of "unofficial courting," she and Sam were getting more comfortable every day, which, much to her angst, meant he was also getting bolder as well, necessitating a wee bit of wrestling on her part whenever they were alone. The thought plagued her all the way to Julie's house where Patrick and Emily took their leave.

"Good night, all," Patrick said when they arrived at Julie and Sam's front walk, their departure causing a strange twinge in Marcy's chest when Emily snuggled closer to Patrick.

"I had a wonderful time, Evan," Julie said at the door, almost shy.

"Me too." He gave her a gentle kiss on the cheek before turning to go. "Good night, Marcy, Sam." Hands in his pockets, he ambled to the street with a whistle on his lips while Julie's soft sigh floated behind.

"Goodness, is he not just the most wonderful man?" Julie stared after him with a lovesick smile, palms crossed to her chest.

Marcy looped an arm to her waist. "He is at that, Jewels, and the admiration is more than mutual, I assure you."

"Oh, I hope so," she said with another sigh. A yawn escaped and she giggled as she gave Marcy a hug, and then one for Sam, along with a pinch of his cheek. "Well, I may be tired, but I won't be falling asleep anytime soon, brother dear, so don't keep my best friend too long, you hear?"

"Be nice, Jewels, and share," Sam said with a tweak of his sister's neck. "You get Marcy alone all night, while I only have her for a few precious moments."

Julie gave him a wink over her shoulder as she slipped inside. "A few precious moments with the likes of you is dangerous enough, so be good." She blew Marcy a kiss and quietly closed the door, leaving her alone with her brother and a stomach tangled in knots.

Taking her hand, he led her over to the white wicker

swing where she and Julie had whiled away so many summers, the memory of happy days spent with a family she loved calming her considerably. Moonlight washed the porch with an ethereal glow that felt almost magical, and when Sam tucked her close with a gentle kiss to her hair, it was as if Marcy had come home.

His fingers idly played with a stray curl on her neck, and she sighed against his chest, contentment purling through her veins. This is what she longed for—a closeness with Sam that meant they belonged to each other and that someday his family would be hers. She closed her eyes to breathe in both his scent and the hope of a future with the man and family of her dreams.

"Marcy."

She lifted her head, heart thudding when he bent to caress her mouth with his own. Warmth seeped through her body as he slipped his arm to her waist, drawing her close with a slow and languid kiss. His mouth trailed to her temple, his words warm in her ear. "I'm in love with you, Marceline," he whispered, "and I want to court you."

She jerked back, eyes wide as she studied him in the moonlight. "Courtship?" she said weakly, her pulse pounding at the very sound of the word. "B-but what d-does that mean?"

He playfully tugged at her lip, his voice husky with desire. "It means I want you, Marcy, sooner rather than later."

Her chest heaved with shallow breaths. "Is this … like a … proposal?" she whispered.

His chuckle was warm against her mouth. "Yes, Marceline … as in marriage."

"Marriage?" she breathed, searching his face for any sign of consent. "You're actually proposing, then?"

His chuckle feathered her cheek as he bent to

deposit a kiss on her nose. "A pre-proposal, Marcy, if you will. Not with a ring just yet till I save enough money, but a token of my intent, nonetheless." He reached into his pocket and placed a small box into her hands. "Open it," he whispered.

With quivering fingers, she lifted the lid and gasped at the gleam of a silver heart on a delicate chain. "Oh, Sam, it's beautiful, but it cost too much—I can't accept it."

He took the necklace from the box and opened the clasp, holding it out with a jag of his brow. "Tell me—if it were an engagement ring, would you accept it?"

"Well, yes, of course, but this isn't a ring—"

"No, not yet, but a pledge of my love and commitment all the same." He reached behind her neck and fastened it, and the silver lay cool and beautiful at the hollow of her throat. Sam traced a finger down the chain, skimming her skin with lovely shivers as he fondled the heart. "Consider this the promise of my heart, Marceline ... until I put the ring on your hand."

"Oh, Sam!" She lunged to kiss him, and he groaned, near devouring her until she was limp in his arms. A sense of warning shuddered through her, and she reluctantly pushed him away. "I need to go in ... Julie's waiting ..."

"Stay," he whispered, hands sweeping the length of her back and the curve of her hip, coaxing her, teasing her while his mouth nuzzled her lips. "We're promised to each other, Marceline—please, just a while longer ..."

The thrill of the promised engagement merged with the intensity of his kisses, weakening her will to deny him this one simple request. After all, they were almost engaged, so what harm could be done with a few minutes more? Goodness, this was the moment she'd longed for since she was a little girl—to be promised to Sam O'Rourke and he to her! The very thought made her dizzy in his arms. Soon she would be an O'Rourke, part of the family she loved and adored, and completely cherished by this man she would marry.

Eventually ...

"I had a wonderful time, Patrick," Emily said as they mounted the steps of her front porch where the crisp scent of autumn leaves and wood smoke filled the cool night air. "Thank you for taking me to the Fall Promenade."

"It was my pleasure, Em," he said quietly, wondering if he'd done the right thing in deciding to see her again. Of all the women he'd wooed, she had been his favorite and the woman he'd spent time with more than any other. *Until Marceline Murphy.* The malaise that always settled with thoughts of Marcy lighted on him now as he gently buffed the arms of Emily's cloak. "We had talked about the Fall Promenade the last time we were together, so I just thought it fitting to ask you."

"I'm glad," she whispered, standing on tiptoe to brush a gentle kiss to his lips. "I've missed you."

A twinge of regret cramped in his chest. Regret that she'd been hurt by his absence, regret that he'd taken advantage of her in the past.

Regret that she wasn't Marcy.

She laid a gentle palm to his cheek. "I don't have to be in until eleven, so we have a few minutes to spare. Would you like to sit on the steps and talk a while?"

He paused, knowing full well Emily didn't expect a whole lot of "talking" from the old Patrick O'Connor, but the new? Releasing a quiet sigh, he took her hand

and led her to the first step, tugging her down beside him. She shivered, and he hooked her close, his gaze on the harvest moon overhead instead of her face.

"You seem different," she said quietly, the familiar scent of rosemary and mint stirring memories of kisses shared on these very steps in the past.

Before Marcy.

The edge of his lips tipped in a faint smile. "I am."

She pulled away to study his face in the moonlight. "Why?"

Marcy's image invaded his mind, and he inhaled a deep breath before releasing it again, wishing he could do the same with his feelings for Marcy. "I've been volunteering at the St. Mary's Center of Hope, and it's changed how I think about some things."

"Like what?" she asked with a tilt of her head.

He laughed, hardly believing the words about to come out of his mouth. "You know, philosophical things—like what I want in life, the type of man I want to be ..." He swallowed hard. "God ..."

"God?" she whispered, and he grinned at the expanse of her eyes.

"Crazy, I know." His smile faded. "But I met someone with a deep faith in God at the center, and between Father Fitz and her, I'm beginning to see things in a whole new light."

"Her?" She paused while a muscle shifted in her throat. "Is ... she why I haven't seen you for a while?"

He took her hand in his, idly caressing her palm. "She is," he said carefully, "but there's nothing between us now, which is why I wanted to start seeing other girls again, particularly you."

She nodded, her gaze locked on his hand as it gently stroked hers. "I see." She looked up, and he winced at the vulnerability in her eyes. "I think you know I care about you, Patrick, so I'd like to help put her out of your mind if I can." Squeezing his hand, she bent close to skim her lips against his, racing his pulse when she deepened the kiss.

Heat scorched his body, reminding him just how long it had been since he'd held a woman in his arms other than sharing a dance at Brannigan's. *Or wrestling a dishrag at the center ...* The very thought dampened the desire that Emily provoked, and with a sudden flash of temper, he jerked her close and kissed her hard with all the passion he'd denied since Marcy had stolen his heart. She melted into his embrace and with an angry surge of old habits, his hands explored the curve of her hips, the length of her thigh, his blood pumping hot while his mouth wandered her throat. If he couldn't have Marcy's love, then by thunder, he'd kindle love where he could, searching for the one woman who could drive her from his mind.

A rogue who so casually equates lust with love.

His mouth stilled on her throat at the memory of Marcy's words, the soft shudder of Emily's moan freezing every muscle in his body. *God forgive me ...* His eyes shuttered closed as he gently pushed her away. "You need to go inside," he whispered, rising to his feet and pulling her along. He led her to the door and turned the knob, pressing a kiss to her forehead before prodding her through. "I'll see you soon, I promise."

She stopped him with a touch of his arm and a sweet gloss of tears, her voice barely a whisper. "Thank you, Patrick … for a wonderful evening and for …" A knot ducked in her throat. "Making me feel so special just now …"

He smiled. "You are, Em, and don't let any man ever forget it." He ambled down the steps, conscience light, but heart heavy while regret thickened the walls

of his throat.
Especially a man like me.

Chapter Twenty-Three

Heart sprinting, Marcy bounded up the steps of her front porch, ripping her coat off as she bolted into her house and flung it on the brass rack by the door. Giddy with excitement, she barreled into the kitchen where her mother was fixing tea for her grandmother who had just arrived from Ireland.

"Mima!" she screamed, skidding to a stop in front of a petite version of her mother, chest heaving as she gave her a ferocious hug. "It seems like forever since I've seen you, and I've missed you so much!"

A husky chuckle too low for the tiny woman in her arms rumbled in her mother's cozy kitchen that smelled of pot roast and apple dumplings—her grandmother's favorites. "And I, you, Marceline." Her blue eyes sparkled like the wisps of silver in her blonde hair as she cupped Marcy's cheek. "You can be sure I'll be having words with the Almighty someday, darlin', as to why the two months I'm here for the holidays go by in a blink while the others drag like a dirge."

Marcy laughed and hugged her again before hurrying over to do the same with her mother. "So ... what can I help you with, Mother?"

Bridget Murphy nodded toward the table with a grin

that almost glowed. "Sit, Marceline. The water's on the boil, and you can join us for tea. I was so excited waiting for Mima to arrive, I did everything but paper the walls," she quipped with a chuckle. "Cleaned the house, made dinner, dessert, cookies, set the table and picked my nails raw, so now it's time to enjoy family."

Tears pricked Marcy's eyes as her mother handed her a cup and saucer before guiding her to the table with a plate of fresh sugar cookies. Ten months a year she was alone, an only child with no real family of her own except Mother and Papa, but for two glorious months, the house blossomed with a fuller, deeper, noisier love.

Family!

Marcy couldn't stop the giggle that rose in her throat from the sheer joy of Mima's presence. The familiar scent of rosewater and the clean smell of freshly starched linen flooded her mind with wonderful memories. She sat on one side while her mother sat on the other, both touching her grandmother's arm as if to make sure she were real.

"So, young lady," Mima said with a lift of her pert but prominent chin, "your mother tells me you're in charge of the fundraiser for St. Mary's?"

Marcy nodded, more excitement bubbling at the thought that Mima would be here for the play. "I am, Mima, and it's been such a wonderful experience, working with Father Fitz and Sister Francine, and serving at the St. Mary's Center of Hope."

Mima squeezed Marcy's hand, blue eyes twinkling. "I am so proud of you, Marceline, for taking this project on. Bridget tells me the annual Christmas play is the main support of the parish center that helps the poor, and with your love of the arts and drama, I cannot imagine how wonderful it will be. Tell me about it."

A Light in the Window

Marcy giggled, the very sound breathless with anticipation. "Oh, Mima, it's called *A Light in the Window*, and it's based on our Irish custom of placing a candle in the window on Christmas Eve through Epiphany to welcome the Holy Family." Marcy clasped her hands in delight, eyes sparkling, no doubt, as much as her mood. "I found it in a book of Irish plays at the library, and it's the perfect story for our fundraiser! It's about a poor family of six where the parents sacrifice to give their children a wonderful Christmas." She chattered nonstop for several minutes about the play, the rehearsals, and the center, barely taking a breath while her grandmother watched her with true affection. Replenishing with a deep draw of air, Marcy released it again in another joyous giggle as she lifted her cup to her lips. "I can't wait for you to see it and meet all the people involved," she said, taking a thirsty sip of tea.

"*A Light in the Window*, is it?" A soft smile lined Mima's lips as her eyes took on a faraway glow. "Sure, it's a tradition that harkens back to when I first met my dear Matthew."

"Really?" Marcy set her cup down to stroke Mima's thin wrist, her voice gentle. "Why? Is that how you met Grandfather?"

"It was indeed, darlin'," her grandmother said softly, a glaze in her eyes that might have been tears. "He was on his way home for Christmas, you see, from the university, and the handsome devil stole his friend's horse on a dare. Bucked right off, he was, hard as you please, not twenty paces outside our gate during a storm." She grinned and tore her gaze from the past, her smile lighting on Marcy once again. "He saw the light in our window, you know, and much to my parent's alarm, it was love at first sight."

Marcy clasped Mima's hand. "Oh, Mima, I never

knew that—that's so romantic!"

She chuckled with a swipe at her eyes. "Not to Mam and Da, I can tell you that, but in time, they came to love him too, and a fine husband he made in the end, to be sure." More tears glimmered as she reached to clutch Bridget's hand. "Aye, and a glorious father too."

"He was at that." Bridget dabbed at her eyes with the hem of her apron, popping up to fetch the tea at the shriek of the kettle. She poured Marcy a fresh cup and refilled hers and Mima's.

"And speaking of 'romantic,'" Mima said with a gleam in her eye, "your mother tells me you've been seeing a young man ..."

Marcy took another quick gulp of tea, the steam heating her face as much as Mima's question. "Yes," she said with a glance at her mother, stomach clenching at the tight press of Bridget's lips. "I'm actually seeing Sam, the brother of my best friend Julie."

Mima nodded slowly. "Ah, yes, Samuel O'Rourke—the rogue that Bridget worries about."

"Mother!" Marcy shot Bridget a pleading look. "Sam has matured over the last year, and he comes from a wonderful family that I just happen to love."

"Humph," Bridget said with a sniff. "It's not his family I'm worried about, Marceline. Samuel O'Rourke was a hooligan growing up, along with that O'Connor boy, and now the two of them terrorize mothers everywhere." She slid Mima a wry smile. "Especially me now that he's taken a fancy to Marcy." She sighed, shooting her mother a look of concern as she warmed her hands on her cup. "He and that O'Connor boy are just a wee bit too fast, if you ask me. Unfortunately, Marcy's clearly smitten, so maybe you'll have more luck convincing her to look elsewhere than I have."

Marcy squirmed in her seat as always when her

mother expressed her displeasure over her relationship with Sam, but now with two sets of probing blue eyes boring into her soul, she suddenly felt outnumbered. She squared her shoulders and took another drink before setting the cup down, determined to win both her mother and Mima to Sam's side. Sucking in a deep breath, she chose her words carefully. "Yes, it's true that both Sam and Patrick may have veered off the path of respectability at one time—"

"'Veered'?" Her mother said with a high lift of brows. Her lips quirked. "A mile-long detour might be a wee more apt."

Mima chuckled and patted her daughter's hand. "Give the girl a chance, Bridge. Marceline has always been a trustworthy daughter, so let's hear her out."

Bridget grunted, the sound inconsistent with the golden hair and porcelain skin of a well-bred beauty. "Yes, she has, except when it comes to the O'Rourke boy. It seems she's been smitten with him from the age of eight, even fawning over him in her diary."

"Mother!" Marcy jolted straight up in the chair while her cheeks pulsed with heat. "You read my *diary*?"

Bridget's lip tipped on one side as she reached for a cookie. "Of course I did, Marceline," she said without apology, chin elevated with dignity. "As any respectable, God-fearing mother worth her salt would do."

"B-but, but ... it's private!"

Head tilted in sympathy, Bridget smiled at Marcy. "Just to the public, darling, not to mothers who care, right, Mother?"

Mima chuckled. "Aye, darlin', although if I'd been more diligent, I might have prevented that bothersome husband of yours from stealing you away from our blessed isle."

The lilt of her mother's laughter defused Marcy's shock for the moment, coaxing a grin to her lips when Bridget stuck her nose in the air with a regal pose. "That 'bothersome' husband, I'll have you know, paid to sail you to us in a berth fit for a queen, knowing full well your presence will tax him sorely."

Mima grinned. "And what a dear boy he is at that," she said with a chuckle, then gave Marcy a wink. "So you've been smitten since the age of eight, is it?" She chewed on her cookie thoughtfully, eyes in a squint. "Why?"

Marcy blinked, lips curling into a grin. "Goodness, Mima, who's to say just why a young girl loses her heart to a boy? Maybe it was because he was always kind to me while the other boys—*especially* his best friend Patrick—treated me like the plague. When Julie and I wanted to play tag or crack the whip or hide and seek with the older children, Sam would take our side, making the others let us play, even taking great pains to hide us in the best spots." Marcy sighed. "I was at Julie's so much, that I guess I got to see who Sam really was inside—his playfulness with his sisters, his tenderness with the younger ones, and even his humor and teasing with his parents. And goodness, when it came to protecting Julie from boys when she got older?" Marcy grinned. "She told me Sam's worse than a lioness with her cub."

"Ah, common ground with the boy, eh, Bridge?" Mima sent her daughter a pixie grin before her gaze shifted back to Marcy, her smile fading into soft concern. "And his faith in God, Marceline? Where does the boy stand on that?"

Marcy dove for a cookie, anything to deflect the blush bruising her cheeks. "Well, as a matter of fact,

Sam accompanies me to church every week and volunteers at the center and with the play, both he and Patrick."

Her mother chomped on another cookie, gumming her lips with a dubious air. "Humph ... I'm still not convinced those two didn't run afoul of Father Fitzgibbons somehow, earning those tasks as punishment." She chewed while she considered her suspicions, eyes in a squint. "Two rogues who work by day and play by night just don't up and dish out soup to the poor or paint scenery." Her lips skewed to the right. "Unless it's painting the town red."

"Mother, really," Marcy said with a shake of her head, smiling in spite of herself. "Can't you give Sam credit where credit is due? He and Patrick are just growing up, finally coming into their own as men, which doesn't surprise me the least bit, given the caliber of family Sam comes from. I mean, you like Mr. and Mrs. O'Rourke, don't you? And Julie is like a daughter, after all."

"Yes, I like the O'Rourkes just fine, and Julie is a gem, no question." Bridget popped the remainder of her cookie in her mouth, brushing her hands free of crumbs like she wished she could do with Sam, no doubt. "But Samuel O'Rourke has probably seen the inside of Father Fitzgibbons' office more than the blessed man himself." She rose to warm up their tea, refilling each of their cups before she replaced the kettle and sank back in her chair. Drawing a long sip, she squinted at her daughter, her cup barely hiding the twitch of a smile. "According to Father Fitz's housekeeper, Sam and the O'Connor boy were in trouble so much, the two of them may as well have moved in and set up camp."

Mima chuckled and leaned back in her chair, arms folded to assess Marcy through curious eyes. "You didn't answer my question on his faith in God," she said quietly. "I can't imagine a troublemaker would have too much of that."

Marcy's tongue made a quick pass, well aware that Sam's faith was as tepid as her tea, but he *was* changing.

Wasn't he?

"No," she began slowly, "I suspect neither Sam nor Patrick have exercised their faith like they should have over the last few years, but I've seen indication of that changing in both of them. Goodness, Patrick counsels with Father Fitz on a regular basis, I understand, and Sam ..." She scrambled mentally for anything that would convince her mother and grandmother that Sam was worthy of her hand and her heart. When nothing came to mind, she huffed out a sigh and forged on. "Well, Sam is an O'Rourke, for pity's sake, a family with a sound moral foundation and faith in God, so I have every confidence he will follow the same path." She swallowed a gulp of tea.

Sooner or later ...

Mima's gaze sharpened, her mouth compressed into that same thin line of doubt she'd seen in her mother. "Do you?" she whispered.

Marcy blinked, Mima's question railroading her confidence. Hands shaking, she took another quick glug of tea as she considered the unwelcome query. Sam professed faith, but Marcy seldom saw it in action other than at the center, especially in the carnal sense of late. It was becoming clearer all the time that his once honorable and protective behavior the first three months seemed to be giving way to more and more passion. Although her own faith had been strong enough to keep him in line the last few weeks, he was clearly veering from chaste kisses to more ardent ones. He was a man with a voracious appetite for pleasure, Marcy was beginning to realize, be it from a bottle or from the lips of a woman.

She shivered, fingers absently fondling the silver heart and chain at the base of her throat. He said he'd committed his heart to her, but doubts suddenly niggled … doubts she'd refused to see before now, conveniently buried deep in her desire to be a part of his life and his family. But Mima's query found its mark, probing into fears and doubts hidden well beneath the surface that now festered in the light of her reluctant reflection—and Mima's. Did he still spend his time at Brannigan's when he wasn't with her? Dancing and flirting with other women? She'd never really asked, side-stepping the issue for fear of the truth, but surely now that he'd committed to her … Eyes flickering closed for the briefest of moments, she vowed to find out for sure. To ask the difficult questions she'd put off for far too long … She sucked in a deep breath to steady her nerves before she opened her eyes to face Mima again. "I have faith, Mima," she said quietly, "that God will answer my prayers for a man who embraces Him as fervently as I. That may not be Sam just yet …" A lump bobbed in her throat. "But I have faith it may be him in the future."

Mima nodded before her frail hand settled on Marcy's arm. "You know, Marceline, our faith in God is very much like that light in the window that your Christmas play depicts. We are God's abode, and His light shines through the windows of our lives into a dark and desperate world. Many may pass, enjoying the beauty of the light from afar, but few will be drawn to knock at the door, willing to embrace the Light of the World." Her hand rose to gently cup Marcy's cheek, a tenderness in her eyes that always warmed Marcy's soul. "Guard your heart well," she said softly, "for a man who will respond to the light in the window, for therein lies a gift of God like no other, except that of His Son."

Moisture stung, and Marcy silently nodded, unable to speak lest she unleash the tears from her eyes. Her heart ached at the thought that when her prayers were all said and done, Sam might not be the one.

Without a word, Mima rose and enveloped her in a warm embrace while her mother did the same, standing beside her with a gentle knead of her back. "We trust you, Marceline," her mother said, her voice caressing along with her hand, "to make the right decision. But more importantly, daughter, we trust God."

"But how will I know?" Marcy's voice was a broken whisper. "That I'll make the right decision?"

Mima bent close, her words warm and husky in Marcy's ear. "Not to worry, darlin'—the decision may be yours, but the strength and wisdom will be all His. Because never forget ..." Mima tipped her face up, shoring Marcy with a deep faith carefully honed by time. "God honors those who honor Him, and He always answers their prayers."

Her heart quickened at Mima's word while thoughts of her struggles with Sam pummeled her mind. *Those who honor Him ...* She closed her eyes, and peace descended while her lips moved in silent prayer. *Oh, Lord, please—let that be me!*

Chapter Twenty-Four

Patrick scanned the nearly empty dining room of the St. Mary's Center of Hope, never more grateful his volunteer shift was almost over. Outside the storefront windows, snowflakes drifted, blanketing the street with a peaceful mantle of beauty that hid the pock marks and smells of a cobblestone street littered with garbage, oil, and manure. He nodded at several rag-tag diners just leaving, his smile as deceptive as the snow, concealing a malaise that settled like the ice crystals outside—bitter and cold.

His eyes flitted to the clock over the now-deserted serving line, where Miss Clara was stacking fresh plates for tomorrow's lunch. *Almost seven—closing time, thank God.* He bobbled the dishrag, wishing he could wipe his melancholy away as easily as the debris and dirty dishes from the tables. His gaze shifted to where Marcy coddled and cooed with a baby at the kitchen table while its mother and two small siblings finished up their free meal in the dining room, and his lips tipped in a faint smile. The woman was downright obsessed with babies and family, yet another reason for Patrick's glum mood. *I doubt a man could find a better mother for his children.* His thoughts ached with a familiar longing before the smile died on his lips. But they would be Sam's children—not his.

Dishrag in hand, he bent over a dirty table with a heavy exhale, scouring food encrusted on the wood. For the first time in his life, he had no interest in women, not if it couldn't be Marcy, and the very notion rankled. Although they'd talked here and there, he hadn't really spent time with Emily in over a month—not since the night of the promenade—and his visits to Brannigan's had become almost as scarce. An occasional drink with Sam or a forced dance with a woman left him with no taste for more of the same. Not since Sam indicated he and Marcy had progressed from an "unofficial courtship" to an "almost official proposal." Far from "official" for Sam, Patrick knew, but iron-clad to Marcy, no doubt, a silent promise of engagement that would wait until he officially put a ring on her hand.

Releasing a quiet sigh, Patrick assessed the smattering of tables yet to be cleaned, occupied by only a handful of diners who appeared to be in no hurry to leave, each obviously savoring Miss Clara's custard pie and hot coffee for as long as they could. His eyes settled on Luther who chatted with a frail woman across his table, and Patrick shook his head with a one-sided smile. Even sweet, disheveled Luther appeared to have a lady love, his eyes sparkling with interest that had little to do with the pie.

Armed with dirty trays, Patrick paused by Luther's table, offering the lady a smile. "Evening, Luther, Cora." He nodded at the snow crusting the grease-penciled window. "Need me to top off your cups with hot coffee before you brave the cold?"

"No, thank ye, Patrick." Luther lumbered to his feet with a toothless grin, buttoning a threadbare coat. "I need to get this lady home afore we get snowed in."

Slipping Cora a wink, he offered an arm patched at the elbows. "Ready, m'lady?"

Cora rose with a smile and the manner of a well-bred woman despite moth holes and grime on her dark woolen coat. With a shy smile, she hooked her arm through Luther's, her lopsided silver bun belying the youthfulness of blue eyes that had seen better times.

And haven't we all. The beautiful sound of Marcy's laughter from the kitchen wrenched in Patrick's chest. Gritting a smile, he picked up Cora and Luther's empty trays, grateful there were only two more weeks till the play and only a month and a half till the new year. A new year when he could move on with his life, pouring his heart into college rather than a woman he could never have.

"No!"

Patrick's head shot up at Cora's frantic cry, his trays clattering back to the table when he spied Luther tussling with another man.

"Hey, hold on, there," Patrick shouted, prying the two men apart. Luther lunged and Patrick pulled him back, locking his arms behind. "Settle down, Luther, this is no place for a street fight." His gaze narrowed on the other man, a surly diner who'd been at the center earlier in the day, a brooder he just assumed wanted a warm place out of the cold. Patrick had never seen him before, but the stranger's belligerent manner had prickled the back of his neck. Mouth slashed in a scowl, the man's greasy black hair obscured dark eyes as brutally cold as the jagged shards of ice that plunged from the gutter outside. "What's the problem?" Patrick said.

Luther jerked from Patrick's hold, chest rattling with breathless heaves while he carefully steered Cora behind. "The problem is this no-good bum is trying to force Cora to go with him, and she don't want to."

"She's my gal, not his," the surly man bit out.

Patrick shot him a warning glare before turning to Cora. "Is that true, Cora?"

She shook her head, eyes on the floor as she picked at a fingernail poking through a hole in her glove. "N-not anymore."

Patrick ducked to peer into her face, his tone gentle. "Cora, do you want to go with him or with Luther?"

She edged closer to Luther's side, shaky fingers grasping onto Luther's arm. "Luther," she whispered, flinching when the other man spit out a curse.

"Okay, mister," Patrick said, "you best leave now. This is a church kitchen, not a barroom, so don't come back unless your attitude improves."

Obscenities spewed as the man shoved past Luther and Cora, snow swooshing into the dining room when the door flew back and slammed to the wall.

"What's going on out here?" Marcy cried, alarm tingeing her tone as she handed the baby back to its mother. The woman quickly herded her children out the door.

"A minor spat, that's all," Patrick called over his shoulder, locking the door behind the mother with a nod and a click of the bolt. Arm to Luther's shoulder, he steered Cora and him to the kitchen, pulling two chairs out for them to sit down. "Luther, I'd like you and Cora to stay here for a few minutes, just till I make sure that guy is gone." He glanced up. "Is that all right with you, Miss Clara?"

"Well, laws, I should say so," Miss Clara huffed on her way to the stove. She poured two cups of coffee and delivered them to the table. "Marcy and I have desserts to deliver to the rectory for the board meeting tonight, but we'll be back lickety-split while you sip on this coffee, you hear?"

"Thank you kindly, Miss Clara, Miss Murphy." Luther glanced up at Patrick with a tight smile. "Appreciate you clearing the area of bad rubbish, Patrick. Cora's been trying to avoid that scalawag all week now, and I just as soon not meet him in the streets."

Patrick slapped Luther on the back. "You bet. Sit tight, and I'll be right back." Slipping his coat on, he waited while Marcy and Miss Clara bundled up and then followed them out the door, escorting them to the rectory before scouting the area in front and back. He strolled several blocks all the way around to make sure the troublemaker was gone, then returned to the kitchen where Luther and Cora were just finishing their coffee. Ready to be on their way, they thanked him profusely before slipping out the back door.

"Nothing like a little excitement to take my mind off things," Patrick muttered, wiping down the last of the dirty tables before carting the trays to the sink. He glanced up when the back door squealed open to usher in a blonde-haired beauty along with a gust of snow. "Go home, Marcy, I'll finish up." Avoiding her gaze, he proceeded to scrape the food from the trays, aware she was watching him intently. Their friendship had suffered since their water fight that night when he'd butted heads with Sam, but it was just as well. It gave him no pleasure to see the lovesick look in her eye whenever Sam was around, so their prior close friendship was no longer an option. At least, not for him, although he suspected Marcy didn't quite understand.

"I'm supposed to meet Sam in the church vestibule in about fifteen minutes," she said in a tentative tone, "but I'd like to help till he arrives."

He exhaled loudly, hanging his head. "I'm almost done, so you may as well go." He glanced at her out of the corner of his eye. "Really, Marcy—go."

"Patrick, I ..."

He turned back to his task, refusing to look at her. It was hard enough being near her with no hope of anything other than stilted friendship, but to look at her was sheer torture, knowing she would always belong to Sam. "What?" He scrubbed the dirty trays, his tone gruffer than intended.

"I ... miss our friendship."

His hand stilled in the dirty dishwater while a nerve flickered in his cheek. Steeling his jaw, he continued scrubbing, harder than before. "We can't be friends right now," he said quietly. "Someday, maybe ... but not right now."

"Why?" It was a frail whisper, uttered by a frail little girl.

He shook his head, grunting a hollow laugh. "You really don't understand, do you?"

"I understand that I value your friendship."

Water sluiced all over when he slapped the rinsed trays on the counter. He jerked a dishtowel from the hook and shot her a hard glance while he dried each of the dishes. "And I value Sam's, which is why you and I can't be close. It's no good for Sam, and it's no good for me."

"I just don't see why we can't all—"

He hurled a tray on the counter and turned, fury burning in his eyes. "Because I'm in love with you, Marceline," he snapped, "and I *don't* want to be around you."

She stared, mouth ajar and pink blotches bleeding into her cheeks like scarlet ink on porous paper. "I ... I'm sorry ... I ... I didn't know ..."

Head bowed, he kneaded the bridge of his nose with the ball of his hand, blasting out a noisy sigh. "Well, that's neither here nor there. Sam's my best friend, and you're the woman he wants, so end of story." He reached for the dishrag and wiped the counter down, ignoring her feeble footsteps into the storeroom that doubled as Evan's office.

Her panicked cry froze the blood in his veins, heart stopping before he bolted across the kitchen into the storeroom. She stood white-faced, body quivering as she stared at the open safe where Miss Clara kept the grocery money. All anger forgotten, he gripped her arms while his gaze locked on her ashen face. "Marcy—what's wrong?"

Her bloodless lips started to quiver and then her body followed suit, rivulets of tears streaming from her eyes. "I-it's ... i-it's ... g-gone ..."

His gaze flicked to the hollow safe and his stomach cramped while he kneaded her arms, fingers caressing in an attempt to stem the flow of her tears. "It's just grocery money, Marceline, and not much because Miss Clara went shopping earlier this week, remember?"

She looked up, her gaze pitiful as ragged heaves wracked her small frame. "N-no, n-not g-grocery m-money," she stuttered, throat convulsing while her quivering fingers pushed stray hair from her eyes, "t-the ... t-he m-money ..."

"What money?" He gave her a little shake when she didn't answer, as if her mind was in shock. "Answer me, Marceline—*what* money?"

A sob broke from her lips. "The f-fundraiser m-money, from t-ticket and c-catalog sales ..."

His skin iced as cold as the frost on the windows. "How much?"

She collapsed against him then, and he swallowed

her up in his arms, her body wracking his with painful weeping. "A-all of i-it ... over five h-hundred d-dollars ..."

He stared before his eyes weighted closed with a silent groan. Stroking her hair, he rested his cheek against her head while his heart wrenched at the familiar scent of lilac water and Pears soap. "You're sure it was in the safe? You didn't give it to Father Fitz or Sister Francine or anyone else?"

She shook her head, sobs shuddering his body while her agony shuddered his soul. "I ... I ... m-meant t-to take it t-to Father F-Fitz tonight when we d-delivered the d-desserts, b-but I forgot ..." Her fingernails dug into his chest as she hung on to his shirt, wailing as if someone had died. His heart twisted. Not just "someone," he realized, but many "someones" whose hope died the moment those funds were stolen from the safe. She trembled in his arms, both her body and her voice. "I ... I p-put a d-donation in this m-morning, b-but I locked the s-safe after, I'm almost c-certain ..."

Rubbing her back with gentle fingers, he led her to the table to sit, then pulled his chair alongside hers. He took her hands in his. "Marcy, listen to me—this will all work out, I promise. We'll find that money somehow, along with the person who took it."

She shook her head, face sodden with tears. "No, w-we won't. It's g-gone, I j-just know it, and p-people will s-starve ..."

The barest hint of a smile tipped his lips as he leaned to embrace her, her flair for drama evident in the life-and-death angst of her tone. "No they won't, I assure you. Life goes on in the gravest of trials, and this loss—if that's what it is because I truly believe we'll recover the money—is but a mere pebble in the road, not likely to tumble you into a sea of abyss." He pulled away and handed her a clean handkerchief from his pocket. "Here, darlin', blow, then we'll discuss what must be done."

His eyes softened as she gave a shaky nod and blew her nose, looking so much like a little girl he longed to protect that his heart stuttered in his chest. She started to hand his handkerchief back, then blushed before clasping it to her chest. "I'll g-get this back to you, I p-promise."

He gave her a tender smile. "It's not my chief concern at the moment. Are you sure Miss Clara didn't take the money to Father Fitz for you?"

She shook her head, more tears trailing her cheeks. "N-no ... s-she was the one who r-reminded me to g-go get it ..."

"Then think back—were you or Miss Clara gone from the kitchen at anytime during the day other than a few moments ago when Cora and Luther were here?"

She swallowed hard, brows pinched in thought. "No, I don't think so ..." Her lips suddenly parted in a sharp intake of air as she pressed two fingers to her temple. "Wait! Yes, I d-did leave briefly this afternoon before the s-supper rush while Miss Clara was on an errand because I wanted to search the church storeroom for some props. Rupert and Rose were here, so I didn't think anything of leaving, but I remember now that when I came back, everyone was gone."

He exhaled slowly, recollecting the ruckus going on when he'd arrived at the center. The street had been chaotic with people, horses, and fire carriages trying to extinguish a blaze across the alleyway. The incident had caused quite a stir, vagrants suspected of starting a fire in a cellar stairwell with wooden crates and boxes in order to keep warm. He nodded, his thoughts on the two elderly volunteers who'd just begun working at the center over the summer. "Yes, Rupert and Rose were out front with the rest of the crowd as I recall, watching the firemen put the fire out across the street."

Beautifully shaped brows pinched in an uphill slant, her agony evident in the gouge of deep ridges above her nose. "But I closed the safe, Patrick, I swear—"

He quickly cut her off when her lip started to quiver again. "I think it sticks sometimes, or at least I remember Miss Clara asking Evan to oil it in the past." He sucked in a silent breath, giving her a reassuring smile. "So the first thing we're going to do is look one more time, okay?" She followed as he marched back into the storeroom to scan both the inside of the safe and the area around it to make sure the money envelope hadn't been dropped.

More tears welled in her eyes when they came up empty-handed. "It's n-no use ... it's g-gone, and now we'll never f-find it ..."

He took the handkerchief from her hand and gently swiped at the new tears on her face. "Yes, we will—where's that faith of yours, Marceline?"

Her blubbering continued, voice trailing off into another wretched wail. "I g-guess-it was s-stolen along with the m-money ..."

His chuckle was soft and low. "Well, then we'll use my bit of faith, near honed to perfection by you and Father Fitz." He bent near to tuck a finger to her chin. "Did you not listen to Father Fitz's homily last Sunday? 'In nothing be anxious; but in everything by prayer and supplication with thanksgiving, let your requests be made known unto God.'"

She blinked, her sobs ceasing with an expanse of eyes.

He grinned, dabbing her cheeks with the cloth. "Yes, Marceline—rogues do pay attention in church from time to time. So then ... we pray, we tell Father Fitz, and we call the police, yes?"

She nodded dumbly, shock apparently stealing her tongue as well as her grief.

"Fair warning, however—this is not my strong suit. I've only heard Father Fitz pray out loud on my behalf once or twice, but I doubt you or the Almighty will mind, eh?" Taking her small hands in his, he closed his eyes. "Father, we're in a pickle here and we need Your help. Please give Marcy the grace and peace to know this will all turn out, show us exactly what we need to do, and please help us recover the money. Amen." He opened his eyes and pushed the handkerchief back into her hand before pulling her to her feet. "All right now—dry your eyes, blow your nose, and let's go see Father Fitz."

Her chin began to tremble, striking terror in his chest. He gripped her arms with a gentle smile, his tone light but firm. "Enough with the tears, darlin', or I'll be bawling right along with you and no good at all."

More tears pooled nonetheless before she launched herself into his arms, clutching him so tightly, his heart climbed in his throat. "Oh, Patrick, I am so grateful you were here right now—you're just what I need!"

His eyes sheathed closed, the fit of her body against his as natural as breathing. *And you're just what I need, darlin', but it obviously wasn't meant to be.* Tamping down his bitter regret, he patted her back and pulled away, tucking his finger to her chin once again. "I'm glad I could be here for you too," he said quietly before helping her on with her coat and grabbing his own.

And if it were up to me, Marceline, he thought with a squeeze of his chest, *I'd be there forever.*

Chapter Twenty-Five

Stomping his snow-caked boots on the stoop of Brannigan's Pub, Patrick opened the door to his past, the smells of cheap booze and even cheaper women a painful reminder of Marcy's effect on his life. He peered through the smoky fog, searching for Sam with a grim press of his lips, angry that Marcy was plagued with worry—not only about the welfare of the lost funds, but that of her "unofficial fiancé" when he didn't show to take her home.

He pushed his way through the noisy throng, Ragtime drifting through the haze along with laughter and off-key crooning as several of the more inebriated patrons sang along with Tommy Thomkins' piano.

"Well, the saints be praised—my prayers have been answered tonight!"

He halted mid-crowd when a shapely redhead grabbed him and kissed him hard on the mouth, the taste of stale beer on her tongue roiling his stomach. Peeling her arms from his waist, he forced a tight smile. "Can't stay, Clarisse, I'm looking for Sam—have you seen him?"

Her lips pushed into a pout as she briefly glanced over her shoulder. "He's been sitting at the bar all night, but he might be in the loo, not sure." She cozied up with a clear invitation in her eyes. "But I guarantee you, Patrick," she said, seduction warm in her tone, "I'd be a lot more fun than your partner in crime."

He gave her shoulder a tender squeeze, remorse softening his words for all the times he'd taken advantage of women like her. "A tempting offer, my friend, but I have serious matters to attend to." He bent to press a soft kiss to her cheek. "Be good, Clarisse."

"I always am," she said with a saucy wink, "and nobody knows that better than you."

Regret stabbed as he made his way to the bar, speaking to those who greeted him on the way. He slid onto a stool and hailed the bartender before craning his neck to survey the crowd. "You seen Sam, Lucas?" he asked when he turned back to the bar.

"I have, indeed, but I'm afraid he's indisposed right now." Lucas inclined his head toward the back room, his smile more of a scowl. "Drank near half his paycheck, I'll wager. Pert near blackened some bloke's eye before I tossed him in the back room to save both his hide and my bar." He reached for a mug. "You need a brew?"

"No, not tonight, but thanks. I just need to find Sam."

"Well, hopefully he's sober by now—plied him with hot coffee an hour or so ago, but you'll be needing to sober him up for anything noble, I'll warrant." Lucas nodded toward the door at the back of the bar where a hallway of rooms hid all caliber of sin. "But help yourself—third room on the left."

Patrick strode down the darkened hall, shame scalding the back of his neck at the various lewd sounds seeping through the doors, wondering how he could have ever been drawn to such empty pursuits. Jaw twitching, he knocked on the third door and waited.

"It's taken." Sam's rusty voice croaked on the other side.

Patrick opened the door, eyes squinting to adjust to the lack of light. "Sam? It's me—Marcy needs you."

Movement rustled the bed as a bare-chested shadow lumbered up, hand to his eyes and a growl in his throat. "What the blazes are you doing, O'Connor? Can't you see I'm busy?"

Fire singed Patrick's temper, burning the sockets of his eyes when a blonde rose to clutch a sheet to her unbuttoned blouse. He focused on Sam, a spasm in his jaw that matched that in his fists. "Yeah, I can see that—busy betraying Marcy." He spit out the words like venom. "You're almost engaged, O'Rourke, or have you forgotten?"

"The key word being 'almost,' O'Connor, so stay outta this."

A nerve pulsed in Patrick's temple as he glared, his words as clipped and blunt as the fists clenched at his sides, just itching to rearrange Sam's face. "I'll give you exactly twenty seconds to get dressed and out of this room, O'Rourke, or so help me, I'll tell Marcy you're too busy in bed to be where she needs you to be."

"You wouldn't," Sam hissed. His eyes bore into Patrick's.

"Oh, you bet I would. You don't deserve a woman like her, and God knows she doesn't deserve a man like you if this is how you intend to treat her."

Sam grappled for his shirt on the floor, his glassy gaze fused to Patrick's while he methodically put it back on. "I'm warning you—it'll be the end of our friendship if you tell her."

"It's the end of our friendship either way," Patrick

ground out, teeth clenched so tight, his jaw ached.

"You don't mean that." Sam wobbled to his feet. His fingers were clumsy as he attempted to button the fly of his trousers. "We have too much history, too much alike to let a woman come between us."

Patrick took a step forward, fists hard as rock. "Marcy is not just any woman, you blackguard—she's supposed to be the woman you love."

Sam had the gall to laugh. "Aye, the woman we both love, if truth be told, which is exactly why you won't tell her because it would kill her, and well you know it." He slowly buttoned his shirt, eyeing Patrick with a wary look. "Look, I'll make you a deal. I fully intend to remain faithful to Marcy once my ring is on her finger because as you know, she's not a woman prone to satisfy a man's needs without the gold band in place." He sat on the bed to put on his shoes, the woman beside him all but forgotten while his gaze locked with Patrick's. "And we're men with needs, Patrick, the both of us. But ..." He slowly rose to his feet, hands propped to his hips. "If you insist on being Marcy's advocate and protector, then I'll make the engagement official with a ring sooner rather than later, faithful to the core."

Patrick's eyes flicked to the woman and back, his voice thick with disgust. "You don't know how to be faithful, O'Rourke."

A spark of anger shot from eyes spidered with red. "Ah, but that's where you're wrong, my friend—I know how to do a great many things." His smile was casual and cool, but Patrick didn't miss his steely tone. "Especially how to persuade Marceline that I have needs to be met."

White-hot fury exploded in Patrick's brain and he lunged, fist coiled in rage as he bludgeoned Sam's jaw, the force of his blow hurtling O'Rourke to the wall. The woman in the bed screamed and jumped up, clenching her blouse closed as she fled from the room. Patrick stood over him, chest heaving and voice brutal while Sam rubbed his face with the back of his hand, shock glazing his eyes. "You ever talk about Marcy like that again or do anything to compromise her, and I swear— I'll hurt you in ways you never dreamed possible." He backed away, too afraid he'd hit him again, his words burning like acid on his tongue. "Now, get your sorry carcass over there and pick her up at the rectory like you told her you'd do."

Sam sat up, eyes shuttered closed for a brief moment before a low groan rumbled from his throat. "No, that wasn't tonight, I swear—" He shielded his face, as if trying to recall, then groaned again when he apparently realized his mistake. He peered up, his guilt obvious from the deep ridges in his brow. "Blast it, Patrick, I must have misunderstood—I would have never forgotten Marcy like that."

"No, but you sure in the devil would betray her with another woman quick enough, wouldn't you?"

Patrick's scorn struck like a cobra, causing Sam to wince. He gouged shaky fingers through tousled hair, his voice hoarse and his breathing heavy. "You wouldn't understand."

"Try me," Patrick said, a sneer twisting his lips. "I'd love to hear your noble excuse for betraying the one woman you claim to love."

Sam's eyes bulged with anger. "Curse you and curse your blasted pretty face." Hunched on the edge of the bed, he put his head in his hands.

"What the devil is that supposed to mean?" Patrick snapped.

Sam was silent for several moments before he

spoke, his words bit out in pain. "It means there isn't a woman alive except Marceline Murphy who prefers me over you."

"What?" Patrick stared in disbelief, then stabbed a finger toward the hall. "You're bloomin' daft, O'Rourke—a lass just left your bed, for pity's sake. Women crawl all over you."

Sam glanced up, face sculpted in stone. "Aye, Patrick, they do, providin' the Southie Adonis turns them away first, then naturally his loyal side-pal will do." Bitterness spewed from his mouth. "But even then, some only in hopes of getting to you."

Patrick scowled, his tone curt over the absurdity of Sam's claim. "You're out of your mind, O'Rourke. If that's true, then why is Marcy in love with you?"

Sam shook his head, eyes in a cold stare. "I honestly don't know," he said quietly, his whisper as tormented as his face. "But I can tell you one thing—it's the only time it's ever happened, and I refuse to let her go."

Mouth slacking, Patrick gaped at his so-called best friend, his anger ramping up all over again. "So Marcy's nothing more than a *contest*—is that it?"

Sam stared him down. "In the beginning, yes," he said, his manner intense, "but I've been seeing the woman for over five months now, Patrick, and as God is my witness, I've fallen in love with her."

Patrick's lip curled. "Yeah, that's why you were in bed with somebody else." He took a step forward, hands clenched. "You have no intention of marrying her, do you?"

A muscle jerked in Sam's throat. "You and I both know I've never claimed to be a marrying man, but Marcy's changed that, I swear, and I plan to make the engagement official in the new year."

"While sleeping with other women, no doubt."

Patrick seared him with a look, eyes itching hot.

Sam looked away. A tic pulsed in a cheek hollowed by drink and fatigue. "I told you you wouldn't understand," he whispered.

"Oh, that's right, your bruised ego over something you've imagined in that harebrained head of yours. You're sick, O'Rourke, you know that?"

A hollow laugh grunted from his friend's lips as he closed his eyes to knead the bridge of his nose. "Aye, I do," he said quietly, releasing a heavy sigh before he looked up to meet his gaze with a haunted one of his own. "A sickness I can't seem to fix."

"What the devil are you talking about?"

Sam buried his hands in his pockets, head bowed. "I mean throughout our entire friendship, Patrick, I've been nothing but an afterthought in people's minds when it comes to you. Not as bright or handsome or charismatic as the beloved Patrick O'Connor. Nor favored by teachers or even the management at the *Herald*. I've spent so many years trying to measure up—with women, in school, at work—that sometimes I ..." His eyes shuttered closed. "Almost *feel* as if it's a sickness. Like I'm driven by this insatiable craving for affirmation ..." He quickly looked away, shame evident in the slump of his shoulders. "Especially of—as Marceline would say—'a more carnal nature.'"

Patrick blinked, jaw distended. "You're lying."

Sam looked up then, the truth naked in his eyes. "I wish I were. Marcy's the best thing that's ever happened to me, and I don't want to lose her."

Patrick slashed a hand toward the bed. "Then stop all this, Sam. Commit to her and tell her the truth." His back straightened with a thrust of his jaw. "Or I will."

Sam nodded slowly, a quivering breath shuddering from his lips. "I will, I swear." He lifted his chin, facial muscles tight with determination. "As God is my witness, I plan to do everything in my power to be faithful to her, Patrick, you have my word."

"Your word." Patrick's tone made it sound like an obscenity. "Your word used to be golden, O'Rourke, but not after this." He shifted with a slack of his hip, hands slung low. "And I'm guessing Marcy thought she had your 'word' too."

Ruddy color bled into Sam's face. "I have never told Marcy I wouldn't see other women—"

"No, but you conveniently let her assume it, didn't you, Sam? The all-powerful silent commitment that goes along with an 'unofficial engagement.'" He spit the words out like a curse. "The perfect means to keep her for yourself while you do what you bloomin' well please."

"Blast it, this is all new to me, committing to one woman," he shouted, fingers trembling as he raked a hand through his hair. "Give me a chance to make it right."

Patrick studied him with a keen eye, his respect for Sam wavering even if his affection was not. Sweat beaded on Sam's brow while Patrick remained silent, considering the best course—both for Marcy and his closest friend. He trusted Sam with his life, but something had changed since Marcy, shaking his trust. He finally huffed out a noisy sigh. "One last chance," he emphasized with a stiff thrust of his finger, his stance as deadly as the threat implied. "You settle down and commit to the woman now or cut her loose, do you hear? But if you commit, O'Rourke, so help me, I will be watching you like a hawk, and if I catch you with another woman other than harmless flirtation over a beer or a dance ..." He squared his shoulders, hands falling firm at his sides while his jaw calcified to rock.

"You'll not only risk losing Marcy, my friend, you'll risk losing me."

Sam nodded, gaze dropping to the floor. "Agreed." He exhaled heavily, then mauled his face with his hands. "Was Marcy mad when I didn't show?"

A grunt parted from Patrick's mouth. "Worried sick is more like it. Over you *and* the five hundred dollars somebody stole from the fundraiser."

Sam's body froze for the briefest of moments before his head shot up. "What?"

Patrick strode to the door and glanced back, tone hard. "Every dime she's earned for the fundraiser—gone, just like that. She's devastated, O'Rourke, and you're the one she wants, although only God knows why." He turned to go.

"Patrick—wait." He clawed the back of his neck before delivering a contrite look. "I'm ... sorry for what I said about Marcy—I didn't mean it. You just made me mad, and I ... only said it to get under your skin." He slipped his hands in his pockets, gaze locked on Patrick's feet and his manner considerably humbled. "I do love her, even though my actions don't always show it, and I swear ..." He looked up then, a glint of resolve in black eyes that burned with intent. "This won't happen again."

Patrick nodded. "You're right, because if it does, you'll pay." He moved toward the door without another word.

"And, Patrick ..."

Pausing, he shot a glance over his shoulder, hand on the knob.

A lump shifted in Sam's throat. "You're ... not going to tell her, are you?"

Patrick studied his best friend for several moments, wondering how two friends who had been so very much alike could now be so different. Sam had a selfish streak when it came to women, true, but he'd always given Patrick his all. The rest of Patrick's anger seeped out on a quiet sigh. "Not if you tell her the truth first and treat her right. And be there when she needs you—like now. She'll be at the rectory a while filing a report with the police, so get a move on."

Sam expelled a loud sigh of relief. "I'm on my way." He took a step forward and stopped, worry etched in his face. "Are we okay, then ... you and I?"

Patrick's pause was longer this time. He wanted to turn his back on him, but that would be like cutting off his own arm. But then Sam's deceit with Marcy was slicing into his heart, so he was dashed if he did and dashed if he didn't. His mouth went flat. "Yeah, we're okay." His brow jagged high in warning. "Unless this happens again."

Sam rubbed the side of his jaw with a sheepish grin. "It won't. And I deserve more than your fist, Patrick, so thanks for knocking some sense into me."

"Yeah, you do, you clown, and don't think I won't do it again." Patrick exhaled loudly, all energy sapped. "Do me a favor, O'Rourke ..." A sick feeling settled in Patrick's gut as he peered up at his friend, jaw tight. "Before you lay a hand on Marcy, clean yourself up. She deserves far more than the touch and scent of another woman."

Sam nodded, the rise and fall of his chest sagging into a slump of shoulders.

Without another word, Patrick left through the back door, a gloom invading his mood as dark as the shadowed alley behind the pub. A woman like Marceline Murphy deserved so much more. His stomach cramped. Not the least of which was a man she could trust.

Chapter Twenty-Six

Despite the bitter cold, Sam had never felt warmer, happier—*cleaner*—than he did now, with Marcy tucked beneath his coat as he shielded her from the swirling snow on the walk to her house. He ducked his head close to hers, the scent of lilac water and lavender from her hair stirring his heart as effectively as the woman in his arms. Somehow she brought out a fierce protectiveness in him, something a woman had never done before other than his sisters.

Along with a fierce possessiveness.

The sudden memory of Patrick's deep-rooted affection for Marcy—Sam refused to call it love—made him grip her closer. He knew full well that if she ever found out about his indiscretions—either tonight's or those in the future should he slip despite his intent to remain faithful—she would end it. And there was no doubt in his mind whatsoever that if Sam were out of the picture, even for a brief time, Patrick would swoop in faster than a seagull over Massachusetts Bay, robbing Sam of the woman of his dreams—*and* Patrick's. He ground his jaw hard, in total contrast to the feather-light snowflakes that fluttered from the sky, delicate, pure, and light. *Like Marcy*—the only woman who had ever made him feel decent and whole for the first time in his life.

Thoughts of Patrick's obvious infatuation suddenly soured his mood. He loved Patrick O'Connor as if the same blood traveled their veins, and it pained him to know he deprived his best friend of the one woman he wanted. Guilt niggled. Almost as much as it exhilarated him to finally best the one man he all but idolized. His lips went flat. *Along with everyone else, apparently.* Except for Marcy, that is, and the thought warmed Sam more than the heat from her body, snuggling close to his.

Truth be told, Patrick was the only reason Sam was with Marcy in the first place, and he owed the man a debt of thanks. Yes, Marcy was beautiful and smart and kind and more of a lady than he'd ever encountered before. But it was Patrick's obsession with her that had truly turned his head, opening his eyes to a rare chance to succeed where Patrick could not. From the first toss of that coin, Sam knew Julie's friendship with Marcy gave him an edge in this battle of charm, allowing him to forge a closeness with Marcy that Patrick never could. From little on, Julie had made it clear Marcy had a crush on Sam, the one boy who turned her head and her heart, and he had thrived in that secret devotion.

Unlatching the snow-encrusted front gate, Sam ushered her up the flagstone walk to her front porch, hoping the late hour of eleven meant her parents and grandmother were already abed. He was in dire need of time alone with her for a few moments in the parlour, and he sensed she needed him as well. He pressed a kiss to her hair and twisted the knob of her front door, pushing it open. A groan lodged in his throat when a blaze of parlour light shafted onto the snowy porch to sparkle the dusting of ice crystals like a thick layer of salt.

"Marcy?" Her mother's concern was obvious from the high pitch of her tone as she hurried into the foyer. "Where on earth have you been?" Her eyes flicked from her daughter's face to Sam's and back, and his body tensed as always at the muted disapproval in Bridget Murphy's eyes.

"Oh, Mother!" Marcy shot into her mother's embrace with another agonizing sob, breaking Sam's heart as she shuddered in Mrs. Murphy's arms.

"Bridget?" Within several of Marcy's painful heaves, her father strode from the parlour, newspaper dangling from his hand and Marcy's grandmother on his heels. "Good grief, Marceline," he said in a tight tone that conveyed his angst, "are you all right?"

She nodded and pulled away from her mother's hold, voice nasal from weeping as she stepped back, a bare inch in front of Sam. "Y-yes, Papa, I'm fine, but I'm afraid the fundraiser for St. Mary's is not ..."

She lapsed into another round of tears, and Sam couldn't stop himself—he gently turned her into a tender hug while stroking her hair, offering her family a somber gaze over Marcy's shoulder. "My apologies for the late hour, Mr. and Mrs. Murphy, but the fundraiser money—some $300 or so—was stolen from the safe tonight at the center, and Marcy was detained at the rectory to file a police report."

Her mother's gasp rent the air. "Oh, heavens, no!"

"Thank you, Sam, for bringing her home," Marcy's father said with a grim smile. He extended his hand to the parlour. "Shall we discuss this sitting down?"

Sam nodded and led Marcy to a blue French-style sofa with graceful mahogany trim, opting to sit beside her on one side while her mother hovered close on the other. He helped Marcy off with her coat, then did the same with his own as her mother looped an arm to her daughter's waist. Perched on the edge of a floral wing chair, Marcy's grandmother watched with folded hands and keen blue eyes that always made Sam nervous, as if she were studying him under a microscope.

"How did this happen and when?" her father asked, his gentle tone edged with worry for a daughter Sam knew was the apple of his eye. Like Mima, he hunched on the edge of his leather gentleman's chair, arms stiff on parted knees and hands clasped while he searched his daughter's face. His salt-and-pepper hair was carefully slicked back and dark moustache neatly trimmed, the consummate image of the railroad vice president he used to be. His blue eyes crinkled at the edges with a fan of fine lines on a distinguished face that was clearly aging well.

Marcy sniffed and proceeded to relate the weepy details of a nightmare that had robbed her of her usual peaceful countenance as much as it had robbed the center. Her hoarse and heavy tone tore at his gut, and Sam fought the urge to slip an arm to her shoulder and cuddle her close. But Marcy's family already had misgivings about his reputation; he certainly didn't need to add fuel to the fire. He released a silent sigh, well aware he had a lot to prove, not only to Marcy and her family, but to himself.

Can I be all she needs me to be? A thought occurred that he should pray about it, like Marcy always prodded him to do, but just as quickly, the notion fled. Prayer was something for women, priests, and weak-minded people, his father was fond of saying, his stock rebuttal whenever his mother badgered him to go to novenas. As stubborn as his mother was religious, his father was of the opinion that able-bodied men didn't need to bother the Almighty with every little thing, a leaning he quickly passed on to Sam. *Along* with his long-held belief that men—*especially* his son—needed to sow wild oats before they settled down, a point of view not shared by his mother.

"Well, Marceline," her father said when Marcy was through with her account of the robbery, "I don't know how, but I do know that God will intervene on your behalf, you mark my words." He nodded at his wife and mother-in-law, the barest of smiles edging his lips. "If I've learned anything from these two stubborn ladies here, it's that God always has the last say when it comes to His own, especially when we pray." He leaned to squeeze his daughter's hand, paralyzing Sam to the sofa when this imposing man of dignity closed his eyes to deliver a prayer while the others followed suit. Feeling awkward, Sam promptly did the same, head bowed and heart thudding. At the close of Mr. Murphy's prayer, Marcy threw herself into her father's arms, more tears welling when he bundled her on his lap to rock her in his arms. "Aw, darlin', you'll see—God will turn this around. And how about we begin right now?"

With a firm pat of Marcy's back, her father pulled a checkbook and ink pen from his vest pocket and commenced to writing a check while Marcy watched, eyes wide as saucers. "A hundred dollars? Papa, no," she cried, staring at the check he'd just written. "This is too much, and we can't afford this right now."

He chuckled and prodded her off his lap, rising to his feet to press a kiss to her cheek. "I had an excellent interview today that has given me hope, darlin', so let's consider it our contribution to the fundraiser—your mother's, Mima's, and mine. Or if it makes you feel any better, you can always pay part of it back when the money is found." He caressed her face with the palm of his hand. "And if not you, then God will, so take the money, daughter, and let's all of us get these tired, old bones to bed."

"Speak for yourself, Kiernan Murphy," Mima said with a clipped brogue that held a hint of humor. "My bones are strong and spry, I'll have you know."

He grinned. "Aye, and with a hard head to match." He arched a brow at his wife before he sent her a wink. "It's best we head up, woman, if I'm to have the strength to spar with your mother."

Marcy lifted on tiptoe to deposit a kiss to her father's cheek. "Good night, Papa," she said with the first smile Sam had seen since he'd picked her up at the rectory. She gave him a fierce hug. "I love you so much."

He patted her back and nodded at Sam. "I appreciate your support of Marcy tonight and for bringing her home."

Sam rose. "I care about Marcy a great deal, Mr. Murphy, so it was no hardship, I assure you." His gaze darted to Marcy and back while he fiddled with the coat in his hand. "If it's all right with you, sir, I'd like a few words with your daughter before I head out. I won't be long, I promise."

"All right, Sam," Mr. Murphy said with a cautious air, "but not too long, please. Marcy's had a trying evening and needs her rest."

"Yes, sir."

Marcy's mother and grandmother each gave her a hug and murmured their good nights before Mr. Murphy shepherded them out the door. Sam didn't breathe till he heard the squeak of the stairs, and then twining his fingers with hers, he tugged Marcy down to the sofa, tucking her close. "It's going to be all right," he whispered, slowly buffing her arms. "You'll see.

The police will find the thief."

She nodded and warmth expanded in his chest when her arms slowly curled around his waist with a sigh. "I know—I felt it the moment Papa prayed."

"And you still have ticket and concession sales to count on, you know, even if the ad money and presales are never recovered."

A reedy sigh parted from her lips. "That's true."

He pressed a soft kiss to her cheek. "I ache for you, Marceline, and I'm so sorry."

His pulse sped up when she turned and burrowed into his hold, as if she couldn't get close enough. "I know—me too."

"If I could bring the money back, I would, you know that." He paused, his throat suddenly dry as he feathered her arm with his thumb. "But there is something I can do, and I hope and pray it will lift your spirits."

She glanced up, her tender look swelling his pride. "What's that?"

He shifted to cup her face in his hands, his manner gentler than ever before. "I love you, Marcy, I know that now, and my heart grieves when you grieve. Seeing you suffer tonight has jolted me, made me aware that I want to be there for you always." He bent in to caress her lips with his own, his kiss almost reverent. "I don't have the money for a ring just yet, but I will soon, and I'm asking you to marry me. Nothing unofficial this time, my love, but engaged in the open for all to see—soon."

She clutched his arm, eyes shining. "Oh, Sam, do you mean it? Really and truly?"

He chuckled. "I do," he said in a husky tone.

Her wispy giggle floated in the air as she blinked up at him. "But why the change of heart?"

He sat back, cuddling her close. "Patrick."

She jerked up to face him. "Patrick? What do you mean?"

His heart stalled as he averted his gaze to the baby grand piano in the corner of the parlour. Guilt churned in his stomach. "Well, you see—Patrick found me at Brannigan's tonight, Marcy, because as I told you earlier ..." He drew in a fortifying breath as he looked at her again, determined to keep his promise to tell Marcy the truth—however vague it might be. "I thought it was tomorrow night I was supposed to pick you up, not tonight."

She nodded, his mention of Brannigan's dimming the luster in her eyes.

Sam cleared his throat, far more comfortable with evading the truth than facing it dead on, but he couldn't risk her hearing it from Patrick instead of him. "I know you're not fond of Brannigan's, but a man needs a place to relax with his friends, have a brew every now and then, especially after a rough shift like I had tonight. But when Patrick found me, he lost his temper and bruised my jaw because I was ..." He swallowed hard, absently rubbing the spot where Patrick had knuckled him. "Chatting with a woman I think he might have his eye on, and so he took a shot at me, ranting and raving how he was going to tell you, insisting I was betraying you."

Those beautiful blue eyes blinked while a sadness welled in their depths that twisted his gut.

He gripped her shoulders, his eyes burning with intent. "What I'm trying to say, Marcy, is that up to now, it's been second nature for me to flirt and tease with pretty women, and I ..." He worked his throat to fight the parched taste in his mouth. "I told myself that as long as we weren't officially courting, that such ...

innocent flirtations ... were not only commonplace, but ..." He quietly gulped. "To be expected."

More moisture pooled in her eyes and he groaned, swallowing her up in a fierce hug. "Oh, Marceline, I swear—I was too stupid and thick and selfish to think that you might construe it as betrayal until Patrick landed that blow, and now I want to make it right." He pulled away, searching her gaze with his own. "I want to commit to you body and soul, my love, if you'll have me, and if you'll forgive me for being the dolt that I am." Sweat beaded the back of his neck as he awaited her answer, not all that sure she wouldn't throw him out on his ear.

The air fused hot and thick in his lungs when she turned away, silent for several heart-wrenching seconds before she finally met his eyes with a tentative glance of her own. "Of course I forgive you," she said quietly, gaze dropping to her lap while she picked at her nails, "but given our commitment, your behavior is a shock, I won't lie."

"Marcy—"

"No—hear me out, please." She looked up then, and he could see the hesitation in eyes misty with hurt. "I care about you a great deal, Sam, and it's always been a dream of mine to be part of your family ..." She averted her gaze while a hint of pink dusted her cheeks. "And lately," she said softly, her voice trailing off, "the dream has grown to include being your wife ..."

"But ...?" Sam whispered, not daring to breathe.

Drawing in a shaky breath, she finally looked up, her face gentle except for the wet resolve in her eyes. "But in light of what you've just confessed and the way your ..." The muscles shifted in her throat. "... passions have escalated when we're alone, well I ... I must admit that it does give me pause ..."

A muscle convulsed in his throat. "I can change for you, Marcy, I swear it."

Her lips curved in a sad smile. "Not for me, Sam," she whispered, "change for yourself and for God—so your life can be all He wants it to be."

His facial muscles tightened as he nodded his head. "All right, my love, what do you need me to do?"

She nibbled at the edge of her smile. "Well, for starters, Mr. O'Rourke, you can stop tempting me with kisses that weaken my resolve." The smile dimmed as her tone sobered. "It's important to me to keep our relationship chaste and pure until we marry." She caressed his jaw with the palm of her hand. "And it's especially critical you pursue God as much as you pursue me."

He nodded again, gaze on the floor. "All right, then, consider it done." He rose to his feet. "Beginning now—see me out?"

She exhaled and walked him to the foyer, her hand tucked in the crook of his arm before she stood on tiptoe to press a kiss to his cheek at the door. "Good night, Sam—you've definitely lifted my spirits tonight."

He slipped his coat on and then cupped her face in his hands. "I hope to lift your spirits far more in the future, my love, once I become the husband you need me to be." Grazing her cheek with his thumb, he slowly bent to brush a kiss to her lips, aching to kiss her with all the passion she provoked inside. But there was no way he would risk losing her again, not with the threads of their relationship so tentative at the moment. He expelled a sigh and gave her a tender embrace, then paused as an unsettling thought marred his mood. Flirtations were one thing, he suddenly realized, but if Patrick ever disclosed Sam's sexual infidelities in a fit of anger, it could ruin everything. He swallowed hard, opting for a bit of insurance as he lowered his voice to a whisper. "Marcy ..."

"Yes, Sam?" She snuggled in to his hold.

"I'm concerned about Patrick."

She glanced up, a furrow etched in her brow. "Why?"

"Because he fancies himself in love with you and something in my gut tells me if he were to get angry enough—or desperate enough—he just might ..." His eyelids weighted closed with regret. "Well, he might bend the truth a wee bit to show me in a bad light, you know? Maybe even imply I made advances in the hopes you would turn me away."

"I don't believe that," she whispered, cheeks braised as if the subject made her uncomfortable. She shook her head, her disbelief evident in the two tiny puckers that creased the bridge of her nose. "You and Patrick are closer than brothers, Sam. I don't think he would do that."

He lifted her chin with the tip of his finger, gaze wary. "Brothers have been known to war over women," he said quietly, hoping beyond hope that it never came to that between Patrick and him. "And keep in mind a woman has never turned him away, so you're a challenge, my love. Patrick's a very competitive man, you know, who's never lost with a woman before, so when he lost the bet over you—"

"The bet?" she whispered, head tilting.

Gulping down his pride, Sam drew in a sharp breath, not sure if what he was about to reveal would hurt his chances with Marcy or help them. "I know it was wrong, Marcy, but Patrick and I were both so taken with you, that he and I tossed a coin to see which of us would woo you first, and Patrick won the toss—"

She took a step back, jaw gaping in disbelief. "I was a bet? A wager?"

Sam clasped her arms, repentance thick in his tone. "In the beginning yes, but I fell in love with you, Marceline, deeper than I ever dreamed possible, and as God is my witness, I want to make you my wife." He gently buffed her arms, head ducked and gaze tender. "I only tell you now so you know what a blow it was to Patrick's pride that you turned him away." He exhaled slowly. "He's not a man to accept defeat easily, my love, especially with women. But once my ring is on your finger, he'll relent, you'll see." He bent to deposit a gentle kiss to her cheek before pulling back, contrition etched in his face. "So ... am I forgiven?"

He didn't breathe until he saw the faint curve of her lips, although there was a bit of a scold in her tone. "You're lucky I'm not adverse to the toss of a coin, Samuel O'Rourke, but it's best you know right now that I am not a proponent of gambling."

"Yes, ma'am," he said, gently tugging her close, "no gambling in the O'Rourke household, you have my word. Only absolute certainties—such as how I plan to make you happy, my love." He nuzzled her lips with a goodbye kiss before opening the door and stepping outside. "Good night, Marceline. And save Saturday afternoon for me after the play practice, all right? I think it's time to scout out some rings."

"Oh, Sam!" Her face was so aglow that for a brief moment, he almost regretted his plan for a long engagement. He strode down her snowy front steps, tugging up his collar to ward off the cold.

Almost.

Chapter Twenty-Seven

Marcy blew her whistle, and all heads pivoted her way as she stood up from her seat next to Sister Francine in the first row to address choir and cast. "Bravo, everyone—this has been your best rehearsal yet!" Her smile tipped into a grin. "Which is good, considering our first show is this weekend. Choir angels, be sure to pick up your costumes from Miss O'Rourke before you leave tonight and everyone—don't forget we have dress rehearsal at six sharp tomorrow night. Come dressed and ready to go, and principals need to arrive a half hour earlier so Miss O'Rourke and I can make up your faces, all right? Good night, everyone, and thank you."

Shrieks, giggles, and the rumble of feet stomping down the stage steps filled the auditorium with an almost electric excitement. A veritable adrenaline buzz had everyone feverish with anticipation and so keyed up that Marcy hadn't slept a decent wink for the last two nights. She slipped her script into Papa's attaché and snapped it shut, turning to Sister Francine with a shaky expulsion of air and an even shakier smile. "Well, Sister, if we aren't ready by now, we never will be," she said with a sudden rush of jitters.

A Light in t

Sister Francine's deep
ease the tightness in
Marceline, if ever a cast
gave Marcy's cheek an a
moon-shaped face eclips
done a masterful job, an
be our finest fundraiser yet.

Marcy's smile faded, thoughts of the stolen ...
stealing her joy.

"There, there, child," Sister Francine whispered, giving Marcy a powerful hug, "it's in God's hands now, remember?"

A frail sigh fluttered from Marcy's lips before she jutted her chin in a show of confidence. "Yes, it is, Sister, and I thank God for that."

Sister Francine eyed several boys from the choir who were darting between the rows in a game of tag, then adjusted her habit with a firm tug of meaty hands. "Go home and get some sleep, Marceline," she ordered, "and I'll lock up after I rein in a few ruffians."

Marcy grinned at the shriek of Sister Francine's whistle, which promptly sent the intended "ruffians" fleeing in all directions as if pursued by the Angel of Death. Shaking her head, she glanced up at the near-empty stage where Julie was distributing the last of the costumes to several giddy angels who appeared as if they might take flight at any moment. "Jewels—you almost ready to go? Sister said she'd lock up."

"Sure," Julie called, patting an angel's head before shuffling her music into a neat pile. She closed the fall board of the piano and hurried down the steps to hook an arm through Marcy's. "Come on—Evan asked to walk me home, so we have to pick him up at the center."

Marcy balked. "Oh no, he might want to take you to

Julie Lessman

, so I'll just walk home alone."

 will not," Julie said with a jut of her jaw. asked me to make sure Evan or Patrick or ebody walks you home since he had to work night, so no argument."

"It's not that far, really." Marcy released a weary sigh while Julie prodded her down the hall and out the door to the courtyard.

"Both Sam and Daddy gave me express orders to have an escort whenever we walk home at night, which only makes sense, and you know it. Goodness, since that young woman was attacked on the North End last month, we can't be too safe."

Marcy rolled her eyes while Julie dragged her toward the center where lights glowed through the back windows. "That was outside of a brothel in the North End, for pity's sake, not a Southie residential neighborhood." She sighed again when Julie tugged her through the door where Evan had blueprints sprawled all over Miss Clara's kitchen table while Patrick looked on. Tillie gnawed on a cookie nearby, swinging her legs in a chair while she waited for Patrick to walk her home.

Evan glanced up, his gaze immediately lighting on Julie. "You two are done early," he said with a pleased smile.

"Sister Francine offered to lock up for us, so we took her up on it." Julie closed the door with a shiver, cheeks rosy from the cold. She sauntered over to tug on Tillie's braid before peeking over Evan's shoulder. "What's this?" she asked while Marcy hovered at the door, anxious to get home. When Tillie waved, Marcy sent her a wink as Julie squinted at the plans.

Leaning back in his chair, Evan exhaled, pointing at the blueprint he and Patrick had been studying. "We've been batting ideas around for future expansion of the center. I'd discussed the possibility of an overnight shelter with Father Fitz, and he asked me to draw up some plans, so I did." He scratched the back of his head with a pencil. "But it'll be years before it sees the light of day, I'm afraid."

"It will, though," Patrick said, arms folded while he lounged back in his chair, "if I know you, Evan, and probably sooner than you think." His casual gaze connected with Marcy's for the briefest of moments, making her feel anything but casual as she quickly plucked off her gloves.

"Absolutely," she agreed, her cheeks as pink as Julie's, no doubt, but not from the cold. She hadn't seen Patrick since he'd comforted her the night the money was stolen, over two weeks ago. *The night he told me he was in love with me*, she reminded herself, quickly averting her gaze to Evan. "Goodness, Evan, you've already made such strides in the short time you've been here."

"Thanks, Marcy." Evan rose and rolled the blueprints, gaze flicking to Patrick. "And your input has been invaluable, Patrick—thank you. You have so much experience with construction, its seems, so I really appreciate all your time and advice."

"It's my pleasure." Patrick shuffled to his feet and pushed in his chair. "Well, I best get Tillie home."

"We're heading to Robinson's, so why don't you join us?" Evan asked, and Marcy inwardly moaned, time at Robinson's with Julie, Evan *and* Patrick the last thing she needed. "After all, I owe you one for all the help you've been."

Tillie bounded into the air, cookie crumbs spilling down the front of her patched corduroy jumper. "Yay, Robinson's!" she shouted in glee, peeking up at Patrick with hope in her eyes. "You promised you'd take me soon, Patrick, remember?"

Patrick tweaked her pigtail with a sympathetic smile. "Sorry, Till, can't tonight, but soon, I promise." He slid his coat off the chair and slipped it on, buttoning it with a smile that seemed suddenly stiff, at least to Marcy. "Thanks for the invite, Evan, but I'm meeting friends after I walk Tillie home, so I should head out."

"Oh, rats," Tillie mumbled, snitching another cookie from a plate on the counter before allowing Patrick to button up her coat. Cookie clenched in her mouth, she waited patiently while he helped her on with her threadbare gloves, finally twirling a scruffy scarf around her neck.

"Another time, then." Evan shook Patrick's hand.

The back door flew open, and a blast of cool air swooshed in along with a ruddy-faced Father Fitz, coatless and chest heaving from his obvious jog to the center. "Sweet chorus of angels, but it's frigid out there," he said, quickly closing the door before buffing the arms of his cassock. "But at least that blessed heat wave two days ago has melted most of the snow." His gaze found Marcy, and he flashed a broad grin. "Ah, just the person I was hoping to find," he quipped, latching her arm to steer her to the table. "Perhaps you better sit down, young lady."

The blood in Marcy's cheeks plummeted all the way to her toes as she stared up at Father Fitz, heart racing as if she were the one who'd just sprinted the courtyard. "What is it, Father?" she breathed, hoping it was good news.

"Only the answer to your prayers, Marceline—and mine." Bending over, he clasped her shoulder with a firm grip, then gave her a wink. "The money's been found."

A gasp popped from Marcy's lips followed by a high-pitched squeal when she launched to her feet, flinging her arms around his neck in a hug. "Oh, Father, I'm going to cry, I just know it!"

"The saints be praised!" Julie said, as giddy as Marcy. "Where, Father?"

"Well, it seems one of our young ladies found it tonight after play practice during an impromptu game of hide and seek. Buried under a mound of leaves, it was, beneath a bush in a dark corner of the courtyard just outside the center." He patted Marcy's back before he chucked a finger to her chin, affection in his smile. "Go home, Marceline, and get some sleep—I suspect your worry over this has robbed you of much-needed slumber."

Marcy suddenly felt as limp as the egg noodles Mother cooked for dinner, her eyes sparkling with a near sheen of tears despite the fatigue of her body. "Your suspicions would be correct," she said with a sigh of relief so loud, Father Fitz chuckled.

"Do we have any idea how it got there?" Evan asked.

Father Fitz paused, lips pursed in thought. "No earthly idea, I'm afraid, but perhaps whoever took it hid there and then dropped it by accident or out of fear during that awful snow that finally covered it up. Or perhaps guilt got the best of whomever and they simply buried it there, hoping it would be found after the thaw." He shrugged his shoulders, then dazzled them with a beatific smile as his gaze honed in on Marcy. "My personal favorite, of course, would be that it was an angel of mercy on a mission from God who heard the fervent prayers of what Mr. Farrell has fondly referred to as our own 'angel of mercy.'"

"Aye, Father Fitz, hear tell those angels of mercy can be a wee bit clannish," Patrick said with a smile. "Especially those of Irish descent."

Father Fitz's laughter boomed in the kitchen as he made his way to the door, tossing an imp of a smile over his shoulder that would have made a leprechaun proud. "I have heard a rumor to that effect. Well, the money is safely tucked away in the rectory, Marceline, so sleep well, eh? Good night, all."

"Good night, Father," Marcy called while the others echoed her farewell.

"Oh, Marcy, I am so relieved!" Julie giggled while she hugged her with all of her might. "This calls for a celebration at Robinson's."

Marcy chewed on her lip. "Jewels, don't be mad, please, but all I want to do is fall into bed, so you and Evan go and enjoy yourselves."

"Oh, boo," Julie said with a frown. "Well, all right then, but we'll walk you home first, won't we, Evan?"

"Absolutely," Evan said, pushing in his chair. "It's no problem at all. I just need to close up here, then we can be on our way."

Marcy arched a brow, one side of her smile sloping up. "It's in the opposite direction by at least six blocks, Evan Farrell, so I refuse to let you and Julie waste your time, especially in this weather." She tugged on her gloves with a determined air. "I'll be fine."

"Patrick!" Julie spun around, halting Patrick and Tillie on their way to the door, where Marcy suspected he was hoping for a clean getaway. "Sam made me promise I wouldn't let Marcy walk home alone, so would you mind walking with her?"

A flush crept up the back of his neck as he turned, his manner way too awkward for an overly confident rake such as himself. A knot dipped in his throat when his gaze met Marcy's. "Not at all," he said with a smile that seemed a bit forced. "It's actually not that far out of our way, right Tillie?"

"Right!" Tillie said with a jut of her little chin. "Then I can swing while you hold my hands."

"Patrick, seriously—you have plans. I can walk by myself, truly."

"Absolutely not. Sam would never forgive me, nor would I forgive myself." He opened the door and inclined his head, brows arched as Tillie bolted into the courtyard to make angels in what was left of the snow. "Shall we?"

She huffed out a sigh and followed Tillie out. "Good night, you two," she called over her shoulder, tossing Evan and Julie a wry smile. "Be sure to celebrate for me."

Patrick closed the door behind her, his sudden silence as stiff and foreboding as Miss Clara's rosebushes in the moonless night—dark, ominous, and rigid with ice.

"Patrick—"

"Marcy—"

Both spoke and stopped at the same time, easing the tension somewhat when Marcy offered a nervous giggle. "Thank you for walking me home," she said quietly, "especially when I know it's the last thing you want to do."

He stared straight ahead, jaw firm and hands in his pockets while he watched Tillie roll around in the snow. "That's not true—I have no problem walking you home."

"Don't you?" She peeked up, his shadowed silhouette as obscure as the gloom of night. Her voice held a touch of tease. "I've seen hooligans happier to go with Sister Francine than you with me."

A faint smile flickered at the edge of his lips as he bent to make a snowball, neatly pitching it at Tillie as she lay, swishing arms and legs in the snow. "That's because those hooligans are not likely to lose their heart to the likes of Sister Francine," he muttered.

She felt an ache in her chest despite the jest in his tone.

His smile spanned wide when Tillie sat up to spit out the snow he'd showered her with. "Come on, you little angel, before I clip your wings—we need to get you home."

"Just one more, Patrick, please?" Bouncing to her feet, Tillie promptly flopped back down a few feet away, flapping her limbs for all she was worth.

Marcy released a frail sigh. "I'm so sorry," she whispered, "I never meant—"

"I know." He exhaled a heavy breath, head lifted as if to watch the clouds of warm air that swirled away. "Any more than I meant to care as much as I do. But you and Sam will be happy, and I'll survive." He glanced at her out of the corner of his eyes, his smile dull. "And someday soon, I hope, I'll be happy for you two as well."

She nodded, forcing a bright smile when Tillie rejoined them. Grasping their hands, the little dickens proceeded to drag on their arms, giggling when Patrick swooped her up on his shoulders instead.

"You were a godsend the night I discovered the money missing," she said, anxious to steer the subject away from his feelings. Hurrying to keep up with his long strides, she was grateful Tillie was preoccupied with trying to reach snowy limbs overhead. "I don't know what I would have done if you hadn't been there, Patrick, and then you were kind enough to find Sam ..."

"Yeah, I'm a real regular guy." His tone was as flat as his smile.

She chewed on her lip, sneaking a glimpse at his angular profile. "Thank you," she whispered.

He grunted. "Yeah, well, if you ever needed the man, that was the night."

"No," she said carefully, head tilted as she studied him. "Not just for finding him ..." She hesitated, a glimmer of tease in her words. "But for dressing him down."

A shower of snow suddenly rained on them both. "Hey, you little minx," Patrick bellowed, squeezing Tillie's leg when she managed to snatch at a bough. The little girl's giggles rose in the air as Patrick continued to tickle, shooting Marcy a confused glance. "What are you talking about?"

A lump bobbed in her throat. "I'm talking about the bruise to his jaw ..." A faint smile tipped the edge of her lips while she dusted snow off Tillie's leg. "The one that knocked some sense into him."

His brisk pace suddenly slowed. "He actually told you, then?" he asked, his voice laced with shock before it climbed an octave. "The whole truth about other women?"

Her smile faded and she nodded.

He released a low whistle, the sound piercing the air, which Tillie swiftly mimicked. "I gotta admit, I didn't think he would, but I'm glad."

"Me too," she whispered, and she smiled when Tillie bounced on his shoulders in time to a Christmas carol she decided to sing.

He shook his head. "I'll tell you what, Marceline, you are one in a million, and so help me, if I ever catch Sam making advances to another woman again—"

"Hey, Patrick," Tillie shouted, the snowscape

muffling the shriek of her voice, "we're almost there!" Her skinny arms wound around his head as she held on for dear life, fingers buried deep in his dark curls. "Can you give me a fast horsey ride before I'm home, please, please?"

"You bet, darlin'." He gave Marcy a wink. "Don't go anywhere, Miss Murphy," he said, nudging Tillie's hands up from his eyes so he could see, "I'll be right back."

"Bye, Miss Murphy ..." Tillie's goodbye floated in the air as they took off, Patrick's husky laughter merging with the little girl's squeals while the two sprinted to Tillie's building a quarter block away. It was a sight to bring a smile to anyone's face.

Except hers ...

"So help me, if I ever catch Sam making advances to another woman again ..."

Her legs felt like lead as they lagged to a dead stop, parted lips wheezing shallow air while Patrick delivered Tillie to her door. She stood paralyzed in the same spot, her heart as jagged and frozen as the icicles hanging from the eaves of Tillie's flat. "Advances?" she whispered.

"He fancies himself in love with you, Marceline, and something in my gut tells me if Patrick were to get angry enough—or desperate enough—he just might ... well, he might bend the truth a wee bit to show me in a bad light, you know? Maybe even imply I made advances in the hopes you would turn me away."

Something stabbed within, as if one of those icy shards had gouged her very soul, and when Patrick finally jogged back, his smile faded into concern. "Are you all right?"

She shook her head, staring at him as if he were a stranger, her body going cold when she realized who he was—the same man who toyed with Emily Fischer over and over again, and heaven knows how many others, all the while pursuing his quest to steal Marcy's heart, no matter what it took.

"I will never give up, Marceline ..."

Nausea curdled in her stomach as she took a step back. "Sam wasn't making advances," she said, her whisper harsh in the night. "He was just talking to her."

Patrick's body stilled, brows arched in disbelief. "That's what he told you? That he was just *talking* to her?" He shook his head again and started to turn away, jaw sculpted tight.

She grabbed his arm to stop him, blood pounding in her brain. "How dare you imply it was more!"

"*Imply?*" He scrubbed his face with his hands, exhaling loudly before he finally looked up. "Fine. I can see you're only interested in his version of the truth, Marcy, so let's just drop it, shall we?" He continued walking.

She hurried to catch up. "He told me it was nothing more than an innocent flirtation, and I believe him."

He grunted again. "Good. You're going to need a lot of faith in him, darlin', because he's been known to stretch the truth with women."

"Oh, and I suppose Emily Fischer knows nothing about that."

He whirled on her so fast, she staggered back. "He's-not-a-marrying-man, Marceline," he hissed, a nerve pulsing in his cheek, "and you need to know that."

Her eyes blazed right back. "You're wrong! Sam proposed the night the money was stolen, and we've already been shopping for rings, so his 'version of the truth' as you call it, carries far more weight than that of a man who's lied repeatedly to Emily Fischer and heaven knows how many others."

"He gripped her wrist, his eyes singeing as much as his hand. "So he finally proposed, did he? If I were Sam, you would have had a ring months ago."

She jerked free, her mouth ajar. "So, he was right, then," she whispered, hardly able to believe she'd allowed this rogue to pull the wool over her eyes. Fingers quivering, she pushed a loose hair from her cheek. "A competition with Sam to win me?" She backed away, shaking her head while shock trembled her tone. "He warned you might try something like this, but I didn't believe you'd stoop so low as to sabotage my relationship with a man who's like a brother."

Her body jolted when he clutched her arms and gave her a sound shake. "No, it's not like that," he shouted. Then just as abruptly, he dropped his hold and spun away, as if suddenly aware how threatening he appeared. A swear word hissed in the air as he mauled the back of his neck.

"Isn't it?" Marcy leaned in, fists clenched at her sides. "Then what do you call a toss of a coin if not gambling with a girl's heart, desperate to add a notch to your post? Sam said you couldn't stand it when a woman turns you away, and now I see it's true. The high and mighty Patrick O'Connor and his almighty ego, so powerful you'd even resort to lying to jeopardize my relationship with your best friend."

"Lying?" he whispered, his face a mask of pale shock. His tone hardened to granite, along with the tight line of his jaw. "I don't lie to people I love, Marceline," he spat out, "unlike my '*best friend.*'"

"Lies," she whispered, sick inside that Patrick O'Connor was every bit as unfaithful to his best friend as he'd been to the countless women he'd wooed. She shook her head, stepping away while water welled in her eyes. "My heart breaks for you, Patrick, truly, because if you keep on as you are, you will drive everyone away with no one to love." She clutched her arms to her waist and lifted her chin, the icy sting of the wind all but freezing the saltwater streaming her cheeks. "I'm sorry, but I don't trust you," she whispered, her voice dead like her so-called friendship with the Southie's number one rogue, "so I'm asking you to leave me alone, please, and to stay far away from me and my relationship with Sam."

"Marcy, wait—"

But she couldn't. Ignoring the plea in his tone, she spun on her heel and started to run, tears blinding her eyes to a vile indictment she refused to believe. It was Patrick O'Connor's unscrupulous reputation she'd feared in the beginning, and it was that same reputation rearing its ugly head once again. Only this time, it stabbed through her heart because she had actually started to trust the man. A man who would turn on her as quickly as he had on his best friend, apparently, and all for the sake of his all-powerful pride.

And ye shall know the truth, and the truth shall set you free.

Hand to her mouth, she sobbed as she ran, wondering why the truth hurt so very much. She heaved to a stop at her gate, a sharp pain in her heart that matched the one spearing her side. With a resolve born of betrayal, she forced Patrick from her thoughts to dwell on Sam, clinging to the one man who was willing to lay down his past to secure a future—*with her.* For all his lukewarm faith and flirtatious ways, Sam O'Rourke had been her champion since she was a little girl, the rogue who had actually treated her with respect and vowed to tame his passion to win her hand. The favorite son of a family she loved.

Chest heaving, she sagged over her gate. Wet prayers salted her lips while bitter tears slipped from her eyes, a woman desperate to escape the lies of a man she could no longer trust.

And clinging fast to a man she hoped that she could.

Chapter Twenty-Eight

Hands poised on the pull cord for the house curtain, Patrick watched from the wings while the cast took their bows for the first performance of the week, applause thundering through the auditorium. The moment was painfully bittersweet, a sense of pride and relief that Marcy had pulled off one of the most daunting and successful fundraisers in St. Mary's history. The glow of success could be seen, heard, and felt everywhere—in the cheers and whistles of the crowd, in the flush of children's cheeks, and in the twinkle of pride in the eyes of the adults. It was a shimmering radiance that sparkled and shone more than the tinsel that glittered on the Christmas tree at the back of the stage, and Patrick almost regretted it was over.

Almost.

Sister Francine called Marcy and Julie to the front of the stage while cast and audience stomped and whooped so loud, Patrick's ears ached. But not as much as his heart. Gaze fused to the back of her bell-shaped gown, his eyes trailed from that crown of corn-silk curls atop her head, past pale-blonde wisps that feathered her neck, down the gentle curve of her red chiffon dress, his heart bleeding that she would never be his. Hands clasped with Julie's, the two of them bowed to more tumultuous ovation, the flush of Marcy's fair neck evidence of her discomfort with all the praise. Patrick was certain she was as relieved as he when Sister Francine nodded his way to bring the curtain down, and easing the rope through his calloused hands, he slowly lowered the drape.

His heart stalled when Marcy flashed a smile his way, only to sink when Sam stepped up behind him with a small bouquet of holly berries. "I'd say Marcy has a rousing success on her hands," he said quietly, his sorry attempt at restoring communication only straining Patrick's nerves tighter than the pulley rope in his palm.

Lips clamped tight, he turned and ignored Sam altogether, striding past flighty angels buzzing around and buoyant cast milling about to snatch his coat from a hook by the back stage entrance.

"Patrick ..." The plea in Sam's tone followed him down the steps, but he was too afraid to respond, unwilling to spoil everyone's night with the bitter words that tainted his tongue. No, his words—and his fist—would have to wait because the last thing Patrick wanted to do was ruin Marcy's evening and everyone else's. No, not tonight. Not with his so-called best friend. Not after what Sam had done.

"We need to talk," Sam called, the strain in his voice ricocheting down the dark and deserted corridor that led to the exit in the back of the building.

Patrick hurled a heavy door open with a hard slam, eyes burning in his sockets while fury burned in his gut at finding Sam at Brannigan's last night with yet another girl. A habit he'd picked up again, according to Lucas, on the nights he thought Patrick was working. He shouldn't care now that Marcy had turned on him so, but he did. The door closed with a thundering bang as he stalked through the courtyard like a madman, his path little more than gashes in the new-fallen snow. He ground his jaw. Gashes that he'd like to put in Sam O'Rourke's face with his fists if he could, and the very thought made him sick to his stomach.

"A sickness I can't seem to fix."

Sam's words that night at Brannigan's whirled in his brain like a bout with the flu, making him nauseous and queasy and not sure what to do ... *or* when. Bile rose in his throat at the damage he'd cause—to Marcy, to Sam, and to the friendship he and Sam shared. Regret lanced his heart, and Patrick halted midway in the snowy courtyard to put a hand to his eyes. No, not just friendship—*kinship*—as if they shared a tie well beyond the press of bloody wrists at the age of eleven. A blood tie that meant blood would be spilled when Patrick betrayed Sam like Sam had betrayed Marcy. He sucked in a harsh breath of frigid air and continued to walk, his guilt like shards of ice needling his mind over what he had to do. Because Marcy needed to know that when it came to broken vows, the only thing faithful about the man she loved ... was that he'd be faithful to betray her again.

"O'Connor—stop!" Sam's voice rang across the courtyard, the bitter angst of his tone matching that of Patrick's gut, but he kept on walking, head down and jaw tight.

"Why don't you handle this like a man instead of slinking away?"

Blood gorged Patrick's temper as he spun around, fury seething in his chest like a bellows. "What the devil would you know about being a 'man,' O'Rourke?" he raged, fists itching for revenge.

Sam's long legs ate up the distance between them, his black eyes burning coals in a pallid face when he stopped two feet away. "I know a man doesn't let a woman come between him and a near brother."

Patrick spat in the snow, fury rising like bile that needed somewhere to go. "It's you who's come between us, O'Rourke, you and your lies to a woman who deserves better."

Sam cocked a brow, his manner insolent. "They all deserve better, Patrick, but neither of us have ever given it, have we? So I wouldn't be throwing stones if I were you." He latched his thumbs to the pockets of his woolen coat and exhaled loudly, his face taut as he studied Patrick through wary eyes. "I made another mistake," he said quietly, "drank too much brew, it's true, but I have no intention of doing it again. You're my best friend—can't you just let it go?"

Patrick's laugh was brutal. "Sure, O'Rourke, I'll let it go. You just end it with Marcy tonight, and you and I'll be bosom-friends once again, no questions asked."

Sam's jaw calcified, along with his tone. "You just can't stand it that Marcy chose me, can you? The Southie's number one rogue, bested by number two."

Patrick stepped forward, blood throbbing in his veins as his voice rose along with his temper. "I'll tell you what I can't stand. A lecher of a man who would throw away the best thing that ever happened to him." He bludgeoned a finger toward Sam's face, eyes on fire and his voice a loud rant. "You best tell her, Sam, or I will."

"Tell me what?" Marcy stood with Julie and Evan at the back door, a shawl draped over her shoulders that she clutched at her waist. Her red chiffon dress fluttered in the icy breeze as if she were a ghost of Christmas past.

Sam jerked around. His breath billowed into a thundercloud that hovered like a portent of gloom.

"Nothing, Marcy—he's just at it again, spinning tales to try and steal you away."

Like a torch to his temper, Sam's words detonated months of frustration and fury, and with a hiss of a curse, Patrick tackled him from behind, landing them both in the snow in a scramble of fists.

"Patrick—stop!" Marcy flew across the snowy courtyard, her screams no more than a distant voice as Patrick delivered a hard clip to Sam's jaw, hurling him into the yard with a split lip that splattered the snow.

"Sam, please—no!" Marcy pleaded, but Sam ignored her, rebounding with hands knotted, stunning Patrick with a sharp blow to his cheek.

The metallic taste of blood unleashed Patrick's rage, and with a curse that defiled the night, he lunged, ramming Sam into the snow once again to hammer him without mercy.

Evan tried to intervene while Julie shouted for them to stop, but Sam rallied with a lightning thrust to Patrick's gut that sent him flying, leveling him in the snow before diving on top.

"Sam, please—*stop!*" Marcy begged, but to no avail. Wheezing hard, he continued to pummel.

Patrick dislodged him with a violent heave and rolled to his side, surprising Sam with a blunt kick that slammed him flat on his back.

Blood in his eyes as well as his mouth, Patrick lumbered to his feet, attempting to charge until Evan braced him from behind. "Enough, Patrick—it's over!"

Patrick slumped to the ground, chest heaving as he wiped the blood from his nose.

"Sam!" Marcy dropped to her knees, red chiffon splayed across the snow like the blood on Sam's pale face. "Are you all right?"

He nudged her away, rubbing the side of his lip with

the sleeve of his coat. "I'm fine, Marcy, go back inside."

She whirled around to sear Patrick with a look, wildfire in her eyes that cauterized him to the spot. "How dare you ruin this night," she whispered, all gentleness charred in the blaze of her anger. "You are hateful, Patrick O'Connor, and I want you to leave!"

Patrick stared, the tears streaming her cheeks wrenching his heart far more than her words ... yet far less than if she didn't know the truth. Stumbling to his feet, he slowly rose to his full height, shoulders square and jaw taut, ignoring Marcy to focus on Sam. "Tell her, Sam," he rasped, chest heaving, "or I will."

Marcy jumped to her feet, fists clenched and anger shimmering off of her in waves. "Get out!" she screamed. "I won't listen to your lies."

Inwardly he winced, but his gaze remained steady. "No, you'd rather listen to his." His eyes flicked to Sam. "Tell her the truth, Sam—or I will—*now!*"

Sam stood to his feet, his eyes cold slits of rage. "I'll tell her the truth, Patrick, but it won't be what you want to hear. The truth is you're so besotted with a woman who won't have you that you'll stop at nothing to break us up."

Patrick took a step forward, fists knuckled into rocks by his side. "No, O'Rourke, the truth is, you're so besotted with other—"

With a loud roar, Sam bulldozed Patrick to the ground, stealing the wind from him for several seconds while he battered with his fists.

"Sam—*stop!*" Marcy and Julie screamed in unison before Evan jerked him back, restraining him while raspy breaths pumped in Sam's chest.

"I ... don't ... want to ... fight ... with you," Sam hissed, gasping for air while his eyes pleaded with

A Light in the Window

Patrick. "Please ... why don't you ... go home ... and leave ... us alone?"

Head pounding from the slam to the ground, Patrick clambered to his feet, as winded as Sam. He wiped the side of his mouth with the back of his hand. "I'll go," he said with battered breathing, "as soon as you tell her the truth—"

Marcy spun around, eyes glinting with wet fury. "You want the truth, Patrick? The truth is I don't believe you no matter what you say. From everything I know about you, everything I've heard, you're the one notorious for breaking women's hearts, for betraying them with other women and using them." A heave shuddered her chest and her eyes glittered like shards of shattered blue glass. "I want you to leave—*now.*"

His heart writhed as if those very shards had impaled his chest. "Marcy—"

"No!" Her voice was a hoarse command, eyes flickering while she cut him short with a hand in the air. The muscles of her throat spasmed as she chilled him with a gaze as frigid as the snow beneath her feet. "You say you have feelings for me," she whispered, tone harsh, "but if you really cared about me, you would cease this vile charade and *leave-us-alone!*"

A deafening silence prevailed, filled only with the violent drum of his throbbing pulse. His ragged breaths boiled into the air like acrid smoke of a hellish inferno, incinerating any hope that Marcy would ever receive the truth from his lips.

"If you've ever heeded a warning before, Patrick, heed this: your history for toying with women's affections will not only backfire, but it's an affront to God that may well cost you the woman you love."

His eyelids sank closed at the memory of Father Fitz's words, as if they bore the same weight that crushed his very heart. Nodding slowly, he stooped to retrieve his battered flat cap from the snow, eyes downcast as a knot of pain jerked in his throat. "My apologies, Marcy, to both you and Sam." He swallowed hard. "And please know ... I ... I wish you well." He slapped the cap against his thigh several times, then paused while it dangled limply at his side. "And you have my word," he whispered with a finality that shivered his heart, "I'll leave you alone."

Not a word was spoken as he turned to go, trudging through the snow with shoulders slumped as if they carried a treacherous burden. *"I'll leave you alone,"* he'd promised, the weight of that reluctant vow echoing in his brain. His heart wrenched in his chest as his sigh clouded the air. *Like Sam when he betrays you, Marceline ...*

Over and over again.

Chapter Twenty-Nine

Marcy's heart was pounding faster than the cards were flying around the O'Rourke's kitchen table, one eye on her hand and the other on the six spoons in the center. *Two queens, two queens, two queens ... three!* Her adrenaline ramped up as more cards flashed by, just waiting ... *waiting* ... for that fourth queen to appear. A muted boom from the grandfather clock in Mrs. O'Rourke's parlour heralded the hour of eleven while the family indulged in a fast-paced game of spoons before ending the evening with dessert. Mind focused on the win, Marcy thought it was the perfect activity to celebrate—and de-stress—from a week of performances in which there was only one left to go.

In the seat beside her, Sam snatched cards faster than she could discard them while Max hunkered down in his lap, content to watch his big brother play with the family. Her heart lurched when everyone lunged for the prized utensils, and she quickly followed suit, accidentally gouging Sam's hand when she stole the spoon from his grip.

"Ow!" He jerked away to gape at the scratch bleeding on top of his knuckles, his jaw sagging into a grin of disbelief. "Marceline Murphy, you are a diabolical she-cat, you know that? I just may need stitches..."

Mr. O'Rourke leaned back in his chair with a spoon in one hand while he tweaked his wife's neck with the other, a roguish glint in his dark eyes. "There's a lot to be said for a woman with spunk, my boy."

Julie laughed, waving her spoon in her brother's face. "Don't worry, Sam—Marce can always stitch it for you after all the practice she's had with costumes."

"Besides," his mother said, raising up to peer across the table at his wound with a twitch of a smile, "it's nice to know you've finally found a woman who can draw a little blood if need be."

"Thanks for the support, Mother," Sam said with a wry smile, sucking on his knuckle. His lips took a slant while he peered at Marcy out of the corner of his eye. "If I don't bleed to death first."

The twins giggled shyly while little Erin, perched on her mother's lap, seemed genuinely concerned. "Do you want me to kiss it for you, Sammy?" she asked with a blink of wide eyes.

Sam winked at his little sister before regarding Marcy with a cheeky smile. "No, Sweet Pea, but thanks anyway. Marcy did the damage, so I think Marcy needs to be the one to kiss it, don't you?"

Marcy laughed and took his hand to examine it. "Here—let me see it, you big baby." She squinted at his knuckles, feeling a bit guilty about the bleeding abrasion, but having way too much fun with the tease. "Where? I don't see anything."

"It's not so much the wound on my knuckles that's bleeding," he said with mock drama, hand over his chest, "but the one in my heart."

Laughter filtered around the table as Marcy rolled her eyes.

"Well, the woman just put you out of your misery, son," Mr. O'Rourke said, shuffling the cards, "because now you have SPOON and you're out. So everyone else has SPOO except for Marceline, I believe." He winked at Marcy. "Is that correct, young lady?"

Marcy nodded, nibbling at the edge of her smile. "Yes, sir, I have SP." She snuck a peek in Sam's direction.

"Only because you cheat," he muttered, grabbing her hand under the table to give it a squeeze.

"I seem to remember some cheating of your own, Samuel O'Rourke," she whispered back, "during a certain game of keep away, as I recall."

Julie handed Sam her spoon and shooed him away from the table. "Here, go dish up dessert—losers have to earn their keep."

"I'm going, I'm going," Sam grumbled good-naturedly.

"Small pieces for the children, Samuel, if you please," Mrs. O'Rourke called while Sam rose to cut the pie.

Quickly dealing the cards around the table, Mr. O'Rourke glanced up when a knock sounded at the back door. He flashed a rakish grin so reminiscent of Sam, that Marcy suddenly realized how like his father he actually was. She turned to see Sam open the door to the pretty sixteen-year-old daughter of the next-door neighbor, whose face lit up with a burnished glow when she smiled up at him.

"Charlotte!" Mr. O'Rourke called, "I swear you get prettier every time I see you, eh, Sam?" Marcy watched as Sam's father scanned the girl head to toe with an appreciative air. "You're definitely no longer that little girl who used to steal my blackberries, I can tell you that."

"No question about it," Sam said, tugging Charlotte into the kitchen with his pirate grin. Marcy paused when he casually slipped his arm to the young girl's waist in a playful squeeze, lingering several seconds too long to suit Marcy.

Charlotte blushed at the praise of the O'Rourke men, hugging a large rectangular cake pan to her chest as she grinned at Sam's father. "Thank you, Mr. O'Rourke—you and your son sure know how to make a girl feel pretty."

Marcy whirled around to study her cards, hardly seeing them at all for the thought that popped in her mind. Yes, as a matter of fact, they *did* know how to make a girl feel pretty—a father/son duo who seemed to enjoy women more than most. And men who were definitely proficient at teasing and flirting with the opposite sex. Maybe too much? Marcy wondered, Sam's words coming back to haunt.

"What I'm trying to say, Marcy, is that up to now, it's been second nature for me to flirt and tease with pretty women ..."

Second nature. And maybe like father, like son? All the times Mr. O'Rourke fawned over his wife and even Marcy on occasion never bothered her before and, in fact, was something she even admired, something she'd wished her father would do. She'd always appreciated the fact that Sam's father was an affectionate man who enjoyed doting on his wife and children. But something in Mr. O'Rourke's flirtatious manner with Charlotte rankled for the very first time, an almost rakish air that he had clearly passed on to his son. At the thought, a new appreciation for her father suddenly swelled in Marcy's heart.

"I'm sorry to bother you so late," Charlotte said, "but I saw you were still up, so I decided to return the cake pan I borrowed. Thank you for the use of it, Mrs. O'Rourke—the cake sale at school was an absolute success." She tapped the pan against her chest. "Especially your family-size red velvet cake recipe."

"You're more than welcome, Charlotte—anytime. You can just put the pan on the counter, and you're welcome to stay for apple pie if you like."

"I'd love to, but I have homework to do, I'm afraid," Charlotte said, and Marcy peeked over her shoulder in time to see her bat her eyes at Sam. "Algebra, you know, so if I run into trouble, Sam, I just may need your help again."

Marcy blinked. *Again?*

"You bet," Sam said, gently tugging the cake pan from the girl's chest before he ushered her to the door.

"Good night, everyone," Charlotte called, and Marcy wondered why the wink Mr. O'Rourke gave Charlotte bothered her so much.

With little or no effort, Marcy won at spoons, but she didn't know how since her mind definitely wasn't in the game anymore. When Mr. O'Rourke declared her the winner, she absently nodded and smiled at the family's good-natured ribbing, diving into Mrs. O'Rourke's famous apple pie along with the usual laughter and chatter around the O'Rourke's kitchen table. Only tonight, the revelry seemed somewhat flat, and for the first time she could ever remember, the warmth and longing she always experienced with this family didn't seem as strong.

"Are you ... all right, Marcy?" Mrs. O'Rourke rose to collect dirty dishes from the table, a hint of concern in dark eyes that conveyed a mother's affection. "You seem a bit quiet."

Marcy rose to help, along with Julie while Sam and his father finished up a second piece of pie. "Yes, ma'am, I'm fine, just a little tired from the play this week, I suppose." She set the dishes on the counter and stifled a yawn. "I hate to say it, but I'm actually relieved tomorrow is the last performance so I can finally rest up."

"Well, tomorrow's Saturday, thank goodness, so I plan to see that you and Julie sleep in as late as possible, all right?" Mrs. O'Rourke rolled her sleeves and poured more dish soap into the dishwater she'd warmed earlier, sympathy in her gaze. "You'll both need all your energy for the final performance and the cast party after." She turned at the sink to smile at her husband as he tucked a sleepy Erin to his shoulder. "If you carry Erin up, dear, Julie can get her ready for bed, then I'll be up shortly after I finish these dishes."

"Will do, my love." He glanced at his twins, both as sleepy-eyed as their little sister, then nodded toward the hall. "Come on, girls, it's time to call it a night, so let's head up." His eyes flicked to Sam, who held a drowsy Max in his arms. "If you'll take care of Max, Sam, I'll tend to the twins."

"Sure, Pop. Come on, Jewels," Sam said, shooting Marcy a wink over his shoulder while he carried Max to the stairs. "I won't be long, Marcy, so don't head up until I come back, okay?"

"Yes, sir." She offered a salute before he and the rest of the O'Rourkes disappeared around the corner, leaving her alone with his mother.

Marcy startled at Mrs. O'Rourke's gentle touch. "Go to bed," she said softly, feathering a stray curl away from Marcy's face. "I can race through these dishes in no time, and you look ready to drop."

"Absolutely not—we'll finish them together."

Sam's mother gave her a tender smile. "You're an answer to Julie's and my prayers, Marceline—I hope you know that. I never dreamed my renegade son would ever settle down so quickly with one woman, but you're obviously the woman he needs."

Oh, Mrs. O'Rourke—I care for your son, I do. But suddenly I wonder ... is he the man that I need? Not sure what to say, Marcy grabbed the dishrag and wrung it out, hurrying to wipe off the kitchen table. She cleared her throat as she cupped her hand to catch the crumbs at the edge, fingers shaking with the motion. "Mrs. O'Rourke," she said quietly, voice hoarse and gaze averted, "do you mind if I ask you something?"

Mrs. O'Rourke glanced over her shoulder, her forearms buried to the elbows in suds. "Yes?"

Marcy carefully shook out the crumbs in the waste basket, then returned to the sink to rinse out the rag. "Since Sam and I have been courting, I've been noticing how much like his father he is, and I was just wondering." She paused to take a deep breath, finally meeting Mrs. O'Rourke's gaze as she snagged the dishtowel from the hook off the icebox door. "I know you're a woman with a deep faith, which you've clearly passed on to Julie and your other daughters, but ..."

"Why didn't it take with Sam?" she asked softly, her dark eyes as piercing as her son's.

Marcy nodded with a chew of her lip.

Mrs. O'Rourke issued a heavy sigh and continued to wash. "Well, it certainly wasn't from lack of trying on my part, I can tell you that. Unfortunately, Samuel is his father's son, and I wish I could tell you differently."

"Unfortunately?" Marcy whispered, shocked that the woman who appeared to adore her husband would have anything negative to say about him at all.

Mrs. O'Rourke's hands stilled in the water while she stared straight ahead, as if lost in her thoughts. "Yes, 'unfortunately.' You see, although Sam's father is a good man and I love him desperately, our faith has never been ... how shall I put it?" She glanced over at Marcy, her smile somewhat sad as she continued to wash. "Evenly yoked, I suppose, as the Bible likes to say. Oh, my husband believes in God and goes to church, of course, but I'm afraid he draws the line at the vestibule door, especially when it comes to the role of a man in the church." She finished up the last of the dessert plates and utensils, then grabbed another dishtowel to help Marcy dry, her tone melancholy. "It's near broken my heart to see Sam follow in the path of his father as a young man—promiscuous, rebellious, a surface relationship with God." A frail breath drifted from her lips. "But his father insists that's how a young man should be before he settles down, and I'm afraid he's curtailed my influence at every turn."

"Did it ... bother you that Mr. O'Rourke wasn't as spiritual as you when you married him?" Marcy whispered as she and Mrs. O'Rourke each dried their last dish.

Mrs. O'Rourke hung their towels on the icebox handle before turning to Marcy with a half chuckle. "Not really, because I was so much in love that I never gave his wild past a thought or was able to see past that rakish smile." She shrugged her shoulders, all at once looking far older and more tired than her years. "Besides, as a young woman in love, I'm sure you can understand, I wasn't exactly thinking about God when Mr. O'Rourke would kiss me."

Marcy's gaze dropped as heat pulsed in her face.

Mrs. O'Rourke's gentle touch drew Marcy's gaze to tired eyes where sympathy shone. "Marcy, deep down Sam's a good man like his father—he just needs a good woman to steer him right. And whether or not you are that woman, you need to know—most men are not prone to embrace God like we women, so when it comes to a deep faith, sometimes we just have to settle for a wee bit less than we hoped."

Mary's eyelids drifted closed. *Please, God, I don't want to settle ...*

Her eyes opened when Mrs. O'Rourke tucked a finger to her chin with a patient smile. "My husband and I have a wonderful marriage, Marceline, and a beautiful family, so the good news is, despite my settling in this one area, there's been little to no damage done."

No, only to your son ...

She patted Marcy's hand. "I best head upstairs to make sure all is well, but I'll send Samuel down to say good night posthaste. Sleep well, my dear." She pressed a kiss to Marcy's hair, the familiar smell of lavender not as comforting as it once had been. "You're good for my son," she whispered, giving Marcy's shoulder an affectionate squeeze, "so I don't want you to worry. Sam will make you a fine husband someday, I promise."

Marcy nodded. "Thanks, Mrs. O'Rourke. Good night."

She watched Sam's mother make her way down the hall while her words echoed in her brain. *"Sam will make you a fine husband someday, I promise."*

Marcy leaned against the counter with head bowed while a thought entered her mind that pricked as much as the sudden tears in her eyes.

Yes ... but was it a promise she could keep?

Chapter Thirty

Marcy nibbled a sugar cookie and smiled, content as she waited for Sam to refill her punch at the final cast party in the St. Mary's Center of Hope. Enjoying a rare moment alone while Julie and Evan left to congratulate Father Fitz and Sister Francine, she breathed in the fresh smell of pine from the fir boughs decorating the middle of the dining-room tables, each flickering with a candle in honor of the last production that just ended. In the kitchen Miss Clara and her volunteers were still baking up a storm, the heavenly scent of cinnamon and nutmeg wafting through the center. Gone were the wooden tables sanded and varnished to a gleam by Sam and Evan and Patrick over the summer, replaced instead with delicate layers of tissue paper laden with trays of Christmas cookies, some still warm from the oven.

Expelling a weary but satisfied sigh, Marcy's gaze wandered a room looped with festive red and green paper chains cut and painted by grade school children from discarded newspapers. Raucous laughter erupted from a table of white-robed boys with halos askew. Each devoured cookies during games of gallows on the tissue with oil crayons provided by Sister Francine. Grateful tears pricked when Marcy spied Tillie and Holly giggling over a game of noughts and crosses with newfound friends, then glimmered with joy at a rosy-cheeked Julie who smiled up at Evan through lovesick eyes. *Oh, Lord, just look at what You've done—friendships forged and friends in love, all in the process of reaching out to the poor!* Julie's face aglow, Marcy had never seen her best friend happier, and with a sudden cramp in her chest, she wished she could say the same for herself.

Her eyes lighted on the hearth and mantle scenery Patrick had built, and her heart immediately constricted over the friendship she'd lost. At Miss Clara's request, he and Evan had delivered it here after the play as a fitting party backdrop to hang stockings filled with candy canes for each of the children. But looking at it now only reminded Marcy of the hateful way she had treated him, something she sorely regretted once her anger had cooled. She was not a woman prone to temper, yet he had evoked an anger in her like no one had since Nora's shameful fiancé, and Marcy suspected it was because of the threat Patrick posed to her peace of mind.

Goodness, she'd dreamed of being Julie's sister and belonging to a close-knit family like the O'Rourkes since she'd been a little girl, and secretly smitten with Sam for almost as long. Patrick's blatant attempt to steal her affection by casting aspersions as to Sam's fidelity—and this from the Southie's king of infidelity, no less—had infuriated her. But now that the strain and stress of the play was over and Sam indicated he and Patrick were at least speaking again, she regretted the rift. She couldn't count the times she'd longed to apologize over the last week of the play, but he avoided her—producing a dull ache inside akin to a splinter that festered inside her heart, painful to the touch. Another heavy sigh drifted from her lips. It was just as well, she supposed. With the feelings he claimed to have for her—if one could believe a rogue used to sweet-talking his own way—friendship would be difficult, at least until after Sam and she had been married a while.

If we get married ... Marcy's heart skipped a beat at the tiny prickle of doubt she didn't want to acknowledge, the one that had embedded itself over the last few weeks, infecting her peace of mind and threatening her dreams.

"Here you are, my love." Sam deposited a fresh glass of punch on the table in front of her, along with a saucer of Miss Clara's iced oatmeal cookies, still gooey from the oven. "Fresh punch and cookies for the lady of the hour."

Her smile was tender as she gazed up at him, amazed at how much closer they had become since the quarrel with Patrick, as if the near-loss of a friend more like a brother had shaken Sam to the core. Suddenly attentive to a fault, he now spent every moment of his free time with her, opening his heart in ways he never had before. The fight with Patrick had devastated him, he said, prompting him to badger his "best friend" for forgiveness until the friendship was slowly being restored. Or nearly so, given that Sam now passed most of his time in Marcy's company rather than Patrick's. Pulling his chair out, he sat down beside her and grinned like a little boy while he snitched one of her cookies, and with a rush of affection, she pressed a soft kiss to his cheek.

His grin broadened as he gave her a wink. "Mmm ... if I get a peck on the cheek for stealing one of your cookies, what might I get for stealing a kiss?"

"A piece of my mind," she whispered with a warning crook of her brow, "if you dare make advances in front of the parish priest."

A Light in the Window

His deep chuckle blended with the revelry in the room. "As long as it comes with a piece of your heart, Marceline, you'll hear no complaints from me." His forehead puckered as he glanced around the room, his heavy exhale following on its heels. "I see Patrick didn't show."

Her wistful sigh matched his. "No. It would seem I'm a deterrent to your best friend." She squeezed his hand. "I'm so sorry."

"Don't be," he said quietly, his smile conspicuously absent. "It's hardly your fault for being the beautiful woman you are." He feathered the edge of her jaw with his thumb, gaze reflective. "He'll come around before we marry, I promise. Has to," he said with a quick swig of his punch, the smile surfacing once again. "Who else could be my best man?"

A loud clanging captured everyone's attention when Miss Clara banged a serving spoon against a cast-iron pot. "Listen up—Father Fitz has something to say."

The conversation and laughter subsided except for the lilting flow of Father Fitz's chuckles, which immediately expanded Marcy's smile into a grin. "Thank you, Miss Clara," Father said with a short bow in her direction, "for that most auspicious introduction. You can rest assured, my dear woman, that after tonight's raging success, you may well find that new cook stove you've requested nestled under your tree."

Miss Clara beamed while laughter circled the room.

Father Fitz paused, slowly scanning the faces before him with pride in his eyes. "Seldom have I seen a fundraiser this cohesive, a group of people who have bonded together more beautifully than those in this room. You have unselfishly given of your time, your talents, and your love to bless the less fortunate, and I have no doubt whatsoever that the Almighty is smiling down on each and every one of you this night. I want you to know that I have never been prouder of a group of people in this parish than I am of this cast and crew. You are ..." A sheen of moisture glimmered in his eyes as his chin trembled almost imperceptibly. "The Body of Christ in action and in the truest sense—the purest expression of what Christmas is really all about. You have my undying gratitude and that of Sister Francine, Evan, Miss Clara and indeed, the entire parish, for a job remarkably well done."

Applause and cheers broke out as a tear trailed Marcy's cheek. Sam pushed his handkerchief at her, and she nodded her thanks before returning her attention to the front of the room where Father Fitz held up his hands. "Before we disperse for the evening, I would be remiss if I didn't address three very important issues." He raised a finger, silver brows lifted high. "One—our thanks to the Almighty, Who not only convened the best group for the job, but blessed their efforts beyond measure." Waiting for the clapping to die down, he continued with a second finger in the air. "Two—when I said 'blessing our efforts without measure, however, I didn't mean to imply we met our goal of eight hundred dollars."

Gasps sounded all over the room as Marcy's breath hitched in her throat, silence settling like a shroud. The serious demeanor of Father Fitz's face slowly eased into an elfin smile while mischief twinkled in blue eyes that sparkled with a bit of the devil. "No, I'm afraid we've set a very awkward precedent for future fundraisers at this church, ladies and gentlemen, for not meeting our goal or even coming close ..." He paused for effect. "But exceeding it by well over five hundred dollars."

No one breathed for a split second, and then with a

lusty swell of whoops, shrieks, and stomping feet, the room thundered with clapping and cheers while Marcy swayed in her seat, too dizzy and stunned to utter a single sound. *Over thirteen hundred dollars?* Only when Sam plucked her out of the chair to embrace her did comprehension dawn while moisture brimmed in her eyes.

Father Fitz hoisted his palms once again, stilling the gathering to a quiet buzz before he added a third finger to his count. "And finally, number three—it is my privilege and joy to honor the young ladies without whom none of this would be possible." Hands clasped behind his back, he jutted his prominent chin in Marcy and Julie's direction while a grin tugged at his lips. "Miss Murphy and Miss O'Rourke, would you please come forward?"

The room exploded with shrieks and whistles and the deafening clomp of more feet as Sam prodded Marcy up with a squeeze of her hand and a palm to her back while Evan followed suit with Julie. Uncomfortable with praise, Marcy's cheeks burned as hot as Miss Clara's ovens in July, gaze skittish as she stood between Father Fitz and her best friend.

"Marceline," he began in his most regal tone, "the people of St. Mary's parish, the Center of Hope, and the cast and crew of *A Light in the Window* would like to thank you and Julie for masterminding not only the single most successful fundraiser in St. Mary's history ..." He winked. "But in the diocese as well."

Joyous pandemonium broke loose among the crowd while Julie grabbed Marcy's hands and screamed, jumping up and down before she finally flung her arms around her best friend's neck. "Oh, Marcy," she cried, her giggles reverberating in Marcy's ears, "can you believe it? We did it!"

"Ladies," Father Fitz said loudly enough to subdue the chaos in the room, "as a small token of our appreciation, we'd like to give you a memento, not only of the incredible job you did, but hopefully to remember each of us by—cast, crew, and staff."

Sister Francine approached with two small tissue-wrapped packages, handing one to each of the girls, followed by a pinch on each of their cheeks. "You deserve this and more for a truly excellent job." Stepping back, she stood on the opposite side of Father Fitz, hands clasped at her waist as she watched them open the gifts with a wide smile that was a mirror reflection of Father's.

With a huge grin, Julie tore into the tissue paper while Marcy did the same, squealing with delight when each unwrapped a beautiful snow globe. "Look, Marce, it's our play!" Julie exclaimed, shaking the ball to watch the snow drift over a bough-trimmed window aglow with a candle.

Marcy shook her globe, lips parted in awe while tears welled in her eyes. She giggled when Father Fitz pressed his handkerchief into her hand, and she absently dabbed the moisture that blurred the drifting snow into a fuzzy fog of white.

"All right, one and all, our party has come to an end, but on behalf of Sister Francine, Evan Farrell, Miss Clara, and the parish—may your Christmas be as wonderful as you've made ours. God bless and good night."

Laughter, hugs, and the scraping of chairs marked the end of a wonderful evening, but much like her snow globe, the next half hour was little more than a blur to Marcy as people crowded around to congratulate her and Julie. Miss Clara and her volunteers were busy cleaning up while Sam and Evan helped, and when the last cookie had been eaten and the punch all put away, Marcy sagged against Sam's chest as he pulled her into his arms. "I do believe you may have to carry me home tonight," she said with a sleepy smile, relishing the citrus scent of his shaving soap.

"It would be my pleasure, love," he whispered, thumbs grazing her waist.

Eyes closed, she savored the comfort of his arms, a chuckle in her tone. "Or to Robinson's first, if Julie and Evan want to celebrate, so I hope you've energized with enough punch and cookies."

He tipped her face up, a smoldering look in dark eyes that warmed her to her toes. "I don't need punch or cookies, Marceline," he said in a husky voice, "the taste of your lips is all the adrenaline I need." He startled her when he grazed her mouth with his own.

"Sam, please ..." she whispered, biting the edge of her lip as she nervously glanced around. She twisted from his hold with an awkward smile, grateful everyone was gone except for Julie and Evan in the dining room and Miss Clara and a few volunteers in the kitchen. Hoping to deflect her embarrassment with a bright smile, she spun on her heel, energy rebounding. "So, Julie and Evan—shall we celebrate at Robinson's?"

"Sounds good to me," Julie said with a grin while Evan helped her on with her coat. She glanced up. "Is that all right with you, Evan?"

He paused for the briefest of moments, somber eyes flicking from Julie to Marcy and back. "Uh, sure, Julie."

Marcy blinked, Evan's hesitant tone giving her pause. Her gaze flitted from the instant crimp of concern on Julie's face to Evan's sober manner, and apprehension settled on her shoulders like the coat Sam had just helped her put on. *Is Evan upset with Julie?*

Worry gnawed as she absently reached into her pocket for her gloves and then groaned, pulling out a folded piece of paper. "Oh, goodness—I forgot the check Mr. Mulholland gave me after the play, a last-minute contribution for, and I quote, 'the most fun he's ever had at a fundraiser.'" She slipped it back in her pocket with a sigh. "I guess I need to deliver it to Father Fitz before we go," she said with a final glance in the kitchen. "Good night and thank you, Miss Clara, Rupert, Rose—the cookies and punch were wonderful!"

Julie and Evan echoed her goodbyes on their way to the front door while Sam handed Marcy her reticule with the snow globe tucked safely inside. Hand to her waist, he ushered her out behind Julie and Evan.

Halfway to the street, Julie groaned and slapped a hand to her head. "Oh, drat, I left Mama's crystal candlesticks on the stage, and I promised I'd bring them home tonight." She whirled around with a plea in her eyes. "Sam, would you be a dear and get them for me?"

Sam froze, glancing at Evan as if half expecting him to retrieve them instead. He gave his sister a stiff smile. "Sure, Jewels—where are they?"

She flashed a smile of her own, gratitude radiating from eyes so like her brother's. "I think I left them in the far corner at the left side of the stage, in that tattered box Mama stores them in, you know?" She chewed on her lip. "I think."

A grin tipped one side of Sam's mouth. "You think?" He shook his head and reached for Marcy's hand. "Never mind, we'll find them."

"Actually ..."

Everyone turned at Evan's remark.

"I forgot Father Fitz said he needed to see both Marcy and me before we left tonight," he said, offering a conciliatory smile along with a slight shrug of his shoulders. "So, Julie, maybe you and Sam should go after the candlesticks and head on over to Robinson's, then Marcy and I will meet you there as soon as we're done."

Sam paused, his gaze lighting on Marcy. "No problem, Evan—we'll wait."

"Well, I know Father Fitz wanted to go over some numbers, Sam," Evan said with a nervous scratch at the back of his neck, "so I'm not all that sure how long it will take. I'd really feel much better if you just took Julie to Robinsons to save us a booth."

"Okay ..." Sam said slowly. "We'll see you at Robinson's, then." He looped an arm around his sister's shoulder. "Come on, Jewels—we should have time to cart those candlesticks home before we head over." He sent Marcy a wink. "See you there, love."

"All right, Sam." Marcy smiled. "And nab the back booth if you can, Jewels," she called.

"Sure, but hurry every chance you get, okay?" Julie's smile over her shoulder was marred by a tiny pucker above her nose. "We have a lot to celebrate."

"Will do." Evan watched them head toward the auditorium and released a heavy exhale, unleashing clouds of smoke that rolled into the cool night air.

"Are you all right?" Marcy asked, head tilted with concern. "Is everything okay between you and Julie?"

His jaw seemed tight as he hooked a hand to her arm to escort her to the rectory. "Yes, everything's fine between Julie and me ... or at least it was until tonight."

Marcy's heart stopped along with her feet as she turned. "Evan? Tell me, please—what's wrong?"

Facing her, he buried his hands in his pockets, his lips now as compressed as his jaw. "It's not about Julie and me, Marcy," he whispered, "it's about Sam."

Marcy's body went to stone, the air in her lungs

refusing to budge while Evan stared at her with empathy in his eyes. "Please forgive me, Marcy, but you need to know—Patrick was telling the truth about Sam."

She stumbled back as if he'd slapped her, cheeks stinging from the assault of his words. "I cannot believe, Evan Farrell, that you would take that scoundrel's word over that of Julie's own brother! What in heaven's name is wrong with you? Patrick only befriended me in the first place to steal me away from Sam, but it's obvious that he's cozied up to you and everyone at the center so much that you're blind to his reputation with women."

"Yes, Marcy, I know his reputation with women, but I also know how much he's changed over the last six months and what kind of friend he's been to me." Sorrow slumped his shoulders as he looked up beneath weighted lids, the kindness in his eyes sapping her anger. "And to you ..."

She spun around, unwilling to see Patrick in a positive light, reluctant to trust a man who'd drawn her in more than she cared to admit.

And fearful of what that might mean ...

"Sam and I are friends," Evan whispered, "but Patrick has spent so much time at the center over the summer that he and I ... well, we've forged a deep bond, and I ..." She heard his weary expulsion of air. "Well, quite frankly, I trust him."

Her breathing shallowed as she shook her head, fighting the urge to put her hands over her ears, but Evan only continued, his voice laced with the same pain that now seared her heart. "I can't allow Sam to hurt you no matter how difficult this is to hear for both you and for Julie, but the truth is ... Sam lies to you," he said quietly, hesitating as if the words were too difficult to push from his tongue, "and he sees ... other women."

"I don't believe you," she whispered, her voice no more than a rasp.

Her nerves bucked when his hand lighted upon her arm. "It's true, Marcy. He may tell you he's working, but—"

She whirled around, panic rising in her chest. "He is working!" she screamed.

"Maybe." His voice faded to a whisper. "But not last Thursday night. He lies to you just like Patrick said. He has other women."

Tears stung as Marcy swayed on her feet, her mind suddenly as scattered as the snow in the globe. She tried to make sense of what Evan was saying, but she was too stunned to comprehend, too fearful to believe Sam would betray her like this. Her words quivered with anger along with her body. "I r-refuse to t-take the word of a rogue who's made sport of lying to women, Evan, no m-matter how good of a friend he's become to you."

A muscle jerked in Evan's throat. "I know this is not easy to hear, but you need to know the truth, and the truth is the trustworthy man here is Patrick, not Sam."

"Lies—all lies!" Marcy cried, fear crawling up her windpipe to cut off her air. "I'll tell you what kind of man Patrick O'Connor is—the kind of man he conveniently accuses Sam of being—a liar and a philanderer. You *know* what he did to Emily Fischer and God knows how many others and yet you choose to believe him over Julie's brother?" Her eyes burned as she leaned in, fists knotted at her sides. "Did you know that your almighty Patrick O'Connor forced himself on me in the beginning, and then nearly again after Sam and I were courting?"

Evan's lips parted in surprise.

"*That's* the kind of man who's accusing Sam,"

Marcy whispered, her tone harsh, "and it pains me that a good friend like you whom I love and trust would side with the likes of him. You may believe him, but I refuse to take the word of a man who's made sport of lying to women no matter how much of a friend he's become."

Marcy flinched at the gentle touch of Evan's hand, his eyes steeped in sorrow. "Then how about the word of a 'good friend whom you love and trust?'" he whispered.

She stared, unable to speak as her heart thudded to a stop.

"I saw him, Marcy," he said quietly, "with my own eyes."

Marcy's eyelids shuttered closed as she wavered on her feet, desperate to stop what Evan was about to say, but knowing she could not. She felt his hand on her arm once again, tightening as if to steady her, and this time she didn't fight, too numb to move.

"I needed help at the center one night to move storage barrels that were too heavy for me alone," he whispered, his voice a low drone, "so I asked Patrick. He'd already taken a night shift at work, so he suggested Sam instead, saying he had the night off. But when I went to Julie's house to ask him, she said Sam was working, and then when I asked if she was sure, she insisted that's what Sam told her." Marcy heard Evan draw in a deep breath and release it while her own remained stagnant in her lungs. "I knew then that if Sam would lie to Julie, he had to have a reason ..."

Her body began to shake. "Because he was lying to me ..." she whispered, the very words chilling her more than the cold.

"Yes," Evan said softly. "So I needed to find out for sure, because I couldn't let him hurt you that way ..."

She nodded, unable to speak as she clung to Evan's

hand while it braced her arm.

"I left Julie's house that night and went straight to Brannigan's, hoping against hope that Patrick was wrong and Sam wouldn't be there, but he was ..." She could almost feel the lump that bobbed in his throat. "And he wasn't alone."

"M-maybe ... maybe he was just t-talking to someone at the bar," she said quickly, desperate to absolve this man who'd been her hero, her defender, her dream ...

Evan hesitated, as if his next words were as agonizing to say as they were for her to hear. "I know this is painful, Marcy, but I want there to be no mistaking the truth. I didn't see Sam talking at the bar that night," he said steadily, his free hand gripping hers on top of his own, "and I was greatly relieved when the barkeep said he wasn't there." The pressure of Evan's hand increased, as if bracing Marcy for the truth that she didn't want to hear. "But something didn't feel right, so when I told the barkeep it was an emergency ..." He paused to release a harsh breath that shivered her very soul. "He suddenly changed his tune and directed me to a back room where I found him ..." His voice tapered into a whisper. "In bed with another woman."

Lord, no, please ... Grief broke through Marcy's stupor, and with a heart-wrenching sob, she crumpled into Evan's arms.

"Marcy ...," Evan's voice was gentle. "I can walk you home and tell Julie and Sam you didn't feel well, if you like. Then you can deal with this in the morning."

She pulled from his hold, her face sodden with tears. "No, Evan, we need to see Father Fitz—"

"Yes, well, about that," he said quickly, gaze suddenly sheepish. "I'm afraid I stretched the truth a bit because I needed to talk to you alone, but I've already spoken to Father Fitz about what he wanted, so I figured I'd tag along while you delivered Mr. Mulholland's check, then walk you home."

Marcy's fingers shook as she pushed loose hairs from her face. "No, Evan, really—I'll give the check to Father Fitz, but then I think I'd like to stay and talk to him for a while, maybe clear my mind a bit ..."

Evan gave her a tight hug. "That might be a good thing to do," he said, "and I'll go tell Julie and Sam you weren't feeling well. But ..." He pulled back to study her, concern mingling with the affection in his eyes. "I insist on walking you home after, all right?" She opened her mouth to decline, but he stopped her with a gentle finger to her lips and an air of authority she dare not defy. "No argument. I always have paperwork I can do, so just pop in when you're ready, all right?"

"Thank you," she whispered, more tears blurring her eyes. "You're a good friend."

His smile was tired. "So are you, which is why I had no choice but to tell you, but I'm truly sorry."

He turned to go, and she stopped him with a hand to his arm. "Does Sam know that you saw him?"

He shook his head, exhaling more puffs of frothy air. "I don't think so. It was dark, and I caught him by surprise with a hand to his eyes, but I definitely saw—and heard—him."

She nodded, absently pressing a palm to her abdomen to quell the nausea that roiled inside. "And Julie?" she whispered.

"No, I don't think she suspects anything either. She all but worships Sam, as you know, so I couldn't bring myself to tell you or her until the play was over."

"I appreciate that," Marcy whispered. "This will crush her as much as it did me, I'm afraid."

He nodded. "Well, I best head over to Robinson's, but I'll come right back to my office, so come get me when you're done, all right?"

She forced a faint smile. "Julie is a lucky girl, Evan Farrell—you're a good man."

His mouth tipped in a sad smile. "So is Patrick O'Connor," he said softly, "more than you know."

Patrick O'Connor. Her heart twisted. The man she'd judged all too quickly. *Twice.* Watching Evan walk away, Marcy quickly swiped at her eyes with the sleeve of her coat, then fished the check from her pocket, hoping her face wasn't too mottled from her tears. She slowly mounted the steps and knocked on the door, her nerve diminishing with every second she waited. Just when she'd made the decision to bolt, the door wheeled open in a shaft of light from the parlour, and Marcy squinted with a hand to her eyes.

"Marceline!" Father Fitz blinked, concern etching his brow. "Is something wrong?"

That was all it took for the dam to break, spilling tears down her cheeks faster than Father Fitz could gather her in his arms, soothing with gentle strokes to her back. "There, there now, Marceline, I was just settling in with some tea—what say you join me?"

With a loud sniff she nodded, allowing Father to lead her inside. He closed the door behind her with a finality that left her strangely at peace despite the grief in her heart. It was time, she suddenly realized, the thought hazy like the snow globe had been through the blur of her tears. Time to close the door ...

On broken promises.

On broken dreams.

And on the broken heart she had hoped to never see ...

Chapter Thirty-One

Eyes glazed, Marcy stared at the hearth in Father Fitz's parlour, barely aware of the hot flames as they crackled and spit, the fire warming her limbs, but doing nothing for the chill in her soul. Father Fitz had led her to one of two gold wing chairs angled toward the hearth, given her a handkerchief and left to prepare the tea, allowing her much-needed time alone to weep while she waited. When he returned, he'd handed her the steaming brew and silently sat in the other chair, hands folded on his chest while he studied her through kind eyes etched with worry.

Gaze lost in the fire, she forced a nasal laugh, the sound as hollow as the charred-out logs that hissed and popped beside her, filling the room with the comforting smell of wood smoke and oak. "I'm sorry," she whispered, "you must think I'm crazy."

His low chuckle soothed as much as the warmth of the teacup in her hands. "If tears and heartbreak were indicative of 'crazy,' my dear girl, I'm afraid our institutions would be woefully full." He paused. "What has wounded your heart, Marceline?" he said quietly. "Or perhaps I should say 'who'?"

She met his eyes then and knew in an instant she

had come to the right place. Compassion warmed his gaze like the fire warmed the room, and in a fragile exhale of air, she felt that raw, bitter cold in her soul slowly begin to thaw. In a lifeless drone, her saga of woe gradually unraveled, along with the tangled knot in her stomach. From Nora's lecherous fiancé to Patrick to Sam, she divulged her love for a rogue that apparently hadn't been enough. Not for Sam with his insatiable lust for others and not for her, she suddenly realized, with her insatiable need for God. A need she longed to have met, both in her life and in that of the man she would marry.

When she'd exhausted her tale and her tears, she sat on the edge of her chair, head in her hands and voice as lifeless as she. "Sam may have betrayed me, Father, but no more than I betrayed myself. I knew better than to trust a rogue with little use for God or His ways, but I was swept away by his charm and his family, which I longed to call my own. I had a niggle of doubt deep in my soul that I conveniently ignored," she whispered, "especially lately." She shuddered despite the warmth of the fire. "But I should have known—you can't trust a man with an eye for women."

Father Fitz rose to stir the embers, a shower of sparks hissing into the flue. "Usually, no," he mused, "but there are times when God intervenes and uses a woman such as yourself to change the most blatant of rogues. Sam's mother and father are certainly an example of that."

She grunted and took a sip of her tea. "Well, I certainly tried with Sam, Father, and truly thought he was on his way to being the man God wants him to be." Her dismissive air quickly dissipated with a sudden swell of tears. "I so longed for it to work," she said softly, "to be a sister to Julie as well as a wife to Sam, and a part of a large family I so dearly love." She sniffed and took a sip of her tea. "Longed for it too much, I suppose, given how easily I was deceived. But obviously it wasn't meant to be."

He observed her over the rim of his cup, blue eyes pensive. "I'm sorry to hear that, Marceline," he said before carefully setting his cup aside. Elbows cocked on the arms of his chair, he steepled his fingers to his chin. "But then again, maybe not."

Her cup stilled against her mouth, steam misting her face as she stared, confused by his remark. Shrugging if off, she blew on her tea and sipped before settling back in her chair with a mournful sigh, gaze lapsing into the flames once again. "Ever since Nora was betrayed by her fiancé," she whispered, "I've prayed that God would spare me a similar fate, that He'd bring me a man whose heart longs for the same things as mine—a marriage and family with God at the core. And what do I get?" She shivered. "A rogue almost as bad as Nora's." She grunted again. "Not exactly the answer I wanted."

"Ah, but, Marceline," Father Fitz said, "sometimes the answer He gives unlocks an unlikely door to our dreams, but we're too afraid to enter." He hesitated. "And sometimes it's the very thing we prayed against."

She peered up, face in a squint. "A rogue?" A bitter laugh tripped from her lips as she vehemently shook her head. "I'm sorry, Father, but I could never trust a rogue like Sam again."

"No, not Sam," he said with an absent-minded scratch of his neck, face pinched in thought. "But there is another whose heart you've stolen and with it, I believe, the propensity to ever play the rogue again."

"What do you mean?" she said slowly, not sure she wanted to know.

His smile was kind. "I mean a young man so smitten, Marceline, he has even ventured to explore a deeper faith in God with a doddering old priest."

She blinked before her head wagged back and forth. "No, Father, I'm sorry—I'm through with rogues, be it Sam O'Rourke or his rakish best friend. Men like that love themselves far more than they can ever love a woman, and I'll not settle for a weak imitation."

Eyes softening with fondness, he assessed her with a smile that faded along with his voice. "Aye, and wise you are, but the rogue I speak of harbors a love for you so strong, Marceline, that he's even given away a piece of his soul to express it."

"Patrick?" she whispered, the very utterance of his name clouding her mind.

His head dipped in assent. "I'm sure you're aware that Patrick has scrimped and saved for years now to attend Boston University in the spring?"

She nodded slowly.

"Yes, well, it's been his dream for quite some time to write for *The Boston Herald* someday." He shook his head while a grin inched across his lips. "I'll give him this—he's a cocky lad to be sure." He winked. "Has his eye on becoming the editor, you know ..."

She swallowed hard, the whites of her eyes expanding along with her shock. *No, I didn't ...*

"Yes, it seems he's a man on a mission, our Patrick ... or was ... until he met you." He chuckled and reached for his pipe, tamping tobacco into the bowl. "Never have I seen a rogue quite so discombobulated." He lit it and took a long draw, releasing a curl of smoke that smelled faintly of vanilla and maple. Gentle eyes locked with hers, fusing her to the spot. "The simple truth is—the boy's desperately in love with you, Marceline."

She shook her head long before her name ever left his tongue. "Not love, Father," she insisted with a nip of anger, "lust maybe or pride or just plain obstinance to win the only woman who doesn't want him, but surely not love."

He eyed her while he puffed on his pipe, assessing her through patient eyes. "One does not sacrifice one's dreams for lust or pride or obstinance, my dear," he said quietly. A haze of smoke as foggy as her mind drifted up to hover, thick and motionless like the air in her lungs. "Nor does one silently forsake his own financial future."

She opened her mouth to speak, but nothing came out. Not words, not air. Her throat convulsed as she tried to draw a breath, eyelids twitching as if they, too, struggled to perform. "I ... I don't understand," she whispered.

Father Fitz laid his pipe aside for a moment to lean forward, elbows on his knees and hands loosely clasped. "I mean that the money that was found buried under the snow was not the money stolen from the center."

Her mouth fell open like one of the bass she and Sam had caught that day at O'Reilly Lake, expelling shallow air as if she'd just sprinted around that very body of water. "B-but ... b-but ... I thought the ... the children found it ..."

He dipped his head with a faint smile. "Yes, yes, indeed they did, but I thought that rather curious, didn't you?"

She considered his question, absently grating her lip. "Well, n-no, not particularly. I was just so grateful at the time that I never even thought about it."

He gave a short nod. "Yes, well, I did, but I'm ashamed to say I let it go ..." He reached for a soiled folded manila envelope behind his pipe on the table and handed it to her with a scrunch of his nose, pinching it at the corner with forefinger and thumb. "Until the police delivered this rather unsavory parcel a few days ago."

Pinpricks of shock tingled her skin as she grasped the corner of the envelope like he'd done, dangling it from her hand. Her neat script on the front was marred with grime, but still readable—*A Light in the Window*. She glanced up with saucer eyes, the air in her lungs refusing to budge once again. "T-this is ... " She swallowed the shock in her throat. "The envelope that was s-stolen from me ..."

"Yes, of course it is, Marceline," he said gently. "The police found it on one of the transients that came to the center. There's only about four of the five hundred there, so apparently he's been drinking up quite a storm."

"B-but how ..."

"That's what I wanted to know," Father Fitz said, placing the dirty envelope back on the table. He eased back in his chair and rested his head on a crisp Irish doily, hands neatly folded on his chest. "So I decided to play the sleuthhound, you might say, quizzing the little girl who actually found the money."

"Yes, Rebecca Moriarty, I remember."

The barest hint of a smile played on his lips. "And I discovered something very interesting—she was an unwitting co-conspirator with another girl who was actually a plant."

"A plant?" Marcy said with a squint.

"A ploy, a spy, a lackey if you will, someone sent on a secret mission."

"But ... but I don't understand," Marcy said again.

"Ah, yes, but perhaps you will when I tell you the

little girl in question is none other than our own precocious Tillie Dewey, who, apparently, was tapped to "hide" the money that Miss Moriarty found. Only it wasn't 'the' stolen money, per se, but 'his' money." His eyes honed in on her with keen precision, his voice as faint as she. "The hard-earned funds of a rogue who'd labored well over three years to save for a college education."

Her eyelids flickered closed as goose bumps shivered her arms. She was barely able to breathe, much less speak the name that finally shuddered from her lips. "P-Patrick?"

Father Fitz's voice was as gentle as the slow, heady warmth that curled in her belly. "One and the same, Marceline," he whispered, "the one rogue of the two whose life you changed forever."

Hot tears stung beneath her lids, the magnitude of what Patrick had done for her coursing through her body, her mind, in languid waves of warmth that seeped to the very tips of her fingers and toes. Awareness ebbed and flowed in her brain like surf on a shore, sweeping away the footprints of the man she believed him to be, replaced now by the man that he was, shimmering sand, unmarred by an unholy past. A sob slowly rose in her throat as she slumped forward, head in her hands, weeping tears of grief mingled with joy.

"Marceline."

She felt the stroke of Father Fitz's hand on her hair and slowly looked up, her chest shuddering with frail heaves.

"I'm no prophet, mind you, but if I were, I'd say that God has answered your prayers, young lady, by giving you a good man whose heart is not only redeemed ..." He patted her shoulder, lips in a quirk, "but yours for the taking." He returned to his seat to hunch on the edge as before, hands casually clasped. "Mind you, it's none of my business, but you might say Patrick has become very special to me. He's a young man in whom you've sparked a keen interest in God, something I've been striving to do since his first of many detentions." He absently scratched his jaw with the side of his hand. "And, if I must say so myself, the young man has grown admirably in his faith." He scrutinized her with a sober smile. "So you'll forgive me if I feel a wee bit compelled to ask, Marceline ... do you have feelings for the boy at all?"

She blinked, his question catching her unaware. Her gaze drifted back to the fire, while her mind traveled back to the heated kiss on her porch and the subsequent apology. Memories flashed of his kindness with the poor and elderly at the center, his little-boy playfulness with her and the children, or his willingness to help wherever he was needed. She envisioned his strong, capable body working side-by-side with Evan while Sam supposedly worked extra shifts at the *Herald,* or his keen wit and teasing manner that never seemed to know a sour mood. No question that his fierce tenderness and protectiveness for Tillie and Holly had won her heart as a friend ... but could he win her heart as something far more? Her eyes drifted closed at the image of a man who had probed and plied her with questions about God and her faith while Sam had merely nodded and smiled and went on his way. And then, in a crackling flicker of the flames in the hearth, Mima's words slowly circled in her brain ...

"Guard your heart well, Marceline, for a man who will respond to the light in the window, for therein lies a gift of God like no other, except that of His Son."

Her heart thudded to a jolting stop ... and then in one violent intake of air, she suddenly knew—*this* was a man she could love deeply all the days of her life.

With a silent heave of her chest, she looked up, Father's face foggy from her tears while her quivering fingers trembled to her mouth. A sense of awe filled her soul over the dawning of hope so bright, she wondered how she missed it. *This is the man I've chosen for you, Marceline* ... She blinked several times to clear the moisture from her eyes, lips parting in a sense of wonder. *Oh, Lord do I have feelings for Patrick O'Connor?* Her jaw sagged when the truth struck hard, neatly buried beneath a mountain of fear. "Yes, Father ... I ... believe that I do."

He hesitated, the barest twinge of concern in his gaze. "But do you ... love him, lass?"

She closed her eyes to conjure Patrick's face, and her breath caught at the image of twinkling gray eyes and a perilous smile she'd never allowed herself to enjoy. A languorous warmth slowly swirled in her belly, steaming her cheeks and snapping her eyelids open. She quickly averted her gaze while she chewed at her lip. "I ... don't think so, Father, but I ..." She swallowed hard. "I believe maybe I could."

The planes of his face relaxed into a crooked smile that looked so much like a little boy, a giggle bubbled up in her throat.

He grinned. "Aye, and a fine Christmas it will be for a former rogue who deserves a bit of cheer, I'd say."

A former rogue, yes ... The giggle broke free as she folded her hands to her lips. Then all at once, her laughter died as another "rogue" came to mind. Her eyes weighted closed while her heart instantly squeezed in her chest.

"What is it?" Father Fitz whispered.

She glanced up, grief wet in her yes. "Oh, Father, I worry about Sam—the hurt this will cause and the hurt he'll cause himself if he doesn't change."

Sobriety settled on Father Fitz's features as he nodded, his manner as somber as hers. "Aye, Samuel O'Rourke, the one rogue who failed to heed the light in the window." He expelled a heavy sigh that brought a slump to his shoulders. And then, in a jut of his chin, the heaviness seemed to flee, replaced by a glint of determination in steel-blue eyes when he flashed her a grin. "Well, not to worry. With Mr. O'Connor out of the way, I can now focus on Mr. O'Rourke while I turn the other rogue over to you."

Her smile wavered. "Do you really believe this is what God has in mind?"

His low laughter buoyed her spirits. "Aye, but the real question is, Marceline—do *you*?"

This is the man I've chosen for you, Marceline, the thought came again, and immediately tears welled in her eyes.

"Now, now, young lady," Father Fitz said with a chuckle, rising to his feet, "don't you think you've shed enough tears for one evening?"

A giggle rose on the heels of those very tears as she wobbled up, her head as dizzy as her heart. "Yes, sir." She patted the moisture from her face and then blew her nose, cheeks warm as she gave him a shy smile. "I need to go, Father—Evan is waiting to walk me home, but I'll launder this and get it back to you, I promise."

He patted her arm. "Keep it, as a memento of the night God answered your prayers—and mine." He looped an arm to her waist and walked her to the front door, unhooking her coat from the rack before he helped her to slip it on.

Donning her fur hat, she then looped her scarf around her neck and buttoned her coat, finally digging in for her gloves. Her fingers met the crinkle of paper in her pocket. "Oh! I almost forgot—Mr. Mulholland made a last-minute donation."

She handed him the check, and he eyed the amount with a lift of brows. "Ah, so you've won the heart of Mr. Mulholland, have you, as well as our rogue?" He tucked the check in his pocket with a mischievous wink. "Good job."

Her giggle was soft. "Thank you, Father," she whispered, voice suddenly hoarse with emotion. She blinked to stem the threat of more tears as she tugged on her gloves. "For everything."

He opened the door. "No, Marceline, thank *you*—for the most memorable Christmas I have ever had. Godspeed, young lady."

She nodded and stepped through the door, then whirled around, pulse erratic. "Father—wait. Does Patrick know about the money, that you know it was his?"

His nose puckered. "Actually, no—that was on my to-do list for next week, when I planned to give him the second best Christmas gift he'll receive this year. But seeing you'll be talking to him before I, no doubt ..." He cocked a bushy brow in question, and she blushed her consent. "Then I'll leave that honor to you."

She grinned. "Thank you." Her smile dimmed as she peered up at the priest, a sudden ache in her chest. "But what about his college fund, all that money he saved ..." She gulped, wishing there was a way the center could keep the money and Patrick could too. "Are you planning to return it?"

The grin reappeared on Father Fitz's face as a twinkle lit his eye. "Not to worry, Marceline, I believe I've gone it one better." He waggled his brows. "The editor of *The Boston Herald* happens to be a dear friend of mine, you know."

Face in a bunch, she tilted her head. "I'm not sure I follow …"

He laughed and opened the door, a glint of mischief in tired blue eyes. "Ah, yes. Well, you see, my friend from the *Herald* happens to be thicker than mortar between bricks with the chancellor of Boston University, don't you know. You might even say they're ...." He winked. "Cousins."

Her mouth fell open before a slow grin curled her lips.

"Which brings me to the second best Christmas gift Mr. O'Connor will receive this year, Marceline, but I claim the right to tell him, eh?" Father Fitz leaned close, his voice a loud whisper. "A merit scholarship, my dear, whenever the boy chooses to go."

She couldn't help it—more tears swam in her eyes.

He chuckled. "Merry Christmas, Marceline—may it give you the desire of your heart," he whispered, the sheen in his eyes matching that in her own. "And only the first of many."

Chapter Thirty-Two

"I can walk the rest of the way from here, Evan, but I can't thank you enough for seeing me home." Marcy gave him a warm smile, grateful for Evan's friendship and the joy he brought to Julie.

"My pleasure, Marcy, but ..." His brow creased. "I'd like to see you all the way to your door, if you don't mind, not just to the corner of your street."

"I know," she said carefully, unwilling to divulge her sudden compulsion to walk to Patrick's house—to see him, to thank him, to tell him she was so very sorry. She swallowed hard, her throat suddenly dry. *And* to discover if what Father Fitz believed was actually true. Her smile was shakier this time, the calm of her voice a stark contrast to the jitters doing cartwheels in her stomach. "But I only live six houses down, and I've already held you up long enough. Besides, I could use a quiet stroll by myself for half a block or so, in the cool air." She tilted her head, a gentle plea in her tone. "You know, just to ponder a few things?"

He stalled for a moment, gaze flicking down the street as if to make sure all was well before he honed in on her face once again. "You're sure you're okay?" he asked, clearly hesitant about her request.

She nodded, her smile coming far more easily than she ever dreamed possible given the ache in her heart over Sam. "Absolutely. In fact, Father Fitz gave me a perspective I've never considered before, and I'm ..." She angled her head in thought, feeling the same sense of awe as in the rectory. "Well, you might say I'm at peace."

His sigh of relief rolled into the brisk air, floating up to become one with a starless sky. "I'm glad, and Julie will be too." Empathy laced his tone. "Although for Sam, I suspect it may take some time."

She shook her head, eyes in a squint. "I don't think so, truly ... at least I hope not. Sam and I weren't really right for each other, but I kept hoping and praying we were." She expelled a heavy sigh, the weight of it drifting away like a cloud of surrender in the frigid night air. Her lips tipped in a sad smile. "I suspect I may have been in love with Sam's family as much as with him, which skewed my thinking somewhat." She looked up then, her manner decisive. "But ... God has a better plan for both of our lives, it seems, just not together."

The ridges in Evan's brow disappeared with a ready smile. "I agree, but please know, I'll be praying for you both, especially Sam. Good night, Marcy."

"Good night, Evan." She watched him disappear into the shadows as he returned the way they'd come and wondered if she was doing the right thing. A lone snowflake swirled from the sky to land on her nose and she closed her eyes, face lifted to the heavens. "Lord, from the moment I left Father Fitz, I've had this urge to talk to Patrick—tonight—to apologize and to thank him for what he did for me, and that's what I intend to do. So, if this is silly of me, and I shouldn't be going over there at this late hour, then please let the house be completely dark." She swallowed the knot in her throat. "Amen."

Forging on, she sucked in a deep swell of frosty air to prepare herself for the task ahead, then made her way to Hastings Street as more and more snowflakes danced from the sky. She peered hard at the street numbers, body braced against the cold. Number 17 Hastings, brick house, green shutters—wasn't that what he'd told Tillie that night? Pulse hammering, she hurried on, spotting number 13, then 15, then—*there!* A groan trapped in her throat. Dark shutters, dark house. Her heart sank lower than her frozen toes, and she huffed out a sigh, her breath languishing like a ghost in the winter sky. "All right, Lord," she said with a slump of her shoulders. "Your timing, Your will." Tugging her scarf more tightly around her neck, she turned toward home, head bowed while a flurry of white as thick as that in her snow globe meandered down like a mantle of peace.

The flurries picked up and along with them, her guilt, accumulating in her mind as swiftly as the blanket of snow on the street. Her pace slowed, thoughts of how she'd misjudged Patrick, Sam, and even the O'Rourkes, believing them to be everything she'd ever wanted in a family, but they weren't. She'd been deceived by her yearning for siblings and a house full of laughter and fun, but the very thing she craved most—a marriage with God at the center—had been absent all along. "Oh, Mother, Papa—I am so sorry ..." she whispered, grieved that she had perceived her parent's marriage to be flawed and lacking when they'd given her something the O'Rourkes never could. The most precious gift of all—a faith so deep and true that one was never alone—even in a family without siblings.

Her steps slowed as she peered up at the heavens,

snow dissolving in the track of her tears. "God, forgive me—I've been wrong about so many things. So anxious to please, yet so quick to judge."

"Yours is a faith that's heart shallow," she'd told Patrick once, berating him for a faulty faith when her own had been steeped in pride, her very words exposing her sin.

"To me, it's a matter of faith that is real and alive and deep ..."

And yet it had been the rogue himself who had taught *her*—a woman in love with God—what real faith was truly all about. Laying down his pride, his heart and in fact, his very life, to serve her ... and her God. Her heart squeezed in her chest as tears squeezed in her eyes. "Oh, Patrick, I don't deserve your love, and yet ... I have it."

"The simple truth is—the boy's desperately in love with you, Marceline."

Heart pounding, she lifted her face to the sky. "Lord, please—help me to love this man the way he deserves."

Unlatching her front gate, she opened it and stepped inside, halting when she spied the candle still glowing in her parlour window. A gentle smile curved on her lips at how Mima insisted it be kept lit each night until Marcy came home, a battle she'd won with Papa, although Marcy knew he really didn't mind. It was their heritage and tradition, after all, the symbol of Christ in their lives, and suddenly Mima's words once again drifted in her brain like the ice crystals from the sky.

"Guard your heart well, Marceline, for a man who will respond to the light in the window ..."

Both Mima's words and the glow of that precious candle seemed to seep into Marcy's very soul ... along with an unexpected rush of desire for the man who

might possibly belong there too.
Patrick.

Closing her eyes, she stopped to savor his name on her tongue, shocked at the intimacy she felt, as if her heart knew all along what her mind had refused to see. A shyness came over her at the thought that this man could very possibly be ...

My soul mate. My future. My life.

The magic of the moment swirled around her, fluttering within her chest like the snowflakes in her hair. A giggle escaped and she slowly whirled around, arms extended and palms up, heart swelling with joy for a God whose blessings fell from heaven as freely as the tiny ice doilies she caught with her tongue. For a single moment, the world was soft, silent, and serene ...

And then ... a faint crunch of snow broke her reverie and with a harsh catch of her breath, she stilled on the flagstone walk. A familiar shadow rose from her parent's Adirondack chair, a mere silhouette against the light in the window. *Oh, Sam, no ... I'm not ready to discuss this tonight ...*

Lips pressed tight, she hurried up the walk and then ... *froze* ... colder and stiffer than the icicles hanging from the roof of her porch.

"I was worried," he whispered, voice hoarse with regret as he descended the steps painfully slow, the muted scrunch of snow beneath his feet as deafening as the pulse pounding in her ears. "I ... wanted to make sure you were all right."

She stared as he stopped two feet away, shoulders hunched into his coat and stance awkward as if he feared his presence might offend. "Are you ... all right?"

Her breath was jagged and her body numb, but not from the cold. "P-Patrick," she whispered, "w-what are you doing here?"

"Evan told me what happened," he said quietly. "Said he was going to tell you tonight." He buried his hands in the pockets of his woolen coat, clearly ill at ease. "I can't tell you how sorry I am for both you and Sam."

His words rekindled her grief—over Sam, over her misjudgment of the man who stood before her, and over the hurt she would cause to a family she dearly loved. "No, please—I'm the one who's sorry, for turning on you like I did, for not trusting you."

He shrugged his shoulders, hip slack, head bowed. "Don't—you had no reason to."

"No, I suppose I didn't ...," she whispered, her gaze tracing the chiseled line of his jaw through the haze of the falling snow. Gray eyes that were now almost black probed hers, bleeding with an intensity that told her he cared. She braced herself with a deep draw of stinging air, lacy fluffs of snow kissing her cheeks. "Until now."

He nodded, his gaze on the blanket of powder at her feet. "I love Sam, Marcy, you know that. He's as much a brother as a friend." His eyes lifted to meet hers, so potent she felt the tendons weaken at the back of her knees. "But I couldn't stand by and watch him hurt you like that. You deserve ..." A knot dipped in his throat. "So much more." A heavy exhale threaded past his lips to whiten the air. "So a part of me mourns your loss and Sam's—but a part of me is relieved." He shifted and inclined his head toward her house. "It's cold, and you need to go in. I just wanted to make sure you were okay."

With a stiff smile, he attempted to pass, but she stopped him with a gentle hand, flustered by the strange tingle it sparked in her palm. "Patrick, wait," she whispered, quickly hugging her arms to her waist while she stared at her feet. "I … don't know how … I can ever thank you for what you did."

"It was nothing, Marcy."

"No!" Her whisper was harsh as her head shot up, eyes burning with a fierce gratitude. "It was everything." She gripped his arm again, but this time she refused to let go, her gaze locked with his. "And it's changed *everything*."

He stared, mouth ajar. "I … don't understand."

Water welled in her eyes. "The money, Patrick," she said fervently, "your college fund that you sacrificed for me. Why did you do it?"

She heard the catch of his breath as his body stilled to stone, shallow air rasping across parted lips. "Who told you?" The words were barely audible, halting and slow while he averted his gaze with head down, cheeks ruddier than before.

"The police found most of the stolen money on a transient, and Father Fitz figured out the rest." She paused, unable to hide the hint of humor lacing her tone. "But I'm afraid your partner in crime sang like a bird."

He nodded, a faint smile shadowing his lips.

"Why did you do it?" she whispered.

His gaze slowly lifted to hers. "You know why," he said softly, but if she didn't, the love in his eyes would have given him dead away.

A shaky smile curved on her face. "Yes—finally, Patrick O'Connor—I know why." She lifted on tiptoe to press her lips to his cheek, and in one jolting breath, he slowly turned into her kiss, his mouth not a half inch away. Her heart thundered in her chest as neither of them moved, nothing separating them but ragged air that boiled into the sky like barely contained steam.

The moment was broken when he pulled away and

took a step back, his labored breathing billowing into the night. "I should go ..."

No ...

His smile was tender. "The play was wonderful, Marcy. You should be proud."

Oh, Patrick, I am ... but not of the play ...

He puffed out a sigh. "Well, I guess I'll see you at the center, then. Good night."

He turned away, and in a stutter of her pulse, she grasped his fingers, halting his retreat with a shaky rush of words. "It would appear, Mr. O'Connor," she said with a casual tone that was anything but, "your reputation as the Southie's most notorious rogue has been highly overrated."

Shock glazed his eyes as they flicked from the hand clutching his to her face, muscles shifting in his throat. "What?"

Suddenly shy, she quickly released him, feeling like a little girl when she clutched her hands behind her back. A nervous smile flickered at the edges of her mouth as she teased him with a bold jut of her chin. "A little gun-shy, are we?"

He blinked before a crooked grin stole across his lips. "Aye, Marceline, all it takes is one good wallop to keep this rogue in line." He rubbed the side of his jaw with the back of his glove, then paused, his gaze caressing her face. "Or former rogue, I should say ..."

She arched a brow. "A quick study—I like that."

Her stomach swooped when he moved in close, eyes fused to hers with a heat that made her forget she was cold. "I surely hope so," he said softly, cupping her face in his hands. "I'm in love with you, Marceline, and as God is my witness, from the moment I saw you, no other woman could even come close." Her heart stopped when his eyes sheathed closed to gently brush her lips with his own, more fragile than the snowflakes floating from the sky. "Say you'll let me court you," he whispered, his mouth as warm as the swirls he produced in her belly, "and I give you my word—I will move heaven and earth to win your heart."

Heaven and earth. Her lashes lifted, and she caught her breath at the glow of love in his eyes. No, not heaven and earth, she finally realized, but heaven *on* earth, a state of heart only possible when God Himself knits two people together. Looking at him now, she marveled that it felt so right, so natural to be considering spending the rest of her life with this man she barely knew, and yet ... somehow she felt as if she'd known him—waited for him—all of her life. Eyes warm with affection, she slowly glided her glove along the strong curve of his jaw. "Moving heaven and earth isn't necessary to win my heart, Patrick," she said. "Just move yours closer to God's and there you'll find mine."

Patrick blinked, her statement producing more shivers than a mile-high blizzard.

"Something tells me, my boy, that before a man can truly win the heart of a woman like Marceline Murphy, his own heart must be aligned with God's ..."

He bowed his head and chuckled, his soft laughter bringing a curious smile to her lips. "What?" she asked, head tipped in question.

Shaking his head, he peered up beneath lashes spiked with snow. "You haven't by chance been in league with Father Fitz to save Sam's soul and mine, have you?"

She grinned. "Only in our mutual prayers for you both to be happy."

Throat working, he stared at her beautiful face, not one bit ashamed of the sheen of moisture that sprang to his eyes. He stroked her cheek with his thumb, barely able to believe that God had answered his prayers. "Then please, darlin'," he whispered, voice rough with emotion, "don't stop."

Her eyelids sank closed as he placed the softest of kisses to her cheek, her temple, skimming each eyelid with his mouth before it trailed to deposit a playful kiss to her nose. "But as fond as I am of Father Fitz," he said with a note of levity, "he's not the one who can make my dreams come true." Her eyes fluttered open when he swept a stray hair away from her face, and he found he had no control over the words that tumbled from his lips. "Marry me, Marceline," he whispered. "Tomorrow, next week, next year—I don't care. Just say that you will, and I swear before God and man I will become the husband God intends me to be."

Her soft chuckle floated into the air in a cloud of smoke. His heart raced at the lift of her smile when she cupped a hand to his face. "As inclined as I am to concur this instant, Mr. O'Connor," she said with a definite twinkle, "I suspect you and I should get to know each other a wee bit better, don't you think?"

His grin spanned the whole of his face. "Aye, and a more pleasant prospect I can't imagine." His gaze dropped to her lips before he could stop it, his voice a husky whisper. "Or heaven help me, maybe I can ..."

He quickly cleared his throat and stepped back, noting a sudden blush in her cheeks he couldn't blame on the weather. "Well, then," he said, shocked that his face was as warm as hers, no doubt, "I suspect you are now frozen to the bone and in dire need of a warm bed." Taking her hand, he tugged her up to the front porch and turned the knob, quietly pushing the door ajar. "Get some rest, Marcy." Caressing her with a gentle gaze, he carefully lifted her chin to softly brush his lips against hers, his mouth nuzzling with a reverence he'd never experienced with a woman before. A shaky breath shuddered from his lips as he gently prodded her through the door. "Because you're going to need it, darlin'—I plan to keep you very busy." He heard the final click of the lock and grinned outright.

Aye, Marceline, for the rest of your life ...

Epilogue

"Oh, Julie, it's absolutely beautiful!" Marcy whispered, blinking back the sting of tears as she gazed at the diamond ring on her best friend's hand. She could hardly believe it. *Julie—married!* Swiping at her eyes with the heel of her palm, she swallowed her up in a giant hug, thrilled beyond words that Evan had finally proposed. She quickly pulled away to take Julie's hands in her own. "Oh, Jewels, I couldn't be happier for you!"

But for myself? Marcy forced a bright smile, determined that her melancholy would *not* shadow the joy of Julie's engagement. "Evan is one of the kindest, godliest men I've ever met, and I just know he'll make you happy."

As if sensing the malaise Marcy tried so hard to hide, Julie stroked a gentle hand to her friend's cheek. "It will happen for you too, Marce," she said quietly, sympathy soft in her dark eyes. "You'll see."

Will I? Marcy stared at the ceiling of her bedroom, slumber nowhere in sight as she lay in her bed in the dark. The grandfather clock in the parlour chimed the midnight hour with distant bongs that seemed to echo her gloom. She should be tired after working several nights this week at the center in addition to her final semester at school, but sleep evaded her as easily as love apparently, at least now that she was no longer seeing either Patrick or Sam.

She shifted on her side, pillow bunched beneath her head while her eyes trailed into a faraway stare, tears blurring the hazy beams of moonlight that spilled across her wooden floor. Bathing her room in an ethereal glow, it was as if God Himself had parted the night sky to peek down from heaven, promising her that she, too, would find a man as committed to God as much as he was to her. Just like Julie had.

Marcy rubbed the moisture from her face with the sleeve of her nightgown. *Only rogues didn't have a propensity for either God or commitment*, she thought with a sniff, a lesson she had learned the hard way. First through Nora's heartbreak with an unfaithful fiancé, then Sam's infidelity, and finally with Patrick, a rake too handsome for his own good—and hers—who turned heads faster than Marcy could tally. How could she ever trust a man like that? She sniffed. The simple truth was—apparently she couldn't.

Heaving a mournful sigh, she curled into a ball and closed her eyes, hoping that her dream of working with babies at the hospital would be enough to stifle her longing for babies of her own. At least until God answered her prayer for a mate who would share her deep faith as well as her life ... that is, *if* God chose to. Because there were days, Marcy was reluctant to admit, when it seemed as if He had no such plan at all.

O magnify the Lord with me, and let us exalt his name together ...

The Scripture reading from mass this morning seemed little more than a taunt, haunting her mind with the reality that other than her parents and Mima, when it came to family, she was really quite alone in the world. Born as an only child of an only child, she seemed destined for the same lonely path in her future—no soul mate with whom to share her faith, no babies to love, no family to fill up the lonely places in her heart.

Even as sleep took her away, the heaviness remained, hovering in Marcy's mind until the first light of dawn crept across her windowsill, chasing the shadows away, but not the despair.

It will never happen for you—you will always be alone.

She lay there in her murky malaise, eyes closed and mind drifting somewhere between contemplation and slumber, the room silent except for the faint chatter of squirrels in the large elm outside her window.

And then something moved in the bed and Marcy froze for a split second before she jolted straight up, covers crushed to her chest and eyes spanning wide. The sound of her shallow breathing merged with that of the man beside her and she blinked away the fog of her dream, tears stinging as she stared at her husband.

I honor those who honor Me, the thought came, and Marcy's hand flew to her mouth as moisture brimmed in her eyes. *Oh, Lord, You do, don't You?*

A loud snort erupted from Patrick's mouth as he turned on his side, dark lashes resting peacefully on his handsome face, and her smile broke through the tears like the sun burst through the dark of night. Ebony curls spilled over his forehead while he snored, his bare chest muscled and strong, rising and falling beneath covers pushed to his waist.

A rush of hot blood toasted her cheeks at the thought of an amorous rogue who now focused all his attentions on her ... and *only* her. His wife, his lover, the other half of his soul.

And soon ... the mother of his child. With a tender

caress of her flat belly, she lay back down, giddy at the thought of telling Patrick that she carried his seed, his baby, a gift like no other, at least for Marcy. The answer to her prayers—and, she hoped—his, and the beginning of their family. Over a month late and owning every symptom Mother had told her about, she'd hoped to tell Patrick after she went to the doctor, just to make sure. But watching him now, he looked so much like the little boy she longed to have, so innocent in sleep, eyes fringed with the longest lashes God ever gave to a man, that she couldn't wait to tell him he would soon be a father.

She lay back down on her side, eyes fixed on the single most handsome man she had ever seen. Another dizzy rush of fire swarmed her cheeks. *Or touched*, she reminded herself with a sweet swirl of heat in her belly. Her gaze scanned from the shadow of dark bristle on his angular jaw down a sculpted torso and arms that had held her close every night for the last three months. The familiar scent of spice and pine and Patrick filled her bed and her senses with delicious memories of a man who kissed her, touched her, loved her like she was his most precious possession in the world. A shy smile tipped on her lips. *And, oh Lord, I am!* At the thought, a deep rush of joy swelled within, so powerful that it quivered her jaw and flooded her eyes. Even her parents and Mima, so wary of Patrick's intentions at first, had warmed to this man who had stolen their hearts as quickly as he had stolen Marcy's.

She stared at him now and her heart trembled at how very close she had come to missing God's best. Tears brimmed as she reflected on the day of her wedding, when Sam had paid her a visit in the wee hours of the morning for a private goodbye. He'd taken a job in New York, he said, because he loved her too much to stay, and she'd grieved for this man who still owned a piece of her soul. "I love you, Marceline," he'd whispered, "and I will never forget you," and despite another man's ring on her hand, she knew she still cared for him too.

But, *oh* ... how it paled next to the love she now felt for Patrick, so deep and so strong that it ached in her chest. With a silent heave, she pressed her palm to her mouth while tears slipped from her eyes. *Oh, Lord— how lucky am I? I married the love of my life!*

Beautiful bliss like she'd never known bubbled up before she could stop it, unleashing a giggle on the heels of a joyful sob that lifted her husband's half-lidded eyes. "Weepin' again, are you, darlin'," he whispered, his voice husky with sleep, "over marrying the likes of me?" Not waiting for her answer, he hooked her close with a strong arm and a soft kiss to her hair. "Good mornin', Marceline," he whispered. He slowly shifted to secure her body flush with his. "Although I believe it's about to get better." He eased her back on the pillow with a languid kiss that all but melted her bones to the bed, his warm breath feathering her cheek while his hand feathered the length of her gown.

She couldn't help it—a little giggle squeaked out when his mouth wandered to the hollow of her throat and he lifted his head, a glint of the devil in his eye as he delivered a mock scowl. "Laughing at the Southie rogue, are you?" A wicked grin slid across his lips as he dove for her neck. "Oh, darlin', I'm afraid that's going to cost you dearly."

Ticklish to a fault, she squealed when his mouth buried deep in the crook of her neck, their laughter ricocheting off the walls while she thrashed and rolled under the covers. She stilled when he cradled her face in his hands, his kiss so gentle, a heady warmth purled all the way to her toes. Chest heaving, he seemed to drink her in with a gaze that caressed every single part of her face. "I'm desperately in love with you, Marceline," he whispered, voice hoarse with emotion while the rogue in him gave way to gray eyes so achingly tender, they brought tears to her own. "Deliriously, feverishly, utterly besotted with the most perfect wife God ever gave to a man." He nuzzled the whole of her mouth. Twining his fingers in her hair, he swallowed hard, a hint of sheen in his eyes. "I adore you, Marcy, and sometimes I can hardly contain the joy that you give ... hardly believe that you're actually mine."

She traced his shadowed jaw with shaky fingers. "God has been so good to us, hasn't He?"

A muscle flickered in his jaw as emotion welled in his eyes. "Aye, Marceline," he said quietly, "more than I ever dreamed and everything I ever hoped."

A smile curved on her lips. "Not everything," she whispered, rising to gently sway her lips against his.

He responded with a low groan, taking her mouth with a ferocity that left her breathless. "Tell me, darlin'," he whispered, trailing the line of her jaw to suckle her ear. "Can you guess what I'm hoping for now?"

Her giggle faded into a moan when his mouth strayed to wander the curve of her throat. "Yes, you hopeless rogue, b-but I believe I can go one b-better," she stuttered, body humming from his touch.

His lips paused on her skin before he glanced up beneath shuttered lids, slipping her a dangerous smile. "I don't see how, darlin'."

Chuckling, she closed her eyes and waited while she chewed on the edge of her grin. "Well, you will, Patrick O'Connor, you mark my words ... say, in about eight to nine months or so ...?"

She felt his body seize, still as stone before his head lashed up, eyes gaping as wide as his mouth while shallow breaths rasped from his lips. "W-what d-did you say?"

Her grin melted into a tender smile. "I said, God's about to give us more than we ever hoped for, my love, in about eight to nine months or so." She scrunched her nose. "Give or take a few."

A muscle jerked in his throat, and then he pounced with joyous laughter, kissing her so hard, her giggles collided with a moan in her throat. Yanking back, he cupped her face in his hands, smothering her lips, her jaw, her temple with frenzied kisses while his chuckles tickled her cheek. "I honestly didn't believe you could make me any happier, Marceline, but I was wrong." He buried his face in the hair that trailed her neck. "Pinch me, darlin', please, because I swear I'm dreaming."

"How about I love you instead?" she whispered, the moisture in her eyes a mirror reflection of his when he rose to meet her gaze.

"Aye," he said softly, palm caressing her belly before he traced the curve of her lips with the pad of his thumb. "Practice makes perfect, so we best get started." He gently grazed her mouth with his own, his kiss as tender as the man who held her in his arms. "Because I'll be looking for twins next year, Mrs. O'Connor, and make no mistake."

Her lashes flickered closed while her soft laughter wisped against the rasp of his jaw. "We'll see, Mr. O'Connor," she whispered, her words dissolving into the joy of his kiss. "We'll see."

Acknowledgments

My deepest appreciation and thanks to each of the following who gave of their time and love to work with me on this manuscript—every one of you were a godsend!

To my dear writer friends Cynthia Andreyuk and Sandy Knight for tirelessly poring over this work to make it all it could be, and to sweet Julie Gilmore Graves, who pointed out so many things during my blog tour, that I just may hire the woman next time!

To Natasha Kern, agent extraordinaire and dear friend—what a blessing you are in my life! To the Seekers—sisters all—and especially Mary Connealy, whose name in the endorsement on the cover of this book will sell far more copies than mine.

To my faithful prayer partners in life, Karen, Pat and Joy and to those in my world of writing, Laura Frantz and MaryLu Tyndall—your precious friendships are made all the sweeter with prayer.

My heartfelt gratitude to my daughter-in-law Katie, who despite a ridiculous schedule, took the time to proof it for me as well. And to my daughter Amy whose prayers and support shored me up all the way and whose face on the cover of this book made it as special to me as it is beautiful.

To Keith Lessman, who not only gave me the benefit of his truly invaluable feedback and a killer cover, but his bottomless love, which—along with God's grace—is the wellspring for any romance that I am able to write.

And finally, to the amazing God of the Universe, the other "Love of my Life." Without You, I would be totally and utterly lost—in my marriage, in my life, and for all eternity.

About the Author

Julie Lessman is an award-winning author whose tagline of "Passion With a Purpose" underscores her intense passion for both God and romance. Winner of the 2009 ACFW Debut Author of the Year and Holt Medallion Awards of Merit for Best First Book and Long Inspirational, Julie is also the recipient of 16 Romance Writers of America awards and was voted by readers as "Borders Best of 2009 So Far: Your Favorite Fiction."

Chosen as the #1 Romance Fiction Author of the Year in the **Family Fiction** magazine 2012 and 2011 Readers Choice Awards, Julie was also awarded #1 Historical Fiction Author of the Year in that same poll and #3 Author of the Year, #4 Novel of the Year and #3 Series of the year. She resides in Missouri with her husband, daughter, son, daughter-in-law and granddaughter and is the author of "The Daughters of Boston" series—*A Passion Most Pure, A Passion Redeemed*, and *A Passion Denied.* Book 1 in her "Winds of Change" series *A Hope Undaunted* ranked #5 on **Booklist**'s Top 10 Inspirational Fiction for 2010 and is followed by *A Heart Revealed* and *A Love Surrendered.*

Julie loves to hear from her readers, so please feel

free to contact her through the following:

Her website at www.julielessman.com, on Facebook at http://www.facebook.com/pages/Julie-Lessman/98874268454, *on Twitter at @julielessman,* On the Seekerville blog at http://www.seekerville.blogspot.com/, or on her personal blog, *Journal Jot*s at http://www.julielessman.com/journal-jots1/

A Note to My Readers

Thank you for joining me on the journey of Marcy and Patrick O'Connor, a couple who learned, as I did in my own marriage of thirty-five years, that true romance is a marriage with God in the center. This is a theme of my heart that I weave into each and every romance novel I write because I know first-hand that blessings abound in a marriage, in relationships, and in one's life when God's precepts are front and center.

Although this is Marcy and Patrick's love story, their marriage and epilogue are both based on my own marriage to a man whose love—like God's—makes me feel cherished and whole. In fact, Marcy's epilogue was taken from my life almost to a word, that precious morning when I awoke in much the same way to the startling realization that God does, indeed, do abundantly, exceedingly more than we think, hope, or pray.

I invite you to continue the journey of Marcy and Patrick in both "The Daughters of Boston" and "Winds of Change" series, six books that not only weave a love story for each of their six children, but continue the love story of a rogue and the woman who wooed him to God.

The family saga begins with *A Passion Most Pure*, book 1 in "The Daughters of Boston" series and finally ends with book 3 in the "Winds of Change" series as listed below. Descriptions of each can be found on the "Books" tab of my website at http://www.julielessman.com/books/ and excerpts of my favorite romantic and spiritual scenes for each of my books can be found on the "Excerpts" tab at http://www.julielessman.com/excerpts/.

"The Daughters of Boston" Series

Book 1: *A Passion Most Pure*
Book 2: *A Passion Redeemed*
Book 3: *A Passion Denied*

"Winds of Change" Series

Book 1: *A Hope Undaunted*
Book 2: *A Heart Revealed*
Book 3: *A Love Surrendered*

And now, here's an excerpt from

A Passion Most Pure

The year is 1916, and Marcy and Patrick have just had a fight, which prompts Patrick to return to Brannigan's Pub for the first time in twenty-one years. Ironically, it's at Brannigan's where Patrick encounters a new "Southie rogue" who has been wooing Patrick's sixteen-year-old daughter against his wishes.

Patrick tried to remember the last time he'd crossed the threshold of Brannigan's Pub—certainly not within the last twenty-one years. There'd been no need. From the moment he'd laid eyes on Marcy, she had been all the intoxication he needed. But tonight … well, tonight he needed more, and with lips leveled in a hard line, he once again returned to the dark and smoky confines of the pub that had once been a second home. He looked around. Almost nothing had changed, except for the faces and style of clothing the patrons wore. They still crowded around the same rickety piano and leaned against the same endless cherrywood bar, which looked as if it were polished to a gleam twice a day. The smoky haze was the same, the smells were the same, and the lure and promise of trading in one's problems for a night of revelry was as strong as ever.

Patrick only recognized a few faces, such as Lucas

Brannigan, the proud owner of this, the most successful pub in the Southie neighborhood. And, of course, there was Tommy Thomkins, minstrel to those who found themselves alone and miserable, catering to anyone who would drink up his melodies along with bottomless mugs of beer.

Patrick found a vacant barstool and wearily sat down, wedged between a bloke passed out on the bar and a young couple so entwined they only required a single stool. The sleeping man beside him was snoring loudly, cheek pressed hard on the cherrywood bar. Drool funneled from his mouth into a pool of saliva. Patrick forced himself to stare straight ahead at the endless rows of bottles overhead, each reflected in the smoky mirror behind, each a tonic of choice for various problems of the afflicted. The couple to his right disengaged momentarily to sate their thirst, and Patrick caught the nauseating scent of perfume mingled with sweat and stale beer. The whiff of it reminded him just how much Marcy had changed his life for the better.

The thought of her now brought a strange mix of sadness and longing, and more than a bit of anger. She had never done this before, never questioned his authority or spoken to him with anything other than the utmost kindness and respect. And certainly, she had never turned him out of her bed before. Patrick nodded to the bartender who pushed a foaming mug toward him, the frothy rise of beer tumbling over the edge before slithering into a puddle on the bar. Not unlike, he thought to himself ironically, his own miserable life at the moment—sweet nectar spilling over, horribly wasted.

Patrick brought the mug to his lips. The biting brew tasted strong and good going down, hopefully to wash away the hurt still lodged in the pit of his stomach. He would have only one, he vowed to himself. This wasn't the end of his life, after all, only an argument, a minor interruption in a 21-year love affair that was the impetus of everything good in his life. She would know by his absence just how much she had hurt him, and she would be sorry and ready to welcome him back. Patrick downed the dregs of the mug and blinked in surprise when the bartender magically produced another, its glorious overflow enticing him to succumb.

His sweaty palms hovered around the glass. He was wrestling with pushing it away when he felt the presence of someone standing close, lodged between the hopelessly entangled couple and himself. He blinked up at a pretty woman in her mid-thirties, and his fingers recoiled as if he'd touched a hot stove. Her dark hair billowed loosely about her shoulders while her green eyes assessed him with open curiosity.

She nodded at his beer. "Drink up—my treat. And tell me now, sweetness, just where in the world have you been keeping yourself!" It was a statement of pleasant surprise rather than a question, and Patrick could do nothing but stare, completely caught off-guard by the woman before him. Her smile broke into a delighted grin at the effect she seemed to be having, and she sidled closer until barely inches away, her gaze level with his. "What, cat got your tongue? The name's Lucy, and it appears you could do with some company. We have a table over there—why don't ya join us?"

She waited while he grappled with his response, then noticed the ring on his left hand. If she was disappointed, she never let it show as she rested her hand on top of his.

"Look, it's only a beer with some friends. We'll send ya back to your darlin' wife with your virtue intact, if that's what's worrying ya."

Patrick knew in his gut he should turn and go. Something within desperately wanted to walk away and return home to Marcy, work things out, and hold her in his arms once again. But as the beer took effect, the allure of home seemed impaired, temporarily overshadowed by the irrefutable charm of this place and the girl before him.

Lucy seemed to be holding her breath as she awaited his answer. When a smile pulled at his lips, she exhaled slowly, carefully. Her eyes were gleaming. "I seriously hope that's a yes!"

"It is, at that. One beer with you and your friends. Then I'll be on my way." It was only an innocent drink with friends, he reasoned, nothing more and nothing less. Within the hour, he would be back home with Marcy where he belonged, where he would be right now if she hadn't turned on him so. She had provoked him to this end, he decided, and would soon realize just how much she'd hurt him.

"Everyone, this is—" Lucy turned to Patrick, an unabashed grin on her face. "Saints alive, I was so taken with ya, I completely forgot to get your name."

"It's Patrick ... Patrick O'Connor. It's a pleasure to meet you all."

"Oh no, Patrick, you have it all wrong. The pleasure is all Lucy's!"

The group broke into uproarious laughter as Lucy punched the arm of the sloshed man who'd spoken. Someone ordered a round of beer. They raised a toast to Patrick, and then one to Lucy, and then to no one in particular at all. Their laughter was contagious and their beer ever flowing, and before long, Patrick found himself wondering why he'd ever stopped coming here. Through the fog in his mind, he felt someone tugging his sleeve. He looked up and saw Lucy in a blur, smiling like a trio of angels.

"Let's dance," she said.

And so he did, unsteady on his feet as they slowly moved to the melancholy sound of Tommy Thomkin's soulful ballad. She burrowed in his arms, startling him when the scent of her perfume aroused his senses. She lifted her gaze to his mouth, her lips parted slightly. Closing her eyes, she waited for the kiss she seemed to expect. Painful seconds passed as a war waged within him, and Patrick could hear the blood rushing in his ears. Suddenly, his arms went slack at her waist. He faltered back.

Lucy opened her eyes to see his retreat, and before he could turn her away, she kissed him. Abruptly, he shoved her away, a mixture of arousal and shame in his gut. He stood there, weaving, sweat trickling inside his collar.

Somewhere in the back of his mind, beneath the numbness the beer created and the passion Lucy ignited, an appalling guilt began to gnaw. He thought of Marcy, alone and asleep in his bed, their children slumbering in the rooms down the hall, and a sense of shame began to counter the intoxication of Lucy's seduction.

What had possessed him to do this? He hadn't touched another woman for over twenty-one years, hadn't sought it out or wanted to, ever. But tonight he'd fallen. The virtues he espoused to his own children now returned, a bitter derision of his own failure. *Dear God, forgive me, I've been a fool.* But, surely a fool who could put an end to his folly. Patrick stared at Lucy, his eyes too clouded to see her face. He hesitated before touching her arm. "Lucy, I'm sorry, but I should go. Lucy ... I love my wife."

Lucy's lips quivered into a weak smile. She put her

hands on Patrick's face. "That's as plain as the nose on your face, Patrick O'Connor." Stepping on tiptoe, she kissed him lightly on the cheek. "Go on with you, now."

Patrick nodded, lowering his gaze from her eyes. His body went to stone at the sound of a voice from behind.

"Well, good evening, Mr. O'Connor! Hello, Lucy …"

Patrick's stomach rolled. Slowly he turned to look into the smiling face of Collin McGuire.

"You two make a lovely couple," Collin remarked.

A rush of hot blood flooded Patrick's face as he confronted the man who had been the source of so much grief in his family. He wanted to slap the smirk off his face, to berate him for enticing his daughter and driving a wedge between them. He wanted to hurt him because he stood there judging him for this unspeakable moment of failure, just as Patrick had always judged him. Patrick felt the sweat crawling down the back of his neck.

Collin offered a smug smile while Lucy blinked, totally bewildered. "Collin, do you know Patrick?"

"Lucy, do you know he's married?"

Patrick started to lunge, but Lucy held him back.

"Yes I know he's married! Ya think I'm blind, do ya?"

"This isn't as it appears …" Patrick's breathing was heavy, his face hot. He hated himself for being in a position where he felt the need to explain himself to this rabble. And he hated the superior look on the rabble's face even more.

"Is that so? Well you know, that's often the case, isn't it, Mr. O'Connor? For instance, it certainly looks for all practical purposes as if you were—shall we say,

dancing?—with a woman who's not your wife."
Patrick winced as if Collin had struck him.

"But we both know despite how it looks to the naked eye … " Collin paused, his eyebrows arched in apparent assessment of the situation, "we can find not only a perfectly innocent explanation, but ourselves in grave danger of gross misjudgment, wouldn't you say?"

Patrick's humiliation was complete. Suddenly he felt very tired, very sober, and completely drained of all energy. Shame weighted him down like a ton of steel and guilt. Resigned, he turned to Lucy. "Lucy, I owe you an apology, I owe Collin an apology, and most of all, I owe my wife an apology. I should have never come here tonight. I love her, and I let momentary anger get in the way of that. I was wrong to succumb to your obvious charms. Please forgive me."

Lucy managed a sad smile. "Oh, go on with ya now, Patrick. It was me who came after you, now didn't I? I saw the ring on your finger, plain as day. I was just hopin' it didn't mean all that much, that's all. Go on, hurry home to that wife of yours. I swear by St. Patrick himself she's one of the luckiest women in all of Boston. And don't ya know I'm giving her fair warning. If she ever treats you badly, I promise I won't be letting go quite so easy." Lucy grabbed Patrick's coat from the chair and threw it at him, a feeble attempt at a smile on her face. "Go on, get out of here!"

Patrick caught his coat and nodded before turning once again to Collin. "There's not much I can say, Collin. You're right. I have judged you—a most common error, I suspect, among fathers of the sixteen-year-old girls you've pursued. I apologize for that. And I apologize you had to see me make the biggest mistake of my life. But I don't apologize for being Charity's father. That in itself entitles me to decide whom my daughter may court and whom she may not."

Patrick put his coat on. "You know, Collin, I was a lot like you when I was your age; had quite a way with the ladies, if you will. I certainly broke more than my fair share of hearts, much as I suspect you do. As Charity's father, I prefer you break someone else's heart other than my daughter's, someone who can handle it. For God's sake, she's sixteen and very vulnerable. I know she looks like a woman, but she's just a little girl––*my* little girl."

Some of the arrogance faded from Collin's face as he watched Patrick through wary eyes.

Patrick continued. "You're a man. You need to find the love of a good woman, not a young girl. I found the right woman, and it changed my life forever. Filled me with contentment and happiness I never dreamed possible."

"*Except* for tonight." Collin's voice was quiet.

Patrick's countenance fell. "Yes, except for tonight. Tonight something happened that hasn't in over twenty-one years of marriage. We fought—bitterly. Tell me, Collin, do you know what we fought about? Would you like to know what shattered our evening and sent me bolting into the night? Well, I'll tell you. We fought over Charity. Over whether or not she should have the right to go out tonight. Could we trust her? Was the discipline of confining her to the house for three weeks enough to impact her? These are nervous questions that race around in a parent's mind, sometimes creating an environment of volatility. And so we fought—over whether or not the punishment we gave for seeing you behind our backs was enough. Enough to let her know we loved her, and as her parents, knew what was best for her. Maybe you can tell me. Was it?"

Collin's eyes filled with surprise. "Why don't you

ask your daughter?" he said, his tone belligerent. "She's your 'little girl', after all."

Patrick's anger surged with renewed fervor. "I'm giving you fair warning, McGuire. Stay away from my daughter."

"Or what? How can you stop me except by making it a little more difficult? I have a lot of feelings for your daughter, Mr. O'Connor. She's not just another conquest to me. Charity loves me, and that's pretty tempting for someone who's never had a lot of that in his life. I don't want to be at odds with you, truly I don't. But don't think you can cut me off from Charity's love."

"And what's more important? Charity? Or the fact that you think she loves you?"

The truth of his query seemed to catch Collin square in the gut. For a moment, his gray eyes widened, then clouded to charcoal as he brooded over Patrick's words. Collin jabbed at the back of his neck, cursing under his breath. He leered at Patrick, a muscle twitching in his cheek. "It doesn't matter. Charity loves me. And nothing—not the fact I may or may not love her, nor the fact she's only sixteen, nor the determined dictates of her father—*nothing* will stop that strong-willed girl of yours from seeking me out, nor me her. It's a fact of life, Mr. O'Connor, and one I'm afraid you'll just have to get used to."

Patrick looked at the young man before him and tried very hard to dislike him. He was too good-looking for his own good, too confident and too cocky to suit him. But for all his air of superiority and all the problems he posed to Patrick's peace of mind, Collin was not unlike a similarly cocky Irishman of twenty years past. Before he found the love of a good woman and before he relented to the hand of God in his life. Patrick sighed and put his hand on Collin's shoulder. At his touch, Collin stiffened.

"Nothing?" Patrick's voice was strangely unaffected. "Well, make no mistake about it Collin, I will fight you every step of the way on this, I can promise you that. And I'm very sure you and Charity will do the same. However, my boy, I'm afraid you're forgetting one very important thing." Patrick slapped Collin on the shoulder, then buttoned his coat and headed toward the door.

Curiosity apparently got the best of Collin McGuire as he grabbed Patrick by the arm. "And what might that be, Mr. O'Connor?"

The faint smile on Patrick's lips felt almost peaceful. "Never—and I repeat, *never*—underestimate the power of a father on his knees." And with that he left, leaving Collin, despite the warmth of the pub, very much out in the cold.

Patrick entered the dark foyer and glanced at the clock on the parlour mantle. His heart sank—1:07 a.m. The reality of what had taken place tonight settled over him like a shroud, blacker than the gloom of his house as he slowly made his way up the steps. At the top of the stairs, Blarney met him, his tail wagging to let him know someone was glad he was home, even if Marcy wouldn't be. He scratched the dog under the neck for a moment, then peered down the hall at the door of his room. Would Marcy be awake? He hoped not. He desperately needed some hours of sleep before facing her. But face her he would, come morning. The very thought caused his stomach, full of beer and bitter regret, to churn within. As if in a trance, he moved to the bathroom where he quickly washed his face and brushed his teeth before continuing down the hall to their room.

Carefully, Patrick turned the doorknob to his bedroom, cautiously pushing the door ajar. He peered into the dark and strained his eyes until he saw her small form in the bed. She was buried beneath the mound of covers that always occupied her side. Patrick stopped and listened. The faint rhythm of her breathing could be heard, the mountain of covers slowly rising and falling in harmony with the sound. He removed his shoes and trousers, and then his rumpled shirt and tie. He reached for his pajamas from the hook on the wardrobe and put them on. Walking to the nightstand, he poured water from the pitcher into a glass and added a small amount of Marcy's perfumed water. Swishing the concoction in his mouth, he glanced at the bed and swallowed hard. He prayed it would disguise the smell of beer on his breath. Silently, he crossed the room to his side of the bed, gently lifting the covers. Marcy never moved a muscle, except for the imperceptible motion of the covers as they rose and fell. Patrick eased his way into the bed, gradually stretching his legs to the bottom edge. With a silent sigh, he tentatively began to relax, the peace of sleep quickly pulling at the corners of his consciousness.

Somewhere in the dark recesses of his mind, he heard something move. And then, before the escape of sweet sleep could steal him away, she pounced. Her eyes blazed and her fingernails slashed like a cat stabbing its prey. Bolting up in bed, Patrick fended her off, her claws flailing in the dark as she spat whispered screams. He grabbed her wrists and shoved her back on the bed, holding her down as he arched over her, his breathing heavy and erratic.

"Marcy, listen to me, *please* ..."

She sniffed in the air. "Sweet saints, have you been

drinking? You reek of smoke and ... *is that perfume?*" He had never seen her eyes so wild. "Let me go, Patrick, *let me go!*"

Her voice was so shrill, Patrick glanced at the door in alarm. "Marcy, you'll waken the children. Can't we talk, please?"

She squeezed her eyes shut, as if to make him disappear. "I don't care if I waken the children. Let them see what kind of father they have—a man who stays out all hours of the night doing God knows what! I can't even stand to look at you."

"Marcy, please ... I'm sorry. I was wrong, so wrong. Please forgive me. I love you." Patrick's words were coming in short raspy sounds, fraught with repentance.

Marcy's eyelids flew open, the rage unabated. "You love me? You have the nerve to say you love me, and this is how you show it? You go and get drunk and let women fall all over you all night? You know it's funny, Patrick, but that doesn't exactly say 'love' to me."

"I am not drunk. I've had a few beers, yes, but I did nothing wrong," Patrick lied, and Marcy seemed to sense it the instant the words were out of his mouth. All at once, as if the wind had been sucked from her, she went limp, a look of pain on her face as tears welled in her eyes.

"You're lying. You ... did something tonight, didn't you?" Her voice was barely a whisper. She searched his face as if looking for something, anything to tell her it wasn't true. Patrick lowered his eyes. Marcy wrenched from his grasp, flinching to the other side of the bed. She jumped up, hair tumbling about her nightgown like a banshee. Patrick's heart felt like a boulder in his chest. He got up from the bed and walked toward her, his eyes moist with regret.

Marcy stepped back, her hand in front of her. "No!

Don't touch me. I never dreamed you would do ... anything ..." She seemed at a loss for words, a loss of comprehension.

He stood there, staring with sorrowful eyes. For a moment, she seemed to sway, appearing about to faint. Slowly she moved toward the bed and sat down, as if in a trance, tears streaming freely down her face. Without uttering a word, Patrick quietly sat beside her, attempting to encircle her with his arms. At his touch, she began to pummel him with her fists, a broken wail heaving from her chest. All at once, she collapsed, and her sobs retched against him. With each heave, her frail hand shook, lying limp against his chest. Patrick held her tightly. The sweet scent of lilac soap filled his nostrils, causing his heart to ache for her. He longed to tell her she was everything to him, that no other woman could even come close. That he would be nothing without her by his side, loving him, supporting him. And, yes, despite his many frailties, helping him to be the man God intended him to be. But for the moment, in his abject failure, he remained silent, clutching her until the last whimper subsided.

When they did, he lifted her chin to stare into her swollen eyes. "Marcy, look at me, please. *Nothing* happened. Yes, it's true I had a bit too much brew. And yes, I did dance with a woman." He swallowed hard. "But it meant nothing. *Nothing.* I turned her away. But I was wrong to go there, wrong to leave you. So wrong. Please forgive me. I was angry. And then the drink, it ...it took hold." He shivered involuntarily, clearing his throat in embarrassment. He grabbed her by the shoulders. "Marcy, you have to believe me. Now more than ever, I realize how much you mean to me. How much I need you." A lump formed in his throat, forcing his voice to crack.

She remained limp in his arms, and so he caressed her face with his lips. He whispered his sorrow, telling her he loved her, cherished her, needed her. His lips brushed against hers, and he could feel the fire of his passion burn deep inside. With renewed intensity, he kissed her again. He felt her relent with a startling hunger of her own. Sweeping her up in his arms, he laid her gently on the bed, his lips never wavering from the sweetness of her mouth. In one beat of his heart, he was overcome with love for her. An intense rush of emotion flooded his soul for this woman who possessed his heart so completely. He stroked her face, her neck, her arms with such impassioned tenderness that a soft moan escaped her lips.

"Marcy, I love you," he said, his voice a hoarse whisper, "more than life itself."

She met his mouth violently with her own, and he knew in that one action, she forgave, allowing the intensity of their love to carry them away.

Made in the USA
Middletown, DE
09 September 2025

17312313R00241